D0032718

THE LAST LINE

Lt. Col. Anthony Shaffer
and WILLIAM H. KEITH

St. Martin's Paperbacks

NOTE: If you purchased this book without a cover you should be aware that this book is stolen property. It was reported as "unsold and destroyed" to the publisher, and neither the author nor the publisher has received any payment for this "stripped book."

Note: The views expressed in this book are those of the author and do not reflect the official policy or position of the Department of Defense or the U.S. Government.

This is a work of fiction. All of the characters, organizations, and events portrayed in this novel are either products of the author's imagination or are used fictitiously.

THE LAST LINE

Copyright © 2013 by Anthony Shaffer.

All rights reserved.

For information address St. Martin's Press, 175 Fifth Avenue, New York, NY 10010.

Library of Congress Catalog Card Number: 2013003729

ISBN: 978-1-250-04850-9

Printed in the United States of America

St. Martin's Press hardcover edition / June 2013
St. Martin's Paperbacks edition / September 2014

St. Martin's Paperbacks are published by St. Martin's Press, 175 Fifth Avenue, New York, NY 10010.

10   9   8   7   6   5   4   3   2   1

Praise for *The Last Line*

"Shaffer combines more than twenty-five years of experience in the intelligence community with a background in the military, and the authenticity shows in his first novel, written with the prolific genre-veteran Keith . . . Shaffer and Keith have added another must-follow hero for fans of covert-ops thrillers by Dalton Fury, Vince Flynn, and Brad Taylor. Teller can be a bit of a callous jerk at times, but what he lacks in subtlety, he more than makes up for in a kind of Jack Reacher instinct for taking the right action at the right time."

—*Booklist*

"Chillingly authentic . . . a riveting tale only a true insider could tell . . . cunningly plotted and richly detailed with off-the-books tradecraft, this will be the go-to novel for intelligence professionals and special operators: a noteworthy debut!"

—Ralph Peters, Fox News strategic analyst and author of *Cain at Gettysburg*

"Captain Chris Teller is a skilled and experienced intelligence professional who doesn't always follow the rules. But he may be our best chance of stopping a bunch of bad guys so vicious they make al Qaeda look good. Shaffer is a professional who understands how the military and intelligence agencies work—and sometimes don't work. What they do and how they do it are an important part of this great story."

—Larry Bond, *New York Times* bestselling author

ALSO BY LT. COL. ANTHONY SHAFFER

Operation Dark Heart: Spycraft and Special Ops on the Frontlines of Afghanistan—and the Path to Victory

For Alex—my oldest son, who has helped me see, as he has grown, the world through his eyes, with wonder and appreciation.

—Lt. Col. Anthony Shaffer

As ever, for Brea.

—William H. Keith

Acknowledgments

Mr. Shaffer would like to acknowledge the following individuals directly:

Curt Weldon—a former Congressman and outspoken leader who sacrificed a great deal in his personal and professional life in maintaining his support for me and who convinced me to come forward to tell the truth and change an inaccurate rendering of our nation's history. He has boldly worked to find solutions to challenges that have plagued this country's national security for decades.

Curt—You, sir, are a patriot and I am sure our Founding Fathers would be proud of your legacy.

> —*You will* know the *truth* and the truth
> will set you free.
> —John 8–32

Walter Jones Jr.—Congressman. A man whose soul and integrity are more important to him than political party or reputation. I am awed by the grounding in honor of his actions and his ability to focus on what is real and important, while those around him focus on the temporal and banal.

Walter—The good grace of honor you bring to your office has served your constituents well, brightened the gray halls of Congress, and has made our nation a better, stronger place for your efforts. God bless you, and your family, in all things.

—Send me.
—Isaiah 8

Mark Zaid, Esquire. One of the best lawyers on the planet. When it comes to the First Amendment, it is clear that freedom of speech is often not so, and that in the battle between the government's wish to control information and the right of the individual to exercise their right of same, he has become a fierce warrior.

Mark—The road to truth is full of potholes of process, boundless rules, and roadblocks of government bureaucrats. Thank you for your hard work to keep the traffic flowing.

Men occasionally stumble over the truth, but most of them pick themselves up and hurry off as if nothing ever happened.
—Winston Churchill

Lt. Col. (Ret) David Johnson and Dr. Newton Howard—the executive director and founder of Center for Advanced Defense Studies, respectively.

You have both been the foundation of rock in a world of shifting sands. Thank you for your undying support.

> Prepare for the unknown by studying how others in the past have coped with the unforeseeable and the unpredictable.
> —General George S. Patton Jr.

There are others, field operatives, brave men and women of the intelligence and defense community who do the hard and often thankless job of defending this great nation in shadows and always at great political risk and physical danger. They are all too often only held up when it is convenient for politicians to use them to score political points, who often have to be creative and dynamic well beyond their training to accomplish real things and to protect us all. These brave men and women sign up not for glory or for recognition; they sign up for honor and the simple but highly satisfying accomplishments in doing real, often impossible things. It is in simply being able to accomplish those things they find their reward. It is to their efforts we hope this novel will help bring some light and entertain them (and the public) in homage to the necessity of protecting the American people from its enemies—both foreign and domestic.

PROLOGUE

Even here, the screams were too loud to allow him to pray.

Saeed Reyshahri remained kneeling, facing east, trying again to recite the Surat al-Fatiha, the seven opening verses of the Koran. *"In the name of Allah, the most beneficent, the most merciful, all appreciation, gratefulness, and thankfulness are to Allah alone, lord of the worlds . . ."*

A dry wind whispered across the sere and barren landscape. Behind him, on the other side of the ridge, a woman was begging, desperately pleading. Reyshahri did not speak Spanish, but he could guess easily enough what she was saying.

"¡No! ¡No! Por favor . . . ¡Lárgate! ¡No me chinge! ¡No me chinge!"

Filthy dogs. No respect for women—but worse, *far* worse, no concern for the importance, the *urgency* of his mission. Why had Colonel Salehi insisted on using these . . . these *animals* for Operation Shah Mat? The Sinaloa Cartel's coyotes were . . . ruthless. Mercenary. Reliable enough if you met their price, but vicious and dangerous.

They had their own agenda.

Reyshahri was an officer in the Vezarat-e Ettela'at va Amniyat-e Keshvar—VEVAK as it was commonly known, the state security service of the Republic of Iran. His rank was *sarvan,* equivalent to a captain in the U.S. Army; he'd been a member of the Sepah for ten years, and with VEVAK for three more. For most of that time he'd helped train Hezbollah militias for their struggle against the Zionists.

VEVAK was known neither for sentimentality nor for squeamishness when it came to operations in the field. There were times when raw brutality was absolutely necessary—to fulfill a mission, to make a point, to send a message.

This, however, was not one of those times.

The other women were screaming now, pleading, sobbing.

He sat up straight. It was no use. He'd hoped to combine that day's Dhuhr prayer at noon with this one, a practice called Jam'bayn as-Salaatayn allowed on long journeys. Instead, today he would miss both.

Ernesto Jesús Mendoza topped the rise, grinning, full of swaggering *machismo,* his thumbs hooked in his belt, his assault rifle slung carelessly muzzle down behind one shoulder. "Hey, Arab! You want some of this?" He spoke English, the only language they had in common. "You'd better hurry!"

Reyshahri scowled, despising the man. Reyshahri was *Persian,* not Arab. The trafficker knew the difference, he was certain; either the pig was deliberately goading him or he simply did not care.

Mendoza and his gang were coyotes, human traffickers skilled in smuggling human cargos north across the border into the United States. They were also, he knew, members of the dangerous Sinaloan drug cartel, but this day they were escorting fifteen migrants north—nine men, six women—plus Reyshahri. An hour ago, they'd stopped here beside a dry arroyo. Mendoza's men had herded the immigrants into the gully at gunpoint, separated out the three pretty, younger women from the rest, and dragged them to a patch of bare ground beside a huge velvet mesquite tree nearby, leaving one of their number to guard the rest and keep them quiet.

The coyotes had used this place before. The mesquite tree was festooned with women's underwear—a rape tree, they'd called it. Reyshahri had heard the term before but thought it was either exaggeration or anti-Mexican propaganda.

Reyshahri had not been able to watch what had happened next. It had been time for Asr, the afternoon *salah,* or prayer, so he'd found a private place behind the ridge, ritually washed himself with sand, and attempted to pray.

It had been useless. Those poor women . . .

"We should keep moving!" Reyshahri said, angry. "We could reach Phoenix tonight! If the Americans find us here they—"

Mendoza spat on the sand. "The American *gilazos* could not find their asses with their hands. Don't worry about them!"

It was Reyshahri's *duty* to worry about the Americans, though. Mendoza's cavalier attitude was not helping.

"Leave me alone," Reyshahri growled. He listened to the screams a moment more. "You . . . shouldn't be doing this."

"Hey, the boys just want a little fun, you know?" Mendoza laughed, an unpleasant sound, and then shrugged. "We needed the halt. We have a long way to go after sunset."

Reyshahri wished he could pray, wished that God could give him the guidance he so desperately needed.

The obligatory daily prayer was called *namaz* in Reyshahri's Farsi, a word that meant roughly "to bow." In Arabic, however, the word was *salah,* meaning "connection," a believer's connection with Allah. Here, on the desolate international border between Arizona and Mexico, Reyshahri knew that he'd lost that vital connection, that he was cut off now from his God.

Perhaps it would be better once he reached the American capital and Operation Shah Mat had properly begun.

He listened to the screaming in the distance and hoped so.

CHAPTER ONE

SECTOR CHARLIE 1-1
SECRET CIA TRAINING FACILITY
0225 HOURS, EDT
13 APRIL

Night—as impenetrably black as only a moonless and overcast night in the woods can be. Captain Chris Teller lay full-length on the ground, probing the smothering darkness around him, every sense alert. There'd been no sound to warn him, nothing but the usual chirp and whir and peep of insects and lovesick amphibians at the pond just up ahead, but there was something . . .

There, he caught it again as he inhaled—the faintest whiff of cigarette smoke just perceptible above the mingled scents of leaf mold, earth, and stagnant water. His pursuers wouldn't be stupid enough to smoke in the darkness; he was probably smelling it on someone's uniform.

Someone very, very close now . . .

Yes . . . just ahead, a shadow against shadows. Using averted vision, looking to one side of the figure instead of straight at it, he could make out the shape of a man leaning against the trunk of a massive tree. The head was heavy and misshapen beneath the brim of his boonie hat.

A Klingon, wearing NVD—night-vision device.

Teller waited, not moving, scarcely breathing, not even looking at the man standing nearby. Play sneak-and-peek with the bad guys long enough and you became convinced that the opposition could *feel* you staring at them. The answer was not to stare at them, and to make the mental noise of a rock.

Patience. Steady nerves. He was prepared to outwait the guy, however, to lie on the chilly ground for an hour if need be. He'd done this before . . .

Christopher Thomas Teller had been with the Department of Defense for eight years now, as a case officer for the Defense Intelligence Agency's Intelligence Directorate. A captain in the U.S. Army Reserve, he'd seen action in both Afghanistan and Iraq, in combat zones where it was sometimes tough to figure out who were the good guys and who wore black hats.

Since he'd started working for the DIA, that was more of a problem than ever.

A sharp hiss of static and a burst of unintelligible words sounded from the tactical radio holstered on the man's combat harness. "Yeah," he said. "Red Three."

More crackling mutters, and then the man said, "Negative. Nothing here. Sector Charlie one-one is clear."

While Red Three was distracted by the radio call, Teller, wraith silent, rose and eased forward. The man was angled away from him, his field of vision sharply restricted by the night-vision device over his face. Teller knew he would get just one chance . . .

"Copy that," Red Three said. "Out."

Teller took the last three quick steps and struck, using the heel of his hand.

Karate chops to the neck are pure Hollywood, all for show and largely useless. What knocks a man unconscious is not the blow itself but the force of the brain slamming against the inside of the skull. Strike high and from the side, aiming just above the temple, and if the target is relaxed his head will jerk sharply enough to rattle the brain and induce immediate unconsciousness.

It was a martial arts technique that Teller had practiced long and exhaustively. You didn't actually need to use much force—in fact, too hard a blow to the temple could kill—but your accuracy had to be perfect, especially when the bull's-eye was covered by an NVD harness and the brim of a boonie hat.

Red Three slumped; Teller caught him as he fell and silently lowered the body to the ground. Swiftly, he dragged the night-vision device from the man's head, checked the man's pulse, then pulled a penlight from his pocket and peeled back the eyelids, first one, then the other, making sure to shield the light with his hand. Both pupils were the same size, thank God. If Teller had misjudged and fractured Red Three's skull, it would *not* have been good.

Again Teller smelled cigarette smoke, stronger now, and grinned. Most smokers had no idea just how much their clothing and breath stank to nonsmokers. A good thing, too; he'd very nearly walked into this one in the darkness.

The night would no longer be an obstacle, however. Putting away his light, Teller slipped on the night goggles. Sweet. The unit was an AN/PVS-21, one of the newer Gen III Omni IV systems that let the operator see both with direct vision and with light intensification, as well as by infrared. He flipped the left-side monocle aside; he wanted to keep his night vision in at least one eye. As he switched the unit on, the surrounding forest seen through the right-eye optics became twilight-bright in green monochrome. He could see still black water thirty meters ahead—the millpond. The heads-up display projection overlaid the image with a compass bearing, waypoint, GPS data, and other useful tidbits. To the left, a bright white star bobbed slightly as it moved through darkness.

An infrared target—another Klingon wearing an infrared wand on his utilities about fifty meters off. Teller was going to have to be careful if he wanted to stay unobserved.

He still had a long way to go.

AIRFIELD COMMAND POST
SECRET CIA TRAINING FACILITY
0234 HOURS, EDT

Marine Lieutenant Colonel Frank Procario glanced at the big clock on the wall, then back at the computer screen. "Face it, Clarke," he told the older man seated at the monitor. "Your people have lost him."

"Not freakin' likely," James Edward Clarke replied. He was staring at the monitor as though willing the screen to provide him with more information. An airstrip, running southwest to northeast, appeared at the bottom; the sprawl of the pond was above, to the north. A half-dozen points of light described a rough circle in the woods southwest of the pond, and Clarke pointed at the circle's heart. "We *know* he's in this area, right here. He can't manage more than a half mile an hour or so, not in the dark over uneven ground, not unless he wants to break an ankle. We'll get him."

Procario gave a humorless grin. "We'll see."

Officially, these woods were part of a highly classified training facility, so secret that the government wouldn't even allow it to be named. To anyone in the know, however, it was "the Farm," a rural base tucked away out of sight within thousands of acres of thickly wooded land, close by a broad and slow-moving river. On the other side of a busy interstate running past the perimeter fence, a popular tourist center celebrated America's heritage. A million tourists wandered that historic site each year, never guessing that the main entrance to the covert CIA training facility even existed nearby. Case-officers-in-training routinely used the downtown area of the tourist site as a classroom where they could practice shadowing, brush passes, mail drops, and the other esoterica of tradecraft.

Since the early fifties, some eight thousand acres of the Farm had been given over to woodland, with isolated buildings and training facilities scattered across the property, all but lost among the trees. In the past few years, though, trees had been coming down by the hundreds, and earthmovers had been carving out acre upon acre for new buildings and roads. The War on Terror had been causing the black-ops budgets to boom, and the Klingons had been making the most of it.

Plenty of woodland and swamp remained, however, more than enough for training classes such as this one.

The session was a fairly standard E&E exercise, escape and evasion. They'd driven Teller out in a Humvee and dropped him off at the side of a road three hours earlier. This night's objective was straightforward—orienting alone across three miles of woodland and swamp with a compass. Teller's goal was the 5,000-foot airstrip located a little more than a mile south of the millpond. The catch came in having to make the trek in pitch blackness while evading a half-dozen CIA instructors, all of whom were wearing high-tech AN/PVS-21s and coordinating their movements by tactical radio.

Still, Procario had known Teller for a long time. "I'll put my money on Chris Teller anyway," he said after a long moment.

"Bullshit. We've got the bastard boxed in."

"That," Procario said, his grin broadening, "is exactly when he's at his most fucking dangerous."

SECTOR CHARLIE 1-1
SECRET CIA TRAINING FACILITY
0240 HOURS, EDT

Teller watched the moving infrared target a moment in silence. Getting caught didn't bear thinking about.

Farm instructors had been known to zip-strip trainees they caught, put them through a mock interrogation, even beat them up in the sacred name of verisimilitude. Classes like this one weren't just about proving you could avoid contract security bully-boys like Red Three. They were to demonstrate means of surviving after you were caught.

Chris Teller had already decided that he would be having none of that, thank you. His trainee days were over. He'd been through the Farm's basic indoctrination course eight years ago, and he'd attended several specialization classes since. His presence here this weekend was nothing more than MacDonald's latest attempt to make life as unpleasant as possible for him, something the woman seemed to regard as her sacred duty.

Right now, though, MacDonald wasn't his problem. He had five Klingons on his tail, and they were going to be royally pissed when they found out what he'd done to Klingon number six.

The CIA did not play well with others. Among themselves, they referred to the Central Intelligence Agency as "the Agency" or "the Company" or even "the Firm." Other U.S. intelligence services—and there were fifteen of them at the latest count aside from the Agency—referred to the CIA as "the Empire," a term that inevitably had devolved into the villains of the popular science fiction franchise. The Klingons got the lion's share of the intelligence budget, the Klingons got the attention on Capitol Hill when it came to procurements, and the Klingons didn't like to share the goodies.

For a DIA case officer like Teller, working with the CIA was a necessary evil, something to avoid if possible, to get through quickly when necessary.

This time around, unfortunately, there'd been no avoiding it.

Thirty yards farther along, the ground began growing soft underfoot, the swamp dragging at his boots with each step. He kept going until he reached the water's edge, then stopped, looking back. He pressed the SEND button on the tactical radio. "Man down! Man down!" he called. "Red Three's in trouble, sector one-one!"

There was silence for a moment. Then, "Who is this?"

"Red Three is in trouble!" Teller repeated. He switched off the radio and began wading out into the pond.

The water was cold and utterly black. In the distance, he heard a shout—and his NVDs showed three infrared beacons converging in the woods behind him. Good. If he'd injured Red Three, he wanted the man to get treatment, and the call would also serve as a diversion. After a moment, he pushed off from the muddy bottom and began swimming. The AN/PVS-21 was waterproof to a depth of ten meters; getting it wet in a late-night swim wasn't going to hurt the unit at all. He struck out with a breaststroke, moving slowly to avoid disturbing the water with more than a ripple. Someone might be watching the water, though he doubted it. Across the lake was exactly the wrong direction for someone trying to reach the airfield.

At least, it was for people trying to reach it through the woods. Teller had a different idea.

The pond was a brackish, irregular lake just off the nearby river. Teller was swimming down one of the lake's inlets now. Five hundred yards to the northeast, lights showed on a wooded shore. There was a small suburban community there between the millpond and the river, according to the maps Teller had studied—houses belonging to the Farm's permanent staff or used by long-term guests.

What he was about to try was almost certainly in violation of at least the spirit of tonight's E&E exercise. He hadn't exactly been ordered to stay on a particular route, but there'd been a clear understanding that he was to travel a more or less direct path southeast from the drop-off point to the airfield, sticking to the woods and swamps and staying clear of inhabited areas. The total trek was about three miles; he'd already traveled more than that, backtracking twice since midnight, then swinging well to the north and east to avoid his pursuers.

He maintained a slow but steady pace across the black water with scarcely a ripple to betray his movement. In the distance, shouts silenced the steady chirp of crickets. It sounded like they'd found Red Three.

Eventually his boots brushed against mud, and then he staggered up out of the lake, dripping. A few more yards through a sheltering privacy wall of trees, and he emerged onto a suburban street.

Most of the houses were empty; all were dark. One nearby house had a couple of cars parked in the driveway, a two-door Nissan and a Ford pickup truck. He pulled a small folding knife from a pocket in his utilities. The truck was the easier target—and as a bonus it wasn't even locked. Well, why should it be? This small and quintessentially American community was located deep in the heart of one of the most secure and secret facilities in the United States.

A few moments later, he touched two bare wires to each other and the truck gunned to life. He wrapped the wires together, put the vehicle in gear, backed out onto the street, and drove off toward the southeast.

Fifteen minutes later, once again in the woods, he abandoned the truck at the side of a road, checked his compass, and started walking once more.

Ten minutes more on foot brought him to the airfield. There was some activity on the far side of the runway—vehicles with flashing red lights and a couple of military Hummers. The control tower building was brightly lit; a room on the ground floor had been converted into a temporary command center for the night's festivities.

A pair of contractors met him outside the command center, rough-looking men in camouflage utilities and carrying M-4A1 Commandos. "Hold it right there, asshole," one of them growled.

"I've finished the fucking mission," Teller said. He glanced at his watch—0314, well ahead of his 0600 deadline. "Game's over. Let me through."

"You're damned right, game over," the other merc said with a nasty grin. "You've got some people pretty fucking pissed off at you."

"Including *us,* you son of a bitch," the first merc said.

Teller studied the two. The CIA often employed

contract soldiers—mercenaries—for its sentries, shit details, military ops, and, as tonight, its paramilitary training exercises. They were well trained and generally possessed decent to excellent martial arts skills. Teller might be able to take down one of these two, but not both, not after running through the woods for three hours and pulling a half-kilometer swim in the bargain.

The stuttering *whop-whop-whop* of a helicopter approached out of the darkness.

Those red lights—an ambulance. The helicopter must be a medevac chopper. Shit. He must have hit Red Three harder than he'd realized.

"Okay," he said. "So where do we go from here?"

"I don't know about the rest of us," a new voice said from behind Teller's shoulder, "but *you* are in a world of shit."

It wouldn't be the first time.

"So what else is new?" Teller asked.

SMITHSONIAN MUSEUM OF AMERICAN HISTORY
WASHINGTON, D.C.
1345 HOURS, EDT

Galen Fletcher smiled thinly as the security guard patted him down, checking for weapons. How ironic. He lived in a country awash in guns, and he had to come home, to the nation's capital, to be properly frisked.

The guard finished and waved him through.

"Thank you for your patience, sir."

"Not a problem," he replied, shrugging back into his jacket.

As he moved into the crowded entryway of the newly renovated Smithsonian Museum of American History, the warmth, the *energy* of the place enveloped him. The meetings at headquarters, which had begun at eight sharp, had continued straight through lunch and left him in a bit of a daze, so to help clear his head, he had decided on an afternoon walking tour of the landmarks along the National Mall in downtown Washington, D.C. They'd meant so much to him when he was younger.

Long ago . . . when it was so much easier to believe.

Surrounded by chattering tourists with their cameras and backpacks, the CIA's Mexico chief of station glanced around him, catching a glimpse of his reflection in the polished steel columns—gray hair, distinguished features, conservatively dressed in his usual navy blue Brooks Brothers suit and red tie. He was reminded of how much like an investment banker he appeared—like his father and his father's father. He hadn't chosen that path, though. His had been a life of clandestine intrigue, of service to his country.

Fletcher passed the glass display cases containing trinkets from the country's past—a muscled G.I. Joe action figure, a chipped wooden cradle, a curvaceous Barbie in a black-and-white swimsuit—and headed up the wide staircase. He strolled through the second floor and stooped to inspect a letter by George Washington, squinting to make out the looped script.

If we consider ourselves, or wish to be considered by Others as a United people, Washington had scrawled, *why not adopt the measures that are characteristic of it—Act as a Nation . . .*

He smiled again, reflecting on his life, on a career in the service of his nation. His start with paramilitary and field operations training at the Farm, then the long climb through the ranks. The days of dust and sorrow in Beirut as a young case officer working to solve the marine barracks and U.S. Embassy bombings. His stint in Sudan—what a godawful place—trying to prevent the fall of the government to forces that would be less inclined to see things the American way. The trip to North Korea in 1994 with former president Jimmy Carter on his mission to defuse tensions there; that had been a close one, the time when he'd first recognized his own mortality.

Five years later, he'd had a closer brush with death, when he'd been deputy chief of station in Côte d'Ivoire. He'd helped save the life of the Chilean ambassador in Liberia during a tense stand-off with the Liberian monster Charles Taylor.

That encounter had earned him the CIA's ultimate honor, the Intelligence Medal of Merit. Now, at a time when intelligence collection had never been more imperative to the security of the United States, he knew more than ever the significance of the honor bestowed on him. Honor was at the core of everything he had done, everything he had become, everything he truly cherished.

Fletcher wasn't sure what he was looking for in the museum—if, indeed, he was looking for anything at all. Reaching the third floor, he swung to his left, stopping with a cluster of people in front of a glass case to inspect a rickety high-back wing chair. Faded orange tweed, it looked like, with plenty of stains and a greasy spot where a head had once rested. Archie Bunker's chair from the 1970s TV show *All in the Family,* the sign read.

Fletcher had been abroad during that turbulent period of America's history, but he had watched as the nation had wrestled with its internal demons and had survived and endured—the ultimate demonstration of America's greatness.

Later, when America—when America's *honor*—was betrayed . . . Fletcher's thoughts veered back to what he had discovered in Mexico at the end of his two years as the CIA's chief of station there. In an instinctive gesture, he glanced around and touched his hand to his tie, ensuring it was straight.

Honor.

He had to do this.

Fletcher made his way out of the museum and down its snow-dotted granite stairs. It was chilly for mid-April in Washington, and a gust of wind seemed to claw its way underneath his coat. He'd not yet adjusted to the climate here after the humid heat of Mexico City, and he felt a chill in his bones that was as much psychological as physical. The cherry blossoms, though, provided an orgy of glorious pink among D.C.'s granite and marble edifices.

He struck out across the National Mall, the white dome of the U.S. Capitol Building rising on his left and the soaring Washington Monument on his right, the heavy gray of a leaden sky emphasizing their vibrancy. The magnificent sight brought back that first, sharp sense of patriotic wonder that had overcome him during his first visit to Washington at the age of seventeen. That had been . . . when? '73? '74?

A hell of a long time ago.

Fletcher took a deep breath, drawing in the chilly spring air before releasing it slowly and deliberately.

It was time.

With renewed energy, his pace increased. He headed toward the Smithsonian Castle. As he approached, he made the slight right off the frozen path to stride down the escalator of the Metro, brushing past those clinging to the handrail.

He was warm now in his own knowing, and he felt an inner glow as he pulled out the fare card from the inside pocket of his suit, put it into the turnstile, and descended the stairs to the tiled platform for the Blue Line train headed to Largo Town Center.

The lighted overhead sign indicated a train was approaching, and the embedded red lights on the granite platform edge began to flash as Fletcher moved up to stand with the rest of the crowd. He smiled graciously at the woman next to him, well dressed, with two children—a young boy and a toddler in a stroller.

"You know," he said softly, "you have a beautiful family. It's people like you who make this country great." Surprised, the woman returned Fletcher's smile. Before she could thank him, the roaring train thundered out of the tunnel. He patted the shoulder of the boy.

Then, in one graceful movement, Galen Fletcher stepped off the platform.

SOUTH MONTEZUMA STREET
PHOENIX, ARIZONA
1220 HOURS, MST

They called Phoenix the kidnap capital of the United States, the second in the world after only Mexico City. In recent years, the flood of illegal immigrants north across the border had brought with it a wave of crime, of kidnapping and extortion especially.

At nightfall, the coyotes had marched their human cargo northeast, deeper into the desert, until the light of a vehicle, an ancient and time-worn panel truck, had shone out of the dark. Saeed Reyshahri and the others had been crammed into the back of the truck and told to lie down under a tarp.

The heat and the stink of sweat and fear, the sobbing of the women, the nausea and disorientation all had been miserable. Hours later, they'd met with another, larger truck somewhere outside of Tucson, changed vehicles, and continued driving through the night, this time with a different group of coyotes in charge.

The smuggling operation appeared to be superbly organized, with chains of rendezvous and safe houses, vehicle switches, and well-armed gangs of men stretched across the desert, all the way from deep inside northern Mexico. The actual border crossing near Nogales had been through a network of lighted and well-ventilated tunnels several hundred meters long. Despite his concerns, at no point had Reyshahri even seen an American Border Patrol or customs officer.

Just after dawn, however, they'd arrived here, in a grimy and run-down section on the south side of Phoenix. The *pollos*—"chickens" in the slang of the coyotes—had been herded into a dilapidated house, forced at gunpoint to strip in order to make escape more difficult, and locked up together inside one of the tiny bedrooms. They were guarded by three armed men under the apparent command of a harassed and shrill-voiced housewife with a baby and a toddler still in diapers.

Reyshahri retained a bit more freedom and at least a measure of dignity; they allowed him to sit in the living room with two of the coyotes and a too-loud television set tuned to a Spanish soap opera. Thanks be to Allah he would be leaving soon. A VEVAK agent code-named Kawrd, "knife" in English, would be arriving momentarily to bring Reyshahri's forged ID and to pay the final installment of Reyshahri's transport fee.

It could not possibly happen too soon.

"Hey, Arab," one of the men said in English. He held out a brown bottle. "Wanna beer?"

Reyshahri could only shake his head. Alcohol was *harām* to good Muslims—strictly forbidden. Surely these animals knew that.

The coyote laughed and said something to his partner, eliciting a nasty grin. "They say you also no like women, mister," the second man said. He jerked a dirty thumb over his shoulder at the guarded bedroom down the hall. "You maybe want one of the boys instead? That it?"

"Some of them *muy bonito,* man, very pretty," the first said, laughing.

Reyshahri leaned back on the filthy sofa and closed his eyes. If he ignored them, perhaps they would tire of the sport and leave him alone.

The plight of the fifteen *pollos* in the party continued to weigh heavily on Reyshahri. The rape tree in the desert had only been the nightmare's beginning. He'd heard stories from some of the coyotes during the trip north. One at a time, now, the migrants would be forced to call relatives, either back in Mexico or, often, here in the States, asking for more money. Each had already paid something between $1,800 and $2,500 American to get them this far—a fortune for impoverished families in Mexico. Now the coyotes were demanding more money. If the additional cash—"ransom" was the only possible word for it—was not paid, the immigrants would be forced to work for the cartel, or, worse, taken to a *casa de la violencia* and tortured, often with their relatives listening over the phone line. Human traffickers had been known—with horrible frequency—to send relatives hands or other body parts, or photos of their loved ones being beaten or sexually abused, in order to speed up the payments.

How in the name of Allah the most merciful had he fallen into this nightmare?

Smothered beneath the tarp, packed in with the migrants in the back of the panel truck, he'd missed Fajr, the morning prayer, but he had a feeling that prayer of any sort would be impossible until he got away from

these men. God, in his infinite love and sense of ultimate justice, would understand. *Surely* he would understand . . .

A pounding on the front door brought him out of
increasingly despondent thoughts, as the two coyotes
pulled automatic weapons from behind the furniture.
A moment later, the housewife led Ernesto Mendoza
and another man into the living room.

"Hello, Arab," Mendoza said. "I find your friend,
see?"

Reyshahri didn't know the other man, but he was
dark and bearded and carried a large briefcase. "*Salaam,* Okawb," the man said, using Reyshahri's code
name, "Eagle."

"*Salaam,* Kawrd," Reyshahri replied. Sign and countersign. Kawrd nodded, then spoke in Spanish to Mendoza. He opened the combination lock on the briefcase
and showed the coyotes the contents—ten thousand
American dollars. Reyshahri noticed that Kawrd stepped
back and put his right hand inside his jacket as they
counted it; it was not at all impossible that the Sinaloan
coyotes would take the money and demand more.

There would be other VEVAK men outside, armed
and waiting. Mendoza couldn't be that stupid . . .

"All correct, *señores,*" Mendoza said with a toothy
smile. "It's been good doing business with you, as always."

As always. "Let us leave this place," he said to Kawrd
in Farsi. "It sickens me."

Together, they stepped outside into the cool April

air. Two more Iranian agents were waiting for them beside a rented car. One gave Reyshahri an envelope containing a U.S. driver's license and citizenship papers.

Reyshahri didn't relax, however, until they were well clear of the city.

The mission. He needed to forget the coyotes and focus on his mission.

CHAPTER TWO

Located twelve miles south of Washington, D.C., and just three miles west of George Washington's Mount Vernon, Fort Belvoir is home to elements of ten U.S. Army Major Commands, nineteen different agencies and direct reporting units of the Department of the Army, and some twenty-six different DoD agencies, among many other units. One of these is the United States Army Intelligence and Security Command, INSCOM. Its headquarters is a four-story building, but only two are aboveground. The wood-paneled office of Colonel Audrey MacDonald was on the top floor, with a window looking out across the brand-new headquarters of the 29th Infantry Division (Light), the National Guard unit known as the "Blue and Gray."

That was *his* unit, the unit that had slashed through

the German lines in twenty-one days of blood at the Meuse-Argonne in 1917, that had charged up out of the slaughter at Omaha in 1944. Chris Teller had transferred to the 29th several years ago, after starting off his military career as an enlisted man in the Alaska National Guard. Now, eight years after OCS in Fort Benning and his entry into the murky world of army intelligence, he was a captain, an O-3, though his GS-12 civil service category was the equivalent of an army major.

None of that was of much help now.

"You insufferable, arrogant, insubordinate *idiot*!" Colonel MacDonald leaned back in her office chair and glared at Teller, who stood before her at rigid attention. She was a lean, hard-edged, and no-nonsense woman, a by-the-book officer with an accountant's outlook on life and zero sense of humor. "An Agency contract employee is in the hospital! You could have killed him!"

"But I didn't, ma'am," Teller said. "The situation—"

"You are at attention, Captain, and will not speak unless I ask you a question!" She picked up the report on her desk and shook it across the desk at Teller. "Our . . . colleagues at Langley have filed a formal complaint against you. It makes us look bad. It makes *me* look bad. The *situation,* mister, is that you have crossed the line."

"Permission to speak, Colonel."

She held the glare a moment longer, as if trying to decide whether to hear him out or not. She dropped the damning report back on her desk. "Granted," she said at last.

"This whole thing is bullshit, Colonel, and you and I both know it. The Farm's just pissed because I crossed their barnyard without breaking a sweat."

"You deliberately attacked one of their CEs. The man is in DeWitt with a concussion." She cocked her head. "That doesn't bother you?"

"No, ma'am. Those boys play rough. I wasn't going to mess around."

"You of all people, Captain, ought to know that things *never* go as planned in combat, real or simulated! If you'd misjudged, if you'd hit him too hard, you could have broken his neck, or smashed the side of his skull."

"But I didn't, Colonel. That's the point. To complete the exercise, I needed to change the rules of the game. So I did."

She tapped the report. "You *broke* the rules of the game. Not only did you injure a member of the opposition, you stole his night-vision device *and* you left the established boundaries of the course. You stole a vehicle—a truck, I might add, belonging to the Agency's assistant deputy director of operations. You also strayed outside the assigned operational area, which could have put civilians and nonoperational personnel at risk."

Teller sighed. "Colonel, the before-action clearly stated that I was to move from Point Alpha to Point Bravo without being detected or captured. The exercise was designed to check out a new E&E class designed by Colonel Procario and did not involve live-fire activity. No civilians were put at risk—not unless the CEs decided to use live rounds instead of blanks. *I* was not armed. As for leaving the assigned area . . ." Teller managed a shrug while remaining more or less at attention. "I didn't have a GPS—and every piece of gear I borrowed was returned in working order, period."

"Damn it, Teller, you knew you were supposed to stay southwest of the swamp."

"Did I, Colonel?" He gave her his best look of open, boyish innocence. "I thought that was a suggestion. It sounded like a suggestion to *me*."

"Don't give me your bullshit, Captain Teller," Mac-Donald told him.

"Colonel MacDonald, you sent me down there to test out their E&E exercise and write a report on its potential usefulness for trainees. The exercise was flawed. It was play-acting. In combat, there *are* no rules, no boundaries, no restrictions."

"Indeed?" MacDonald's tone dripped acid. "So . . . civilians, women and children, they're all fair game? Rules of engagement are to be ignored?"

"Damn it, Colonel, that's not what I meant and you know it." Teller was angry now. "When you face an enemy in combat, you don't pull punches, you don't give him the first shot, and you don't decide if attacking him is politically correct. You take him down, and you take him down hard. And you sure as hell don't play by the bad guys' rules!"

"The exercise at the Farm was a game, Captain. Games have rules."

"How do we learn from a game where we have to follow rules? I don't get it."

"No," MacDonald said. "No, you don't. That's why I'm relieving you of duty pending a formal investigation."

"You can't do that, Colonel!"

"The hell I can't. Just watch me. You are dismissed."

"Colonel—"

"Dismissed!"

Teller stared at her for a long couple of seconds, then turned on his heel and strode out of her office.

It wasn't even 1000 hours yet, and he needed a drink.

**SAFE HOUSE, EAST OLYMPIC BOULEVARD
EAST LOS ANGELES, CALIFORNIA
1230 HOURS, PDT**

They'd driven through the night, arriving in the Angelino suburbs well before dawn. Reyshahri and Kawrd— the other VEVAK agent introduced himself during the drive as Fereidun Rahim Moslehi—had stopped in the desert outside of Palm Springs for Fajr, the morning prayer.

It had felt . . . good. God, Reyshahri knew, would forgive him for missing the appointed prayers during his journey north out of Mexico. Here, away from Mendoza and his filthy Sinaloan coyotes, it was possible once again to think about the mission.

The mission began . . . here.

This part of East Los Angeles was a teeming barrio of tenements, housing projects, and houses crammed together in festering, noisy mayhem less than ten kilometers from downtown L.A. The population here was almost exclusively Hispanic, most of them from Mexico. The safe house was a single-family home attached to a mechanic's garage on East Olympic Boulevard, just off the Santa Ana Freeway. Reyshahri noticed a Mexican flag hanging from the eaves of a house across the street, and a brick wall nearby had been daubed with white paint, in letters two meters high: *"¡VIVA AZTLÁN!"*

Excellent. He didn't speak Spanish, but he knew what the words meant.

"Our contact here is Manuel Alvarado," Moslehi told him as they got out of the car and walked up the rotting steps and onto the front porch. Inside, a dog barked.

"Another cartel member?" Reyshahri asked. He glanced surreptitiously left and right. There were guards out, though not obviously so. A group of young men on the street corner. Other men sitting on porches, or lounging casually on front stoops.

"No. But he is a dedicated Aztlanista."

Alvarado answered the doorbell—an old man, white-haired and missing his front teeth. He carried a Smith & Wesson .38 in a shoulder holster over his filthy sleeveless tee. *"¿Quien es?"* he asked, looking at Reyshahri with suspicion.

"This is the colonel I told you about," Moslehi replied in English. "He is with us."

"Okawb," Reyshahri added.

Alvarado gave a curt nod and admitted them. "You'll want to see the . . . stuff?"

"Please," Reyshahri said. "It all arrived safely?"

Alvarado grunted and led them to a locked door off the kitchen. A couple of men with shotguns stood aside for them. "One truck hasn't arrived yet," Alvarado said. "There may have been a problem in Tucson."

"What problem?"

A shrug. "*Los federales*. Maybe a problem. Maybe not. We'll see."

Not good. If the Border Patrol or the FBI had intercepted one of the shipments, it could tip them off to Shah Mat. More likely, though, the Americans would parade the captured materials as evidence that they were winning their vaunted war on drugs, and not think about what that seizure represented.

The door opened into the back of the garage, a huge open space that served now as a warehouse. On every side, crates and cartons were stacked on pallets almost from floor to ceiling. There were drugs, yes, but most of the boxes were filled with something just as dangerous—weapons and ammunition.

Reyshahri pulled up the lid on one crate already opened. Inside were military assault rifles—twelve of them, wrapped in translucent plastic. He picked one up and stripped off the protective covering. It was an M-16A4, factory fresh. Prominently stamped on the crate was the FNH USA logo. Another crate nearby, longer but narrower, carried the Saco Defense Systems logo. Inside, also carefully wrapped, was an M-60E3 light machine gun.

Other crates held ammunition of various calibers, hand grenades, and plastic explosives. Most was American manufactured, though there were a few foreign imports. The RPG-7s were Iranian, manufactured by the Defense Industries Organization, or DIO. They'd reached Los Angeles by way of Syria and Hezbollah.

There were weapons and ammunition enough here to equip a small army—which was precisely why they'd been smuggled across the border from Mexico, a few crates at a time, and at great cost.

Alvarado saw Reyshahri admiring the M-60. "We have our friends within the United States government to thank for most of these," he said, grinning. *"Rapido y Furióso."*

"Fast and Furious." Reyshahri nodded. He didn't need to be fluent in Spanish to translate that. Carefully, lovingly, he replaced the machine gun in its crate. The scandal last year, when the American public learned that large numbers of American weapons had been shipped to Mexico's drug cartels by the U.S. Department of Justice, had been explosive. Operation Fast and Furious, supposedly, had been an attempt to track arms shipments to the cartels, but somehow the government agencies responsible for tracking them had failed to do so. What the American news media did not know, *could* not know, was that the visible scandal represented only a tiny piece of the whole story. The weapons had vanished into Mexico without telling the FBI or DEA a thing about where they had gone.

Now many of them were *here,* smuggled back into

the United States and awaiting shipment to their final destinations. Some had been routed here directly, thanks to the efforts of the operation's allies in Washington.

Operation Fast and Furious was the tip of a vast weapons-smuggling iceberg.

"Your distribution network is in place?" Reyshahri asked Alvarado.

"*Sí, señor.* My people need only the order."

"Then do it. You have the order."

Alvarado's eyes widened. "Immediately?"

Reyshahri nodded. "The longer we delay, the more likely it is that the enemy will discover us."

That, of course, had been the chief danger all along. Operation Shah Mat was so big, involved so many people, and had such terrifyingly far-reaching implications that the secret would not be secure for very much longer. They had to strike *now,* before the enemy was aware of the danger.

"And your part in this game, *señor capitán?*"

"It will happen. Eight, maybe ten days. No more."

The man hissed, a sharp intake of breath. "*Jesús y María.*"

"God willing," Reyshahri added.

EXECUTIVE SWEETS
WASHINGTON, D.C.
1745 HOURS, EDT

Chris Teller paused at the door, then held it open for Procario. "After you, Colonel."

"I hate these joints," Procario said, grimacing. "Why can't you get yourself plastered in a decent dive?"

Both of them were in civvies, Procario in a sports coat, Teller in his usual stone-washed jeans and a gray T-shirt.

"I'll have you know I've done some of my best undercover work here," Teller said.

"Undercover? Or under the covers?"

"Cute."

"Damn it, Chris, this is embarrassing!"

Once, Fourteenth Street had been D.C.'s infamous red-light district, a seedy, noisome patch of inner-city lights and shabbiness where strip clubs, massage parlors, triple-X-rated theaters, tittie bars, and by-the-hour motels had shouldered one another in salacious intimacy with somewhat more respectable businesses such as liquor stores, tobacco shops, pawnbrokers, and quick-loan joints. That had been back in the wild and woolly seventies, when an intoxicated Wilbur Daigh Mills, honorable congressman from Arkansas, had been stopped at 2:00 A.M. one night by Park Police for driving without his lights—and a stripper with the stage name Fanne Foxe had bolted from the car and gone for an impromptu swim in the Tidal Basin.

The 1974 scandal had led to Mills's resigning as chairman of the House Ways and Means Committee. It had also led to an attempt by the city to clean up the Fourteenth Street strip once and for all.

Nowadays, new sex-industry businesses were kept out, and the old ones, the ones grandfathered in, were strictly regulated and ruthlessly taxed. The old Pussycat Revue was now Executive Sweets, a high-toned gentleman's club with a tastefully elegant sign out front and a twenty-dollar cover just to get in. It was, Teller thought, the perfect illustration of a truism. Washington might be dynamic, constantly moving, always changing, and yet the place never, ever changed.

Teller and Procario walked through near-darkness to the front desk, giving a smiling hostess their money under the watchful eye of a bouncer who could have doubled as a linebacker for the Washington Redskins. Beyond the hostess station, the club opened into a crowded pub with dark wooden paneling, subdued lighting, and a haze of cigarette smoke suspended beneath the ceiling's cedar beams, while sultry R&B droned from the sound system. Teller led the way to a table close by the runway, where a bored-looking brunette was taking off her clothes more or less to the music's beat. Other women moved among the tables wearing sequined G-strings, high heels, and smiles, serving drinks or cruising for tips.

Teller liked the place. He'd spent a lot of pleasant evenings here, though sometimes it was tough to remember everything that had happened the next morning. He glanced over at the bar and took in the framed and autographed poster-sized blow-up of a topless Annabelle Battistella, better known to her fans as Fanne Foxe. Evidently, her notorious late-night swim in the Tidal Basin had given her career a real boost, and she'd commanded top dollar for her dancing at a number of area clubs, including the old Pussycat. A brass plate beneath the portrait read THE TIDAL BASIN BOMBSHELL, the *nom d'art* she'd adopted after the Mills incident. Before that, she'd been known as the Argentine Firecracker.

"Did you really do undercover work here?" Procario demanded. He didn't sound convinced.

"Huh? Sure."

"Doing what?"

"Remember that Russian from the trade delegation last year? Turned out to be SVR?"

"Suslov?"

"That's the one. Brought him here and got him hammered. Told him I could pull strings, get him a date with one of the girls."

"And he bit?"

"He bit. Had to work fast, though. The Company was putting the moves on him, too. Snuck him right out under their Ivy League noses. They thought I was taking him to dinner at the Filomena, over in Georgetown."

"Slick."

"I thought so."

"So . . . did you?"

"Did I what?"

"Did you get him a date with one of the girls?"

"Well, that would be between Suslov and the girl, wouldn't it? Strictly after hours. The girls here could get fired if they're caught getting too personal with the clientele, you know?"

A waitress came up to their table, leaning forward to give them a good view. "What would you boys like?"

"Those'll do," Teller said, winking at her.

"Coke," Procario said. "I'm driving."

"Jack Black," Teller added. "with a Heineken chaser."

The woman smiled at them and left, her naked buttocks twitching provocatively to either side of her sequined dental floss. "You got it wrong, amigo," Procario said, watching the play of muscle and bare skin. "I've told you—it's 'martini, shaken, not stirred.' If you're going to be a spy, get it the hell right."

Teller made a face. "Nasty stuff. Anyway, James Bond was a pussy."

"So you've said." It was a long-running joke. "So I take it the McDee drilled you a new one?"

"More or less. I'm suspended. 'Pending formal investigation,' she said."

"Shit. Not again. What is it now, three times in three years?"

"Nah, four, but who's counting? The bitch was setting me up with that gig at the Farm, I swear. And when I come out with my usual panache and dash, she has a squirming litter of kittens."

"Sounds like you need to switch hats."

"Maybe. Why? What do you have?"

"Maybe nothing, but I had a call from JJ this afternoon. Something's popped, something damned big and scary. The Klingons are scared shitless."

"JJ" was John J. Wentworth, an analyst working the Latin American desk in the CIA's Directorate of Intelligence. He was a Klingon, but still one of the good guys, a former marine who hated the interagency rivalries and bickering politics as much as did Teller.

"Do tell. Any ideas what's up?"

"He didn't say."

The waitress returned with their drinks. Teller pulled cash from his wallet and handed it to her, including a generous tip. "Keep it, babe. Is Sandy on tonight?"

"She sure is. Can I give her a message?"

"Nah. I'll just heckle her when she comes on."

The Scotch burned. Cheap stuff, despite the price. It didn't matter. It would get him good and drunk, and right now that was pretty much all he cared about. On the runway, the brunette had been replaced by a blonde wearing a conservative business suit, padded shoulders and all. She seemed a bit livelier than the first woman, more connected with the crowd. Voices in the smoky semidarkness urged her along as she started removing her jacket.

The laws encircling "exotic dancers" in this town were so twistedly labyrinthine they were funny. Across the river in Virginia, the guardians of public morality were stricter than here in D.C.; dancers had to wear G-strings and pasties, though some communities actually went so far as to permit *transparent* pasties. D.C. was more liberal. Bare-breasted was the rule rather than the exception, and sometimes the girls would strip down to their skin, though they weren't supposed to. The local authorities occasionally cracked down on places that called too much attention to themselves. Low-key and low-profile seemed to be the secret.

Just like in intelligence work.

"So what did JJ have to say?" Teller asked after a few moments.

"Just that they're having a brainstorming session at

his office tomorrow. He wondered if we might come by."

"He just has the hots for you."

"Maybe. He thinks you're cute, too."

"You think he's recruiting?"

"It's possible. But the way he was talking, I think they're seriously running scared. There's a rumor . . ."

"What rumor?"

"One of their people stepped in front of the Metro yesterday."

"Shit. Stepped? Or was pushed?"

"Stepped. They're pretty sure he stepped, anyway. There were lots of witnesses."

Teller started to raise his glass to his lips. "Who was it?"

"Galen Fletcher."

That stopped him. Carefully, he set the drink down again, untouched, a cold prickle working its way up his spine. He'd known Galen and respected him. "I hadn't heard that."

"They're working to keep it off the six o'clocks."

"Damn." Galen Fletcher had been the CIA's chief of station in Mexico, working out of the U.S. Embassy in Mexico City. Eight years ago, he'd been one of Teller's instructors at the Farm. Teller, fresh out of his twelve weeks of OCS, had gone through the CIA's training course there for intelligence case officers as a part of his initiation into the Defense Intelligence Agency. Teller remembered Fletcher well—a quiet, cultured man, polite, refined, definitely old school, a *gentleman*.

Very, very good at what he did.

The dancer on the stage was down to skin and little else now, her business suit and underwear scattered along the runway. She finished her dance, working the pole in the center of the stage, then bowed to an appreciatively noisy audience, gathered up her clothing, and sauntered off.

It turned out Sandy was up next.

Her stage name was Bitsie Bright, but Sandra Doherty was an old friend. Teller had been seeing her on and off the stage for a year now; she was fun, perky, and great in the sack. She spotted Teller as she went into her routine and gave him a broad wink.

Teller scarcely noticed.

"Who's his number two?" he asked.

"Dick Nicholas. Deputy chief of station."

Teller grunted. "Don't know him."

"Me neither. I knew Fletcher, though."

"From when you were at the Farm?"

Procario nodded. "We were instructors down there at the same time. Six, maybe seven years ago."

The circles within American intelligence sometimes were remarkably small. The same people kept running into one another, being stationed together, or bumping into one another in the damnedest places at the damnedest times.

"So why would Galen off himself?"

"Maybe we'll find out tomorrow."

"How's that?"

"We have a date with JJ and some of his people at Langley. Ten o'clock."

"Was that what you meant by putting on another hat?"

Procario nodded. "Getting kicked out of INSCOM might be damned convenient right now."

"Maybe."

U.S. intelligence was a maze of overlapping and competing departments—the CIA, NSA, DIA, FBI, and God alone knew what else, all theoretically tied together since 2005 under the director of national intelligence. In fact, since the Office of the DNI had taken over, things had been even more confused and contentious. Everyone was out first and foremost to protect his own little patch of turf.

Teller and Procario often joked about wearing different hats. Though he was currently working—at least in theory—for MacDonald at INSCOM, his real work address was the Defense Intelligence Agency, the DoD's highest-level intelligence service. Technically, Procario was marine intelligence, but more often than not he was working for the DIA as well. Both men had worked for the CIA, though no one on either side of the duty roster admitted to that, and often their assignments were so unofficial they slipped completely beneath the bureaucratic radar of all of the government agencies, offices, and departments.

Which was the way Teller liked it. You could get a lot done when all of your bosses thought you were working for someone else.

So tomorrow they would be discussing things with the Central Intelligence Agency—though at an under-the-radar level to avoid the red tape and the turf wars.

Teller finished his drinks, watching Sandy writhe and twist on the stage above him. He already knew that he wouldn't be going home with her tonight.

Damn and double damn.

He wanted to find out what had happened to an old friend.

CHAPTER THREE

CENTRAL INTELLIGENCE AGENCY
LANGLEY, VIRGINIA
1140 HOURS, EDT
15 APRIL

Located in Langley, Virginia—a subdivision of the nearby town of McLean—the George Bush Center for Intelligence rises from 258 wooded acres on the south side of the Potomac River, a few miles west of downtown Washington, D.C. Teller's and Procario's appointment was in the OHB—the Old Headquarters Building, directly across from the NHB.

They were expected. They checked in at the front security desk, then entered the lobby, striding across the sixteen-foot seal of the Agency set into the marble floor. Off to the left, between the American and the Agency flags, was the Memorial Wall, 103 stars cut into solid marble representing the lives of CIA officers.

He glanced ahead, looking up at the words from John 8:32 carved into the lobby's south wall: AND YE

SHALL KNOW THE TRUTH AND THE TRUTH SHALL MAKE YOU FREE.

Yeah, Teller thought, with just a little bitterness. *Right . . .*

Truth, Teller knew, was a highly flexible commodity in this town.

Three men in conservative business suits emerged from the passageway beneath the legend. Jack Wentworth advanced with his hand out. "Frank! Chris! It's good to see you."

"How's it going, JJ?" Teller asked, shaking the man's hand.

"To hell," Wentworth replied. "In the proverbial gold-plated handbasket. Chris Teller? Frank Procario? This is Ed Chavez and David Larson. Ed, Dave, these are the DoD people I was telling you about."

Hands were shaken. "Pleased to meet you," Chavez said. He had Latino features and a friendly smile. Larson seemed more reserved, possibly suspicious. That was fine, so far as Teller was concerned. He didn't trust them either. The Klingons always worked to remind the DoD clan that they weren't Company, and that the Company was just a bit better than everyone else in the game.

"I've reserved a conference room down the hall," Chavez told them. "I really want you guys to take a look at this and tell us what you think."

The conference room was dominated by an interactive touch-table. "You've heard about Galen Fletcher?" Chavez asked.

"Yesterday," Procario said, "but JJ didn't say what the problem was."

"The problem," Wentworth told them, "is that we're blind in Mexico—and at the very worst possible moment."

Why am I not surprised? Teller thought, but he said nothing.

Wentworth tapped on the tabletop, bringing up a series of images. Pictures glowed on the table's surface, repeated large on the screen built into the wall behind him. "Both of you gentlemen," Wentworth went on, stressing the words to give them special weight, "now have Blue Star clearance."

"Gee, thanks," Teller quipped.

He didn't add that his DIA security clearance was two levels above Blue Star. Even in this age of computers and databases, the various agencies and departments in both the government and the military often didn't talk to one another.

Make that *especially* in this age of computers. An individual's electronic personnel records could be written on more than one level, and how deeply you were able to read them depended on the reader's security classification—and on how open the targeted records might be to the accessing agency in the first place.

Wentworth gave Teller a sharp look but continued. "What you see and hear in this room does not leave it. Understood?"

Procario crossed his arms, his face deadpan. "Of course."

"We'll be good, Mommy," Teller added.

Wentworth flashed Teller an annoyed glare. A photograph of Galen Fletcher appeared on the wall, much larger than life. He was smiling, a pipe in his right hand. Teller felt a fresh pang at the image; Fletcher had been more than a friend, more than a sponsor. In many ways he'd been Teller's mentor, the man responsible for Teller being who and what he now was.

"We're putting it out that Fletcher had personal problems, problems that caused him to take his own life. In a sense that's true."

"In a sense?"

A second face appeared on the wall next to Fletcher's, a much younger man, in his forties perhaps, lean, sharp edged, a bit grim.

"Richard Nicholas," Chavez said. "Our deputy chief of station in Mexico—and a traitor."

"Fletcher brought word to Langley personally four days ago," Larson said. "Nicholas sold us out, possibly starting a year ago."

"He sold our Mexican network to Los Zetas, and probably to the Sinaloans as well. To date we've lost three case officers and twenty-five agents. DEA is losing theirs, too. And we now have reason to believe that our pictures of the cartel hierarchies are false fronts." As he spoke, Chavez tapped commands into the table, bringing up a wall-sized map of Mexico, the southwestern rim of the United States, and the northern half of Central America, all of it divided into a scattered rainbow of colors—but predominantly in yellow and blue.

"This is how the Mexican cartels have carved things up so far, at least as far as we've been able to dope it out. Blue is Los Zetas. Yellow is Sinaloa."

The blue area stretched from the Texas border south along the Gulf Coast all the way to include the Yucatán, spreading inland as far as the Sierra Madre Oriental. The yellow region reached from the borders of New Mexico and Arizona south through central Mexico to Guadalajara, with a small, disconnected pocket down on the border with Guatemala. Other cartel-controlled areas were smaller and more isolated—the Tijuana Cartel in red, tucked in between the northern end of Baja California and San Diego; the Beltrán Leyva Cartel in orange, on the Pacific coast between Hermosillo and Mazatlán; La Familia Michoacana in green from Acapulco to Mexico City itself; the scattered remnants of the once-mighty Gulf Cartel, light blue patches around Matamoros and Tampico. Numerous other colors formed a scattered patchwork around individual cities: Los Negros, formerly part of Sinaloa; the tiny but powerful Juárez Cartel and its armed wing, La Línea; the Oaxaca Cartel; the South Pacific Cartel and the Knights Templar, both fragments of the disintegrating Beltrán Leyva Cartel. A number of photographs illustrated the map—cartel leaders and drug lords.

"The picture is always changing," Larson said. "Shifting alliances, blood feuds, betrayals. Gangs go extinct. New gangs arise from the ashes. The Beltrán Leyva brothers used to be allies of Sinaloa, but since 2010 they've been cozy with Los Zetas. La Familia used to be part of the Gulf Cartel and allied with Los Zetas, but then they switched sides. We think they're pretty much out of the picture, now, but an offshoot gang, Los Caballeros Templarios, the Knights Templar, is picking up the pieces now. They have an armed subgroup that calls itself La Resistencia, claims they're ready to fight and die for social justice."

"So they're revolutionaries?" Procario asked. "Political?"

"When you can buy and sell politicians, judges, police, and military personnel like candy," Chavez pointed out, "they're *all* fucking political.

"The two most powerful cartels are still Sinaloa and Los Zetas. Los Zetas started off as a gang of Mexican elite Special Forces, el Grupo Aeromóvil de Fuerzos Especiales. GAFE." He pronounced the acronym to rhyme with "café." "Superbly trained by U.S. Special Forces. Thirty of them deserted in '99 to form a private mercenary army for the Gulf Cartel, but in 2010 they went freelance. Today they include GAFE deserters, corrupt federal, state, and local police officers, and Guatemalan Kaibiles."

Teller whistled softly. The Kaibiles were another elite Special Forces branch, trained in jungle warfare and counterinsurgency operations.

"The Zetas have pretty much taken over all of the old Gulf Cartel territory," Larson said. "Their big nemesis has always been the Sinaloa Cartel."

"Sinaloa is the really big, bad boy down there," Chavez told them. "At least we think that's the case. It got started all the way back in 1989, when the old Colombian cartels started falling apart. For a while, it was known as 'the Federation,' until the Beltrán Leyva Cartel broke away and set up shop for themselves. We estimate that Sinaloa alone has brought two hundred fifty tons of cocaine across into the United States between 1990 and 2012. God knows how much heroin and marijuana."

"What you're saying," Teller said, "is that all of these alliances and feuds down there keep changing the picture, and now you can't even see what the picture is."

"Exactly. The drug gangs started picking off our agents a couple of months ago. Right now, we have *no* active agents on the ground in Mexico, and we've recalled our last four case officers because we think Nicholas compromised them."

"He fucking blew their covers," Wentworth said, "and now we're deaf, blind, and stupid down there."

Within the Central Intelligence Agency, an agent was a local person recruited to spy for the CIA. A case officer, on the other hand, was an American employed by the Agency to recruit and "run" agents from the local population.

"So you're looking to rebuild your Mexican network," Procario said.

"Yes," Larson said, "but there is a . . . complication." He looked at Wentworth, who nodded.

"We were tracking a possible Trapdoor package to the Yucatán," he said.

"Jesus!" Teller said. "Confirmed?"

"No," Larson admitted. "Not confirmed. But we're ninety percent on it."

"Dave is with WINPAC," Wentworth explained.

WINPAC was the CIA's Weapons, Intelligence, Nonproliferation, and Arms Control Center, a department under the Directorate of Intelligence concerned with monitoring nuclear weapons and the threat they posed to the United States. "Trapdoor," Teller knew, was a code name for loose nukes—atomic weapons or nuclear materials that had gone missing, particularly during the break-up of the Soviet Union and in the chaotic aftermath of civil war, breakaway republics, and Muslim unrest during the nineties.

"We believe," Larson continued, "that two of Lebed's missing suitcases were purchased in 2011 for twelve million dollars—a real bargain. Informants placed them in Karachi this past February. We were attempting to organize a strike force to go in and neutralize them. Unfortunately, they disappeared."

Teller felt a cold chill sweep up the back of his neck. This was nightmare stuff. Lebed was Russian general Alexander Lebed, who'd announced to the world in 1997 that 132 so-called suitcase nukes produced for the KGB were unaccounted for and might be headed for the open market. There were plenty of groups and governments in the world who would like to acquire one or more of the devices and become an overnight nuclear power.

"Disappeared? How?"

Larson shrugged. "We're talking about two devices about yea big." He held up his hands three feet apart, indicating something the size of a large briefcase. "Fifty, maybe sixty pounds each. Karachi is a very busy port, the Pakistanis don't particularly like us right now, and not all of the ships there are well documented. We thought the weapons were on board a Syrian freighter, the *Qahir*. Navy SEALs deploying out of Diego Garcia intercepted the *Qahir* in the western Indian Ocean and performed a VBSS. They came up empty-handed."

VBSS was the military acronym for "visit, board, search, and seizure." Teller wondered how that one had been covered up, since he hadn't heard anything about it either on the news or through official channels. Possibly the State Department had been working overtime smoothing things over back-channel, convincing the Syrians that it was in their best interests to help find two missing nuclear weapons. Or possibly the *Qahir* had simply been reported as lost at sea. Those waters were well known to be the hunting grounds for pirates, and dangerous.

"So we went back to the drawing board," Larson continued. He tapped on the tabletop, bringing up fifteen photographs of different ships. "All of these vessels were reported as departing from Karachi during the last week in March, the time period when we thought the weapons left Pakistan. We were also following up rumors that the ISI had stepped in and secured the devices for themselves." Inter-Services Intelligence, the ISI, was Pakistan's equivalent of the CIA. "The destinations of those ships were scattered all over the world—Jakarta, Sidney, Los Angeles, Southampton, New York. Most of them had multiple ports of call, which complicated things. We focused on the ones heading for U.S. ports, of course. Nothing."

"So we're back to square one," Chavez said. One of the ship photographs enlarged as the others disappeared from the screen. She was an ancient freighter, rust streaked and decrepit. "One of the vessels on our list was a small tramp, the *Zapoteca*. Liberian flagged, but owned by Manzanillo Internacional, a Mexican import-export company. We got curious because Karachi is a long way outside her usual range."

A box of stats opened alongside the photograph, and Teller skimmed down through the information quickly. The *Zapoteca* displaced 1,800 tons, was 252 feet long at the waterline, and had a beam of just over 40 feet. She was single screw; her power plant was a Burmeister & Wain Alpha 10-cycle diesel delivering 1,200 horsepower. She had a range of 3,000 nautical miles at 12 knots and usually carried a complement of ten men. She'd been launched in 1951 by Frederikshavn Vaerft & Terdok; originally she'd been Danish. She'd been sold to Colombia in 1985, then sold again to Manzanillo Internacional in 1996.

Interesting.

"Colombia, then Mexico," Teller said. He exchanged a glance with Procario. "The cartels?"

Procario nodded.

"We checked that," Wentworth said. "The corporations owning the *Zapoteca,* both in Colombia and in Mexico, are legit."

"But mostly she stuck to a coastal run between Barranquilla and either Veracruz or Tampico," Chavez

pointed out. "That's just fifteen hundred nautical miles—
say, five or six days at twelve knots. But from Karachi?
She'd have to take it in two- and three-thousand-mile
legs, refueling along the way. That's over thirteen thousand nautical miles and forty-five days, not counting
the time spent in each port."

"Maybe they were on a horse run," Procario suggested. "Might be worth it. A hell of a lot of heroin
comes out of Afghanistan by way of Karachi."

"That was a possibility," Larson said, "but unlikely.
The Mexican cartels produce their own heroin in
northern Mexico. Why send one ship halfway around
the world for a few more tons of the stuff? So we began
wondering what the *Zapoteca* might be carrying besides drugs, especially when she didn't show up at Veracruz like she was supposed to. We began a rather
intense and thorough search with our NRO assets."
Part of the DoD, the NRO—the National Reconnaissance Office—was one of the sixteen U.S. intelligence
agencies. Headquartered in Chantilly, Virginia, it designed, built, and operated America's spy satellites.
Larson moved his fingers over the interactive tabletop
and brought up a new photograph. It had been shot
obliquely from overhead, from high up and off the vessel's port stern. Enlarged, the level of resolution and
crisp detail was astonishing. You could see coils of
rope on the deck, streaks of rust down her side, and
crewmen going about their work. One man in blue
jeans and a T-shirt appeared to be leaning against the
railing along the fantail, balanced somewhat precari-
ously. The resolution was good enough to show his

head and what might have been a beard, but not quite sharp enough to show facial features.

"What's that one doing?" Teller asked, pointing.

Chavez grinned. "Taking a piss."

Sure enough, Teller could just make out the man's hands, folded together below where his belt buckle might be.

The gesture was so completely human that Teller smiled. The CIA, in his opinion, relied entirely too much on what it referred to as its technological assets—looking at satellite imagery and listening in on cell phone intercepts. Satellites were good if you were tracking tanks or army movements or even individual ships, but they rarely helped you track individual people or figure out exactly what they were doing. You couldn't get inside a person's head with a satellite.

Lines of type at the lower right of the image gave the date and time: 09 April, 1827 hours GMT, just six days ago. Below that were the vessel's coordinates: 16°45'30.80" N; 82°54'34.69" W.

"The ship's position when this was taken was about three hundred forty miles east of Belize City," Chavez said. "The *Zapoteca* appeared to be on course for Belize at the time, not Veracruz."

"Veracruz is on the other side of the Yucatán Peninsula," Larson said.

"I know how to read a map," Teller said. "Why Belize?"

"That's what we wondered," Wentworth said. "We told Fletcher to send a couple of agents down there and check it out."

"And then they disappeared," Procario said.

Wentworth closed his eyes, then opened them again. "In a manner of speaking. On the eleventh, *this* arrived at our Mexican embassy."

The satellite image of the *Zapoteca* was replaced by another photograph. For a moment, Teller's mind refused to register exactly what it was he was looking at. The photo was a bit blurry—probably shot with a cell phone camera—but it showed a desktop, an open cardboard box, and a lot of partially crumpled newspaper.

Inside the box was the grim reality that Teller, as he stared at it in increasing horror, only reluctantly began to accept.

It was a man's head, but horribly mutilated. The ears, the nose, the eyes, all were missing, and the skin, sliced randomly here and there as if by a scalpel, was caked with blood. Black, blood-matted hair was visible, and a black mustache. Below this last was an *x-x-x* pattern of what looked like leather cord sealing shut a bulging, bloody mouth.

"His mouth." Procario began. "What—"

"His penis was stuffed inside, and the lips sewn shut," Wentworth said, his voice utterly drained of any emotion.

"Henrico Javier Ferrari Garcia de Alba," Chavez said, grim. "There was a right forefinger inside the box along with the head, so we were able to get a positive ID from the print. The bastards *wanted* us to know. Recruited by Fletcher himself last year. A member of the Mexican *federales,* the federal police, and something of a campaigner for government reform. He told us he was sick to death of government and police corruption and let himself be recruited so he could fight back. We got a lot of good information from him about high-ranking politicians and military personnel who were owned by the cartels. Forty-one years old. College educated, Universidad de México. Accomplished violinist; wanted to be a professional musician but ended up with the police instead. He . . . he had a wife and three kids. Fletcher wasn't able to find any of them after this—their house in San Mateo showed signs of a struggle—and we think they may have been abducted as well."

"The other agent was Agustín Morales Galvan," Wentworth added. "No sign of him at all . . . at least, not yet. Their last report was from Corozal on the tenth. That's a town on the Yucatán east coast, about eighty miles north of Belize City."

"So," Teller said, "Galen sent those two to Belize to check on the arrival of the *Zapoteca,* and both of them disappeared."

"We have to assume the cartel enforcers got them," Chavez said.

"Which cartel?" Teller asked. He looked at the map of drug cartel territories, still partially visible as a kind of wallpaper behind the photo of the severed head. The Yucatán was highlighted in blue. "Los Zetas?"

"Actually, we're not sure," Chavez said. He touched the tabletop, and the nightmarish photograph mercifully disappeared. "That's Los Zetas territory, yeah—

but there's a chance, a fairly good one, we think, that Los Zetas and Sinaloa have buried the hatchet and are now working together."

A black-and-white surveillance photo came up on the screen, next to Mexico City on the map. Four men stood on a city sidewalk, apparently getting into a car. "This was taken a month ago. The one on the right, behind the open door—that's Carlos Guevara Alvarez, one of the top lieutenants in Los Zetas. The one next to him, holding the door open, is Ernesto Mendoza Flores, a high-ranking member of Sinaloa who specializes in smuggling both drugs and people into Arizona and New Mexico. The one in the back, he's Hector Gallardo, and he's important—the chief lieutenant, aide, whatever you want to call him of one of the *real* big fish. Joaquín 'El Chapo' Guzmán. Head of Sinaloa Cartel, and by conservative estimates now with a personal worth of around one billion dollars. *Forbes* magazine listed him as the nine hundred thirty-seventh richest man in the world—and the sixtieth most powerful."

"So if a senior Guzmán aide is hanging out with Alvarez," Wentworth said, "then there's got to be a truce on, and a pretty solid one."

"And the fourth man?" Teller asked. "He doesn't look Mexican. More Middle Eastern, I'd say."

"*That* is the one who really worries us," Chavez said. "You're right. He's not Hispanic. He's Persian. His name is Saeed Reyshahri. He's Republican Guard and probably VEVAK. Until recently he was an Iranian adviser with Hezbollah in Syria."

"What the fuck are the Iranians doing in Mexico?" Procario demanded.

"That's what we would like to know," Larson said, "very, very badly. We've known for several years that Hezbollah has people in Mexico working with the cartels—and Hezbollah, of course, has ties to Iran. We have the Mexican state in virtual anarchy, the possibility that a couple of small nukes have arrived in Belize on board a Mexican freighter with cartel ties, and now a VEVAK agent turns up in Mexico City with high-ranking members of Mexico's two largest and most vicious drug cartels. That's not good."

"And right at that moment," Chavez added, "someone pulls the plug and our Mexican network goes down. It's not exactly a good time to be in the dark."

"Can you explain to me," Teller said, "what Hezbollah's interest in Mexico might be?" He spoke quietly, his voice and manner wooden. His emotions were still churning after the sight of the severed head, and he was having trouble controlling them.

Wentworth shrugged. "We've known they've been there for several years," he said. "Mostly, they seem to be using the cartel smuggling networks—especially Sinaloa—to bring their own drugs across the border into the U.S. in order to finance their operations in the Middle East. But they're moving people across as well."

"The cartels," Chavez added, "don't just bring drugs into the country. Over the last decade, they've been more and more involved in smuggling illegals across the border as well. The operators are called coyotes, and it's pretty lucrative for them. They bring in between eighteen hundred and twenty-five hundred dollars per person, and lots of times they manage to extort more from the families. Sometimes a *lot* more, usually by locking up the illegals once they're in the States and threatening to torture or kill them. Since they have well-established conduits—a network of underground railways—Hezbollah has been using them to move its own drugs and undocumented people across as well."

"So we need to find out what a known VEVAK agent is doing here, too," Procario said.

"Our *first* order of business," Larson said, "is to get our Mexican intelligence network up and running again. Then we need to find out if someone—possibly one of the cartels—has just smuggled a couple of small nuclear weapons into Mexico."

"Los Zetas with nuclear weapons," Wentworth said. "It doesn't bear thinking about."

"Maybe it's not the cartels bringing in the nukes," Teller said. "Maybe it's the Iranians."

"I don't buy it," Larson said, shaking his head. "If Iran got caught playing those kinds of games, some major Armageddon would come down on their turbans, and they know it. They're not going to risk all-out retaliation over a couple of pocket nukes."

"Just how big a nuclear device are we talking about?" Teller asked. "I thought suitcase nukes were pretty small. What, five or six kilotons?"

"If they're based on Russian RA-115s, yeah. Sixty-five pounds for the device, three- to five-kiloton yield, or thereabouts. That's less than a third the yield of the device that flattened Hiroshima, but it's more than enough to wreck the downtown area of a major American city. They might also be built from old Soviet nuclear artillery shells. Those have smaller yields—half a kiloton up to about two kilotons. Still nasty."

"So what does a Mexican drug cartel want with a pocket nuke?" Procario asked.

"Extortion, most likely," Chavez replied. "All of the cartels have been under a lot of pressure lately, both from the Mexican government and from the U.S., the FBI and DEA. All of the cartels have a history of killing people they perceive as enemies in spectacularly bloody and public ways in order to send a message. 'Back off, or this'll happen to you.' They might well threaten to nuke downtown Mexico City if the government and the army there didn't do what they said."

"Are we sure Mexico City is the target?" Teller asked.

"No."

"Because we also have a Shiite terror group and their Iranian sponsors getting cozy with the drug cartels. Maybe *they're* the ones bringing them in. Maybe they're planning on smuggling those bombs across the Mexican border."

"We've thought of that," Larson said. "For the past week we've thought of little else. But, like I said, the Iranians aren't stupid. They're not going to let Hezbollah screw things for them, either. We know Hezbollah is in Tehran's pocket. Most of us think it's not Hezbollah behind it, but al Qaeda."

"Either way," Wentworth said, "it's not pretty. JJ

said you people might have some ideas. If you do, we'd love to hear them."

Teller exchanged a look with Procario. "Of course we do," he said. "We've got exactly what you need."

21ST CENTURY CITY
SANTA MONICA BOULEVARD
LOS ANGELES, CALIFORNIA
1002 HOURS, PDT

"Hey, you should lay off that stuff, man," the driver said, watching the two in the backseat in his rearview mirror.

"Yeah," the other passenger said. "*Cojones químico.* That's no good, Mannie. We need to be at our best, y'know?"

"I can handle it, man." He'd sprinkled some white powder from a small plastic bag onto a square of paper. "*Solamente una pizca de blanquito, no más.*" He inhaled the powder through his right nostril, then jerked his head back, crumpling the paper. "*¡Ay! ¡Qué bueno!*"

The driver scowled. "*¡Qué malparido! ¡Eres un angurri!*"

"C'mon, c'mon," the other passenger told the driver. "He'll be okay. You got our packages?"

"*Aquí.*" He handed back two large canvas tote bags, the kind with retail logos on them used by green-conscious shoppers in the United States. Both bags were quite heavy and bulged a bit.

"Wait for us," the passenger said, taking the bags

and handing one to Manuel. *"Diez minutos, Ignacio,"* the driver said. *"No más."*

Ignacio Carballo glanced at his watch, then nodded. "Keep the motor running."

The two slipped out of the backseat onto the sidewalk and sauntered toward the looming, ultramodern façade of the shopping center, through two sets of glass doors, and into the main interior boulevard of the mall. The air-conditioning was cool and pleasant.

This was an upscale part of the city, between Santa Monica and Beverly Hills. The shoppers, Carballo noticed, tended to be young, bored looking, and well dressed; even the cutoff jeans and T-shirts looked like they'd come with designer labels. He didn't see a single black or Hispanic face, and for just a moment he felt afraid. He and Mannie stood out in the crowd.

They had to get this started *now,* before a guard or a cop challenged them.

Halfway up the lane of shops and boutiques, Carballo pointed to a Starbucks on the other side. *"Allá,"* he said. "Start there."

"¡Sí! ¡Vámonos a soltarse el pelo, 'mano!"

Carballo shook his head. "Just go! Let's do it!" Manuel Herrera was a good guy, but right now he was flying on that hit of *mosca.* Turning to face back the way he'd come, he reached into his canvas bag with his right hand, removing a baseball-sized steel sphere, a U.S. Army–issue Mk 1 hand grenade. His left hand holding the bag by its carry strap, he hooked his left forefinger through the cotter-pin ring and yanked it free. With his right hand, he flipped the grenade backhand and to the right, sending it clattering into the front of a Frederick's of Hollywood.

Continuing to walk briskly, he pulled another grenade from the bag, yanked the pin, and tossed it into the next shop along, a gift store featuring lots of cut glass ornaments and bric-a-brac. Then to the next shop, counting under his breath. *". . . y tres . . . y quatro . . . y cinco . . ."*

He heard a shrill scream from somewhere behind him, and in the next instant an explosion thundered from the lingerie shop. Glass windows and splinters from the wooden door frame erupted into the central aisle like a shotgun blast. Opposite, the grenade Manuel had tossed into the Starbucks detonated behind the counter. Glass display cases turned into blast-driven shards, razor sharp and deadly, scything through the cluster of customers waiting for their expensive morning coffee.

More screams, shrill and terrified . . . and then the next blast went off . . . and the next . . . and the next. The shopping mall had become a storm of chaos, blood, and death. People were running in every direction, none of them knowing which way to go, just that they had to *run*. Others lay on the polished tiles of the floor, many of them splattered with blood, their own, or the blood of others. When Carballo glanced back over his shoulder, he saw horror. A young man propelled from a shop, colliding with an elderly woman. An overturned stroller, an infant in pink pajamas squirming on the ground nearby. A woman—the child's mother, perhaps—lying on her back, eyes staring at the skylights overhead, her face a mask of blood . . .

Carballo didn't think about it, didn't *let* himself think about it. There was a job to be done. He and Herrera continued to walk down either side of the aisle, tossing grenade after grenade into each shop front as they passed it. Each of them had started with twelve grenades in his bag. Carballo was down to his last three when he saw a mall security cop ahead, running toward him.

Mall cops weren't armed, but they could still be trouble. Without slowing his walk, Carballo reached into his bag, extracted a Mini-Uzi, released the charging handle, and sent a burst of 9 mm rounds slamming into and through the security guard. The Mini-Uzi, a smaller version of its more famous big brother, was less than fifteen inches long with its folding stock removed and weighed less than eight pounds with a full magazine. With a cyclic rate of fire of better than fifteen rounds per second, it sounded like a miniature buzz saw. The security guard flopped backward, arms pinwheeling, and came to rest sprawled across an ornamental tree planter. Carballo turned and loosed the rest of his magazine randomly into a crowd of shrieking people, dropped the empty magazine, and snicked home a new one.

Three more shops, three more grenades. He dropped the now empty canvas bag and strode toward the front entrance. He hoped Mannie was behind him, but he didn't stop to look. Mannie was a big boy and could take care of himself.

As he emerged onto the sidewalk once more, he nearly collided with a a traffic cop in shorts, helmet, and a windbreaker riding a bike. That one wasn't armed either, but Carballo cut him down with a burst from the Mini-Uzi, slamming bike and rider sideways into a brick wall. Other people on the sidewalk shrieked and scattered. Carballo snapped off the rest of his magazine in a quick succession of bursts until the weapon was empty.

More gunfire sounded from inside the mall. It sounded like Mannie was having fun. Kicking up his heels, just like he'd said.

Fuck him.

He reached the idling automobile and yanked open the passenger-side front door. *"Vámanos,"* he said, sliding in.

"What about Mannie?"

Carballo looked at his watch. Nine minutes had passed. *"Un tecado gilún,"* he said. "Leave him!"

As more explosions sounded from the mall, blasting out the glass doors at the entrance, the getaway car sped off down the street.

In the distance, sirens wailed.

CHAPTER FOUR

CENTRAL INTELLIGENCE AGENCY
LANGLEY, VIRGINIA
1318 HOURS, EDT
15 APRIL

"I've never heard of this," Larson said. "Damn it, why weren't we informed?"

The five men had gone down to one of the OHB's employee cafeterias for lunch. As they ate, they continued to discuss the technological twist Teller and Procario had been describing to them.

"Hey, new stuff is coming out all the time," Teller told him. "This thing is still in beta, but it would be easy enough to get you guys a copy, let you try it out."

"So it's like a virus—" Chavez began.

"A very, very smart virus," Teller said.

"—and it just leaps from phone to phone?"

"Right," Procario said. "It's called peer-to-peer transmission."

"And it creates a map of phone use," Chavez said. "That's . . . amazing."

"Hey, welcome to the twenty-first century," Teller told him. "All the thrills of sci-fi, and outmoded Dark Ages concepts like privacy magically become a thing of the past."

The system they'd been describing had recently come from a high-technology think tank in Washington, one of dozens of corporate entities in the town feeding information, analyses, tools, and, occasionally, informed guesswork to the policy makers. Teller knew that something similar had already been field tested by the NSA, but the deep-black National Security Agency didn't like to share with anyone.

The software was called Cellmap.

"So how do we deploy it?" Chavez wanted to know.

"We find a cell phone that's part of the net we want to map," Teller told him. "It would have phone numbers of other contacts. It uses those to locate other phones on the network."

"Kind of like a computer virus making copies of your e-mail list," Wentworth suggested.

"Pretty much. Even if the user didn't save contact phone numbers, the phone would still have a list of all the numbers it's called in its memory. Cellmap nestles down in the phone's memory, gets the list of numbers, and starts sending copies of itself phone to phone. Doesn't need cell towers. Doesn't even need the phone to be switched on. It jumps from phone to phone to phone all by itself—and periodically it uploads to a satellite, which zaps it back to you."

"Pretty soon," Procario told them, "you build up a map of phone connections. Even if the opposition is doing onetime use with call cards, it keeps track of the phone. If they throw the phone away and get a new one, the system is redundant enough to fill in the gap as soon as the new phone comes online."

"Right." Teller nodded. "And the best part? Every cell phone on the network has the potential to become a bug."

"The phone doesn't need to be on?"

"Nope. The phone has a microphone, and the virus operates on *very* low levels of power. You activate a target's phone from here, and it starts transmitting conversations from the guy's pocket."

"I'd heard the NSA could listen in through telephones," Wentworth said, thoughtful. "Pick up on key words and relay conversations automatically, even when the phone is off."

Teller nodded. "They've been doing that for a while, though there are legal issues to using it inside the United States, of course. Cellmap, though, is a lot more flexible, and it puts active bugs in the pockets of everyone in the target network. Doesn't take long, either. A few seconds, even allowing for satellite transmission time."

"Incredible."

"So we need to get someone down to Mexico," Chavez said, "have them find a phone and plant the virus."

"Why can't we plant the virus from here?" Wentworth wanted to know. "We could give El Chapo a call and infect his phone from here."

"Uh-uh," Teller said, shaking his head. "Doesn't work

that way. You have to use a special install program to shoehorn the virus into the phone's memory, and we can't do that long distance. *Yet*."

Chavez looked at Wentworth. "Sounds like a good way to learn if Los Zetas are working with Sinaloa," he said.

"I was thinking that," Wentworth replied. He looked at Teller. "How would you two like to take a little all-expense paid trip south of the border?"

Teller's eyebrows arched up his forehead. "Us? Why?"

"Because sending someone who understands the tech is better than trying to teach someone down there from up here. And because, like we said, we don't happen to have any assets in Mexico right now. And you have a reputation for . . . *unconventional* thinking."

Procario chuckled. "It'll take you off the McDee's radar for a while, Chris."

"There *is* that." He looked at Wentworth. "What would our org chart look like?"

"You'll work for Dave here," he said, nodding at Larson. "You'll be with WINPAC, under the Directorate of Intelligence. Or . . ." He hesitated. "What do you think, Dave. Maybe S&T instead?"

S&T was the Directorate of Science and Technology, which included the Agency's research and development branch.

"No," Larson said firmly, shaking his head. "Absolutely not. That would put them under Colbert, and he would want to be in on the new toy. All the way in, and he wouldn't want to deploy until we owned it. We need boots on the ground down there *now*. Anyway, I'd rather keep them in my stable."

"Fair enough." Chavez grinned at Teller. "So, you cowboys up for this?"

Teller grinned. "Does this mean you're recruiting us?"

A shrug. "Only if you want me to."

"I'll let you know after MacDonald's IG witch hunt is over."

"Jesus," Wentworth said. "You have an inspector general on your ass?"

Teller grinned. "It's an 'administrative investigation,' not the Pentagon Papers. No big deal. Okay, we'll run your little errand for you. What could possibly go wrong?"

"Nada, amigos," Chavez said. *"Absolutamente nada."*

"What's our legend?" Procario asked.

"We'll fix you up as a couple of *norteamericano* journalists," Chavez said.

"Huh." Teller wasn't sure he liked the sound of that. "Haven't the cartels been offing journalists lately?"

"Only Mexican journalists," Wentworth said.

"At least so far," Procario said with a dark chuckle.

"And since you two are clean skins," Chavez continued, "you should escape their radar."

"Clean skins" meant that Teller and Procario were unknown to anyone in Mexico, including even Agency personnel at the American Embassy. They would have to assume that the cartels had their own spies there, seeking to spot fresh CIA officers arriving to take over from the ones blown by Richard Nicholas.

"You know," Wentworth said, "there really ought to be a way to infect a target's cell phone remotely."

"You're thinking about Nicholas?" Chavez asked.

"Yeah. We have his number—"

"Can't do it," Teller said.

"Hey, even if we could, he probably ditched his phone right off," Procario pointed out. "He knows if you get him on the line, you could pinpoint his position by GPS."

"We'll get him from the other direction," Teller said, "when we tag his new buddies and they tag him."

"Speaking of phones," Wentworth said. He reached into his pocket and pulled out his cell phone. There was a new text message, and he took a moment to read the screen. "That was Andy. We need to get to a TV," he said, pocketing the phone again.

"We can use my office," Chavez said. "It's right down the passage outside."

"What's up?" Procario wanted to know.

"Not sure. He just texted me about a terrorist attack in L.A. He says it's all over CNN."

Minutes later, they stood in Chavez's office, staring at a television monitor. Black smoke billowed from the front of a large, modern-looking shopping mall. Fire and police vehicles crowded the street outside, roller bars flashing. ". . . about fifteen minutes ago," a woman's voice was saying. "As yet there is no indication of who is behind the attack, though authorities here say that it might be al Qaeda."

A red marquee banner was running across the bottom, declaring TERROR ATTACK IN SANTA MONICA.

"Not al Qaeda," Larson said. "Not since we capped OBL."

The reporter was still talking. ". . . and eyewitnesses claim that at least three men began throwing hand grenades or explosives into shops inside the mall, then proceeded to fire indiscriminately into crowds of shoppers with machine guns . . ."

"Doesn't sound like AQ," Procario said. "They would've used a truck bomb to try to bring down the whole building."

"They're still lying low, anyway," Teller said. "They don't know what intel our SEALs pulled out of the Abbottabad compound. The sons of bitches have been running scared ever since."

"So who did it?" Wentworth asked.

"Maybe Hezbollah?" Chavez suggested.

"I don't think so," Teller said, shaking his head. "Their number-one target is Israel, and they don't want to get the U.S. *too* mad at them. They don't stand to gain anything by shooting up American shopping malls."

"A lot of us think it's AQ trying to smuggle those nukes into Belize," Larson said. "We can't count them out after bin Laden's death, not by a long shot. They hate us, we know they've been trying to get their hands on tactical nukes for years, and now they just might have done it." He jerked a thumb at the television screen. "This could just be the beginning, the opening move in an escalating campaign. Start with Hollywood shopping malls, and end with a nuke in the D.C. Mall."

"Aw, hell, and maybe it was a disgruntled employee," Procario said. "Wait until we hear something other than hot air from CNN."

"No waiting," Larson said. "I want you two on a plane tonight, if we can swing it. Better still . . . Ed? How about if you go with them?"

Chavez reached for his phone. "I'm on it."

"We don't need an army," Teller said. "We want to stay inconspicuous."

"Three men is not an army," Wentworth said. "I'll feel better about you going if you have some decent backup."

"We'll need something to go on," Procario told Wentworth. "A target. Someone who's likely to have a phone connection with at least one of the cartels."

"We have a contact with CISEN," Wentworth said. "We'll have him meet you, fill you in on local color."

CISEN was the Centro de Investigación y Seguridad Nacional, an intelligence agency under the secretary of the interior but reporting directly to the Mexican president.

"Whoa there," Procario said. "What if this CISEN guy is owned by the wrong people?"

Despite attempts at reform, the Mexican government was riddled by corruption. In a country where a police officer made a few dollars a week and the drug lords could offer bribes of millions, *no* one could be trusted.

"Miguel de la Cruz," Wentworth said, "is as solid a man as you'll find. You can trust him with your lives."

"Funny you should put it that way," Procario said, "because that's exactly what we're going to be doing."

"We could split the team," Teller said.

"What do you mean?"

"I get off the plane by myself and meet this de la Cruz guy. Frank and Ed deplane later and shadow us. If de la Cruz pulls a fast one, they're both there to ride to the rescue. They can also sweep us for tails."

"That sounds reasonable," Wentworth said. "Besides, Ed knows de la Cruz. It'll make contacting him easier."

"You'll all have to go in wired," Larson said.

"Just so we can stay in touch with each other," Teller said. "I don't want the opposition picking up anything unusual about us."

"Agreed."

"Okay," Teller said, nodding. "This is starting to sound like a plan."

"And while we're at it," Larson told Wentworth, "it wouldn't hurt to have them check out Belize City as long as they're down there."

"You want us to check out the *Zapoteca*?" Teller asked.

"It would help," Wentworth said. "We have a brand-new lily pad in Ladyville. That's less than ten miles from Belize City. But we'll need someone to go in and confirm the target, eyes on, before we sent in a strike team."

"Lily pad"—also known as a cooperative security location, or CSL—was the military's slang term for a local facility used by the United States for training in counterterrorism and drug interdiction. Generally, there were no U.S. personnel permanently stationed at these bases, but equipment and supplies could be pre-positioned there, and there was a large runway available so that troops could be flown in on short notice. As such, it differed from a forward operating site, or FOS, a base that usually had a small permanent force of troops or contract employees stationed there.

"I trust you understand," Procario said, "that the

more objectives you pile onto the mission, the more likely it is that *all* of them will fail."

"Hey, it's not like you're being asked to take down El Chapo Guzmán, okay?" Larson said. "You go down there and interact with cartel personnel, do what you have to do to spread your virus. If you happen to be in Belize when you do that, you can swing by and eyeball the docks, see if the *Zapoteca* is in port. Listen, this is crucial. If someone is bringing stolen suitcase nukes into Belize, we need to bring them down, and we need to bring them down *hard*. Understand me?"

"Of course," Teller said. He looked at Procario and shrugged. "Not a problem."

"Not a problem," Procario added, "unless the bad guys have security beefed up in Belize because they don't want outsiders snooping around their nukes. Did you think of that?"

"I'm sure," Larson said with an unpleasant half-smile, "that the DIA can find a way to cope."

"Okay," Chavez said, closing his phone. "We've got three seats on a 747 out of Dulles, eighteen thirty tonight. Nonstop all the way to Benito Juárez."

"Good," Larson said. "I like going by way of Juárez. We don't want to tip off the black hats in Belize that we're interested in the area. These guys can get a private flight from Mexico City to Ladyville, go in quiet without showing our hand."

"You boys up to date on your shots?" Wentworth asked.

"I'm not sure—" Teller began.

Wentworth waved his hand. "Not important. We can

bring your shot records online and give you what you need down in the dispensary. And we'll have your passports and other papers ready for you in a couple of hours."

Teller looked at Procario. "Cheer up, Frank. It's a holiday in the land of sun and fun!"

"Maybe," Procario said. He was staring at the news broadcast as talking heads in the newsroom speculated on who might have launched the terror strike against Los Angeles. "But whether it's Hezbollah, al Qaeda, or plain old home-grown narcoterrorists, we're going to need some heavy backup on this one."

"Like what?" Larson wanted to know.

"Oh, I don't know," Teller said. "How about some U.S. Navy SEALs?"

"We'll see what we can arrange."

"You'd better. I don't want to get shipped home like Henrico Ferrari. I get claustrophobic in small spaces like cardboard boxes. And my feet smell."

CAFETERIA
ECCLES FEDERAL RESERVE BOARD BUILDING
TWENTIETH STREET AND CONSTITUTION AVENUE NW
WASHINGTON, D.C.
1335 HOURS, EDT

"You've seen the news, James?"

James Walker looked up from his meal. "You mean California? Yes."

"And so it begins."

The man placed his tray on the table and took a seat

across from Walker. His name was Randolph Edgar Preston, and he was the assistant to the president for national security affairs, more commonly known as the national security adviser, or simply as ANSA. As a man with direct access to the president of the United States, he was undeniably one of the most powerful men in the world.

"It begins," Walker echoed. Glum, he turned and looked out the large expanse of glass windows along the cafeteria's south wall, a view that took in the Constitution Gardens and the Reflecting Pool just beyond, the abrupt, skyward stab of the Washington Monument off to the left, the Lincoln Memorial to the right. "It begins, but I still wonder if the time is right."

"Why, James! Having second thoughts?"

Walker looked back at Preston, met his eyes . . . then dropped his gaze.

People thought of James Fitzhugh Walker as a small, gray man, as a banker, as an accountant, as a *lawyer,* terms that defined his world of numbers, accounts, banking laws, and the soulless transfer of funds. For twenty-five years he'd worked at the Fed, slowly working his way up the internal hierarchy. For twenty-five years he'd nurtured his career, built his life. If that life was less than exciting, well, James Walker didn't like excitement. He liked things . . . predictable. Sane. Ordered. *Rational.*

"I've had second thoughts, as you put it, all along, Mr. Preston. You know that."

"But you did agree to work with us. To work with the *Program.*"

"People have died, Mr. Preston. If our . . . our involvement comes under public scrutiny—"

"Ah, but it will *not,* Mr. Walker," Preston said. "There is no reason for any of this to go public, is there?"

Preston had a way of looking at him, cold, unemotional, *superior.* Walker felt exactly as he imagined a mouse might feel when confronted by a hungry snake.

"No. No, of course not."

"Good."

It took Walker a moment to work up the courage to ask the question. "So . . . what are you doing over here?"

"Finding you, of course. We're having a special meeting tonight. The Program's Central Committee. At the club. You'll be there?"

Walker wondered for a moment what would happen if he told the man no, if he said he had other plans, even just a quiet night home with his wife and son.

Then he realized that it would make no difference at all. The Program, as it was informally known within the group, lately had come to dominate his life, to *own* it.

"I'll be there."

"Excellent. We'll be discussing the next steps we must take to further the Program. We expect that things will be happening very quickly now."

"I still don't understand," Walker said. "Why the ungodly hurry?"

"For the simple reason, Mr. Walker, that a secret of this size, of this magnitude, cannot be long kept. We are rewriting history, our little group, and the consequences will affect millions, no, *hundreds* of millions of people. The longer we wait, the more likely it is that . . . well . . . a chain is only as strong as its weakest link, isn't that right?"

Walker wondered if Preston had just threatened him. He knew he was the weak link. The others—Logan, Gonzales, Delaney, Fuentes—they'd been in on this from the beginning. They knew the risks, but they'd been willing to push ahead nonetheless. *They* never seemed to have second thoughts.

"We are, all of us," Preston continued, "under a great deal of pressure. But now that things are moving forward for us, the pressure will be less. I promise you that the rewards shall be infinitely worth the current stress and . . . difficulty."

"Directo a México is coming under fire, you know," Walker said. "If Congress gets too interested, it could be bad. I know it's only marginally concerned with the Program, but if it comes under intense public scrutiny, everything could unravel. *Everything.*"

"Directo a México, as you well know, James, is completely legal. You need have no fears on that account. As for Congress . . . well, you leave them to me. They are *not* your concern."

Numb, Walker could only nod.

"Good," Preston said, standing. "I'll see you at the club tonight. *Be* there, James."

Walker watched as Preston—arguably one of the most powerful men in the United States government—walked away. He took a last bite of his barely touched lunch, then pushed the tray aside. The cherry blossoms were at their height—clouds of pink beyond the Reflecting Pool and around the Jefferson Memorial and the Tidal Basin farther south.

Right . . . completely legal. It *was* legal, of course, because the insanely serpentine laws had been written that way to *make* it legal, all while avoiding too much oversight from Congress or unpleasant attention from the media.

Generally, the public thought little about the Federal Reserve and knew even less. Hell, people's eyes glassed over when Walker told them what he did for a living— and that was okay. He didn't want attention, not directed toward the Federal Reserve, and especially not directed toward him.

As for the public, well, these things always were best kept out of the public eye. Someone once had noted that people should never watch how sausage or laws are made, and the same, Walker was convinced, was true of the federal banking system.

Deliberately designed to be independent within the government, Fed did not need to have its decisions ratified by either the president or by Congress. The seven members of the Board of Governors were chosen by the president and ratified by Congress, which also maintained oversight, but most decisions were made by a handful of wealthy and powerful men who did not answer to politicians, to political parties, or to ideologies. The federal banking system was, in essence, responsible only to itself, and that included its need to show a profit.

The public at large, Walker thought, would be distressed indeed to see how the government used the Fed to manage both the nation's economy and its own profitability—too often to dismal effect.

It had taken Directo a México to prove to Walker once and for all just how thoroughly corrupt the system had become.

Four years ago, he'd been given the task of overseeing the remittance program, which was growing increasingly controversial. More and more members of the general public had become aware of it as journalists and editorialists wrote about it, criticized it—and right now the Federal Banking System didn't need to be in the glare of that kind of harsh spotlight.

Directo a México had been launched in 2003 under the U.S.-Mexico Partnership for Prosperity, a joint operation by the U.S. Federal Reserve and the Banco de México. Under the program's provisions, people of Mexican descent could wire money to their families south of the border, using U.S. commercial banks and credit unions to transfer the money directly. The controversial part was that they could make those transfers using only a *matrícula consular,* an ID easily obtained at any Mexican consulate. Since they weren't even required to provide a Social Security number, *any* immigrant, citizen or noncitizen, with or without documentation, could use the service.

The banking fees attached to each transaction were generously low. Supporters of the program pointed out that more money sent to Mexican citizens still living in

Mexico might help cut the tide of illegal immigration north.

Which, of course, Walker knew, was complete and utter bullshit. The Mexican government had long been actively encouraging its more impoverished citizens to emigrate to *el norte,* so that more and more immigrants would send yet more and more money to Mexico. The so-called remittance program was now completely out of hand. Last year, almost twenty-five *billion* dollars had been sent south across the border. Mexico was addicted to that river of cash; money from *el norte* was the country's second-largest source of income after oil. Critics of the program pointed out that U.S. tax dollars were being used to support illegal immigration, and as the recent recession had deepened, people had begun questioning whether the United States could afford to support Mexico's poor.

Of course, when Walker had taken charge of the project, things hadn't seemed all that bad. Banking, after all, was just business. A business was required to make money, to show a profit, and, as Preston had just pointed out, Directo a México was completely legal.

Lately, however, James Walker had become aware of the Program's other aspects.

Anyone could get a *matrícula consular.* No one checked up on the applicant's identity. Legal or illegal, it didn't matter. The drug gangs and cartels that were destroying the Republic of Mexico now were using Directo a México to send money extorted from illegals in the United States south to Mexican banks that were owned and controlled by the cartels, and to launder drug money from the north. The Federal Reserve Bank didn't care. Business, after all, was business, and lately business had been *very* good.

Where, Walker wondered, did you draw the moral line? When did you accept responsibility for evil writ that large?

He thought of Carol.

Carol Marie Sullivan once had been his lover, an indiscretion wildly uncharacteristic of Walker at the time, but which he still treasured now, five years later. In 2011, she'd had the opportunity to take a vice president's position at the Federal Reserve Bank of Phoenix, Arizona. While there, she'd uncovered . . . irregularities. Nothing illegal, but she'd strongly suspected that criminal elements were using her bank and the remittance program to ship money back to Mexico.

Always a crusader, Carol had tried to alert the local news media to the problem.

Of course, the media had not been interested. Certain elements within the banking system were always on guard against unfortunate leaks being made to the press. Carol had written a long e-mail to Walker, expressing her anger and her frustration, and her determination to keep digging.

Two days later, she'd committed suicide—a combination of pills and alcohol. The coroner's report had noted a blood alcohol level of over 0.35.

Carol, Walker knew, never drank. *Never.* She'd claimed to hate the taste of the stuff. Besides, her e-mail, while angry, hadn't sounded like one written by someone about to kill herself. It had been written by a person determined to get to the bottom of a very ugly situation, hinting at wholesale corruption both in the banks and in politics.

Walker was dead certain that Carol had been murdered—but by whom? Cartel enforcers? Or, worse, by someone within the federal banking system? He assumed, *had* to assume, that the murderers had been vicious criminal elements, not bankers and business-men and lawyers.

Not people like *him*.

Phone calls to local law enforcement had been un-helpful. Carol's death was ruled a suicide, case closed.

Which was to be expected. The local cops certainly weren't going to want to open the political snake pit of bank corruption, illegal immigration, and Mexican ma-fias.

Poor Carol.

Walker, riding the tiger now, didn't know how he was going to be able to let go.

If he did, he now was convinced that the same would happen to him.

SOUTH STEPS
ECCLES FEDERAL RESERVE BOARD BUILDING
TWENTIETH STREET AND CONSTITUTION AVENUE NW
WASHINGTON, D.C.
1412 HOURS, EDT

Preston paused between the massive, squared-off pillars at the top of the marble steps of the Federal Reserve. His meeting with Walker had confirmed something he'd been considering for some time. He was going to need to eliminate Walker, sooner, probably, rather than later.

The man was weak. Spineless and weak. Worse, he had a *conscience*.

The Program couldn't afford too much of that kind of thing.

Preston had recruited Walker at the Bohemian Grove two years before. That intimately private gathering of millionaires, bankers, politicians, business executives, and artsy types every July in Monte Rio, California, had turned out to be the perfect recruiting campus for the Program, a way for Preston to bring together the money and the power necessary to pull this thing off. They'd needed Walker for his banking connections with the Hispanic community; control the money and you controlled the people. The Fed's monetary policies even gave the Program a certain amount of control over the Mexican cartels—not much, but some—and that would be vital in the final stages of the plan.

Walker, Preston knew, was still pining over that woman. What was her name? Some VP of a Fed bank in Phoenix. A reformer. A crusader. Now a *dead* crusader, after Mendoza's people had finished with her, managing to make it look like suicide. If Walker suspected that Preston had given the order to off the bitch, he would be turning state's evidence at the Hoover Building in ten minutes flat.

Even if he didn't suspect the connection, Walker

was just not reliable. Somehow, Preston knew, he would have to find someone else to handle the Mexican connections. Gonzales, maybe. A congressman in one of L.A.'s Hispanic communities, Gonzales was more figurehead than anything else—but he was *visible*.

He was bought and paid for, too.

Maybe the Program could dispense with Walker once and for all.

Preston reached the bottom of the street and turned left. The Ellipse was just three blocks east, toward the Capitol Dome.

LOS ANGELES CITY HALL
NORTH SPRING STREET
LOS ANGELES, CALIFORNIA
1520 HOURS, PDT

The crowd had come southwest across the overpass above the Hollywood Freeway just two blocks from city hall and surged down North Spring Street, chanting loudly. "*Libertad, libertad,* give us back our land! *Libertad, libertad,* give us back our land!" Many carried signs and placards, hastily scrawled on pieces torn from brown cardboard boxes. ¡*VIVA AZTLÁN!* read one. JUSTICE! DIGNITY! FREEDOM! read another.

The crowd was met by a determined line of police officers in front of city hall, across North Spring Street behind plastic riot shields.

"*This is the Los Angeles Police Department,*" a voice, hugely amplified, boomed across the mob. "*This is an illegal assembly. You are ordered to disperse now or face arrest. I repeat, this is the Los Angeles Police Department . . ."*

Across the street, on the roof of an office building at North Spring and West Temple, two men armed with M-16 rifles and wearing police body armor took aim at the crowd.

CHAPTER FIVE

"Señor de la Cruz?"

"Miguel, *por favor*. And you are Señor . . . Callahan?"

"*Mucho gusto.*"

"'*Chogusto.*"

"This is the guy I phoned you about," Eduardo Chavez added. "*Es buena gente.*"

Teller shook hands with de la Cruz, a small, wiry man in jeans and a yellow polo shirt. His grip was strong, and he had a direct, intense gaze.

The CISEN officer glanced around, as if checking the futuristic architecture and profusion of tropical plants for possible eavesdroppers. "It's good to meet you, sir. Your presence here is . . . most welcome."

They'd decided to meet de la Cruz in the hotel lobby the morning after their arrival rather than at the airport as originally planned. The change of venue gave them more tactical possibilities—and the palatial lobby of a five-star luxury hotel was less likely than the airport to have cartel spotters.

Security here, Teller was pleased to see, was pretty good, although the plainclothes personnel scattered about the area were a little obvious in their casual nonchalance. A police officer in dark blue and wearing tactical armor patrolled the sidewalk outside the front door, armed with an M-16, and there were security cameras at various points on the ceiling. The Mexican government depended on tourism for revenue almost as much as it did on remittances from Mexican immigrants in *el norte,* and so they went to expensive lengths to make sure those tourists felt safe.

"I have a car outside," de la Cruz told them. "It's been scanned for bugs. We can talk freely there, on our way to CISEN headquarters."

"*Vámanos,*" Chavez said.

Teller wondered, though, if CISEN HQ would be a safe place to talk. He would assume that it was not.

The three of them left the hotel, crossing the street to a white Ford Escort parked in the hotel's front lot. Teller glanced around, trying to spot Frank Procario, but he didn't see the marine. Not that he'd expected to; Procario, as Teller knew from dozens of exercises at the Farm, was one of the best. Their rental car was in the parking lot; it would be up to Procario to get on their tail and follow them. The wire Teller was wearing would provide a signal that would help Procario stay with them, as well as let him listen in on the conversation.

"So . . . you're here undercover, posing as a journalist?" de la Cruz asked as Teller slid into the backseat.

Teller's papers identified him as John Callahan, a reporter for the *Washington Post*. De la Cruz knew him only as Callahan, not as Teller. It was safer that way.

"That's the idea," Teller replied. "Did they fill you in on the mission?"

"You need to find a member of one of the cartels, ideally mid- to high level, and plant some sort of a bug on him."

Teller nodded. De la Cruz didn't need to know the details. "Right."

"And I assume that this is connected with the arrival of two, ah . . . packages from Karachi?"

Teller looked at Chavez in the front passenger seat for confirmation. The Mexicans shouldn't have had access to Trapdoor intelligence.

Chavez returned the glance over his shoulder, then nodded. "Some of us have been sharing information with CISEN back-channel, very informally," he said. "We figured if those packages *were* wandering around in Mexico, it made sense to have CISEN in the loop, helping to find them."

"I see." The news was faintly disturbing. If Mexican police, intelligence, and security services could not be trusted, there was a serious danger here. They still didn't know who was behind the smuggling of the two nuclear weapons, if, indeed, they were on board the

Zapoteca at all. Who in Mexico would want a couple of suitcase nukes?

Worse . . . what would happen if people who didn't know about the nukes found out about them now, and decided to join in the chase?

"We were informed a week ago," de la Cruz added. "Your NRO has been forwarding us satellite images of the *Zapoteca* as she approached the coast of Belize. Unfortunately, your satellites appear to have lost her almost immediately."

"Lost her? She should have reached port five or six days ago," Teller said.

"The *Zapoteca* is not in Belize City," de la Cruz said. "That was her presumed destination, based on her course and speed when she was first photographed. We are checking out other ports along the Yucatán coast." He hesitated. "We have, of course, informed *el presidente*."

"What is your analysis of the situation?" Chavez asked.

"We are assuming one of the cartels is behind it, of course," de la Cruz replied. "Possibly with help from al Qaeda."

"What would al Qaeda have to gain by selling nukes to Mexico?" Teller asked.

De la Cruz shrugged behind the wheel. "Money. What else?"

"I don't think so," Teller said. "If al Qaeda has managed to get its hands on two pocket A-bombs, they wouldn't send them to Mexico. Their beef is with *us*."

"*Disculpe,*" de la Cruz said, "but I must remind

you, Señor Callahan. The entire world does not revolve around just you *yanquis*."

"No, it doesn't," Teller replied, "but the world *does* have to make sense. The drug lords are interested in just one thing—profit. It would hardly be in their best interests to use atomic weapons against their own country."

De la Cruz pulled the Escort out into the seething, chaotic traffic of downtown Mexico City. The streets here appeared to be locked in a perpetual traffic jam, vehicles inching along, horns blaring, drivers shouting and gesticulating at one another. It reminded Teller of downtown D.C. in rush hour, maybe worse.

"The cartels may have those nukes for extortion," de la Cruz said. "At CISEN, we have been looking at one particular extortion scenario with considerable interest. The cartels have been coming under a great deal of pressure lately, from the government, from our military. This is why they have grown so dangerous, so desperate, these past few years. I can imagine them planting a couple of small nuclear devices here in Mexico City and threatening to detonate them if the government does not legalize their operations."

"What, make manufacturing and shipping drugs legal?"

"Exactly. Or, at the least, they might tell us to turn our heads, to ignore their activities at every level. It would be like holding a loaded pistol to our heads."

Teller weighed the possibilities. It did make sense. The different Mexican cartels had been at each other's throats since the beginning, trying to dominate the lucrative drug pipelines north, but they'd also been engaged in all-out war with both the Mexican government and various agencies in the United States, the DEA and the FBI in particular. For a long time, they'd been able to buy or bribe officials in the Mexican government, police forces, and army, but that had become a lot tougher since 2006, when Mexican president Felipe Calderón had launched the first of his country's military assaults on the drug lords. If the cartels could get the government off their backs, they would have a lot more freedom and resources to pursue their war on one another.

If the cartels were feeling the pinch, they might resort to extortion on a new and unheard-of scale.

"It's possible," Teller agreed, "but that still doesn't feel right to me. I still think it more likely that if al Qaeda got hold of a couple of nukes, they'd use them on us, not sell them to a third party."

"So," Chavez said, "where would you suggest we start, Miguel? It doesn't have to be someone as big as El Chapo."

De la Cruz gave a deep shrug. "The *cabrónes* are everywhere here. You just gotta look."

"Which cartel is calling the shots in Mexico City?" Teller asked.

De la Cruz gave a harsh snort. "Which one isn't? Sinaloa, La Resistencia, Knights Templars, LFM . . . they're all pretty active here."

"LFM?"

"La Familia Michoacana. Used to be part of the Sinaloan Federation, until they got greedy. We think they're extinct now, but you never can be sure."

"Okay. What about Los Zetas?"

"Them, too, though they're more east coast, in the Gulf Cartel's old territory. All of the cartels maintain at least some presence here, y'know?"

"Well, if you're going to buy a few dozen *federales* or judges or generals, this is the happening place, right?" Chavez joked.

"There's one guy," de la Cruz said, thoughtful. "Juan Escalante Romero. He's Sinaloa, but the word on the street is he's been playing with Los Zetas, too. He's ex-GAFE. Trained at Fort Benning. And he's tough, *mean*."

"So where would we find him?" Chavez asked.

"Different places. He's all over, really. But there's a Los Zetas safe house we know of, in Iztacalco. He often goes there when he's in town."

"Sounds like we have ourselves an opportunity for a stakeout," Teller said. "What fun." He despised stakeouts—hours and hours of unrelenting boredom for the minute chance of a payoff.

"I'll drive you by there, if you like. Give you a chance to look the place over, and maybe we can find a good spot for an OP"—an observation post.

"Sounds good."

De la Cruz turned off onto a side street, continuing to make slow but steady progress through the noisy, teeming tangle of the congested inner city. Teller glanced back, trying to spot Procario, but failing. The rental was an inconspicuous silver-gray Ford Focus. If it was back there, it was lost among some hundreds of other vehicles packed into the narrow street.

He wanted to believe that the CISEN officer was right, that the drug cartels had brought the nuclear weapons to Mexico with the intent of extorting compliance from the Mexican government. The fact that the *Zapoteca* was involved—again, assuming the weapons were on board her—suggested one or more of the cartels were involved. The cartels would have the money, the ready cash, to purchase a couple of tactical nukes on the open market. Finally, the mere possibility that the former archrivals Sinaloa and Los Zetas were actually working together suggested that something *very* big was afoot.

It made a convincing argument.

He still didn't buy it. If it was not a coincidence that Sinaloa was cooperating with Los Zetas, neither could it be a coincidence that Hezbollah activity was increasing in the region, or that a known VEVAK agent was operating in Mexico. Suppose *they* were involved in the smuggling of two tactical nukes into Mexico or Belize? If that were the case, the situation could be quite different . . . and a *lot* more serious for the United States. Either Hezbollah or their Iranian backers might be planning on using the drug cartels and their smuggling networks to get those weapons across the border into the United States.

The same was true if al Qaeda was behind the operation, but Teller still doubted that they were the masterminds here. While not out of the running yet by any means, al Qaeda had been savaged by U.S. intelligence and military operations to the point that they were now just barely hanging on. They *might* be planning a nuclear strike out of sheer desperation, but it was a lot more likely they were all still lying low in the wake of Abbottabad, waiting for the next predator drone strike, the next SEAL team assault.

They needed information—solid intel. Until they had it, they were groping in the dark.

Perhaps this Juan Escalante would be able to shed some light on things.

LOS ANGELES CITY HALL
NORTH SPRING STREET
LOS ANGELES, CALIFORNIA
1020 HOURS, PDT

". . . and we go live now to reporter Catherine Herridge, on the scene."

Guided by the voice of the studio anchor in her ear, the reporter looked at the lens and began speaking with earnest sincerity into her microphone.

"Yes, Peter. LAPD sources say they still have no clue to the identity of two men who fired automatic rifles from the roof of a building into the crowd gathered outside city hall yesterday afternoon, killing four and wounding seventeen. Two men were taken into custody, but according to one source, both men carried LAPD badges and identification."

On the small monitor set up in front of and below her cameraman, the scene shifted from her face to a tape shot from a news helicopter the afternoon before. Two men could be seen leaning over the wall of a skyscraper, firing indiscriminately into the crowd twenty stories below. Abruptly, a number of uniformed police officers broke out onto the roof. Both gunmen immediately dropped their weapons over the building's side and turned to face the officers, hands in the air.

"Officials so far have refused to make any statement about the two, as to whether they were active-duty police officers, as has been claimed, or even whether they are still in custody."

The scene shifted once again to a close-up of an angry crowd, close-packed behind a yellow police-barrier tape. One Hispanic man was waving a crudely scrawled cardboard sign reading POLICE BRUTALITY!

"While the crowd outside of city hall yesterday dispersed as soon as the shots were fired, other crowds have been gathering at points across East Los Angeles since then to protest what they call police brutality, or excessive use of force against peaceful demonstrators. Congressman Harvey Gonzales, of the East L.A. Congressional District, has personally issued a plea for calm while the incident is investigated."

DISTRICTO IZTACALCO
CIUDAD DE MÉXICO
REPUBLICA DE MÉXICO
1535 HOURS, LOCAL TIME

They'd parked the Escort on Sur 145, a narrow street in the *barrio* of crowded tenements, houses, and shacks. De la Cruz had pointed out the suspected safe house used by Escalante and other members of the Los Zetas cartel, a two-story house with a cracked plaster façade and a decaying front stoop.

"I'd have thought a drug lord could afford something more upscale—something with a Chihuahua at least . . ." Teller observed.

De la Cruz shrugged. "In this part of town, it's best to be inconspicuous. Besides, it's not his home."

"So, how do we know if he's here?" Chavez asked.

"Oh, he's here alright," de la Cruz said. "That's his car parked in front of us. See the sticker on the plate? *Hoy no circula*."

"'No drive today'?" Teller translated. "I don't get it."

"Mexico City has two major problems," Chavez told him, "traffic congestion and pollution caused by traffic. The *hoy no circula* program takes some of those cars, the older ones, off the streets."

"Newer cars are exempt," de la Cruz explained. "But cars older than eight years can't go out on the streets one day a week plus one Saturday a month."

"*Exacto*. His '02 Chevy has a red sticker, and his license plate number ends in '4.' That means he can't take it out on the streets on Wednesdays, or on the third Saturday of the month."

"And today is Wednesday," Teller said. "That must be hell on people who have to commute."

"It forces people to find other ways to get to work," de la Cruz replied. "But Mexico City proper has nine million people living in it . . . and almost twenty-five million people in the metro area. It's the largest city in the Western Hemisphere. Twenty years ago, they were issuing hazardous air warnings for this city 355 days out of the year. Today . . . well, things are a lot better."

"Yeah, the air doesn't seem that bad," Teller admitted. "A little thin, but not bad. I can't see people in the United States giving up driving, though, even one day a week. I think we're addicted to it."

De la Cruz chuckled. "Don't get smug, gringo. I've seen Los Angeles and Washington, D.C., in rush hour. Mark me, you *yanquis* will be doing something just like it soon!"

"Sure," Chavez said. "Remember gas rationing, back in the seventies? It could get that bad again."

"Before my time," Teller said. The steady erosion of basic American freedoms over the past couple of decades was a sore point with him. He decided to change the uncomfortable subject. "So . . . tell us about this Escalante character."

"Here . . ." De la Cruz reached into a jacket pocket and produced a smart phone. "You have net access?"

"Sure." Teller pulled out his mobile phone. With de la Cruz's phone acting as a mobile wireless hotspot, he could exchange contact information with the CISEN agent, then download a file from de la Cruz's phone. He opened it, and began scanning through the information. The attached file photos included several surveillance shots of Escalante, plus one prison photograph, showing front and side views. He was a young man with dark hair, a heavy mustache, and cold, cold eyes.

"He started off working for Sinaloa," de la Cruz

said. "Strictly mid-level management. He oversaw the shipment of cocaine, mostly, up from Colombia, and passed it on to the smuggling networks in Tijuana and Nogales. When the Tijuana Cartel went independent, they put a price on his head, but he went to work for El Chapo and the Sinaloan Federation. Arrested in '99 for bribing police officials, but they let him go—a federal judge in Sinaloa's pocket. He's loyal to Sinaloa, but the word is that he has personal ties to Los Zetas, so he's a floater."

" 'Floater'?"

"Sinaloa and Los Zetas are in an all-out war . . . have been since 2010. But he's able to cross the lines, kind of like having diplomatic immunity, y'know? Floats from one camp to the other, and neither side is able to touch him. We think he's been brokering a truce between the two cartels."

Teller scanned through the information appearing on his phone's screen. "A half-million dollar penthouse in a high-rise condo in downtown Mexico City," he said, reading. "So what's he doing driving a beat-up white Chevy that he can't take out on Wednesdays?"

"Oh, he's got a Mercedes, too," de la Cruz said, laughing. "*And* a Peugeot. And a couple of other hot cars. But . . . remember what I said about being inconspicuous? A Mercedes would be kind of out of place in this neighborhood. When he stays here, he drives his low-profile junker."

"And why does he stay here at all?" Teller wanted to know.

"A girl, of course," de la Cruz said. "Isn't that the way it always is?"

"Maria Perez," Chavez added. "She keeps the place as a safe house, for members of Los Zetas when they're in town. Word is she's a niece of *El Hummer*, Jaime Perez Durán. He's one of the original bigshots of the Los Zetas, so maybe that's how he ended up in both camps, playing diplomat."

"Exactly." De la Cruz nodded. "Escalante has a wife living in his high-rise, so he can't take Maria there. So he visits her here at this place two, maybe three times a week. Probably tells his wife he's staying late at the office. And if it happens to be a Wednesday, well, he *has* to stay that extra day, right? Or the police'll pick him up for violating *hoy no circula*."

"Well, things are just tough all over," Teller said. "Even for drug lords." He stretched and shifted. His long legs had been folded into the back of the Escort for hours now, and he was getting stiff. "Hey, you said we might be able to find a place for an OP."

"Sure." De la Cruz pointed to a pastel-blue painted house across the street and several numbers north from the cartel safe house. "That house . . . there. The guy who owns it, Antonio Vicente Lozano, is a police informant. Strictly unofficial, since if his address showed up on an official record or pay voucher, he'd be dead the very next day. But some of us in CISEN pay him a bit every month out of our own pockets to just kind of keep an eye on the Perez house. He lets us know the make and license numbers of cars that show up out front, how long they stay, that sort of thing. That's how we picked up on Escalante."

"Sweet."

"See the window on the third story, the one with the little balcony and all the potted plants in front of it? A couple of times, now, Vicente's let us rent that room for surveillance." He grinned. "We've picked up some pretty hot action from Maria's bedroom, let me tell you."

"Anything useful?" Chavez asked.

A shrug. "*No mucho.* Escalante's pretty careful about what he says, even around his *tragona.*"

"Let's set it up," Teller said. "And I think we're going to need some special equipment from back home."

SAFE HOUSE, EAST OLYMPIC BOULEVARD
EAST LOS ANGELES, CALIFORNIA
1630 HOURS, PDT

Automatic gunfire sounded outside, and Reyshahri cautiously went to the window. The mob outside filled the street as far as he could see in each direction, and was on the move now, headed toward downtown. The shots had come from a man brandishing an M-16, firing wildly into the air. "Idiots," Reyshahri said in Farsi. "Those bullets have to come down somewhere."

Beside him, Fereidun Moslehi chuckled. "It will attract their police all the sooner," he said in the same language. "And that is what we want, a confrontation, yes?"

"Oh, there will be a confrontation. I have no doubt of that."

There must have been thousands in the crowd, which was made up mostly of young, angry men, but Reyshahri could see women and even children in the mob as well, marching, shouting, punching the air with clenched fists as they chanted.

"*¡Dignidad! ¡Igualdad! ¡Libertad!*"

Dignity. Equality. Liberty. The sincere and honest aspirations of any people. The signs they carried sported the same sentiments. "*¡Justicia!*" Read one. "*¡Fuerza a las Gentes!*" read another. "*¡Aztlán. Libre!*" a third.

Free Aztlán. *That* didn't have a chance, of course. At least . . . not yet.

Aztlán was the mythical ancestral home for the Nahua native peoples; the name Aztec literally meant "People from Aztlán." Beginning in the 1960s, however, the name had been taken up by the Chicano movement and various independence activists to refer to the lands of northern Mexico annexed—some said "stolen"—by the United States after the Mexican-American War in 1847. The idea was a frankly political ploy to give the Chicano independence movement what they felt was a legal right to what was now California, Arizona, New Mexico, Texas . . . the entire U.S. Southwest, in fact, as far north as Colorado, Utah, and Nevada. A number of Latino political action groups in the United States had united under the Aztlán banner—the *Plan Espiritual de Aztlán*, the *Movimiento Estudiantil Chicano de Aztlán*, and NOA, the Nation of Aztlán.

The Latino independence movement had remained fairly low-key for decades, but lately, the Hispanic populations of those states had become more vocal. The

Chicanos were in the majority in large areas of southern California, Arizona, New Mexico, and Texas, and they were beginning to flex their political muscles. Many were talking about the *inevitability* of a new nation, *el Republica del Norte*, that would secede from the United States within the next half century or so.

There were many also saying that it would not be that long, that the new country was being born *now*.

The past twenty-four hours had seen an explosion of rage and determination within the local Chicano population. Not all of it, of course, not even a majority . . . but enough to focus the world's attention on East Los Angeles. Paying those two members of an L.A. drug gang to fire into the crowd outside of City Hall yesterday had blown the lid off, as Reyshahri had known would be the case. The story was flashing through the Hispanic communities of L.A. like lightning: The LAPD had fired into a peaceful crowd of demonstrators! The IDs and badges carried by those two—plus the intervention of a police official on the cartel payroll—had freed both men.

Both men had disappeared a few hours later; there would be no way to question them further.

Was this the beginning of a new nation? Reyshahri doubted, frankly, that the hodge-podge of activist groups and would-be revolutionaries would be able to pull it off. They certainly wouldn't do it on their own. The United States federal government had settled the question of whether individual states could choose to leave the parent country long ago, had done so by winning a bloody civil war. Those people out in the street could shout and chant until they were blue in the face. Once they became too violent, too big of a problem, Washington would declare martial law and send in the National Guard.

That would be the last anyone would hear of *Aztlán Libre* for a long, long time to come.

Still, his superiors back in Tehran had come up with Operation Shah Mat, which they thought had a good chance of success. Reyshahri's first part in this operation was to encourage the independence movements in the southwestern U.S., to help them forge alliances with one another if they hadn't already, and to see to it that the weapons and ammunition smuggled up out of Mexico reached their organizers. Whether or not the Aztlanistas managed to vote themselves free of the States, frankly, was unimportant. What was important was that they be loud, visible, and dangerous for a period of perhaps one more week.

After that, after Reyshahri carried out the *second* part of Shah Mat, none of it would matter in the least.

CHAPTER SIX

Teller was bored.

Stakeouts were, of course, an integral part of intelligence work, and even more so for counterintelligence, when you needed to keep tabs on the opposition. As a newbie, he'd polished just-learned skills dozens of times in training, practicing with senior intelligence officers as his targets. He'd been on plenty of the real thing since, throughout his career, in the streets of Kabul and Karachi, in Berlin once, and even in Washington, D.C., where he'd been keeping an eye on that SVR officer who'd wanted to defect. Of course, on that case he'd needed not only to watch the target but to watch for his *real* opposition from the Company, his nominal allies at the CIA.

In eight years of intelligence work, he'd never been able to get past the mind-numbing boredom of a routine stakeout.

Chavez and Teller had spent the night in the small bedroom on the third floor of Antonio Vicente's house, taking turns sleeping and watching; de la Cruz had gone home for the night. Frank Procario had joined them for a time, then gone to a hotel back at the airport. Teller had phoned in a request for some special equipment, and it would be arriving sometime on the seventeenth.

The two men spent much of the evening discussing the mission and how they could best carry it out, along with all the variants and sequels they could think of, all the possible ways it could go down. If they could catch Escalante in the street—perhaps by pretending to hold him up, or presenting themselves as members of a rival cartel threatening him—they might be able to grab his phone for a crucial few moments while Teller infected it with the virus, then return it to him. Chavez wasn't sure they could pull that off, however, without making him suspicious, and Teller had to admit that it was a long shot. Physical confrontations with the target *always* went the way of Murphy; things never unfolded as planned, and there were always unexpected complications.

Teller also put forward the possibility of the two of them breaking into the safe house—again posing as thieves or rival cartel members—with Chavez holding Escalante and his lady friend at gunpoint while Teller found Escalante's cell phone and inserted the Cellmap virus.

"The trouble is," Chavez pointed out, "Escalante would *know* something was screwy. If he suspected that we were CIA or CISEN, he might assume we'd bugged his phone and get rid of it."

"The big problem," Teller replied, "is that we still don't know the bastard's over there. We've been watching the place for twenty hours now, and we haven't seen him."

"His car's parked out front."

"Yeah, and now it's Thursday and he hasn't come out to drive it home. Maybe he loaned it to his lady friend for the week. You ever think of that? Until we put Mark One eyeballs on the target, get a positive ID, we don't know he's there."

"We could check."

"How?"

"Miguel could go up posing as a census taker or a meter reader or whatever. He could get the appropriate camouflage at CISEN headquarters."

"Possibly," Teller said. "I don't want to spook the quarry, though. The opposition may assume that *anyone* asking to read the meter is an undercover cop."

"They can be paranoid like that, yeah."

"I think I'm going to vote for breaking and entering. At least if we have them at gunpoint, we would be in control of the situation."

"Until Murphy showed up," Chavez said. "But . . . yeah."

"We need the package from Langley," Teller said. "That will give us an edge."

"I hope so," Chavez replied. "I don't like operating in the dark, y'know?"

CENTRAL BUREAU COMMUNITY POLICE STATION
EAST SIXTH STREET
LOS ANGELES, CALIFORNIA
1112 HOURS, PDT

Located just six-tenths of a mile south of city hall, the LAPD's Central Bureau controls operations across sixty-five square miles of Los Angeles, including the downtown business district, Newton to the south, and Hollenbeck to the east. The most ethnically diverse of the LAPD's operational areas, it has a population of over 900,000 people.

Ignacio Carballo walked toward the bureau's front doors, then hesitated, momentarily cowed by the sheer looming size of the edifice. He glanced at his partner, Hernán Jimenez Montoya, shook himself, then forced himself to go on. Despite the warm and sunny Southern California weather, both men were wearing knee-length raincoats, black leather with zippers up the front. Jimenez was wearing a backpack.

A couple of SWAT officers were patrolling outside the front doors of the public entrance, and Carballo braced for trouble. Every police officer in the city, he thought, must be on a hair trigger. The riot in East L.A. was still under way; at last report, a dozen buildings were on fire over there, and last night the mob had turned over a couple of police cruisers. There were rumors that the governor had already declared martial law, though Carballo hadn't been able to confirm that. It didn't matter. *They* told him what to do . . . and he did it. For *that* much money, he would have stormed the Capitol Building in Washington, D.C.

So, into the lion's den. Avoiding eye contact, the two men walked side by side up to the glass doors leading into the building's vestibule.

"Hey, you two!" one of the officers called. "Where do you think you're going?"

"To see the chief of police," Jimenez said.

"Right. What's in the backpack?"

"We are reporters," Carballo said, pulling out the ID he had ready in his raincoat pocket. "The backpack has camera equipment."

The second officer snorted. "You two look ready for the monsoon season."

Carballo gave a careless shrug. "The weather service said rain later today."

One of the cops examined the fake ID, then shrugged and handed it back. "You'll need to check all that gear through inside, you know."

"I know."

One of the cops actually held the door open for them.

Ignacio Carballo had trained with GAFE, the Special Forces, both in Mexico and at Fort Benning, Georgia, with the American Green Berets. He'd fought cartel mercenaries in Juárez, in Nogales, and in Tijuana, as well as revolutionaries in Campeche until a friend had recruited him for Los Zetas. He was tough, well trained, and experienced. Even so, his heart was pounding as he stepped through into the front lobby of the city's central police station, and his hands and face were slick with sweat. There were a dozen police and security people inside, and several dozen civilians.

Two of the security guards waved him forward toward the frame of one of the metal detectors. Casually, Carballo unzipped his coat and stepped forward. Behind him, Jimenez slipped his backpack off his shoulder and advanced toward the conveyor belt for the X-ray scanner.

As Carballo passed through the frame, an alarm sounded, and a red light flashed. One of the guards picked up a wand to give him a scan. "Please remove your coat," he said.

Carballo shot him.

The 9 mm Beretta had been in a shoulder holster underneath the raincoat. As quickly as he could pull the trigger, Carballo squeezed off rounds, pivoting as he fired into the police and security personnel around him. The slide locked open when the magazine was empty; he dropped the weapon. Strapped to his side, muzzle down and also hidden by the long coat, he was carrying an ArmaLite AR-15, its action modified to permit full-automatic fire. In one smooth motion, he unclipped the weapon and brought it up, triggering a long, stuttering burst into the crowd of civilians.

Jimenez was in on the action now, yanking a pull-ring at the top of the backpack and hurling it underhand beneath the line of tables marking the security perimeter. Under his coat he was wearing an M-16 assault rifle, and within a couple of seconds he was adding its shrill thunder to that of Carballo's weapon.

Civilians screamed and scattered. Police officers drew their weapons. One, quicker than the rest, brought his Smith & Wesson semiautomatic pistol up in a two-handed grip and squeezed off three shots. Carballo felt one of the rounds slap him in the chest, hard, staggering him back a step, but the Kevlar vest he was wearing underneath the raincoat absorbed the force of the impact, and he felt nothing more than a thump, like a hard punch in the chest. Turning, his AR-15 at his shoulder, he returned fire and sent the officer stumbling backward and down, the front of his white shirt suddenly blossoming bright red.

For a small eternity of seconds, the two men poured full-auto rounds into the crowd, into the scattering police officers, into anything that moved.

Another round slapped Carballo in the back, much harder this time, and he felt the steel plate inside his Kevlar vest bruise his torso. The two cops with body armor were coming in through the front door, weapons set to semiauto, squeezing off rounds as they came. He didn't know if their armor was hard, like his, or soft, but he took no chances, aiming instead for their unprotected faces. Blood splattered across the glass doors, and then the safety glass crazed as missed rounds smashed through it.

Jimenez thumbed his magazine release, dropping an empty, and snapped a full mag home. *"¡Vámanos, 'mano!"*

Stepping across the two bodies, Carballo and Jimenez

jogged out onto the sidewalk, where a gray van had just swung off the street, bypassing the diagonal parking area out front, and was waiting for them beyond the ornamental shrubbery, its sliding side door open. The two men dived headfirst into the back of the vehicle, as Raimondo Velez fired his M-16 above their heads and into the building's front windows.

"*¡Ándale!*" Carballo yelled, but the van was already moving, tires squealing as it sideswiped a parked car and banged back onto the street. Behind them, the explosives in the backpack detonated with a booming roar, blowing out the front doors of the police station with a blast large enough to shake the building and set off car alarms for dozens of yards around.

Around the corner and one block down Wall Street, they abandoned the van for a less conspicuous vehicle left parked and waiting for them, and ten minutes later they were on the Santa Monica Freeway, heading east.

Behind them, the LAPD's Central Bureau Station was burning.

OBSERVATION POST
DISTRICTO IZTACALCO
CIUDAD DE MÉXICO
1434 HOURS, LOCAL TIME

"Jesus, it took you long enough," Teller said. "What kept you?"

Frank Procario dropped the aluminum-sided case he was carrying on the bed and gave Teller a sour look. "Traffic," he said.

Teller looked at his watch. "You picked up the package six hours ago! How long does it take you to drive five miles?"

"Six hours," Procario said, "when I have to get around a full-blown riot in downtown Mexico City."

"What riot?"

"A big one. A big demonstration, anyway. Yankees go home."

Chavez came in, carrying another equipment case. "Yeah, it's on all the local news stations," he said, putting the case on the floor. "They've declared martial law in California."

"Christ," Teller said. "Leave the country for a couple of days and the place goes to hell. What's going on?"

"Riots in Los Angeles," Procario said. The marine sounded exhausted. "Police officers beating up Latinos in the streets have been filmed with cell phone cameras and iPads, and the footage has been getting a lot of airtime. L.A.'s Hispanic population is up in arms, claiming police officers were seen firing into a peaceful demonstration outside city hall. Lots of big demonstrations have broken out in other cities, in support of L.A.'s Latino communities. Phoenix. San Antonio. Chicago. New York. And Mexico City as well, apparently. Showing solidarity with their oppressed brothers in *el norte*." He patted the top of the equipment case on the bed next to him. "But at least we got the shipment in from Langley."

Teller had called Langley yesterday, requesting the expedited shipment—several bulky metal cases flown into Benito Juárez International by a chartered plane early that morning. "That's great," Teller said. "Let's open 'em up."

The various cases were opened, the equipment inside carefully unpacked. Procario got off the bed and began setting up the scope on its tripod, aiming it out the bedroom window at the cartel safe house. Teller unpacked the AN/PRC-117F and unfolded the antenna. Chavez began setting up the KY-99.

The AN/PRC-117F satellite communications unit weighed just sixteen pounds and was connected to its cruciform antenna by a plug-in cable. The KY-99 was a crypto device employed for greater security.

"The prick's ready," Teller said, grinning. "Let's have the K-Y."

All military PRC radio units, ever since the Vietnam War, were called "pricks." The inside joke within the DIA was that the CIA *always* broke out the K-Y for use with the prick whenever a surveillance target was going to get screwed.

The television monitor went onto a desk next to the window, alongside a laptop computer. Procario finished adjusting the triple-M scope. "I'm getting an image," Teller told him. "Left a little . . . and up. Good. Hold it right there! Perfect!"

The three gathered around the monitor, studying the latest in through-the-wall surveillance technology.

Electromagnetic radiation fills the air, an ocean of electromagnetic waves from the very, very long and low-energy—the longest radio wavelengths—to the unimaginably short and extremely energetic, gamma radiation. Visible light is parked somewhere in the middle between infrared and ultraviolet.

The wavelengths between microwaves and long infrared are known as the millimeter band, with wavelengths from ten millimeters to one, and frequencies of between thirty and three hundred gigahertz. Also known as MMMR, for millimeter microwave radiation, the waves can pass through most materials with ease.

They cannot penetrate metal, and they cannot penetrate water or objects that were mostly made of water, but bricks, mortar, drywall, glass, cloth—all are as transparent to triple-M wavelengths as air is to visible light.

On the monitor on the desktop, the walls of the Perez house across the street were invisible. An open network of pipes, the house's plumbing, was clearly visible, as were wires, nails, metal studs, and other bits of the building's architecture. Hanging apparently unsupported in the middle of the space was a naked, glowing male figure.

He glowed because the human body gives off millimeter radiation, but he was also being imaged by the background microwave radiation. Humans can accurately be described as bags of warm water; electromagnetic radiation, both background wavelengths and that emitted by the body, rendered his clothing invisible but reflected off his skin. The resulting image was a bit blurry but revealed as much detail as the backscatter X-ray scanners that were causing such a furor at airports and other security checkpoints back in the States.

Teller could see that the target was male, that he was leaning back on an invisible chair on the building's ground floor, and that an assault rifle—made visible by the metal components of its receiver and trigger group, barrel, neatly stacked bullets, and other furniture— was leaning against a transparent wall beside him. His hands were propped up in front of him, as though he were reading a magazine.

"That," Chavez said, "looks like a guard."

"I agree," Teller said. "I don't see the woman who owns the place, and that guy looks more like hired muscle than a midmanagement cartel businessman."

This last was pure guesswork, of course, an impression based on the figure's position and the presence of the rifle. Judging from the hazy outlines of walls picked out by pipes and wiring, the man was sitting in a hallway rather than in any of the house's living spaces, a spot where he had a clear view of the front door.

"So," Procario said, "if we take that guy, could we plant Cellmap on his phone?"

"We'd have to kill him to do it, if he's a guard," Teller said. "Besides, if he's street muscle, he won't have that many numbers on his cell."

"Yeah," Chavez agreed. "The higher in the organization, the more phones in the network we could hit at once."

"Even a street thug is going to have the number of someone higher up," Teller said, thoughtful. "Hell, that guy probably has Escalante's number, since he's working for either him or for the woman, so it would probably work. We could reach Escalante's phone through his."

"Just like picking up VD," Procario said. "You sleep with a girl, and you sleep with everyone she's ever slept with, and everyone *they've* ever slept with, and everyone *they've*—"

"Thank you, Mr. Middle School Sex Ed." Teller typed several lines into the laptop, which was processing the image. The raw data would have a lot of weird echoes and reflections from both the building infrastructure and the furniture, but software running on the computer cleaned up the image and even tightened up the details of what otherwise would have been a featureless blob of light. Millimeter imaging wasn't quite good enough to identify a specific face—the eyes, especially, looked curiously blank—but when he enlarged the image as far as it would go, Teller could see the small metal belt buckle resting just below the man's navel and the fastener and zipper below it, see some coins floating next to his hip where his pocket would be, pick out a chain and a tiny cross hanging between his nipples, and see the bright, hard circlet of his wristwatch. Unlike backscatter X-ray images, which rendered the subject bald and baby-skin smooth all over, the MMMR scope could see the man's body hair, picked out in crisp, sharp detail.

Chavez peered closer at the monitor. "Ha! *¡Un cacahuete!*"

Teller didn't recognize the word. "What's that?"

"Peanut. Mexican slang for 'tiny dick.'"

"Ah. I see what you mean."

The observation left Teller thoughtful. He remembered reading about a major scandal a few years back, when a TSA trainee in Miami had beat a classmate unconscious in the facility parking lot with a length of pipe and was then arrested for assault. It seemed the classmate had led other students throughout the afternoon in making fun of the small size of the first man's genitals after he'd gone through one of the new airport backscatter X-ray scanners in a training exercise.

Where and when did the government have the right to subject citizens to what amounted to a strip search without a warrant, and without even the excuse of probable cause? Backscatter X-ray imaging devices were in use at all major U.S. airports, and there was talk of using the far more graphic but much safer MMMR units to avoid exposing American air travelers to X-rays. Not only that, but the new traveling backscatter vans were being used by various U.S. agencies to search for terrorist bombs inside vehicles on the streets. Several right-to-privacy groups were in the process of suing various agencies for their violation of Fourth Amendment rights, but the through-the-wall surveillance devices were so damned useful that those lawsuits hadn't made much headway so far.

What, Teller wondered, was *right*? The lawyers could argue the thing back and forth and never come to a decision, but a court could only make a determination on what was permitted, not on what was morally or ethically right. If de la Cruz had been here, he might object to a Mexican citizen in the privacy of a home being subjected to such graphically revealing scrutiny.

Or perhaps not. Mexicans seemed a bit more relaxed about sex, the body, and natural bodily functions than their *norteamericano* neighbors. Even so, the three intelligence officers already had agreed not to let the CISEN agent see their surveillance setup. It was simpler if they had to answer fewer legal questions.

"Okay," Teller said. "We know there's only one guy in the house, and we know where he is. If Escalante and his girlfriend don't show up soon, we'll take this guy."

"How long do you want to wait?" Procario asked.

"Dark," Teller said. "We'll go in after it gets dark."

OFFICE OF THE NATIONAL SECURITY ADVISER
WHITE HOUSE WEST WING
WASHINGTON, D.C.
1610 HOURS, EDT

Randolph Edgar Preston watched the large-screen television monitor mounted on the wall of his office, his face expressionless. With him were two men, Charles Richard Logan, the CEO of the North American Oil Consortium, and Congressman Harvey Gonzales. Gonzales's congressional district, which gerrymandered through predominantly Hispanic neighborhoods all the way from East Los Angeles out through Pico Rivera and south to Norwalk, was burning on the TV.

"What do you think, Harvey?" Preston asked with almost insulting familiarity. "Are the troops going to put it down?"

"I dunno, Mr. Preston. As soon as one crowd gets dispersed, two more pop up."

"Good control," Preston observed. "Good planning. Your organizers are to be commended."

"Not *my* organizers," Gonzales said. "Most of that's by way of the people with MEChA and NOA. Lopez and Acevedo, and their people. The student groups especially."

"Well, they're doing a splendid job." He chuckled. "I'll bet the Chicanos can *taste* Aztlán independence."

"This independence thing is not going to fly, Mr. Preston," Logan said. "You *do* know that, don't you?"

"What, Aztlán independence? Probably not. But once it starts going international, it definitely will put us where we want to be on the map."

On the television, an attractive blond news reporter held a microphone below her chin, speaking earnestly into the camera. Behind her, the southwest face of the downtown police headquarters smoldered, the front wall blown out, smoke stains on the concrete.

". . . and eyewitnesses say two men walked into the LAPD Central Bureau Community Station at about eleven o'clock this morning," the woman was saying. "They were stopped at the security desk inside the front lobby, and at that point, according to eyewitnesses, they pulled out automatic weapons and opened fire."

Behind her, a number of medical personnel came through, carrying someone strapped to a gurney.

"They're . . . they're bringing one of the victims out now. John . . . John, see if you can get a shot . . ."

Police officers flanking the gurney waved the camera back. "Back off!" an officer growled. There were flecks of blood splattered on one side of his smoke-stained face.

"Unconfirmed reports say that at least twelve were killed in the shootout," the reporter continued, "and at least twice that number seriously injured. One of the terrorists reportedly threw a backpack, which exploded seconds later, causing a fire and severe damage to the front of the building.

"So far, police have refused to make a statement, but one officer who wished to remain anonymous said that it looked like al Qaeda has set up shop in downtown Los Angeles. He told Fox News that this attack was well organized and well planned, like a professionally executed military strike. This is Catherine Herridge, live, for Fox News. Peter, back to you."

"Thank you, Catherine." The newsdesk anchor replaced the reporter's face. "Riots, meanwhile, continue in East Los Angeles for the third straight day since reports and home videos of LAPD officers firing into a demonstration were released by local news stations. For a perspective on the situation, we go in our studio to our experts on urban crises . . ."

"Experts my ass," Preston growled. "The idiots still think it's al Qaeda."

"An easy assumption to make," Logan said. "Al Qaeda has been *the* big bugaboo in this country since 9/11."

"Well, we'll disillusion them of that during the next couple of days. Ah! Good product placement!"

On the screen, footage of a demonstration was being shown—angry Latino faces in a street. A green banner unfurled behind the front ranks read POWER TO THE PEOPLE! POWER TO AZTLÁN!

"In English," Preston added, "so the great unwashed masses can read it!"

Another sign nearby was in Spanish, repeating what was rapidly becoming the movement's catchphrase. ¡DIGNIDAD! ¡IGUALDAD! ¡LIBERTAD!

"I still think Walker's right," Logan said. "You people are moving too fast. This thing could blow up in our faces!"

"Nonsense, Charles. I told Mr. Walker, and I'm telling you. An organization such as ours is too big for the details to be kept secret for long. We strike now, and we strike *hard,* or we risk losing everything."

"If you say so."

"I'll be glad when this is over," Gonzales said. He sounded miserable.

"Harvey, you will be *astonished* at just how quickly things fall into place."

CHAPTER SEVEN

VICENTE HOUSE
LA CALLE SUR 145
DISTRICTO IZTACALCO
2220 HOURS, LOCAL TIME
17 APRIL

A thin, drizzling rain had begun an hour before. Teller and Procario, black ski masks pulled down over their faces, were just about to step into the street when the headlights of a car flared in the darkness, then swung aside. "Hold it," Teller said, and the two men remained frozen in the shadows beneath the house.

"I think we have our target," Chavez's voice said in Teller's ear. "A Peugeot just pulled into a parking place a couple of houses up from the objective. Two people getting out."

"We're on hold," Procario replied.

Teller heard the double slam of car doors, the *click-click* of hard shoes on a wet sidewalk. A moment later, a man and a woman came into view, arm in arm as they turned off the sidewalk and picked their way up the sagging steps of the safe house.

"Target confirmed," Chavez said from his vantage point above the street. "That's definitely Escalante. I assume that's Maria Perez with him."

"If it's not," Teller murmured into the needle mike beside his mouth, "he's a *very* busy fella."

The woman was gorgeous, with long black hair wet from the rain. She fumbled in her handbag for her keys.

"The guard's heard them," Chavez said. "He has the rifle. He's walking toward the door."

The door opened, spilling yellow light into the street. The two stepped through, and the light snapped off as the door closed behind them.

"Okay, they're all standing in the hallway talking," Chavez reported. "You know, this doesn't look like it's going to break up anytime soon."

"We'll wait for as long as it takes," Procario said. He was staring up the street. "Hey, Ed?"

"What?"

"Do we have a tail there? Two cars back from Escalante's vehicle."

"Wait one."

"Now what?" Teller asked.

"I noticed another car pull in behind Escalante," Procario said. "The driver hasn't gotten out."

"You two had better abort and get back in here," Chavez told them a moment later.

Teller pulled off the ski mask with a gloved hand. "Why? What's up?"

"Frank's right. We have another surveil out there."

"Shit. Okay. We're coming back in."

Ten minutes later, the three men were again gathered about the monitor, studying the gray-scale image. The car, its engine still glowing brightly at millimeter wavelengths, was parked on the street perhaps twenty yards beyond the Perez residence. Two figures were visible through the windshield in the front seat, a man behind the wheel and a woman in the passenger seat. At that distance, details were almost impossible to make out, but the woman appeared to have something bulky and partially metallic up in front of her face. Teller used the laptop to try to boost the image resolution, but with only marginal success.

"They're definitely watching the front of the Perez house," Teller said after a moment. "Question is, are they ours or the opposition?"

"Opposition," Chavez said. "You mean as in a rival cartel?"

"Exactly. Maybe Los Zetas and Sinaloa have a truce going, but there are plenty of other cartels out there, and they must be shitting themselves right now at the thought of the two big boys getting in bed together. They might have decided to whack Escalante and break up the party now, while they can."

"Or they may just be keeping an eye on the competition," Procario said. "I never heard of drug cartels using women in the field like that, though."

"No reason not to."

"No reason except the idiot Latino compulsion to picture everything in terms of machismo." Procario glanced at Chavez. "Sorry, man. No offense."

"None taken. It's true. People down here still think in terms of men doing the fighting while the women stay home and cook. Of course, that means women can go places and do things without attracting as much suspicion as a guy, y'know? And the cartels use that. Last year, we picked up a sixteen-year-old girl who'd been trained as a Zeta assassin."

"Jesus."

"We have records of them using a thirteen-year old girl as a runner. Bastards."

"Well," Procario said, "we'll know in a moment."

"Can't tell from her face," Teller said, still studying the image, "but I think that one's a keeper. That's a *really* nice set she has."

"So what if those two are friendlies?" Procario asked.

"CISEN, maybe," Chavez suggested.

"I don't think so," Teller said. "Miguel would have told us, I think."

"We didn't tell him about me being here as your backup," Procario pointed out. "Or about the nudie-show surveillance gear."

"Point. But I was thinking of the Company. Or DEA. Or FBI. Or some other alphabet-soup acronym."

"NSA?" Chavez volunteered.

"Probably not," Procario said. "They're strictly SIGINT, signals intelligence. Electronic eavesdropping, phone taps, that sort of thing. They don't have agents in the field."

"That we know of," Teller pointed out. "Remember, NSA means 'Never Say Anything.'"

Chavez chuckled. "I thought it was 'No Such Agency.'"

"That, too," Procario said.

"No, if it was anyone of ours, I'd have to assume either DEA or CIA," Teller said, thinking out loud. The Drug Enforcement Agency had a history of sending agents and teams into Latin American countries, trying to shut down the tangle of drug pipelines that wound their way up to the United States from and through Mexico, and from Peru, Colombia, and Venezuela. As for the CIA, well, the Empire had a history of not letting one hand know what the other was doing.

"How about it, Ed?" Procario asked. "Your buddies back at Langley have another op going down here? Something they didn't tell us about?"

"It's certainly possible," Chavez said. "The Latin America desk was running scared after losing our network down here. And Larson and WINPAC are scrambling to cover their asses after losing those tactical nukes. They might have several teams on the ground, trying to pick up the pieces, and they wouldn't necessarily tell any of them about the others."

"Hey, heads up," Teller said, glancing out the window. "More people joining the party." Sur 145 was a quiet back street, normally. It seemed to be a lot busier than normal tonight.

Procario readjusted the MMMR receiver, aiming it back at the house. Two men had just gone up onto the porch and were now standing at the door. On the monitor, it was clear that both were armed. One had a revolver tucked in next to his left armpit; the other carried a semiautomatic pistol at the small of his back, riding down into the waistband of his pants.

"Fucking Grand Central Station," Chavez observed.

"It's not a hit," Teller decided, studying the two closely. "They're not armed for an assault. And hit men don't ring the doorbell."

The door opened, and the two men stepped into the hallway inside. "It looks more like a convention," Chavez said.

The two newcomers were met by one of the men inside the house and led into what was probably a living room. Another man, probably Escalante, and Maria Perez were seated on invisible furniture there. They stood up as the newcomers entered.

"I do wish we had a bug in there," Procario said. "It would be nice to listen in on what's going down."

"Once we have Cellmap in place," Teller said, "no problem. Until then, though, we're out of luck. Do we have the sat feed going?"

"Uploading perfectly," Chavez said. The Prick 117F was transmitting everything they picked up through the MMMR scope back to Langley for analysis.

"Fucking technology," Procario said. "We can pick up those guys' *heartbeats,* fer chrissakes, but we can't listen in on their conversation!"

"Yeah, we need a laser mike," Teller said, "but the angle is wrong."

Sending out a tight beam of millimeter radiation, at the rate of some hundreds of pulses per second, the system could analyze the waves bounced back and actually record the heartbeats and respiration of each target. The laser mike sent a beam of coherent light and bounced it off the glass of a convenient window. By measuring the reflected beam very precisely, the system in effect turned the window into an enormous microphone diaphragm, allowing a surveillance team over a hundred yards away to listen in on conversations inside the room.

Teller had thought about having one of those units sent down from Langley with the MMMR but decided against it. For the device to work, you either needed to be directly opposite the target window, so that the reflected beam bounced straight back at you, or you needed to plant a receiver somewhere else, off to the side at the one point where it would pick up the reflection, then transmit the data by radio back to the listening post. The angle of incidence equals the angle of reflection, as the physics boys said; dicking around in front of a house several numbers up the street would have been a great way to attract unwanted attention for the team.

There were also high-tech bugs available that could be placed up against the glass of a target window, sensing the vibrations directly. Or they could plant some more traditional listening devices inside if they broke into the place later.

A break-in, though, simply was not an option. With five people in the target house now, it was far too dangerous to try an armed confrontation.

The woman got out of the car and started walking south toward the Perez house. "Uh-oh," Chavez said. "Another one coming to the party?"

Procario whistled appreciatively at the MMMR screen. "Nice," he said.

"She's carrying," Teller observed. It was possible to make out the shape of a semiauto handgun riding at her waist, probably in a holster worn in front, over her belly. He pointed at the screen. "Is that a *suppressor*?"

"Either that," Procario joked, "or it's one hell of a hard-on."

"Standard field issue," Chavez said.

"Yeah, I'm thinking it's the Klingons, definitely." Teller looked away from the screen and out the window, studying the woman down on the street in ordinary light instead of millimeter waves. The curves and intimate details exposed on the MMMR monitor were wrapped in a dark gray raincoat. There was enough of a glow from a nearby streetlight for him to make out her features clearly.

"Hey," Teller said. "I *know* her!"

Chavez joined him at the window. "Jesus."

"Definitely one of yours."

"You're right. She's DO." That was the CIA's Directorate of Operations. "I don't know her name—"

"Yeah, but I do! Hang on. I'll be back in a moment."

"Wait a second, Chris!" Procario called, but Teller was already through the door.

Yeah, Teller knew her, all right—Jacqueline Dominique, Jackie for short. At least, he *thought* that was her real name. She'd been his lover for a brief but intense fling last fall, before she'd been transferred to Venezuela.

She was tough, experienced, dedicated, and smart,

and she'd been *that* close to convincing him to leave DIA and come over to the Dark Side. It was possible she'd not told him her real name. "Dominique" had always seemed so . . . theatrical. The name of paparazzi bait, a model or a singer, maybe, not a *real* person.

"Watch yourself, Chris," Procario's voice said in his ear as he hurried down the steps from the upstairs apartment. "She's going up to the house."

Which might mean she was undercover. Or . . . the unthinkable. She was a double agent, working for them.

No, he didn't, he *couldn't*, believe that of Jackie. She was too direct, too much the stereotypical straight arrow. You needed a mind like a hyperdimensional corkscrew to play on both sides of the street simultaneously.

Teller stepped out onto the front porch of Antonio Vicente's house. Dominique had reached the front door of the Perez house and was leaning over to the side, pressing something against the corner of the front window. It was too small and too far away for Teller to see what it was, but he assumed it was a listening device— probably one of the dime-sized stick-ons that could pick up vibrations through the glass like the more sophisticated long-range laser mikes. It would include a tiny transmitter to beam what it picked up back to Dominique and her partner in the car parked up the street.

Gutsy—but damned risky. If the bad guys also had the Perez house under surveillance, Jackie was screwed. He watched her straighten up, look around, then turn and walk back down the steps to the sidewalk. She didn't head straight back to the car but continued walking south. Going directly to her car, with possible watchers in the neighborhood, would have been bad technique.

Teller decided to follow her.

MATAZETAS HOUSE
LA CALLE SUR 145
DISTRICTO IZTACALCO,
2245 HOURS, LOCAL TIME

Enrico Barrón leaned into the eyepieces of his heavy army binoculars and gave a wolfish grin. *"Quiero clavar ese culo apretado."*

The Spanish was blunt and vulgar, a desire to "nail that tight ass."

The two were in a second-floor bedroom overlooking Sur 145, across the street and just to the north of the Maria Perez house, where they could keep an eye on it. The two watchers were members of a unit called the New Generation Cartel, but better known as Los Matazetas—"the Zeta Killers." Though their public presentation was of a civilian vigilante group dedicated to wiping out the Zetas Cartel, they in fact were closely allied with the Sinaloa Cartel. The order—a very strongly worded order—that had come down last week from Guzmán himself had directed them to cease all hostilities against the Zetas, and Barrón didn't like it one bit.

However, Guzmán had a habit of turning people who disobeyed his orders over to his special inquisitors, with instructions to keep them alive for as long a time as possible. Barrón had seen some Zetas and others who'd received that special attention from the Sinaloan interrogators, seen them while they were still clinging to the last bloody, shrieking shreds of their lives, and he had no intention of sharing their fate.

"Who is she?" his partner asked, watching now from behind his shoulder. The woman had just stepped off the Perez porch and was walking south down the sidewalk, her ass twitching provocatively beneath a long, lightweight raincoat.

"I don't know, but I'm betting the bitch just put a bug on Escalante's window."

"Huh. Gringo, you think?"

"Of course. She's not one of ours."

"With that chassis? No, unfortunately."

"Not a problem. We'll make her one of ours."

"You want to pick her up?"

"I think we should find out who she is, who she works for, no?"

His partner shrugged. "I think you just want to toss some powder." In Spanish, the phrase *echar un polvo* meant much the same as the English "get your rocks off."

"Hey, I don't see a problem mixing a little pleasure with our business."

"Who's she with?"

"She got out of that green car across the street." Barrón panned the binoculars down and to the right, searching. "Yeah, the driver's still there."

"Okay. You and Carlos take out the driver, then grab the girl. Take Arturo along."

Barrón thought for a moment. "Should we pick the guy up for questioning, too?"

"Nah. Kill him. But *quietly.*"

"It's done. Hey . . . there's someone else on the street now." He pointed south. A tall man in a tan jacket was walking down the east side of the street. "What do you think? One of our new Zetas friends? Or another gringo?"

Barrón drew his Beretta pistol, chambered a round, and tucked it into his waistband. "Doesn't matter. I'll handle him."

A moment later, he, a nineteen-year-old killer named Carlos Gutierrez, and a seventeen-year-old named Arturo Gomez were letting themselves out into the drizzling night.

LA CALLE SUR 145
DISTRICTO IZTACALCO
2256 HOURS, LOCAL TIME

Teller stayed on the opposite side of the street from Dominique, and a good thirty yards behind her. He didn't want to spook her, and he certainly didn't want to engage those superb reflexes of hers before she could realize it was him.

This was, he reflected, a lot like one of the exercises they'd put him through at the Farm eight years ago— giving him a photo of someone and having him find the person and tail him through mobs of tourists. He'd actually been pretty good at it. The trick was to blend in with the crowd and not be obvious about stopping when the target stopped, or following him into alleys or shops.

The trouble here was that it was late and the street was pretty much deserted. There was no crowd to blend with, and no easy way to become invisible on the pavement.

In this sort of situation, you had to focus on staying outside of the target's field of view, muffling the click of your footsteps, and, so far as was possible, not thinking about your quarry. Science didn't recognize the effect yet, but anyone who stalked human beings for a living—snipers in combat, detectives tailing a suspect, or intelligence officers following an enemy agent—knew that humans had a remarkable ability to *feel* when someone was following them. Call it telepathy, ESP, or magic, there was something to it, like when he'd felt the Klingon in the midnight darkness at the Farm. From what he'd seen of Jacqueline Dominique, she had that sixth-sense thing down to hard science. Sneaking up on her would *not* be easy.

She passed the mouth of a narrow alley but then turned right at the next intersection, vanishing behind the corner of a building. Teller had already decided that she was simply walking around the block in order to return to the car and her partner. That way, if someone had challenged her at the Perez house, she could have claimed to be lost and asking directions. Avoiding the alley was good basic tradecraft; alleys were great places in which you could be trapped, and too often they proved to be one-way cul-de-sacs.

If Jackie was boxing the block, the alley would give

him a shortcut, assuming it cut all the way through. If it didn't, he could double back and meet her when she approached her car.

"Hey, Frank?" he murmured.

"Go." Procario and Chavez were monitoring his wire.

"I think she's boxing the block. I'm cutting through an alley to head her off."

"Just watch yourself, buddy," Procario replied in his earpiece.

"Don't worry about that. It looks to me like I'm in the clear."

Glancing up and down the street and seeing no one, he started across, heading for the narrow and uninviting black slit of the alley.

LA CALLE SUR 145
DISTRICTO IZTACALCO
2257 HOURS, LOCAL TIME

Barrón eased the Chevy van out of the narrow driveway, pulling into the street and turning left. In the passenger seat, Carlos Gutierrez chambered a round in his Browning Hi Power, which had been threaded to accept the long, heavy tube of a sound suppressor. The passenger-side window was already rolled down.

"It's the dark green car," the voice of his partner said in his ear. "Two back from Escalante's white Chevy."

"I see it," Barrón replied. "Wait one."

He pulled the van up alongside the green Escort and braked to a halt. Gutierrez extended his arm through the window, talking aim with the Hi Power. The driver only had time to turn his head to his left, eyes widening, and then the 9 mm pistol gave a harsh chirp, bucking in the gunman's hand.

Glass crazed and shattered. Gutierrez fired again, then again and again and again, snapping off round after round into the face and neck of the man seated at the Escort's wheel. Blood splattered across the inside of the Escort's windshield as the driver slumped over. Calmly, Gutierrez got out of the van, stepped up to the Escort's driver's side, and reached in with the Hi Power, placing the sound suppressor up against the driver's head just below and behind the ear. He triggered two more shots, then climbed back into the van.

"Amateurs," Barrón said, and he accelerated the van slowly south down the street.

LA CALLE SUR 143
DISTRICTO IZTACALCO
2301 HOURS, LOCAL TIME

The next street to the west of Sur 145 was, illogically enough, Sur 143. Teller didn't know where Sur 144 might be; the alleys here were far too narrow to have their own names or numbers. At the far end of this one was a wooden fence twelve feet high. He pushed off from an overflowing trash can, caught the top, and chinned himself up and over. This was beginning to look more and more like a damned exercise at the Farm, complete with obstacle course.

"Chris! This is Frank!" He sounded worried.

"Go ahead."

"Trouble. A van just pulled alongside the green car. Guy in the passenger seat just killed the woman's partner."

"Shit. How?"

"Professional-style hit—handgun with a sound suppressor. The van took off south, but it turned right at the next intersection."

Down the street Jacqueline Dominique had taken. "Okay. I'm on it."

"Be careful, Chris. Someone made them."

"Right."

Obviously, someone had been watching the Perez house and noticed Jackie going up on the porch. She and her partner had been burned, as tradecraft slang so succinctly put it.

Ahead, the narrow alley opened onto Sur 143, the next street to the west. Teller reached the sidewalk and saw Dominique off to his left, just rounding the corner. She was still a good thirty yards away.

He was about to step out and flag her down when a pale gray van came around the corner behind her, lights glaring in the night. The sliding cargo door on the vehicle's right side was open, a man crouching inside. As the van screeched to a halt, Dominique turned, but the man in the back had already leaped onto the sidewalk just a few feet behind her. The passenger-side front door swung open, and a second man jumped out, lunging for her, a heavy gold-chain necklace flashing incongruously in the glow from a streetlight.

At least they hadn't simply gunned her down in the

street. They intended to abduct her, and that gave Teller a slim chance.

He pulled out his personal weapon, a ten-round Glock .45 semiautomatic riding in a belt holster high enough to stay hidden beneath his jacket. Stepping into the open, Teller braced the pistol in a Weaver stance, two-handed, right arm straight, left arm bent with the hand supporting the right. Thirty yards is a *long* range for any handgun; he ignored the man behind Jackie— too risky—and drew down on the man coming out of the front of the vehicle, squeezing off four quick shots.

Thunderous gunfire echoed off the buildings across the street, and the passenger-side window on the van crazed from the impact of at least one round. The target spun, aiming a pistol and returning fire, the harsh chuff of a suppressor mingling with the whine of a round passing Teller's head, the sharp ping of a ricochet from bricks to his left. Teller fired twice more, and the other stumbled, going down on all fours, though whether he'd been hit or was simply diving for cover Teller couldn't tell at that distance.

Dominique couldn't get at the pistol she was carrying under her raincoat, not quickly enough, at any rate. Instead, she slammed the heel of her hand into her attacker's face, sending him sprawling back through the open cargo door. The man on the ground started to get up, but she pivoted sharply and planted the toe of her boot beneath his chin, kicking *hard*.

Teller was already running toward the fight as fast as he could, his .45 still gripped in two hands out in front of him. He wanted to stop the van, and momentarily considered shooting at the right front tire, but rubber tires don't puncture as easily when hit by gunfire as they seem to do in the movies, and the van could still get well clear of the area running on a flat. Instead, he aimed for the windshield, trying to hit the driver.

Again, there were no guarantees. The angle of a vehicle's front windshield can deflect bullets even as they punch through, but at least he could wreck the driver's vision. He put three more rounds through the windshield, turning glass to a crazed white web.

One round left. He saw a clear shot at the guy with the gold chain, who'd just been slammed back into the van's side by Jackie's kick. As he staggered forward, Teller fired again. The man spun sharply to his right, then collapsed on the pavement.

Teller thumbed the magazine release, dropping the empty to the sidewalk, reaching into his jeans pocket to pull out a loaded magazine and slap it home into the pistol's grip. The man Dominique had hit in the face had grabbed the sliding door and was tugging it shut, and the van was already accelerating wildly down the street, sideswiping a parked car as it moved. Teller came to a halt, let the locked-open slide snap a round into the firing chamber, and began shooting, pivoting to his right as the van screeched north up the street. He put five rounds into the vehicle, then held his fire as it careened behind some parked cars.

It was gone.

Dogs barked in the distance, and Teller heard the slam of shutters banging closed across the street. Neighborhoods like this one tended to stick their collective head in the sand when they heard gunfire on the street nowadays.

"Who the fuck are you?"

He turned, breathing hard. Dominique stood fifteen feet away, her pistol with its awkward sound suppressor now gripped tightly in both hands, aiming directly at him.

Carefully, Teller raised his hands and stepped farther into the illumination of the streetlight, letting her see his face.

"Chris?"

"Hello, Jackie. It's been ages. You never write . . . you never call . . ."

Then she was in his arms.

CHAPTER EIGHT

LA CALLE SUR 143
DISTRICTO IZTACALCO
2304 HOURS, LOCAL TIME
17 APRIL

"Who is he?" Jackie Dominique asked.

Teller grimaced as he squatted by the body of the man he'd shot, studying his wallet. Over twenty thousand pesos in bills, a Mexican driver's license and some other ID, a color photo of a pretty girl, several credit cards. Flashy rings and a heavy necklace that looked like gold. According to the license, the man's name was Carlos Gutierrez Sandoval. His address was in Nogales, up on the Mexico-Arizona border. He was nineteen years old.

For answer, he handed the wallet to Dominique.

Teller pocketed the pistol, a Browning Hi Power, and three magazines of 9 mm ammo, but searched every pocket in vain for a cell phone. *Damn*.

Reaching into his own pocket, he pulled out his cell

phone, flipped it open, and took several pictures of the dead narcoterrorist's face. He also photographed the driver's license.

"Frank?"

"Go."

"They tried to abduct Jackie Dominique. I shot up the van, took down one Tango, but two others got away."

"Ed wants to know if Ms. Dominique is okay."

He glanced at her. Her face was flushed, she was breathing hard, but she didn't look more than lightly shaken. "Yeah, she's fine. Listen . . . you guys might be exposed."

"We're already breaking down the OP. We won't learn anything else here tonight. That meeting at the Perez place is starting to look permanent."

As he listened, he lifted the left arm of the body on the street, examining the elaborate tattoo. There were hearts and flowers, the red, white, and green of the Mexican flag, and the word MATAZETAS running from elbow to wrist encircled by twining roses. He took a photo of that as well, then keyed in a transmission code.

"Okay," he said. "I'm uploading some photos of the Tango for you to shoot back to Langley. But I don't want to go back there with Jackie, in case they're watching the place. We'll meet you back at the hotel, probably tomorrow."

"Roger that. Good luck."

He dropped the limp arm, thoughtful, and pocketed his phone. "Yeah . . . You too."

The Matazetas, he knew from his briefing back in

Langley, was an arm of the Sinaloa Cartel, and that fit if this kid was from Nogales. *Zeta Killers*.

He checked through Gutierrez's clothing again, still looking for a phone, then abandoned the search. He took the money from the wallet instead. The current exchange rate was around thirteen or fourteen pesos to the dollar; twenty thousand pesos was around fifteen hundred dollars, and if he and Jackie were going to go to ground overnight, they would need cash. He had a thousand pesos and a few hundred dollars on him, plus a cash card, but the card might allow him to be tracked, and right now he wanted to disappear for a while.

Both Sinaloa and Los Zetas maintained what amounted to small armies, for their wars with each other and with the Mexican government. Teller was unwilling to make any guesses as to how sophisticated their surveillance techniques or technology might be.

He also pocketed the dead man's credit cards. A check on those and what he'd purchased recently might be of some use.

"We need to go back and pick up James," Dominique told him. "James Grant, my partner. He's waiting in the car—"

"No, we don't. He's dead."

"My God! How?"

"My people have an OP overlooking the Perez house. They saw the bad guys drive up and take him out before they came after you."

"Oh, Christ." Her shoulders slumped, and she seemed to fold up a bit inside.

"My people will take care of the body," he said.

Rising, he gently took her arm. "C'mon. We need to get out of here. There may be more of those people around, or the guys in that van may come back for us. And the police will show up sooner or later. We don't want to have to answer their questions."

"You told your people you weren't going back to your OP?"

"That's right. They're getting ready to hightail it. You and me are going someplace else, just to be on the safe side."

"Like where?"

"Someplace," Teller told her solemnly, "where I can get a drink."

Los Gatos was a bar and restaurant a few blocks away, on the fringes of a commercial neighborhood better populated than the barrio streets where they'd just met. Inside it was smoky and noisy, a nearly full house. Teller scanned the crowd as he stepped in past the vestibule, trying to get a feel for the place. Lots of blue-collar types, a few students, but no obvious tourists. Tourists would have offered a bit more camouflage for the two of them, but the place was public enough that no one was going to try to get at them here.

Probably.

"We need some insurance," Teller said, looking around. An enormous man was hunkered over one end of the bar, tattooed, bald, with a ragged goatee and muscles bulging with steroids. Teller suspected that the man might be the Los Gatos bouncer. "Wait here."

He walked over to the end of the bar and spoke with the giant for a few moments. Money passed from Teller's hand to the other's and quietly disappeared. *"Gracias, amigo,"* Teller told the man, and he rejoined Dominique.

One advantage to Los Gatos was the knowledge that they could have a conversation without being easily overheard. They found an empty booth toward the back of the place.

"Dos cervezas," Teller told the waitress when she showed up a moment later.

"¿Que tipo, señor?"

"Me gustaría una Corona, por favor," Dominique told her.

"Y Negra Modelo por mí. Gracias." As the waitress walked off, Teller said, "I think your accent's better than mine."

"It should be. I've been working the Latino beat for three years now, and living in Venezuela for six months."

"So how's Venezuela?"

"Anti-American in public. Quietly taking all the help from Big Oil and U.S. technology they can manage."

"So I've heard."

"Well, what brings you to Mexico City, Chris? Other than your charming penchant for rescuing damsels in distress?"

"I could ask you the same thing," he told her.

"Is it business?"

"Of course. You?"

"Of course. Your cover?"

"Journalist."

"Me, too."

"Not exactly the safest of choices right now," Teller told her. He shrugged. "I considered circus clown, but I knew your friends in the station here have the corner on that market, and I'm trying to keep it low-profile. The role of *journalista* works for the paper-shufflers, but I wouldn't care to have the opposition think I was with the press."

"And that's assuming the government isn't the opposition . . . or in bed with them."

"Either way, it's not a real healthy environment here for reporters at the moment."

"You're thinking of those two women in Iztapalapa?"

Teller nodded. "The bastards have been targeting reporters, media people, even people on the Internet for a while, now."

The recent spate of cartel attacks against the media had been so shocking, so violently bloody, that they seemed deliberately designed to frighten off anyone reporting on the spiraling violence in Mexico. In early September of 2011, two female Mexican journalists had been abducted off the street. Their bodies, stripped naked, bound hand and foot, beaten, and strangled, had turned up in a park in the neighboring district of Iztapalapa the next morning. That was less than three miles from the spot where Teller and Dominique were sitting now.

There was more, and much worse. A few days after the Iztapalapa murders, two young people, a man and a woman both in their twenties were found dead, hanging from a pedestrian bridge in Nuevo Laredo just across the river from Laredo, Texas. The male was hanging from his wrists, savagely mutilated, his right shoulder gashed so deeply the bones were exposed. The woman was tied by both hands and feet, topless, her entrails dangling from three deep slashes in her belly. Both showed evidence of torture, their fingers and ears mutilated. Notes left on the bridge promised the same for anyone who posted about the cartels on the Internet or through a Twitter account.

Late in the same month, Maria Elizabeth Macias Castro, the newsroom manager for a Nuevo Laredo newspaper, had been found, partially undressed, decapitated, her severed head displayed on a nearby ornamental piling. A sign on the piling indicated she'd been killed because of her posts on a local electronic social network.

Since 2000, over seventy journalists had been killed or had disappeared in Mexico, and there'd been other overt threats against people simply posting about the cartels on the Internet. The sheer blood-drenched viciousness of so many torture-murders clearly was intended to send a back-off message to anyone and everyone writing about the violence in Mexico.

Yet the CIA seemed stuck on "journalist" as a cover for officers going into Mexico. There were reasons for that; legal restrictions in the United States made most other mobile professions—medical personnel, say, or Peace Corps volunteers or church officials—illegal, and reporters were among the few people who could travel around asking questions without attracting unwanted notice. Still, Teller felt a bit exposed in a country where people who asked questions about the drug cartels tended to disappear—or else be found disemboweled or headless and left on public display.

What worried Teller most about the torture of those two kids in Nuevo Laredo, however, as well as Castro's death, was what they said about the cartels' technological abilities. People on social networks used nicknames; on the placard left beneath her head, Castro had been identified only as "Laredo Girl," her network pseudonym. It suggested that the cartels had intelligence units capable of tracking people through their Twitter accounts, of finding them despite the supposed anonymity of social networks online. Teller remembered reading about the note left with the bodies hanging from the bridge: *This is going to happen to all of those posting funny things on the Internet. You better fucking pay attention. I'm about to get you.*

Empty threat, mindless machismo and bravado? Or did the cartels—probably Los Zetas in those two particular cases, since one note had been signed "Z" and the other "ZZZZ"—actually have the expertise and technology to track down anonymous individuals on the Internet?

The cartel killers seemed to possess the sophistication of many legitimate intelligence agencies, a disquieting thought for someone in Teller's line of work. If they could hack e-mail accounts or track people by their Twitter posts, they likely had the equipment and the trained manpower to plant sophisticated listening devices or to track someone remotely, by means of RFIDs, for instance. Los Zetas had gotten their start as Mexican Army Special Forces; some of them must be people with intelligence training as well.

It was just possible that some of the Zetas had gone through one or more spy courses at the Farm. *That* was a nasty thought.

Their beers arrived, and they sat in silence for several minutes, quietly drinking. Teller gulped his, hard and fast, and ordered another. Dominique nursed hers, absently playing with the wedge of lime perched on the rim of the glass. "Thank you, by the way," she said after a while. "You probably saved my life tonight."

"Don't mention it," Teller replied.

"Well . . . maybe I can make it up to you. Later."

"Maybe you can." He was already turning over possible hides. Los Gatos would close in another couple of hours. He'd checked the times on a plaque by the door. They would have to find a hotel; it was not a good idea to go back to their own rooms downtown, the Hotel Hilton at Azueta for him, the Holiday Inn Zócalo for her.

He thought for a moment, then added, "You know, Jackie, we *could* work together. Pool our resources."

"I'm not sure that's a good idea," Dominique told him. "I've been made, somehow. But they don't know about you yet."

"Maybe. But they saw me on the street just now—and

it's possible they spotted our OP at the Perez house, too. We can't take anything for granted right now."

"So what do we do? Pack up and go home?"

"No, I don't think so. There's a lot we can do yet."

"They must have spotted me in front of the Perez house."

Teller nodded. "Right. We saw you plant a listening device on the window. The opposition likely was watching, too, from another building."

"Damn. James and I talked about that possibility before I got out of the car, but we didn't see any sign of a lookout, and we *had* to know what was going on." She shrugged. "Calculated risk."

"The opposition is pretty slick." He grinned at her. "*We* were watching you through a triple-M scope from across the street. Maybe they were doing the same."

She made a face. "So I should have sold tickets. See anything you like?"

"Very much so."

"Pervert."

"Exhibitionist."

"*You're* the one with the high-tech peep-show gear. What did you see in the Perez house?"

"Does that mean you're willing to pool information?"

"Maybe. Depends."

"On what?"

"On what you decide to share with me."

"Well . . . besides a full-body massage that I'm willing to throw into the deal, what do you want to know?"

"For a start, what's your mission here? What are you

doing in an unhealthy neighborhood at ten in the evening, besides rescuing me?"

"Re-creating the CIA's network in Mexico." That wasn't the whole story, of course, and it was general enough to sidestep the *really* sensitive topics, like two missing nuclear warheads, but it would do for a start.

"Yeah? For who?"

"JJ Wentworth." He decided not to mention Larson. The WINPAC man's involvement would bring up issues about nuclear weapons, issues he wasn't ready to mention just yet.

Teller felt a deep and genuine reluctance against sharing anything with the CIA. The Klingons always played their own game, by their rules, and they did not play well with others. Information they shared usually had strings attached, and they always had their own agenda. Right now, he didn't want to get sucked into that any more than was necessary. Not only that, there was no way to tell, at this point, where Jackie's loyalties really lay.

Jackie Dominique was a friend, and she'd been his lover. That didn't mean he trusted her.

"Wentworth." She shook her head. "Don't know him."

"It's a big company."

"Does that mean you're working with us now?"

"No," he said with a sharp emphasis that surprised him. He caught the surprise in her eyes and lowered his voice. "No, not at all. I'm just . . . helping out."

"Hm." The hint of a sparkle in her eye suggested that she might have her own ideas about that. Dominique had wanted him to go to work for the Agency ever since they'd met early last year. "We'll have to see what we can do about that."

MATAZETAS HOUSE
LA CALLE SUR 145
DISTRICTO IZTACALCO
2335 HOURS, LOCAL TIME

Barrón's partner, Agustín Morales Galvan, ran his finger down the list in the telephone directory, paused, then thumbed another number into his cell phone, his eleventh call so far. Unless they were hiding in someone's house, they must be in a public place at this hour—a bar, a hotel, a late-night restaurant. There were only so many places they could be, and Morales had connections with most of them.

"Los Gatos," a voice said on the other end of the line. Morales could hear the clink of glasses and the rumble of conversation behind the barkeeper's voice.

"Hola, Luis," he said. *"Este es Calavera."*

He could almost feel the man on the other end of the phone go cold. *"Sí, señor."* Yes, sir. The nickname "Calavera" had a double meaning in Mexican Spanish. *Una calavera* could be a swinger, the life of the party, a libertine.

It also meant "skull."

"I am looking for a person," Morales said, continuing in Spanish. "A woman . . . tall, very beautiful, black or very dark brown hair, wearing a dark gray raincoat. She may be with a tall man, good-looking, light hair, in a black turtleneck, tan jacket, and jeans. Have you seen them, friend?"

"I . . . I have, sir. Yes! Those very people came in together maybe ten minutes ago."

"Excellent! Some of my people will be there shortly."

"Is there . . . will there be trouble, sir?"

"Only if they start it, Luis." Morales snapped the cell phone shut. He looked up at Barrón and Gomez, standing in front of him. Barrón had blood on his face and was trying to stop the bleeding with a handful of toilet paper.

"Los Gatos," he told them. "No screwups this time, understand?"

"No, sir."

"Bring both of them in. I suspect that they are . . . former associates of mine."

Agustín Morales had worked for the Sinaloa Cartel for ten years now. He had military experience—four years with the Mexican armored corps, in intelligence, and he'd had special training in the United States. The far-flung Sinaloan intelligence network was almost entirely due to his efforts and his skill. Largely, those efforts had been directed against the Mexican government and against the American DEA, but for the last couple of years more and more of his attention had been focused on Los Zetas and their attempts to seize control of *all* narcotics trafficking and networks in Mexico. He didn't like the Zetas, and he didn't trust them—wild, bloodthirsty animals, animals who killed for fun, or to drive home messages with horrific shock. He'd helped create La Nueva Generación—nicknamed "the Zeta

Killers"—to counter their rampage, and perhaps turn down a notch the murderous violence engulfing the country.

Which was why he was as angry at his orders tonight as was Barrón. They were here, in a Sinaloan safe house, in order to provide security for another meeting between a couple of Zeta and Sinaloan big shots: Escalante and Ortega. It was so damned tempting to just send in a team of Matazetas and kill the Zeta bastard—but Morales knew the value of following orders, and he knew discipline.

Two years ago, he'd actually allowed himself to be recruited by the CIA case officer working out of the U.S. Embassy . . . what was his name? Fletcher, that was it. Morales had been in a position to learn a lot about the CIA's attempt to infiltrate both the Sinaloa and Zetas organizations. He personally had helped interrogate that *policía* bastard working for the CIA, Garcia. It had been his idea to send Garcia's head to CIA headquarters as a warning.

"We'll get the son of a whore for you, Calavera," Barrón promised him. "*And* the bitch."

LOS GATOS
DISTRITO IZTACALCO
2340 HOURS, LOCAL TIME

"How much do you know," Dominique asked him, "about something called Trapdoor?"

"Has to do with tracking nuclear warheads, doesn't it?" he replied carefully, keeping his voice neutral.

She nodded. "Specifically, over a hundred small tactical warheads stolen after the Soviet Union broke up. Suitcase nukes, some people call them."

"I've heard of them."

"The CIA thinks two of them may be headed for Mexico on board a ship from South Asia."

"The *Zapoteca*," he said, keeping his voice low.

Her eyes widened. "You *know*?"

"One of your people, Dave Larson, briefed me. WINPAC."

"Shit."

"Are you angry I already know? Or angry they didn't tell you they had a second string to their bow?"

"*Damn* it! Larson is the one who sent me down here," she told him. "Am I supposed to be here backing you up? Or are you backing *me*?"

Teller had been distracted and wasn't paying complete attention to the conversation. There were two men at a nearby table, and for the past several moments he'd been warily noting their behavior. One was quiet enough and wasn't calling attention to himself. His friend, however, was loud, more than half drunk, and getting rowdy. He'd just reached up under a waitress's skirt, and when she shrieked and slapped him, he grinned and pulled out a thick sheaf of pesos, waving it under her nose.

"I'm sorry," Teller said. "You were saying?"

"I asked you who was the backup for who, you for me or me for you."

"Doesn't matter," he told her. "Just so we don't get in each other's way."

"What's so interesting behind me?"

"I think we have some drug-gang people over there," he said quietly. "One, anyway. He's flashing bills and acting like a dick."

"That doesn't make him a drug lord."

"Not by itself. But he's wearing patent leather shoes that must've cost a couple of hundred dollars, and a jacket and silk shirt that set him back a lot more than that. He's pushy, won't take no for an answer. Acting like a big shot. And when he moved just now, I think I caught a glimpse of leather under the jacket. He's carrying."

"Are they watching us?"

"No . . . don't turn around. I don't think so. But I think we'd better get out of here." He tossed a generous tip on the table, and together they stood up and began threading their way toward the front door. As they passed the table, the noisy one leered at Dominique. "Hey, *chichuda!*" he called. The word was a mildly offensive endearment in Mexican Spanish, a reference to the size of her breasts. He reached for her.

"*Frénalo a poco, macho,*" she told him, fending off the hand. The slang phrase called him a tough guy and suggested that he should put on his brakes.

The guy's eyes darkened, and he came to his feet. "*No seas una chuchafría, puta,*" he said in what he must have imagined to be a dangerous tone.

"*Tómala con calma, amigo,*" Teller told him, placing a hand on his chest. "Simmer down."

"*¡Te voy a reventar!*"

"Take me apart, you little insect?" Teller said pleasantly, still speaking Spanish. "I don't think so." Smiling in his most disarming fashion, Teller put his arm around the enraged but baffled man's shoulders and pointed toward the end of the bar, where the big man with the football-player physique was drinking. "See that guy? In our organization we call him 'Manuel el Loco,' and he's my hired gun. Only . . . he doesn't usually need a gun, you know? Because he can take people apart with his bare hands."

"Manuel el Loco" glanced up from his drink just then, saw Teller looking at him, and gave a big smile. Teller tossed him a two-finger salute, and Crazy Manny gave a little wave in reply. The wind spilled from the tough guy's sails.

"I suggest you leave me and *mi comay,* my girlfriend, alone, *comprende*?" Teller said, still friendly.

"S-sí. Comprendo . . . señor."

"Bueno. Hasta luego."

He followed Dominique out of the restaurant.

MATAZETAS HOUSE
LA CALLE SUR 145
DISTRICTO IZTACALCO
2359 HOURS, LOCAL TIME

"Hey, Calavera?" It was Barrón's voice.

"Dígame," Morales replied. "Tell me."

"The targets aren't here. We talked to Luis, the bartender. He said they just left, five, maybe ten minutes ago."

"Okay."

"You want us to drive around the streets, looking for them?"

Morales thought for a moment. "Go ahead—but they've probably gone to ground at a hotel in the area. I'll get back to you."

"Yes, Calavera." Barrón sounded relieved that Morales hadn't responded with anger. In fact, he'd half expected this. A few calls to hotels and taxi services in the area, some threats, a bribe or two, and he would find them, no problem.

He reached again for the telephone directory.

CHAPTER NINE

HOTEL ESTRELLA
DISTRICTO IZTACALCO
0225 HOURS, LOCAL TIME
18 APRIL

"Again?" she whispered, her ears close by his ear.

They lay together in an uncomfortably soft hotel bed, nude and slick with sweat and deliciously entangled. A neon sign outside the window leading to a second-floor fire escape flashed yellow and green light across the ceiling in regular patterns, and an ambulance siren wailed in the distance.

Teller groaned, and stretched. "I don't think I can," he admitted. "Oh, but that was *good*."

"Better than your exotic dancer friend?" Dominique asked. "What was her name . . . Titsie Tight?"

"Bitsie Bright. Let's not start *that* again, okay?"

They'd had a major blow-up over Teller's relationship with Sandy Doherty just before Dominique had left for Venezuela. Damn it, he'd never pretended that his relationship with Jackie was an exclusive one.

"Sorry," she said, relaxing against him, her head pressed up under his chin. "That wasn't fair."

"No, it wasn't." He gave her a squeeze. "But it was justified."

"So . . . what did you tell that creep in the bar, anyway? You never said."

"The big guy I talked to when we first went in?"

"Yeah."

"I told him I was the producer for a movie, and that some of the stars were going to be in Los Gatos tonight."

"And he believed you?"

"Well, slipping him a thousand pesos helped. Told him it was to take out an option on his services, that he was exactly the type we wanted for the big fight scene, and we'd have him sign a contract tomorrow."

"I repeat," she said, sounding dubious, "he *believed* you?"

"Hey, pay people enough money and they'll believe any damned thing you tell them. When lover boy looked like he was going to be a problem, I pointed to the big guy and told the cockroach he was my bodyguard."

"Pretty slick."

"I thought it would help if those guys in the van came in. If they didn't come in shooting, that is."

"What if they had?"

"Then you and I probably wouldn't be screwing one another's brains out in a cheap hotel right now. You can't cover *every* eventuality, but you do your best to cover what you can."

"Do you really think those guys in the van are still looking for us?"

"I don't know. You asked me earlier what the targets were doing in the Perez house. The answer is, some kind of meeting, maybe a low-profile summit between cartel leaders. And Juan Escalante is believed to be brokering a truce or deal between Sinaloa and Los Zetas, a cease-fire. My guess is that you got spotted by a Zetas security detail, and they want to know who you are and who you work for."

"Maybe they think we're from a rival cartel."

"That's probably their big concern. There are a lot of small fry, besides the big two. None of them will want an alliance between Los Zetas and Sinaloa, and they could do a lot of damage by hitting that meeting, maybe making it look like the cease-fire had collapsed."

"Makes sense. And that means they want to capture us for questioning, not just shoot us down in the street."

"They'll also want to know if maybe we're working for the U.S.," Teller added. "You could pass for *una Latina hermosa* easily enough with that hair—but me, I look like a gringo. They probably think I'm alphabet soup. CIA, DEA . . ."

"The TLA."

Teller didn't recognize the acronym. "What agency is that?"

"Three-Letter Acronym," she replied, laughing. Her hand, resting on his chest, began to wander, teasing.

"So what is Escalante's connection with nuclear weapons?" Teller asked. "Mmm. That's nice . . ."

"We're not sure. WINPAC thinks one of the cartels might be smuggling them in to destabilize the country."

"That's what I was told. Doesn't make sense, though."

"Why not?"

"In case you hadn't noticed, love, Mexico is *already* destabilized. Worse than Colombia ever was back in the eighties. It's on the point of becoming a failed state now, and I'm not sure there's any power on earth that can stop that."

"Well, a pocket nuke or two would certainly hasten the process." Her hand continued its teasing, becoming more aggressive.

"Sure, but what would be the point? The cartels have already infiltrated the government, the police, the army, and the judicial system, either with people or with bribes or through terror. Before long, Mexico is going to be as bad as Somalia, with warlords and gangs running everything."

He let his own hand begin wandering, and she gave a small gasp. "Oh! But we *really* should get some sleep . . ."

"Eventually."

"Mmm. It *does* appear that you're ready for another go."

"More like another come. You haven't answered my question."

"Which one?"

"Any ideas how Escalante's connected with the

nukes? You said you were sent here to investigate Trapdoor. You were surveilling Escalante. You didn't just pick him at random."

"No. He was of interest because WINPAC tagged him with the Kilo."

"Kilo?" He shook his head, confused. "I don't understand. As in kilos of cocaine?"

"No. As in a Russian Kilo class submarine."

Teller's hand stopped moving. "You're kidding me."

"You weren't briefed? The Zetas have purchased a Russian diesel sub. Maybe 'rented' is the better word. It's been on the market for quite a while."

Yes, it had—and the game quite suddenly had just escalated to a whole new level.

During the Cold War, NATO had assigned code names to Soviet submarines based on international alphabet flags—Charlie, Delta, Echo, Foxtrot, Golf, and so on—and the Kilo class had been one of the most successful of the lot. Diesel powered, intended as an attack sub rather than an ICBM boomer, the boat was so quiet that U.S. sonar operators referred to it as "the black hole," and it had given naval strategic planners fits. Displacing 2,900 tons submerged, 241 feet long, and with a crew of fifty-two, Kilos had a range of well over 7,000 miles on the surface or, as was more likely, if they used a snorkel underwater. Their endurance was estimated at around forty-five days.

First launched in the early 1980s, Kilos had become an important export item for the Soviet Union, then for the Russian Federation that followed it. Algeria, China, India, Poland, Iran, Romania, and Vietnam had all purchased Kilo submarines, and Egypt and Venezuela were expected to make purchases soon.

Back in the 1990s, a new wrinkle had surfaced, as it were, with rumors that the Russians were attempting to rent a Kilo class submarine to one of the Colombian drug cartels, complete with a trained crew—one year for a reported one million dollars, plus operating expenses. The thought of an ultraquiet modern submarine hauling multi-ton lots of cocaine north and off-loading them on deserted American beaches had been a nightmare scenario for the Drug Enforcement Agency and others. According to information developed by the CIA, however, the cartel in question had gotten spooked and backed off. Evidently, the idea was too crazy even for the Colombian drug cartels; a million dollars was pocket change for them, but they'd elected to stick with more traditional methods of smuggling—like having human mules swallow condoms filled with cocaine to get them through customs.

"The Mexican cartels have been using subs lately," Teller observed, "but those are homemade jobs, custom-made."

The earliest, back in the 1990s, had been semisubmersible only, designed to be almost invisible to radar. More recent designs were fully submersible. They were called narco-subs, drug subs, or, amusingly, Bigfoot submarines, because authorities had heard rumors about the things for years but never seen one. Since the mid-2000s, though, a number had been seized, both by local police or military authorities and by the U.S. Coast Guard. A typical narco-sub was between 40 and

80 feet long, could travel up to 2,000 miles, could submerge to 300 feet, and had a crew of three or four—though some had been captured and found to be under remote control. The largest could carry around twelve tons of cocaine.

One report Teller had seen mentioned forty-two individual submarine sightings by the U.S. Navy in the first six months of 2008. The DEA estimated that about a third of all the cocaine moving from South America to Mexico was coming in by submarine; the Colombians, especially, were pioneering the use of submersibles in narco-trafficking. U.S. Intelligence believed that FARC—the Fuerzas Armadas Revolucionarias de Colombia, Marxist-Leninist guerrillas—had been cooperating with the Mexican cartels to build the subs in order to pay for their revolution.

There were so many of the do-it-yourself subs out there that hiring a Russian Kilo now seemed like overkill. Still . . . since they were built on the cheap, they weren't particularly quiet. How much cocaine could a Kilo boat smuggle in—and how hard would it be to pick it up and track it?

"When did all of this go down?" Teller asked.

"A couple of months ago. I found out about the sub being transferred to Venezuela first, but then it was transferred to Los Zetas. We think it's in the Yucatán someplace, but we haven't been able to find it yet."

"The Yucatán. Where we think the *Zapoteca* was headed."

"Exactly. And you can see why WINPAC is . . . concerned."

"Yeah." Suppose the final destination of those two suitcase nukes wasn't Mexico after all. Suppose there was another target, one located somewhere on the U.S. eastern seaboard, for instance. Narco-submarines didn't have the range to reach, say, New York City, but a Kilo did. Easily.

A couple of five-kiloton nukes detonating between Battery Park and Governors Island would wreck lower Manhattan and might force the evacuation of all five of the city's boroughs and much of northern New Jersey as well. Compared to that, the destruction of the World Trade Center towers would seem like minor vandalism.

"It still doesn't make sense, though," Teller objected. "Why would the Mexican cartels want to nuke a target in the United States? They want live, paying customers, not radioactive ruins."

"I don't know," Dominique admitted. "Extortion, maybe?"

"Yeah, well, if the Zetas leadership has been watching too many James Bond films, maybe. Damn."

"What?"

"I really need to plant my bug."

"What bug?"

He told her about the Cellmap virus, about how it would map out the drug-smuggling networks and also let Langley listen in through cartel cell phones. "If they *are* smuggling those nukes north," he concluded, "they're having to coordinate a lot of different factors. Getting the weapons transferred off the cargo ship and onto the sub, for a start. If we could listen in, we might have a better idea of what's going on."

"We need to find the *Zapoteca*," she suggested.

"Yeah. I—" He stopped, listening.

"What is it?"

He touched his finger to his lips and sat up, staring at the crack of light under the door to the room. He'd thought he heard something in the hallway outside . . . a creak of old floorboards, perhaps. Now he saw a shadow flicker past the light.

The Estrella was something less than a four-star luxury hotel. The ceiling tiles were water stained and drooping in places, the floors and bed were sagging, and paint was peeling in places on walls and doorjambs. Teller would have preferred to find a higher-class hotel, if only because he and Dominique would have been better able to blend in and disappear at a place like the Hilton or the Holiday Inn, places where gringo *turistas* didn't stand out like a couple of big hairy spiders on a dinner plate.

Taxis were too easy to trace, though, and they'd needed to find a place within a short walk of Los Gatos. The Hotel Estrella was one of four or five places within half a mile of the bar, so he'd decided to risk it.

Now he was wondering if he'd made a mistake. He heard urgently whispering voices.

Quietly, he reached underneath the mattress, his fingers closing around the grip of his locked and loaded .45. Beside him, Dominique rolled over to her side of the bed and picked up her Beretta Px4 Storm, a 9 mm subcompact, custom fitted with a sound suppressor.

A metallic click sounded in the lock. The security chain was on as well, of course, but that wouldn't hinder a determined attacker for long. This hotel didn't have anything as sophisticated as dead bolts—another point in favor of the Hilton.

The door snapped open, banging against the chain. Dominique rolled off the mattress, dropping to the floor with the bed between her and the door, as Teller leaped for the room's tiny desk, scooping up the rickety chair beside it. The door banged inward again, and again, and on the fourth attempt wood splintered as the security chain pulled free. As the door flew all the way open, Teller hurled the chair with a sidearm swing, aiming for the silhouettes backlit by the lighting in the hallway.

The chair going out collided with gunmen coming in. Wood splintered, and one of the attackers went down in a flailing tangle of arms and pieces of disintegrating chair. Teller brought his pistol up in a two-handed stance and fired, the boom of the powerful semiautomatic handgun ringing off the hotel walls.

From behind the bed, Dominique cut loose with three fast shots, the noise muffled somewhat by the suppressor but loud enough to wake the neighbors if the .45 hadn't done that already. At least three figures were down now in the doorway, two of them still moving. Teller fired again into the tangle—and then the fire escape window at his back exploded inward, and something struck him, hard, in the ribs. The blow knocked him forward and down, but he managed to hold on to his pistol as he fell, turning, firing at a half-glimpsed shadow on the fire escape outside. Dominique turned as well, firing through shattering glass until the shadow outside folded and dropped.

"Chris! Are you okay?"

Rising to his feet, Teller reached around to his back, high up, just beneath his right shoulder blade. His hand came away slick with blood, and it hurt to breathe.

"I'm fine," he said. "Just nicked."

Dominique picked her way through the shattered glass, pistol ready.

"Watch out, don't cut yourself," he said. He picked up her shoes and handed them to her, then found his own. There was glass everywhere, and he shook a couple of shards from his left shoe before slipping it on.

"I think this one's dead," she said, coming back from the window. "Looks like a 12-gauge. Here, let me see your back."

"No time. Get your coat. We're out of here." He could hear shouts and loud voices from elsewhere in the building. Even in this part of town, a gunfight inside a hotel was going to bring the police, and quickly. A moment later, a fire alarm went off with a harsh, angry bray, sounding over and over again. Someone had pulled an emergency alarm to evacuate the hotel.

Teller took time to find his pants, pull them on, then fish the cell phone from his pocket. He made his way across to the room's inside door, stooping to examine the three bodies there.

Correction—one KIA and two wounded. One of the wounded was unconscious and wouldn't last much longer; one round had gone through his left lung, the wound bubbling and whistling. The other was whimpering, curled into a fetal position with his hands laced over his belly, blood pooling beneath him. Neither of the wounded men was paying attention to Teller. Quickly, Teller pulled the wallets from all three.

He found cell phones in their pockets. Jackpot!

Teller also found an unopened pack of cigarettes in the dead man's shirt pocket. Quickly, he stripped off the cellophane and used it to cover the sucking chest wound on the first wounded gunman. He retrieved a pillowcase from the bed and used that to pack the other's belly wound. That ought to hold them until an ambulance arrived.

He then jacked a connection cable from his cell phone to one of the others and punched in a four-digit code. The question was how long it would take the virus to load into the target phone.

It took less than five minutes for Dominique and Teller both to get dressed and collect their things. Teller went to the fire escape and looked down into the hotel parking lot.

"No one down there," he told Dominique. "If these four have backup, they'll be waiting for us either in the lobby or right outside the front entrance. We'll go down this way."

Teller went back to the door and checked the progress of his download. It was still going. Damn. They couldn't wait much longer. If the police didn't show up, curious hotel guests or management might—though chances were they would be cautious after hearing gunfire.

Dominique took a sheet from the bed and wrapped it around her hand, using it to smash broken glass from the window frame, clearing the way for their escape.

"We're good to go," she said. She nodded at the tangle of bodies on the floor. "You think those two will make it?"

"Maybe."

"Why'd you help them? They're bloodthirsty murderers."

He shrugged, still watching the phone download in process. "They're also human beings. Drowning in your own blood is a horrible way to die."

Ten minutes. Come on come on *come on* . . .

A light winked green on the display of his cell phone. Swiftly, he unjacked the cable, pocketed it and his phone, and slipped the other phone back into the pocket of the gut-shot gunman.

"Let's go," he told her. "I'll go first and check it out."

He wanted to make sure that someone wasn't down there in the parking lot, hidden out of sight, watching that window. He took a moment to check the body on the fire escape platform—dead with a round through his forehead—then clattered down the extended fire escape ladder without attracting any attention that he could see, though the wound in his back shrieked at him as he moved. Dominique was right behind him. "Where now?" she asked, coming up against him.

"Downtown," he decided. "My hotel. It's only a few miles."

"Well, I must say you certainly know how to show a girl a good time."

"Hey, that's me," he said, grinning. *"Una calavera real."*

The rain had stopped, though the streets and sidewalks were still wet. Two police cars, sirens ululating, pulled in at the front of the hotel, followed closely by an ambulance.

A crowd had already gathered out front, mostly hotel guests, to judge by the range of undress and dishabille—underwear, negligees, and even blankets pulled over shoulders.

Teller took Dominique's arm, and they began strolling north toward the city center.

OVAL OFFICE
THE WHITE HOUSE
WASHINGTON, D.C.
0905 HOURS, EDT

"Good morning, Mr. President."

"Randy."

"I have the report you wanted."

"Thank you." The president looked up from what he was reading, then leaned back in his office chair. He looked exhausted, gray, *old.*

Well, it had been that kind of week.

"In two hours," the president said, "I have a meeting with the UN ambassador. He's going to tell me all about a resolution proposed by Mexico, UN Security Council Resolution 2855. What the hell am I going to tell him?"

Randy Preston glanced around the office. The two

men were alone for the moment. A large flat-screen television monitor was on against one of the walls, the sound low but still audible. It was tuned to CNN and was running coverage of the continuing riots in Los Angeles as well as, since yesterday, in Phoenix, San Antonio, El Paso, and Chicago.

"I'm afraid, Mr. President, that there may be nothing you can say. Nothing we can do."

"The hell there isn't. If the Security Council tries to pass such a resolution, I shall order our ambassador to veto it."

"That might buy us some time, sir," Preston said, "but we may well be up against the inevitability of history."

"*Fuck* history. I will not be known as the president who gave away half of California and Texas!"

"Of course not, sir."

"UN resolutions are not binding!"

"No, sir."

"You're my national security adviser. Give me some advice I can use!"

Preston shrugged. "I would suggest that you agree to study the situation, to give the resolution due consideration, and promise to respect the rights and aspirations of citizens in those states. You might also give thought to pulling back the National Guard. That battle in East Los Angeles last night—that was bad. Made us *look* bad."

"Those troops are in there to restore order. They're not coming out until order has been restored."

"Yes, sir. But keep in mind how much this looks like the Arab Spring."

"This has nothing to do with the goddamn Arabs!"

"Maybe not, sir. But to the world at large, it looks exactly the same."

In December of 2010, popular demonstrations led swiftly to the overthrow of the government in Tunisia. Protests in Algeria, Jordan, Saudi Arabia, and other nations in the region resulted in various government concessions. By early February of 2011, full-scale revolt had broken out in Egypt, leading eventually to the ousting, arrest, and prosecution of Hosni Mubarak and two prime ministers, and a general takeover of the country by the military that was still being protested. Yemen and Bahrain faced serious public disorder, and Gaddafi's forty-two-year dictatorship in Libya had at last come to an end in all-out civil war.

"Egypt, Libya, and Syria," Preston said. "Those were the worst—revolution or civil war. In each case, there were instances of soldiers firing into crowds of civilians. Thousands died, and there was a world outcry, with demands for intervention by the UN or by NATO."

The president stared hard at Preston. "Surely you're not suggesting that we're going to be attacked by NATO."

"I'm saying, Mr. President, that American police and army personnel have fired on demonstrating civilians in Los Angeles and other American cities. Right now, our allies in Europe see that as the exact moral equivalent with Gaddafi's African mercenary snipers killing civilians in Tripoli, or al-Assad's butchers machine-gunning protestors in Damascus and Daraa. They see us as having supported a NATO offensive against the Libyan government to ostensibly protect endangered civilians.

"They'll likely ask what can be done to protect American civilians in an identical situation."

"The situations are not identical, damn it. This . . . this Aztlanista movement is threatening to cut up our southwestern states to create a whole new goddamn country, by force if necessary! This *will* not stand!"

Although the text had not yet been released, Resolution 2855 was expected to call for a popular referendum within the southern portions of several states in the U.S. Southwest, under UN oversight, with an eye toward creating a new and independent country. The newborn nation, popularly known as Aztlán, would be carved out of the southern halves of California, New Mexico, Arizona—the new border roughly running along the 35th parallel—and the southern quarter of Texas, more or less along the 30th parallel. Such a division, if it actually came to pass, would abruptly change the nationality of roughly thirty million citizens of the United States.

"I will *not* be known as the president who presided over the dismemberment of this country."

Preston looked at him with something strangely akin to affection. In fact, he hated the man, but the president was so arrogant, self-serving, politically motivated, narcissistic, and so damned *predictable* that manipulating him scarcely offered any challenge at all. Just wind him up and point him in the right direction.

To be fair, the political system in the United States had been teetering on the brink for a long time. *Money* ran the country, not the people, not democracy. The president had inherited a hell of a mess from his predecessors—as all presidents do—and no man was good enough, strong enough, or smart enough to keep the whole chaotic, jury-rigged structure from crumbling. Few people knew it yet, but the United States of America was in very serious trouble. The final collapse had already begun, and it was accelerating.

Exactly what Preston and the other members of the Project had been aware of for some time.

"Mr. President," Preston said, picking his words carefully, "the Aztlanistas don't stand a chance. We all know that. Hispanics are, what? Thirty-eight percent of the populations of California and Texas? Less than that in Arizona and New Mexico. They are in the strong majority in the southern portions of those states, of course, but there is no constitutional provision for letting only part of a state vote on an issue like this. If there was a vote tomorrow, the referendum would easily be defeated, with or without the UN getting involved."

"Damned straight." The president seemed to relax somewhat. "And most Hispanics know they've got it *good* in this country. Even the illegals are better off than they'd be if the states they're living in broke away and became a fucking third-world country!"

"Exactly, sir." Preston knew that one of the biggest problems the Aztlanistas faced was the fact that only a small percentage of all Hispanics in the United States actually supported them. Lopez and his bunch were noisy, but they didn't speak for all Mexican immigrants. *Yet.*

"But it's the *idea* of the thing, of the UN meddling in our internal affairs!"

"Yes, sir." Preston didn't need to add that the cold fact of the matter was that ever since the United States had become the world's sole remaining superpower, the country's relationship with the United Nations had gone from bad to abysmal.

"There was that call for the UN to intervene in the 2012 elections," the president said. "Remember that? They do not have that *right*!"

"Of course not, sir. However, Resolution 2855 is going to make us look bad, *very* bad, just by coming up for a Security Council vote. It's going to be a public relations disaster for us, and we're going to need to dig to put a good spin on it."

The UN Security Council was a fifteen-member group charged, under the UN Charter, with "responsibility for the maintenance of international peace and security." Five members were permanent: the United States, the Russian Federation, the People's Republic of China, France, and the United Kingdom, each of which had veto power. Resolutions were nonbinding, but could become binding if they were made under Chapter VII of the UN Charter—"Action with Respect to Threats to the Peace, Breaches of the Peace, and

Acts of Aggression." A vote by nine of the fifteen members was needed to affirm a given resolution.

"And how do we put a 'good spin' on something like this?"

"We've weathered worse, Mr. President. Careful handling of the news media. A lot of political maneuvering behind the scenes, backroom deals, that sort of thing. Some judicious arm-twisting, if necessary. If we threaten to pull out of the UN—or even just threaten not to pay our arrears up there—they'd cave pretty quickly."

The United States had withheld payments to the UN before in order to shape its foreign policies. Currently, the back-owed bill amounted to well over a billion dollars.

The president picked up a pen and scribbled on a notepad in front of him. "I like that."

"But I recommend that you not threaten to do that yet, not at your meeting with the ambassador. Just have him suggest that we're looking at ways to contain the violence, including pulling out the troops. See if he can delay a vote."

"I will *not* pull out the troops, Randy. Not when the only alternative is complete anarchy."

Preston nodded. "No, sir. You asked for my advice, and I've given it. I should remind you, though, both the Russians and the Chinese have already publicly compared us to Syria."

"Damn it, Randy," the president said, "this is outrageous! The United States of America is not going to quietly go along with this! I will *not* give in to these . . . these rabble-rousers!"

"I agree, sir, *if* we can do so without murdering our own people."

Something that, Preston knew, was already a foregone conclusion.

CHAPTER TEN

"We've got some data back on those credit card numbers you picked up," Chavez told Teller. "I think you'll both be interested in this."

At 3:00 A.M., Teller had woken Procario up with a phone call and had him come pick them up. His back was hurting, the streets of Mexico City were dangerous at night, and he didn't want to get dragged into any more firefights. By a little past three thirty, the two of them had been back in the two-room suite at the Azueta Hilton, filling in Chavez and Procario on the evening's events. Chavez had uploaded the credit card numbers over the satellite link back to Langley and checked with Operations to see if the Cellmap intel was coming through yet.

Teller and Dominique had hit the sack before an answer had come back. They'd slept—*just* slept—until well past eight.

It had been a long night.

Awake again, they'd joined Procario and Chavez in the other room. "Let's see it," Teller said.

Procario had set up a laptop computer on the desk and had just finished downloading pages of text from Langley. The information showed recent purchases for all of the men.

"This is Carlos Gutierrez Sandoval," he said, pointing, "late of Nogales."

"The guy from the van who had all the money in his wallet," Teller said.

"That's him. Seems he was a big spender. He ran up over thirty thousand pesos' worth on that card in the last week alone. Clothes . . . jewelry . . . and until two days ago, he was spending it all in Chetumal and in Corozal."

"Chetumal? Where the hell's that?"

"Corozal is in Belize, isn't it?" Dominique asked.

"Have a look," Chavez said, calling up Google Earth on the screen and zooming in toward the eastern coast of the Yucatán Peninsula.

Yucatán thrusts almost four hundred miles due north into the Gulf of Mexico, tropical and low-lying enough that most of it is cloaked in jungle. The western and northern portions of the peninsula belong to Mexico. South is Guatemala, while a narrow, rectangular strip of the southeastern coast is occupied by the tiny nation of Belize.

"Chetumal is right here," Chavez said, pointing at the screen to a spot on the eastern Yucatán coast half-way down the peninsula. "It's in Mexico, on the mouth of the Rio Hondo and smack on the border with Belize." His finger tracked south. "Corozal is nine miles south, in Belize, right here."

The coastal region there, Teller noted, was actually a sheltered inland waterway, the Bahía de Chetumal, an arm of pale blue sea around ten to fifteen miles wide and zigzagging from north to south. Those two towns actually lay on the western shore of the bay, cut off from the darker ocean almost forty miles to the east by a south-jutting peninsula—Costa Maya, the Maya Coast—and by Ambergris Caye, a slender island more than twenty miles long reaching toward the south. Beyond that, farther south still, a broken barrier of small cays stretched from Ambergris Caye almost all the way to Belize City. Chetumal Bay, isolated from the ocean, was cloaked in jungle and possessed numerous inlets, lagoons, and coves, plenty of places where a ship might disappear.

"Okay, so what was our big spender doing way the hell down there?" Teller asked.

"Possibly he was helping with this," Procario said, and he called up a photograph, an aerial view of a dock with a freighter tied up alongside.

"The *Zapoteca*!" Teller exclaimed. "You found her!"

"We found her," Chavez agreed.

"How come it took so long?" Dominique asked.

"That four-hundred-mile stretch of coastline," Procario said, "from Honduras all the way up to Cozumel and Cancún, has dozens of bays, small towns, inlets . . . lots of places where you can easily park a small freighter, and this area in here"—Procario swept his fingers up the light blue waters of Chetumal Bay—"this isn't usually navigated by large ships. It's shallow, and the sea approaches are protected by the second-largest barrier reef in the world. All of the main ports in the eastern Yucatán are directly on the ocean, like Cancún, or in places with easy access to the ocean—Belize City or Ladyville. We had our satellites looking for the *Zapoteca* in places like Belize City, not way off the beaten track in Chetumal."

"Exactly," Chavez said. "Not only that, but there was a good chance the *Zapoteca* had gone on to Veracruz and we'd missed her. That was its original destination, remember. Or she could have put in at Campeche or some other port along the way."

"Like Coatzacoalcos," Chavez said. "Big oil-refining and -shipping port over four hundred miles west of Belize, beyond the other side of the Yucatán. Or Ciudad de Carmen. Most of our satellite time was spent watching Carmen and Coatzacoalcos."

"Satellites are wonderful," Teller observed, studying the photo on the screen, "but even something as big as a cargo ship can easily get lost in all that ocean."

"So how did you find the ship?" Dominique asked.

"We got to wondering," Chavez said, "what your friend Gutierrez was doing down there besides buying gold jewelry."

"And we had an interesting confirmation, something that focused our attention on that area," Procario added. He began typing on the keyboard, bringing up a new display.

Teller watched a map of all of Mexico come up, from the U.S. border down to Guatemala. An instant later, blue dots began to appear, one at a time at first, but then faster and faster and still faster, beginning as a tight, solid blue cluster around Mexico City but spreading rapidly outward, creating clusters and constellations that blanketed the country, with heavy concentrations at the major cities—Mexico City, Veracruz, Tijuana, Nogales, Nuevo Laredo, a dozen other urban centers. Lots of blue icons scattered across into the United States, Teller noticed, and throughout Guatemala and Belize as well.

"Is that—" Teller began.

"Yup," Procario said, grinning. "First phone-home from Cellmap. It's working."

"My God, there're a lot of them."

"They're still running the analyses at Fort Belvoir," Procario said. He glanced at Chavez. "*And* at Langley. Eventually, we'll be able to zoom in on any one of those dots and turn that phone into a covert listening device."

"How are they picking up the geographical data?" Dominique asked.

"Those are just the phones that have GPS trackers built in," Teller said. "Devices like iPhones. Tracking older phones is tougher."

"Yeah," Procario agreed. "It can be done by triangulating off cell towers and Wi-Fi servers, but that'll take more time to process. This gives us a damned good start, though."

Teller pointed at the east central coast of the Yucatán, where a mass of blue dots had congregated at the bend in Chetumal Bay. "So what's going on here?"

"That," Procario said, "was our confirmation."

"It could be a local smuggling operation," Teller suggested.

"A lot of drugs come up into Mexico from South America by sea," Chavez said. "The old Colombian cartel pipelines. And lots of it comes into Mexico at Chetumal. It's a major port of entry for the stuff. But this made us take a closer look—"

"And the *Zapoteca* was there," Teller said, completing the thought. "We'll need to go check it out."

"While you two were napping," Procario said with a grin, "we were making reservations. You and me are booked on a three-o'clock puddle jumper to Chetumal."

"What about me?" Dominique asked.

"You're with me," Chavez told her. "We'll do some Company business here in Mexico City, while these two army types check out the ship."

"Just keep in touch this time," Teller told Dominique, "okay?"

SAFE HOUSE, EAST OLYMPIC BOULEVARD
EAST LOS ANGELES, CALIFORNIA
1340 HOURS, PDT

Saeed Reyshahri moved back grimy curtains and stared out the back window. From here, you could see smoke rising from behind the buildings to the north, great, boiling clouds of it.

East Los Angeles was burning.

This was the fourth straight day of rioting. The poorer sections of the city, it turned out, had been powder kegs on short fuses, waiting to explode. Local television stations now showed nothing but news reports and scenes of the riots—young men emerging from smashed storefronts carrying flat-screen TVs and pushing shopping carts full of clothing and electronics, overturned cars and burning buildings, the angry faces of chanting and banner-waving mobs, lines of police in riot gear, National Guardsmen patrolling trash-littered streets with M-16s.

What was amazing, at least to Reyshahri's way of thinking, was the fact that most Latinos in Los Angeles weren't even taking part, save as occasional targets of mob violence. The mobs had started by looting Asian- and black-owned businesses, but the violence had rapidly spread to Hispanic shops as well—and now to housing projects, apartments, and even suburban communities as far east as West Covina. An aggressive barrio minority was now burning everything its members could reach.

When the troops and police responded, they seemed unable to tell the difference between rioters and peaceful citizens, and there'd been a number of ugly incidents. The news stations were estimating a death toll of over two hundred, at least ten of those at the hands of the police. Thousands had been injured, inundating hospitals and medical services throughout the city, and thousands more were homeless.

The arrival of troops had not slowed the rioting in

the least, so far as Reyshahri could tell. Guardsmen had cordoned off the downtown area and parts of Commerce and East L.A. itself, but the rioting crowds and demonstrations had spread faster than the troops could move. There was talk now of bringing in helicopter gunships and armored vehicles. The death toll was already higher than in the six days of rioting in the wake of the Rodney King jury verdict, back in 1992.

He heard a knock on the door and turned away from the window.

"Hey, Eagle," one of the safe-house Mexicans called, using his code name. "They're here."

Reyshahri let the curtain fall back into place and walked into the living room, where Moslehi and three of the Mexicans were standing with two newcomers. They were big, tough-looking Hispanics. Both had dark smudges on their faces, and one had gauze wrapped around his left forearm.

"Eagle," Julio Prieto said as he walked in, "Knife, I want you to meet a couple of our Brown Berets. This is Ignacio Aceveda Juárez and Angel Lopez Villalobos. They're the men I was telling you about."

Reyshahri shook hands with both men. *"Mucho gusto,"* he said. "It's very good to meet you both."

"You are the Arabs we were told about?" Lopez asked. He didn't look impressed.

"That's right," Reyshahri said. By now, he was becoming accustomed to being misidentified as an Arab. If it helped the mission—and it was absolutely vital that Iran's involvement be kept out of this affair—then so much the better.

The Brown Berets were a Chicano nationalist activist group that had been around since the 1960s. They were prominent in the fight for Hispanic civil rights, for organizing against police brutality, and for carrying on the crusade for Chicano self-determination.

Reyshahri had been directed to meet with these men before traveling east to carry out the main part of Shah Mat. It was vital to coordinate with them before things went up. Those orders had not, in fact, come from Tehran, but from the mysterious man in Washington, D.C., Reyshahri knew only as "Duke."

He felt uncomfortably poised between his own organization and this cabal within the United States government that had put the whole thing in motion.

"So, the Duke guy," Aceveda said. "He said you would have something for us."

"That's right. If you can prove you're who you say you are."

"Hey, Eagle," Prieto said, angry. "These are *mis compadres*—"

"Está bien," Aceveda said, waving the man off. "He is right. The phrase you want us to say, *señor,* is 'checkmate.'"

"Good," Reyshahri said, and he pulled a sealed envelope from his jacket pocket. Aceveda took it, tore it open, and examined the contents.

Aceveda's eyes widened as he read. *"¡Diablo!—"*

Lopez took the letter from Aceveda and read it as well. "You're not fucking serious, man."

"On the contrary, *señor*. I am very serious."

"¿Bombas atómicas?¿Estas loco?"

"Think about it, *señor*," Reyshahri said. "How else is your Aztlán going to become reality?"

"But . . . but . . ." Lopez waved the letter. "This is *crazy*!"

"Duke promised you a way to declare independence." He flicked the edge of the letter with his hand. "Without this, you declare independence, the U.S. Army moves in, and you end up either dead or in prison. If we pull this off, believe me—the Americans are going to be too busy with other problems to pay any attention to *you*."

Reyshahri waited as the two read the letter again.

Not for the first time, he wondered how this mysterious "Duke" had gotten wind of the two tactical weapons. The man, obviously, was highly placed in American intelligence—possibly the CIA, possibly higher, perhaps even as high as the National Security Council. There were rumors among the higher ranks of VEVAK that someone within the NSC had turned.

Reyshahri didn't trust the man, whoever he was. It was quite possible that this whole drama was an elaborate sting operation—like the one precipitating the diplomatic clash a few years ago, when the Americans had accused Iran of fomenting a plot to kill the Saudi ambassador to the United States. Two Iranian Quds Force agents had been arrested, supposedly for trying to hire an assassin from a Mexican cartel who'd turned out to be a U.S. informant. Nonsense, of course. If Tehran had wanted the Saudi pig dead, he would now be dead, and without the use of Mexican thugs to do it. Either the whole affair had been a clumsy attempt by the CIA to discredit Iran on the international front, or MEK—an Iranian dissident group—had tried to embarrass the Tehran government.

Either way, VEVAK was playing it *very* cautiously. Tehran could not afford to be linked to those two weapons.

Even so . . . the opportunity was simply too good to pass up. Reyshahri's superiors had tested Duke for the past six months, using channels through the Iranian Embassy in Mexico City. The CIA's deputy chief of station there, a man named Nicholas, had been the conduit. The answers Duke had sent back—hard intel about U.S. foreign policy, about American military strength and deployments in the Middle East, about their cyberwar attacks against Iran's nuclear program, about American agents in Iran, Iraq, and Syria—*everything* so far had checked out.

If the Americans were trying to entrap Iran, would they have used the deputy chief of station? No. No, unthinkable.

So Saeed Reyshahri found himself in California, telling two leaders of the Aztlanista movement that Washington and New York were about to be destroyed, and that in the chaotic aftermath, they would have their chance to create their new country.

"That letter gives you the timetable," he told them. "The weapons by now are already on their way to their targets. You have until the twenty-second."

"Four days," Aceveda said, shaking his head. "It is not enough time!"

"It is the time you have, *señor.* I am told you will

have . . . help. Duke's people have planned this out carefully. There is a U.S. congressman, Gonzales."

"We know him. He has been active with our movement, supporting it, for a long time."

"He will step into temporary leadership of the area, when government control breaks down. You and your people will rally behind him, declare him to be *el presidente* of your new republic." He pointed at the letter. "It's all in there."

"I see it," Lopez said, still reading. *"¡Jesús, María, y José!"*

"The lands stolen from us!" Aceveda said, almost reverently. "They will be ours again! This makes it possible, Angel!"

Aceveda folded the letter and began to put it in a pocket.

"No," Reyshahri said, holding out his hand. "That gets burned here, in my presence."

"Huh? Why?"

"To make absolutely sure it doesn't find its way to American intelligence."

"You don't trust us, Arab?" Lopez demanded. "We're trusting *you* not to inform on us! Seems to me the trust ought to go both ways, *verdad*?"

"We don't trust *anybody*," Reyshahri said, taking back the document. "It's not about trust. It's about survival."

"But we need to show this to our people."

"Why? Are you saying they don't trust *you*?"

"They trust us with their lives!"

"Good. Then tell them what you saw here. Tell them

that in four days, the United States government is going to be in utter and complete turmoil, and that that is when you must strike. Understand?"

"*Sí,*" Aceveda replied, nodding slowly. "*Comprendemos perfectamente.*"

"Very good."

Later, after the two men had left, Reyshahri stood again at the window, watching the smoke from the burning sections of the city.

He'd not told the two Aztlanista leaders what was in store for them, of course. He knew the type. They were so . . . idealistic. So fervent. They *believed.*

As it had been explained to Reyshahri by his superiors in Tehran, the Aztlán independence movement was doomed. They would declare their new state when Washington was in flames—but sooner or later the flames would be extinguished, and the American army would move in.

From Tehran's perspective, that was acceptable. Sacrifices must be made in every daring venture—especially *other* people's sacrifices.

Aztlán would provide some months of diversion, time in which Iran would put its military plans into operation. By the time the U.S. flag again flew over Los Angeles, Iran would have consolidated its position, would be dug in from Baluchistan to Lebanon—a new Persian Empire that no one, not the Israelis, not the Americans, could ever challenge again.

He produced a cigarette lighter and carefully burned the document he'd shown the two Aztlanistas to ash.

"Moslehi!" he called as he whisked the last of the ash from his fingertips.

"Saeed?" Moslehi said, coming into the room at his back. "Is there a problem?"

"Not at all, Fereidun," he replied, "but we've done all that we can do here. Call and put us on a flight to Washington. It's time for the next phase of the operation."

Moslehi's eyes widened. "Thanks be to God" was all he said.

CHETUMAL
YUCATÁN, MEXICO
1715 HOURS, LOCAL TIME

The ancient Beechcraft B200 Super King Air, a twin-turboprop commuter plane flying for Aerolíneas Ejecutivas, dropped toward the runway with queasy suddenness. The aircraft, with seating for thirteen, was cramped, noisy, and prone to midair bumps. As the landing gear came down, it sounded to Teller as though something important had just dropped off.

"I don't know, Frank," he told Procario, strapped into the seat beside him. "I keep expecting to see the pilot walk back here any moment, wearing goggles, a white scarf, and a leather aviator's jacket."

"Nah," Procario said, "he won't come back here. He's too busy up front flapping his arms."

The Beechcraft cabin seated thirteen, but only five of the other seats were taken on the seven-hundred-mile flight to Chetumal—one by a passenger with the bored look of a frequently flying businessman, the others by tourists in sunglasses and bright-colored shirts, with cameras and straw hats. They'd talked among themselves nonstop throughout the flight. Mexican tourism, apparently, hadn't yet been affected much by the narco-trafficking violence, but that, Teller reflected, was only a matter of time.

Ignoring the chatter from the front of the cabin—something about camera prices at duty-free ports—Teller looked down out of the window to his right. They'd made their descent from 27,000 feet over mile upon verdant mile of unending jungle, a thick and tangled sea of green interrupted now and again by patches of cleared farmland, isolated puffs of cloud riding above their shadows, or the startlingly white exclamation of an ancient Mayan ruin rising above the surrounding forest canopy. Now the canopy was flashing past almost close enough to touch . . . and then the end of the runway appeared out of the jungle, rising to meet them, and the Beechcraft touched down seconds later with a solid thump. Minutes later, they were stepping off the boarding ladder and onto the tarmac.

Chetumal International Airport was located just to the west of the city center. The waterfront was perhaps two miles from the tiny airport terminal; they phoned for a licensed taxi to pick them up; the local *públicos* were far too risky. Too often, wealthy tourists and businessmen were kidnapped off the street and held for ransom by gangs using private taxis. The vehicle took them to the Holiday Inn downtown. They checked in, swept their room for bugs, put together the special gear they would need for some low-tech surveillance, and decided to walk the ten blocks down to the wharf on foot.

Teller and Procario were dressed as tourists, wearing the stereotypical bright floral shirts and with digital cameras slung around their necks. They still carried papers indicating that they were journalists with the *Washington Post,* but tourists would stand out a bit less in this part of the world. Neither man was armed for what they expected to be an initial look-see at the target. Too many complications could ensue if the local constabulary stopped them for one reason or another and found out they were carrying.

"I wasn't expecting a city quite this big," Teller admitted as they stepped out onto the street named Héroes de Chapultepec and began their stroll down to the docks. "Or this clean."

"Population of a hundred thirty thousand and some," Procario told him. "Capital of the state of Quintana Roo. Not your typical third-world border town, no. As for being clean . . . well, they have to keep it pretty for the gringo tourists, right?"

"Well, tourism hasn't let them forget about the Mexican-American War down here. 'Heroes of Chapultepec'?"

Procario chuckled. "Not by a long shot. These folks have *long* memories."

The street name was a reference to an incident in the U.S. invasion of Mexico back in 1847. *Los Niños Héroes,* the Boy Heroes, were six cadets of the Mexican Military Academy, aged between thirteen and nineteen. During the U.S. assault on Chapultepec Castle at the gates of Mexico City, they chose to die at their posts rather than surrender to the invaders. One, Juan Escutia, had wrapped the castle's flag around himself and jumped from a parapet rather than let it fall into American hands. Mexico still celebrated the last stand of *Los Niños* with a national holiday in September.

They turned left off of Héroes de Chapultepec and began the long stroll south on De los Héroes.

Mexico, Teller reflected, was in an extraordinarily awkward position right now. Intensely proud, imbued with a soaring, patriotic love of flag and country, many modern-day Mexicans still deeply resented the Mexican-American War of over 160 years before, and its outcome—the loss of the northern part of their country from Texas to California. The unpleasant proximity of the *norteamericano* giant just to the north today both chafed and worried them; with the country on the verge of descending into anarchy, they must dread the possibility of U.S. military intervention—a *second* Mexican-American War.

Chetumal possessed a single commercial pier, a concrete wharf extending south from the city a thousand feet into the bay. With two lanes of traffic, one going out and another coming back, and lined down the eastern side with palm trees, the quay provided docking for the water taxis and other local transport cruising the azure waters off the city. The quay was long enough to accommodate cruise ships, and Teller wondered if that was the idea. Since 2001, Disney World had run its own built-from-scratch native village at Costa Maya, on the Caribbean forty miles across the bay to the northeast, created just for the cruise-ship trade, and other towns in the area must have lusted for the influx of tourist dollars.

There was also the seamy underside of the local economy. According to CIA reports, 37 percent of all of the South American cocaine headed for the United States passed through the port of Belize, less than seventy miles to the south. The port of San Pedro, at the southern tip of Ambergris Caye, was notorious as one of the filthiest, most corrupt towns in the area, where the police provided security for incoming drug shipments and human-trafficking operations without even bothering to change out of uniform. Chetumal was the main port of entry from northern Belize into Mexico, and it was a sure bet that a lot of those narcotics were coming across the border here.

There were no cruise ships at the long quay, but there *was* a dilapidated-looking freighter streaked with rust—the *Zapoteca*.

Their second mission objective was at last in sight.

CENTRO DE CISEN
MEXICO CITY
1745 HOURS, LOCAL TIME

Jacqueline Dominique smiled as Miguel de la Cruz took her hand and kissed it in courtly, old-Mexican fashion. *"Mucho gusto, Señorita Dominique,"* he told her. "I trust you've recovered from your . . . experience of last night?"

"I'm just fine, Señor de la Cruz," she told him. "Thank you."

"A terrible thing. My department can provide an escort for you immediately, if you wish."

"Not necessary, *señor,*" she told him.

"It's important that we maintain a low profile, Miguel," Chavez added. "You know that."

Or at least, Dominique thought to herself, a lower profile than gun battles in the streets . . . or in city hotel rooms in the middle of the night.

"I suppose," de la Cruz replied. "But so beautiful a woman, openly assaulted by *los narcotrafficantes* . . ."

"Let's drop the machismo bullshit right now, Señor de la Cruz," she said. "I can take care of myself, and you do *not* need to coddle me."

De la Cruz didn't look convinced, but he seemed to resign himself to her attitude. He gave a small shrug. "Very well. I asked you to come here because we have some new information on one of the men in the Hotel Estrella last night." He turned the monitor on his desk so that they could see. "We know this one."

Dominique leaned forward to read the display. The photograph of a bearded young man glared back at her, sullen and blunt.

She read the name on the file. "Yussef Nadir Suwayd?"

"His ID read Pablo Tomás Rios," de la Cruz said, "but we've been watching him for a while. He's Palestinian, almost certainly Hamas."

"That's the one I shot in the stomach," Dominique said. "He didn't have the beard last night."

"No. Just so you know, we do suspect him of being al Qaeda."

Dominique suppressed an exclamation at this piece of misinformation. Hamas and al Qaeda hated one another and rarely could be found working together. Was de la Cruz genuinely misinformed, or was something deeper going on here?

"He survived?" Chavez asked.

"So far. He is in critical condition at Hospital de Jesús. Same for the other one, the man shot in the chest. We haven't been able to question either of them as yet."

"You have them under guard?" Chavez asked.

"Of course."

"And just why do you think he's al Qaeda?" Dominique asked.

"We've had numerous reports lately that al Qaeda is planning . . . something big here in Mexico. A terrorist plot. Something perhaps involving nuclear weapons."

"An extortion scenario," Chavez said. "Threatening Mexico City with nuclear weapons, either for money or to make the government ease up on the drug cartels."

"Exacto."

"Which still doesn't answer the question," Dominique pointed out, "of why Yussef Sawayd here would be helping cartel assassins or kidnappers."

"Obviously, you have come under suspicion, *señorita*. We believe that this cabal wanted to kidnap you—and possibly Señor Callahan as well—for questioning." He closed the computer file. "And that brings us to the second reason I wanted to talk with you. CISEN is going to insist, Miss Dominique, that you either accept a security detail, or that you leave the country. It is too dangerous here for you now."

"Now just a damned minute—" she began.

"Lo siento mucho, señorita," de la Cruz told her, "but the decision has already been made. At the *highest* levels."

"You're throwing me out of the country?"

"We are . . . urging you to leave. For your own safety. Trust me, *señorita*. The cartel interrogators are brutally vicious to a degree you cannot imagine, without mercy, without conscience. If you were to fall into their hands . . ." He shook his head. "Please do not force us to act *diplomatically,* Señorita Dominique."

"This is hardly necessary, Miguel," Chavez said. "Your agency and ours—we have an understanding."

"As I say, the decision has already been made. It is out of my hands. *¿Comprende?*"

"Comprendo," Dominique told him. *"Yo comprendo perfectamente."*

CHAPTER ELEVEN

CHETUMAL WATERFRONT
YUCATÁN, MEXICO
2134 HOURS, LOCAL TIME
18 APRIL

"I'm hungry," Teller said. "Want to spell each other, get some chow?"

"Sounds good," Procario replied. "Nothing happening here anyway."

"From the sound of things," Teller said, gesturing with his smart phone, "all the excitement is happening north of the border." He'd been using his phone to pull down news from the United States. The riots in major cities across the Southwest sounded bad. Worse was troops firing into civilian crowds. *Not* good . . . not good at all.

The two of them were sitting on a bench beneath a palm tree at Chetumal's marine terminal just across the pier road from the *Zapoteca*. From here, they had a good view of the entire port side of the vessel, including the single gangway amidships. There was some minor activity on board—crewmen moving about inside the superstructure or on the aft deck—but for the most part the ship appeared to be empty and deserted. The line of white numerals down her rust-streaked bow at the waterline showed she was riding high in the water. They'd checked with a port authority official earlier, and for five hundred pesos under the table he'd told them that the ship's cargo—jute from Pakistan—had been offloaded the week before. The *Zapoteca* had docked at Chetumal on April 10, eight days earlier. It had taken, the port authority official told them, two days to get the necessary clearances, and the cargo had been off-loaded over the next four days. Chetumal wasn't a usual port for cargo vessels, which meant no cranes were available. The bales of plant fiber had been unloaded by hand.

Which meant the *Zapoteca* had been standing empty for two days now.

"I think if the bombs were aboard her," Teller said, "they'd have been taken off by now. Eight days! Christ!"

"Might not be that bad," Procario replied. "The nukes would have been hidden, probably underneath all of that jute. They wouldn't be able to get at them until the holds were empty."

"We're talking about a couple of suitcases, Frank. Some seaman could have had them in his cabin and taken them ashore the first day they were in port."

"Maybe. But if they wanted to play it safe, those suitcases would have been kept someplace where a nosy customs agent wouldn't see them. Like underneath a couple hundred tons of jute fiber."

"Well, Mexico City hasn't been vaporized yet," Teller said. "Or any city in the U.S."

"We're still going to need to check that ship," Procario said. "We can't afford to make assumptions and miss the obvious."

"Which is?"

"That the bombs might still be on board. And if they're not, there might be traces of them, something to prove the bombs *were* there."

"Radioactivity."

"Which is why we brought the Geiger counters."

Teller frowned, knowing all the ways radiation could be shielded. You could spoof Geiger counters with kitty litter if you had enough of it.

"We'll need to be in close—real close—for *that* to work, Frank. Any idea as to how we're going to get on board?"

Procario looked thoughtful. "We might go back and talk to our new friend at the port authority. Maybe for a few hundred pesos more, he'll let us pretend to be customs officials."

"Possibly," Teller said, "but most of the customs people—and that includes our friend—are in the pay of one or more of the cartels. That's the way it works in this little shithole corner of the world. I'm worried that he's already reported us to Los Zetas, just because we were asking about the ship."

"Calculated risk."

As Jackie had found out last night, a calculated risk

was a great way to get burned. Teller was about to say something to that effect when he saw movement on the ship. The sun had set some time ago, but the quay was lit by streetlamps, and there were lights on board the ship. A lone merchant seaman was coming down the gangway.

"Well," Teller said, "if we want to talk to someone who might have answers . . ."

"I'm with you there. Not here, though."

"I think I'll see where he's going." Teller watched the man amble past on the far side of the street. "You stay here and keep an eye on the ship."

"I'd feel better about it if you had backup."

"I'll stay in touch. Besides, it's easier following a guy one-on-one than with two. Less obvious."

When the seaman was a good hundred feet down the quay, Teller stood and started after him. He stayed far enough back to stay off the guy's radar, remaining in the shadows where possible. At the shore end of the quay, the seaman turned right, walking along the coast highway on the northern, inshore side of the road. Teller followed.

The streets were relatively deserted for a Friday evening, Teller thought. They'd seen a few tourists since their arrival, but between Cancún and Costa Maya, Chetumal was relatively off the beaten track for gringos.

His target swung left suddenly and entered a bar-restaurant, El Cocodrilo. Teller waited on the street for a few moments, then followed him in.

Inside, the place was smoke-hazed and dark. A

twelve-foot crocodile, stuffed and blackened by years of cigarette and cigar smoke, hung from the ceiling above the bar. As his eyes accustomed themselves to the dim light, Teller spotted his quarry, sitting alone at a table in a large alcove off to the right.

Again Teller looked around for insurance in case he needed it, but no football-linebacker types presented themselves. He found a table where he could keep an unobtrusive eye on the target. When a waitress came to the table, he decided to go ahead and order *paella de marisco* and a beer. The place seemed clean enough, and there was no reason not to go ahead and take care of dinner as long as he had the opportunity.

Halfway through his seafood and rice, a man in a rumpled suit walked into the restaurant carrying a briefcase. He walked up to the seaman's table, they spoke for a moment, and then the man set his briefcase on one of the two remaining chairs and sat down in the other. Teller was interested to note that it was the weary-looking business traveler he'd seen on the flight down from Mexico City. The two talked for about ten minutes, and then the businessman abruptly stood, shook the seaman's hand, and walked out.

He'd left the briefcase on the chair.

The seaman stayed there, nursing his beer, and Teller tried to decide which way to go. Clearly there'd just been a handoff, probably of money. If a covert payment was made in this part of the world, it had to do with drugs, smuggling, or bribery—and quite possibly all three. Should he follow the businessman or stay with the seaman?

He decided to stick with the original plan, to stay with the sailor. It was dangerous changing targets mid-mission, and the businessman might be a mule, a courier or go-between who knew nothing. The seaman, on the other hand, if he'd just received payment, might know a very great deal indeed.

There still didn't seem to be an easy way to approach the man, who remained at his table, nursing a beer. If Teller confronted him, there'd be no way to force him to cooperate here in public.

Inspiration arrived a few minutes later, however, in the form of two men, one heavyset, the other skinny and tall. Both were a bit unsteady, evidently well along into an evening of bar-crawling. The older, more portly of the two wore a white sports coat with an outrageously vibrant tie—the sort of neon-hued strip of painted silk sold in souvenir shops throughout those Mexican towns that relied on the tourist trade. The other, a kid barely into his twenties, wore a bright T-shirt advertising the Costa Maya resort.

He thought for a moment, then nodded to himself. This could work . . .

Leaving a tip at the table, Teller walked over to the tourist with the bright tie. "My God!" he said, grinning broadly. "Another couple of yankees! *Damn,* it's good to see you!"

"Well, not quite a *yankee,* mister," the big man said with a soft drawl born in the Deep South. He looked Teller over, head to foot and then back again, taking in the flower-print shirt and the expensive camera around his neck. "Name's Sam Winters, of Peachtree,

Georgia." He indicated his friend. "This here's my . . . partner."

"Greg Coleman," the other said.

"Callahan," Teller told them. He let just a bit of Deep South into his own voice. "John Callahan. Can I buy you boys a drink?"

"Well, I sure wouldn't say no—"

"Sammy, do you think that's a good idea?" The skinny one sounded suspicious.

"I know, I know," Teller said, raising his hands. "*Never* trust a stranger! I just had a quick question for you. What'll y'all have?"

"I'll have a beer."

"Sure. Me, too."

"*Tabernero!*" Teller called. "*Tres cervazas, por favor!*"

"Hey, you speak the lingo real good."

"Thanks," Teller said. He dropped his voice to a more conspiratorial level. "Listen, I know this'll sound crazy as hell, me being a total stranger and everything . . . but . . . you see my friend at the table over there? Dungarees and a briefcase?"

Winters squinted into the gloom. "Yeah . . ."

"He was just telling me how very much he admires your *tie*! Where on *earth* did you get it?"

"What . . . this?" Winters touched the neckpiece. Up close, Teller could see that it was decorated with flamingoes and palm trees—not exactly a coherent fashion statement. "Why, Cancún. Little shop on the waterfront. I forget the name."

"See, my friend is shy. I mean, *really* shy. He just

couldn't get up the nerve to come ask you himself, so I told him I'd find out for him."

"I wish I could help you, but there are so many little shops there." He turned to Coleman. "Was it La Playa?"

"Well, it doesn't really matter," Teller said. Their beers arrived, and he picked his up, raising the glass to salute the two. "Hey, enjoy your stay, okay?"

"Why, thank you, Mr. Callahan."

"No, thank *you*."

Carrying his glass, Teller walked back across the restaurant, passing his own table and approaching the seaman, who was just starting to get up.

"Going somewhere, sailor?" Teller asked, speaking Spanish.

The man gave a start and clutched the briefcase against his chest. "Who are you?"

"Juan Escalante," Teller told him. He was fishing, curious as to whether the sailor knew the real Escalante.

"You don't look Latino." The man was suspicious, but not because of the name. He was also scared. Good. "You look like a gringo tourist."

"My mother was from Seattle." Teller pulled out his wallet and flipped it open to his driver's license, snapping it shut immediately before the other had time to read it. "El Centro de Investigación y Seguridad Nacional. You may have heard of us?"

The man's grip on the briefcase tightened, and he gave a sharp negative shake of his head. "What does CISEN want with me? I've done nothing wrong!"

"Relax, *señor*." Teller gave him his friendliest smile. "We're not interested in you. We're interested in the man who was just here with you."

"I know nothing about him."

"Of course, of course you don't. What is your name?"

"Federico Castro."

"And what were the two of you talking about, Federico?"

"He . . . he wanted to sell me something."

"What?"

"A watch. He had a watch with the strap cut. I think he must have been a thief. I told him to go away."

"I see. And what's in the briefcase?"

"Nothing. Papers. Listen, you have no right—"

"*Cálmate*, Federico. I know you are lying. I watched him bring that briefcase in here and leave it with you. I notice you haven't bothered checking what's in it. Do you trust him that much?"

The man's eyes widened slightly, then narrowed. "Listen, I've done nothing, *nothing*! Leave me alone!"

"Or what? You'll call for the police?" Teller considered the man for a moment. He was terrified and retreating deeper and deeper into his denials. Teller needed to turn up the heat a notch or two. "I have news for you, friend. CISEN has . . . connections down here. A working arrangement with some of the major business concerns in the area. You understand?" As he spoke, Teller absently touched his forefinger to a puddle of moisture on the tabletop beside the man's beer, then dragged it swiftly across the surface, forming the letter *Z*. Leaning forward, he said again, "You understand?"

Castro gave a small gasp, a short, sharp intake of breath. Drops of sweat were standing out on his forehead now. Yes, he understood.

"What is the name of the man who just left you?"

"*Señor* . . . I . . . no." He shook his head. "*You* do not understand. It would mean my life to tell you anything!"

"It will mean your death if you do not." Teller tapped his fingertip beside the *Z* on the tabletop for emphasis. Los Zetas had a certain reputation.

"You . . . your people are supposed to be in on this! Working with him, a part of the program!"

"Not all of us agree with the program," Teller told him. He nodded at the briefcase. "And the man who gave you *that* is not . . . trustworthy. It seems that he stole from the wrong people."

"Look . . . I did what was asked of me. I deserve to be paid!"

Until that moment, Teller had not been absolutely certain that the briefcase contained payment. Castro had just confirmed that.

"I agree. Don't worry. You may keep your payment. As I said, it is the *delivery boy* we are interested in."

"Julio. He calls himself Julio."

"I see," Teller said dryly. "And what is his *real* name?" Teller was fishing here, and taking a small chance with the attempt. Julio might well be the courier's real name, but in this kind of dealing he was almost certainly using an alias.

"You know the answer to that."

"Of course," Teller lied. "But we need to know if you know."

"I was told his name was . . . Hamadi. Mohamed Abdullah Hamadi."

Teller was careful not to betray his surprise. "Correct. And where is the . . . shipment?"

Castro blinked. "At the warehouse, of course."

"*Which* warehouse?"

Castro's eyes narrowed. "There is only one. I don't think you know. You're playing a game, you're trying to trick me!"

It was time, Teller decided, to play his last card.

"My friend, did you think I came in here alone?"

"What?"

He nodded toward the bar at the far end of the restaurant, where Coleman and Winters were sitting with their drinks. "See the big man? The one with the tie?"

"Yes."

"One of my associates."

"I don't believe you."

"Hm. Believe or not, as you wish." At that moment, Winters looked up, and Teller caught his eye. The big man grinned.

Teller grinned back. "You wouldn't know it to look at him," he said through the smile, "but he happens to be one of our best assassins. If I give the sign, he will follow you out of this place, hunt you down, and strangle you with his tie."

As he spoke, Teller touched just below his throat, moving the fingers up and down to indicate a tie.

Winters's grin broadened, and he reached up and took hold of the neon tie, jigging it up and down.

The blood drained from the frightened man's face, and he sagged back in his chair. *"Dios mío."*

"You *will* answer my questions. What warehouse?"

"The usual one, the one on Santa Elena, by the airport."

"And when did you make the delivery?"

"Two days ago. Wednesday."

"Hamadi was there? He took delivery?"

"Yes. There were four or five others there with him."

"Uh-huh. Other Arabs?"

"One of them was. I'm not sure about the others. I didn't hear their names. But I heard him talking to one of the others in what sounded like Arabic."

"Were there two . . . packages?"

Castro nodded.

"How big? How were they packaged?"

"In wooden crates." He indicated a size with his hands. "About a meter and a half by a meter by a meter, more or less."

"They were heavy?"

Again a nod. "A friend off the ship helped me. We had to use a handcart."

"How heavy?"

"I don't know. Thirty, maybe thirty-five kilos."

"And why didn't they pay you then?"

"I don't know. I wanted them to. Hamadi . . . he said they needed to check the merchandise, that he would meet me here tonight."

"So the packages met with their approval, I suppose. Have you checked?"

The man shook his head.

"Let's have a look."

The man was reluctant, but Teller told him, "It would be a shame to choke out your life with such a garishly hideous tie around your throat."

"Here."

"You open it."

Teller had considered the possibility that the briefcase contained not money but a bomb, a cheap means of getting rid of a witness. The odds were against that, however; between their reputations and having more money than God, the cartels would be more likely to let him live so that he could make other deliveries in the future. The briefcase clicked open without incident, and the man turned it so Teller could see.

"Well, well." Not money—but four brick-sized bundles of white powder wrapped in clear plastic. Perhaps two kilos. If it was already cut, at a hundred dollars a gram it would have a street value of $200,000.

Teller was glad he'd been careful and simply accused Hamadi of stealing from the wrong people instead of openly assuming that the briefcase contained money. There'd always been the chance that the payoff had been in barter.

The revelation raised an uncomfortable ethical dilemma for him, though. Two kilos of cocaine represented a staggering toll in human addiction, suffering, and crime. He wasn't working for the DEA, it wasn't his job, but he hated to see that much of the white powder making its way north to the streets of some U.S. city. Even knowing that two kilos was a drop in the ocean compared to the hundreds of tons that made it north across the border every year, he didn't want to let it go. Several options occurred to him. He could revert to his role of CISEN officer and confiscate the stuff, or pretend to put the seaman under arrest. That would call too much attention to him, however, when he needed to stay out of the light. If the sailor put up a struggle, he might have trouble talking his way out of it when the police showed up.

He could not put the mission at risk, even for two kilos of cocaine.

There might be a way to stop it, though.

"I'd like a sample," he said. As he spoke, with his left hand he slipped open a zippered compartment on his camera case, reaching in with a finger and emerging with a slender black sliver of plastic perhaps a third the length of a toothpick. He kept his hand below the table, out of sight.

Castro hesitated, then nodded—perhaps while thinking of garish ties. Careful not to alert other patrons in the bar to what was happening, Teller reached into the briefcase with his free hand, worked one end of a sealed plastic bag open, then touched the finger of his other hand to the cocaine inside. As he did so, the action blocked from the sailor by the partially open briefcase itself, he pressed the RFID chip into the bag, burying it within the powder. He made a show then of pulling out his finger and rubbing a taste of the powder stuck to it across his upper gums . . . and felt the characteristic cold, tingling numbness of the drug's touch.

His estimate of the drug's street value went up to half a million. "Well, that tells me what I need to know," Teller said, resealing the opened bag and closing the briefcase. "Thank you."

Castro snapped the briefcase shut and took it back. "You . . . you're letting me go?"

Teller gave a careless shrug. "Of course. It's Hamadi we want, not you."

The RFID tracking chip, Teller reflected, wasn't a perfect answer to his ethical dilemma. It would respond to a radio signal from a tracking device, locating the shipment, but only across a fairly short range—a few hundred feet at most. Once this shipment vanished into the multiple pipelines funneling hundreds of tons of cocaine north across the border, it would be almost impossible to find it again, save by the most extraordinary chance.

But the drug would be cut again at least once before it was sold on the streets, and when it was there was a good chance that the chip would be found. Whoever found it would have to consider the possibility that someone was tracking that particular shipment of drugs. The distribution network might be disrupted; the source of that batch of coke would be suspect. Federico Castro might find himself in considerable trouble with whoever he was planning to sell the stuff to.

Teller read the relief in Castro's face and decided to push just a little harder. "One more question," he said.

"Yes?"

"The two packages. Where are they going?"

"How should I know? To the north."

"Do you know by which route?"

"No." He hesitated. There was fear in Castro's eyes again.

"I think you do know. Shall we go have a word with my friend over there?"

"Look . . . I just heard Hamadi talking with one of the others. They were speaking Spanish, so I understood. Hamadi mentioned taking them to the ruins."

Las ruinas. The way Castro said the words, it sounded like a specific place, a place name, rather than a general description of a place.

"And what happens to them there?"

A shrug. "Who knows? The submarine, I suppose."

"They're taking the crates away on a submarine?"

"Look, Hamadi simply had me bring the . . . the two crates here from Karachi! I don't know anything else! I swear!"

"Do you know what those devices are?"

"I was told . . . I was told that they held special chemicals for processing drugs. That's *all* I know! Please!"

Teller let a very relieved Castro leave after that, waited for a few moments, then strolled out of El Cocodrilo, exchanging another friendly wave with Winters and his friend as he passed. He rejoined Procario on the bench across from the *Zapoteca*.

"I think," he told the other, "that we have a lead."

"Really? The guy saw the nukes?"

"Better than that . . . and he knows where they are now. C'mon. We have to put a call in to Langley."

It promised to be a long night.

HOLIDAY INN ZÓCALO
MEXICO CITY
2315 HOURS, LOCAL TIME

Jacqueline Dominique hit ENTER, then leaned forward to watch as data flooded down from the satellite and across the screen of her laptop. This, she thought, was going to be a game changer.

She and Chavez had returned to her room at the Holiday Inn, and she'd spent the past several hours trying to get clearance from Langley to go deep black—operating inside of Mexico without the knowledge or approval of the local government. She was still awaiting word on that; such requests involving mere administrative details would likely not be reviewed until regular working hours tomorrow. In the meantime, Chavez had gotten her a seat on a flight back to Washington leaving Benito Juárez International at three thirty the following afternoon, just in case.

In the meantime, Teller had uploaded the results of his investigation in Chetumal to Langley, but he'd included her in a blind cc. His report mentioned two crates that likely were the missing nuclear weapons hidden in a warehouse, and an informant's statement that a submarine was hidden somewhere close by, at a place identified as "las ruinas."

"Ruins" could mean any of a thousand locations across the Yucatán. Fifteen hundred years ago, the Mayan Empire had been at its height, with immense stone cities scattered across the jungles of what one day would be southern Mexico, Guatemala, Belize, and Honduras. Those cities, with names like Chichén Itzá, Tikal, and Copán, fascinated the modern world and continued to draw visitors from all across the globe to marvel and wonder at the stark, forest-choked relics of a vanished civilization.

Which ruins the informant was referring to was as yet unknown. However, Teller's report had discussed the probability that the submarine must be somewhere close by Chetumal. It made sense. The *Zapoteca* had brought the weapons from Pakistan to Chetumal; from there, they were being transferred to a submarine that would take them to their final destination. That implied that the submarine and the ruins were relatively close by.

Dominique called up a mapping program and began studying satellite images pulled in from the servers at Langley. The NRO had photographed the entire region extensively while searching for the *Zapoteca* over the past few days. She concentrated on satellite images of the coastline within a few miles of Chetumal. Each image had three versions, one in visible light, one in infrared, and one at radar wavelengths. She spent a lot of time going back and forth between the three, looking for anomalies.

Her bosses back at Langley, she thought, would not have approved. Image analysis was properly carried out at the National Reconnaissance Office in Chantilly,

Virginia, or at CIA Headquarters itself. Field officers might be given the final, highly polished results of a satellite pass, but they certainly weren't encouraged to look at the raw data and make their own assessments.

A friend in the Office of Imagery Analysis—a department of the Agency's Intelligence Directorate—had broken the rules and given her access to these pictures. The original set, ordered to find the hiding place of the *Zapoteca,* covered so many thousands of square miles of water and jungle that weeks would pass before a full analysis would be available.

Chris Teller's discoveries in Chetumal had sharply narrowed the search field, and Dominique knew what she was looking for.

Thirty minutes later, she found it and reached for her phone.

CHAPTER TWELVE

CHETUMAL HOLIDAY INN
YUCATÁN, MEXICO
0215 HOURS, LOCAL TIME
19 APRIL

"I think," Teller said, studying the screen, "that Jackie's onto something. Look at this!"

Teller and Procario had returned to the hotel at around midnight and spent the next couple of hours composing a report to zap back to Langley. They'd found an e-mail attachment waiting for them, a collection of very large image files sent by Dominique to Teller's computer.

On the screen, a photo taken from space looked straight down on water and jungle.

Within the sheltered, inland waters of Chetumal Bay, a smaller, deeply cut bay named for the fishing town of Corozal extended westward into the jungles of northern Belize. The southern coast of Corozal Bay was actually a slender peninsula, like a fang extending three miles east into the blue waters of the Bahía de Chetumal.

On the northern coast of the peninsula, ten miles southeast of Chetumal, was a point of land and a cluster of white stone ruins called Cerros.

Teller zoomed in on the point, an equilateral triangle cloaked in forest extending north into the azure waters. A dirt road connected the site with the village of San Fernando two and a half miles to the southeast and, in roundabout fashion, with Corozal across the bay on the northern coast.

"Okay," Procario said, looking over Teller's shoulder at the screen, "she's found some Mayan ruins ten miles from Chetumal. There are other ruins closer."

He was referring to the ruins at Oxtankah just seven miles north up the coast from Chetumal. Both Teller and Procario had spent some time earlier that morning going over the local maps, looking for *las ruinas*.

"Yeah," Teller said. "But take a look at the same thing in IR."

He shifted the satellite imagery to infrared. The waters of the bay turned black and cold, the land areas warmer, a deep blue green. Several brighter and hotter spots appeared scattered near the coast.

One object hot enough to show as a brilliant yellow glowed right at the line between jungle and bay.

"Huh," Procario said. "What is *that*? Too big and hot to be a truck."

"How about a Kilo class diesel submarine snugged up against the shore?"

Nothing showed at visible wavelengths. The submarine, if that's what it was, had been pulled close enough to the shoreline that it was well masked by the dense jungle canopy extending over the water's edge. Radar seemed to show something reflective enough to be metallic, though the water itself showed up as bright and hard under radar.

"At least two hundred feet long," Procario noted, reaching past Teller's shoulder to use the software's ruler tool to measure the radar footprint. "Maybe two hundred twenty."

"About the above-water length of a Kilo-class submarine resting on the surface."

"And the heat signature is about where the exhaust vents would be."

"That's what I was thinking."

"How old are these?"

"Two days."

"Not good. If the diesels were running, they were getting ready to take her out then. She's probably already left."

Two days at twelve knots—that meant the sub could be anywhere at all within over five hundred nautical miles, maybe even off the northwestern coast of Cuba and approaching southern Florida. If those two mini-nukes were on board, it was very bad news indeed.

"Or she'd just arrived two days ago," Teller pointed out. "Or they were charging her batteries, running her pumps, checking her engines—any of a dozen possible things."

"Right there," Procario said, pointing, "that could be an open forward hatch. Yeah. It must be hot as hell inside."

"Exactly. I think they were running the air pumps to cool off inside."

"Makes sense."

A submarine was a tiny, enclosed metal cylinder with over fifty people stuffed inside. In the tropics, even sitting on the water's surface and tucked back into the shade of the trees, it would be sweltering inside, stinking of sweat and diesel fuel. The crew might well have decided to take a chance and fire up the engines in order to circulate fresh air through the vessel.

"Way too big to be a home-grown narco-sub," Procario said. "We need a team in there, and we need it *now*."

"I agree," Teller said. He picked up his phone. "Let's see how long it takes to arm a lily pad."

AVENIDA DEL PIÑÓN
MEXICO CITY
0920 HOURS, LOCAL TIME

"The traffic is horrible," Chavez said.

"Maybe it's a sign," Dominique told him. "I should stay put."

She was angry. Her department head, Charles Vanderkamp, had ordered her back to Langley, siding, apparently, with de la Cruz and CISEN.

"I don't think you'll be able to convince them," Chavez said. "Vanderkamp sounded pretty insistent."

"He's just pissed that I found the submarine on those photos instead of him."

"Well, you did kind of go outside the SOP," Chavez reminded her. "Ah, that's what the holdup is. Another demonstration."

A sea of marching people was visible ahead, marching northwest along the broad and tree-lined expanse of the Avenue del Piñón. At the forefront, protestors carried an enormous green banner: *LA PRIMAVERA DE LOS LATINOS.*

The Latino Spring. They'd been hearing that phrase a lot over the past couple of days—a deliberate parallel with the "Arab Spring" of 2011. It wasn't referring to an independence movement within Mexico but showed solidarity with the Aztlanista movement back in the United States.

A traffic cop just ahead was gesturing, moving traffic off the avenue and onto a side street. Flashing lights showed where police vehicles were forming a roadblock. Traffic continued to crawl forward as the main thoroughfare leading from downtown out to the airport was diverted.

"I didn't break any regs," Dominique told him.

"No, but you're probably due for the official you-need-to-be-part-of-the-team lecture. If you're lucky, they won't accuse you of being a cowboy."

"I'm beginning to think Chris has the right idea. Do what's right, and fuck 'em if they don't like it."

"I guess you are due for the cowboy lecture. Uh-oh."

"What?"

"Idiot," Chavez said. He was watching his side mirror.

Dominique turned, looking back. A motor scooter was making its way past the traffic jamming the narrow street, traveling on the sidewalk to pass them. Pedestrians were leaping out of the way to avoid being hit. Abruptly, the scooter bumped back onto the street, coming up alongside the rental car carrying Chavez and Dominique. The driver was wearing a black motorcycle helmet, anonymous. He reached into a saddlebag, pulling out a package . . .

"Get out!" Chavez screamed. *"Out of the car!"*

Acting on instinct, Dominique yanked the car door handle and threw herself into the street. The scooter was already accelerating, racing ahead up the street. Chavez threw his own door open . . .

The explosion struck her like an incoming ocean wave, slamming her over as flame seared the air above her head and bits of metal and glass snapped past her. She didn't have her handgun, not when her next stop was going to be the airport and a security check. Rolling over, she looked up at the car, its interior twisted and flame-licked. "Ed!" she yelled, trying to rise to her feet. "Ed!"

Chavez had caught the full fury of the blast, which had peeled open the left side of the car. Close by, people screamed, or simply lay on the pavement, motionless, while others came to help. Storefront windows on both sides of the street had been blown out; the street was covered with glass.

Dominique realized she was bleeding, her face cut . . .

She made it to her feet at last. A man grabbed her by her shoulders and guided her toward the front step of a storefront. *"¡Señorita! ¿Estás herida?"*

"No, no . . . I'm okay . . ."

A second man arrived to help, pulling a handkerchief from his pocket and pressing it to her forehead to stop the bleeding, but she waved both of them off. She had to get out, get out *now* before the police showed up. With a government as corrupt as this one, the police who got there first would be there to finish the job.

Sirens wailed close by.

CERROS RUINS
YUCATÁN, BELIZE
1227 HOURS, LOCAL TIME

Teller lay on his belly beside a low stone wall covered with odd glyphs and ornate carvings, using his binoculars to peer down at the coast two hundred yards to the southeast. The triangle of land jutting out into the bay gave them a good vantage point looking back at the shore from across the water. Unfortunately, the coast there, deeply shaded by the jungle canopy, was heavily indented. A submarine could easily be hidden in there close to shore and remain invisible. Through binoculars, Teller could see something that might be a wooden pier running along the shore, however, and a curtain beyond, like dark green haze, that might be the hanging folds of a large camouflage net.

Of the expected Kilo class submarine there was no trace.

Beside him, Procario was aiming the Lightweight Laser Designation Rangefinder (or LLDR) at the presumed location of the sub. "I'd feel better about this if we could see the damned thing," he said.

"It might be behind that netting," Teller told him.

"Maybe. We'd need to get closer to see for sure."

"That," Teller said, "would not be a real good idea."

Procario slapped a mosquito on his cheek, leaving a tiny smear of blood. "Bloodsuckers."

"Hey, welcome to beautiful Belize. Land of mystery, enchantment, and mosquitoes the size of Cessnas."

They were just ten miles south of Chetumal, across the waters of Corozal Bay. Belize was a former British colony, with town names like Sand Hill, Bermudian Landing, and Teakettle Village standing in amusing contrast to the sea of Spanish and Mayan names around them. One town in particular, Ladyville, located eight miles up the coast from Belize City, was the location of a new lily pad, a cooperative security location where prepositioned supplies and equipment could be used by American forces engaged in operations against narco-terrorists.

Teller and Procario had rented a car and driven south early that morning, crossing the border into Belize at the tiny, duty-free enclave of Santa Elena, following the Northern Highway until they found the road to the fishing port of Corozal, then driving around the curve of Corozal Bay to the much tinier, sleepier village of San Fernando.

North of San Fernando, the road had been blocked off by a chain and an orange sign reading *CAMINO CERRADO*—"road closed."

They'd found a place to park the car, off the road and well back under the trees, and set off cross-country, navigating by compass and lugging their equipment in heavy backpacks—their satcom gear and the thirty-five-pound LLDR. An hour's hike through fairly open jungle had brought them to a cluster of low hills and the triangular headland on the bay. A number of Mayan ruins rose from the hilltops, including a kind of white stone platform overlooking the water, with ancient, worn steps leading to the top. The jungle here gave way to open ground and patches of brush; they'd found this vantage point alongside the wall so that they could look down at the presumed submarine pen without showing their silhouettes at the crest of the hill.

The road-closed sign had discouraged the arrival of any sightseeing tourists, obviously. The ruins, normally open to the public—or at least to archaeologists— were deserted. But they'd seen an armed guard at the foot of the hill, though, sitting on a block of carved masonry smoking a cigarette, and there were at least two more guards in the jungle close to the pier. *Something* was going on back there in the jungle, something those guards didn't want outsiders to see.

There seemed to be no way to get down there without being seen.

"Let's call in the hired help, then," Procario said after another moment.

"Right." Teller pulled out the handset for the AN/PRC-117F satcom. "Gray Fox, Gray Fox," he called. "This is Flashlight. Ready to burn."

"Flashlight," a voice came back in his earpiece. "Gray Fox OTW." *On the way.* "Two mikes."

"Copy, Gray Fox. Be advised that the primary target is not in sight. Repeat, not in sight."

"Copy that. Our orders are to go boots-on-the-ground and check it out up close and personal."

"Roger. Target will be a wooden pier at the water's edge. Come on in."

Turning, he looked back to the east, searching the sky, but there was nothing there yet. "Gray Fox," he thought, was a mildly amusing homage to the incoming unit, still one of the most highly classified operational units within the U.S. military.

Created in 1980 to conduct intelligence for a planned second attempt to liberate American Embassy hostages held in Tehran after the disaster at Desert One, the United States Army Intelligence Support Activity—usually shortened to ISA—had gone by a number of names over the years. Commonly known simply as "the Activity" within the intelligence community, its official operational names had included, among others, Centra Spike, Cemetery Wind, and Gray Fox.

As "Gray Fox," the ISA had helped track down Colombian drug lord Pablo Escobar in 1993. Since 2005, they were no longer identified by two-word Special-Access Program code names but were referred to under the general heading of Task Force Orange, or by the more cryptic—and classified—acronym OMS. Their name was changed every couple of years for security reasons; informally, though, they were still referred to as "the Activity"—and evidently a mission planner at INSCOM had dredged up the old Gray Fox code to identify the helicopter assault team now headed for Cerros from the Ladyville lily pad.

Technically, the ISA, under INSCOM direction, was intended as intelligence support, tasked with gathering HUMINT and SIGINT for a variety of classified operations. In this instance, however, it was being employed as a primary ops unit rather than in a purely intelligence-support role. The incoming strike was tasked with securing the stolen nuclear weapons first and foremost; a second, parallel raid was being mounted at this moment on the warehouse at the Chetumal airport. Gathering intelligence was the secondary objective this afternoon, including most especially information on the intended targets—and on just who was behind this nightmare of submarine-deployed A-bombs.

In Teller's opinion, the Activity was definitely the right team for this mission. Teller had worked with the ISA before, in Afghanistan and doing cyber ops, and knew just how good they were. Delta Force was supposed to be the best, but these guys were one notch better.

"Flashlight, Gray Fox," sounded in his earpiece. "One mike. Light 'em up."

"Copy, Gray Fox. Light is on." He nudged Procario. "Paint 'em."

Procario had already lined up the small, tripod-mounted AN/PED-1 LLDR, sending a series of invisible, coded pulses of infrared laser light down and across the water to strike an exposed bollard at the side of the makeshift pier. Scattering off the target, the light would be picked up by the receivers on the incoming helicopters, guiding them in for a precise strike.

The two sentries on the stone blocks at the bottom of the hill were still smoking. They looked like locals—smugglers, probably, or rebels, or both. Revolutionary groups had used the profits from drug smuggling to fund their activities for decades—nothing new there. Teller still didn't believe the drug cartels were behind the import of nuclear weapons. They had the money, certainly, but not the motive.

Neither did Hezbollah, despite reports of their being involved with the cartels, and despite Castro's identification of Mohamed Hamadi as a Hezbollah operator. Even the Iranians—long the power behind Shiite Hezbollah—didn't have a motive to launch a nuclear attack on Mexico.

Might Iran launch a nuclear strike against the United States, using a Russian Kilo class sub? Well, that was why the Activity was coming in hot right now. Prisoners might be able to shed some light on whoever was behind this plot, and on exactly what their motives might be.

Teller heard it first, a faint, fluttering tremble in the air, coming across the bay from the north. The sound grew steadily, swelling to thunder . . . and then two MH-60L Black Hawk DAPs roared in scant feet above the water, zeroing in on the invisible spot of infrared light reflecting off the pier. DAPs—Direct Action Penetrators—were specially modified MH-60 helicopters used by the 160th Special Operations Aviation Regiment, the Night Stalkers, for covert strike operations. Riding clouds of spray raised by their prop wash, the two dead-black helicopters flared and went nose-high as they approached the jungle, then rose, one slowing to a graceful hover above the tree canopy as the other banked sharply left. The two sentries stared openmouthed for a moment, then threw down their weapons and bolted, vanishing into the jungle. The lone man sitting on the ruins jumped up and started running in the other direction, racing all-out up the slope of the hill toward Teller and Procario.

"I've got him," Teller said. He reached for his M-4A1 carbine, left leaning on the wall beside his pack. As the man drew closer, less than fifty yards, Teller aimed his weapon at the ground in front of him, snapped the selector switch to burst fire, and put three quick-spaced rounds into the earth. *"¡Alto!"* he yelled, and the man skidded to a confused stop. *"¡Levante las manos!"*

In response, the man raised his hands, looking around wildly for the source of the command. At his back, ISA commandos were fast-roping from one of the Black Hawks, vanishing into the trees behind the pier. Teller heard a chattering burst of full-auto gunfire and a shrill yell. The second Black Hawk circled over the jungle like a hungry predator, ready to provide close fire support.

"¡Ven! ¡Ven!" Teller shouted. *"¡Ahora bajar!"*

Still shouting in Spanish, Teller ordered his prisoner to come closer, then to get down on the ground. More gunfire sounded from the objective, and then the circling Black Hawk stooped, the M-230 chain gun slung beneath its left stub wing shredding the forest canopy with 30 mm shells at a rate of better than ten per second. Explosions ripped through the forest, throwing fragments of leaves and bark above the treetops as someone back in the woods began screaming.

For a long moment, the jungle was silent again, save for the heavy *wop-wop-wop* of the two aircraft.

Another civilian broke and ran from the jungle's edge, carrying an M-16. Teller raised his M-4 and fired another burst. *"¡Alto!"*

The man with the rifle stopped, looked up the hill directly at Teller, and raised his weapon. Teller fired again, a three-round burst that hit the man just as Procario fired as well, multiple rounds catching him in a vicious crossfire that kicked him back and knocked him down.

Teller could see movement through the trees now and raised his M-4 once more—but the figures emerging from the tree line were anonymously garbed in Kevlar, helmets, and close-assault gear. One turned toward the hill and raised his hand in silent salute.

"Flashlight, Gray Fox."

"This is Flashlight. Go."

"Fox One reports AO is secure. You can come in now."

"Copy that. We have a prisoner up here."

"Well, welcome to the party, then, Flash. The more the merrier."

HOSPITAL DE JESÚS
MEXICO CITY, MEXICO
1523 HOURS, LOCAL TIME

"Hello, Ms. Dominique. How are we feeling now?"

Dominique opened her eyes. De la Cruz was standing by her bed, accompanied by two other men in plain, dark civilian suits.

"I don't know how *you're* feeling, Señor de la Cruz," she said, "but I'm doing just fine."

"*Bueno.* You had us worried."

"It was an ambush. A man on a motorcycle . . ."

He nodded. "I know. I came as quickly as I heard. I am . . . distressed to hear that Señor Chavez was killed."

"So am I." She reached up and touched the bandage wrapped around her head. The gash was still tender; not all that bad—only a minor cut—but a scalp wound could bleed like nobody's business. "Thank you for coming. Maybe you can tell the doctors that I'm okay, that I want my clothes and I want to leave. *Now.*"

She'd been having trouble communicating with the doctors. They'd sent her up here, to a private room, straight from the ER, and told her nothing save that the police wanted to talk with her. She'd not been badly hurt; they hadn't even needed to give her sutures, using a butterfly strip instead to close up the cut on her forehead.

"I am afraid, *señorita,* that things are not so simple," de la Cruz told her.

"I'm not hurt," she told him. "Not badly enough to be put in the hospital. There's no need for me to remain here."

"Of course not. My . . . associates and I are here to take you to another location. A *secure* location."

Dominique was instantly suspicious. "And who are they?"

"CISEN officers, like myself. This is Señor Martinez, and that is Señor Cobos. They have some questions to ask of you."

"Where are you taking me?"

"As I said, a secure location."

"Not the airport?"

"No. Things have . . . changed. Ah . . . here is the orderly with your clothing. We'll step outside while you dress."

When she was alone in the room, Dominique got out of bed and went to the window. The streets of Mexico City crawled and clotted and honked far below—about five stories down. The window was sealed; there was no escape that way.

Her cell phone, ominously, was missing from her pocketbook. Possibly it had fallen out and gotten lost in the street or in the car during the explosion, but its absence worried her. If someone had taken it deliberately, taken it to cut her off from Langley or Teller . . .

Reluctantly, she began dressing. Her first order of business, however, was to pull a cheap ballpoint pen from the pocketbook and clip it to the front of her bra, between the cups. Unscrewing the pen, she made an adjustment to the credit-card-thin sliver of circuit-covered plastic hidden inside. Then she put on the bra so that the pen would ride unnoticed when she put on her shirt.

As insurance it wasn't a hell of a lot—but it was all that she had right now.

CERROS RUINS
YUCATÁN, MEXICO
1603 HOURS, LOCAL TIME

The submarine, as Teller had feared, was gone. There was plenty of evidence that it had been there, however. A thin rainbow sheen of oil coated the water along the crude wooden pier that ran parallel to the shoreline; two pickup trucks farther back in the jungle still had several dozen 55-gallon drums that once had held marine diesel fuel, and a large dump of empty drums farther back in the jungle showed where they'd been depositing their empties.

ISA commandos moved through the jungle encampment with silent precision, picking up and bagging everything that might be useful for intelligence analysis—not only laptop computers and thumb drives but briefcases, trash, and the contents of dead men's pockets. A photographer moved everywhere taking high-resolution pictures of everything, including the faces of seven dead narcoterrorists laid out in a line in front of the wood and concrete-block shack that had been their headquarters.

In fact, a small village had been built here in the light-dappled shadows beneath the forest canopy: tents and small buildings, a fuel storage tank, a small machine shop powered by an electrical generator, storage sheds for food, equipment, weapons, and plastic bags filled with cocaine—everything necessary, in fact, for a secret drug-smuggling submarine base hidden in the jungle. The ISA troops had captured twelve men, including the one Teller had nabbed. Arrangements had already been made to bring in a big CH-47 Chinook helicopter transport from Ladyville to fly the prisoners out.

Teller and Procario had been going through the stash of recovered digital intelligence: two laptop computers, several external hard drives and thumb drives, and briefcases full of papers. The computers all appeared to be password protected, but that, Teller knew, wouldn't be a problem once they got them back to Langley. The Agency's technical experts could crack all but the toughest computer security safeguards, and anything *they* couldn't read would be passed on to the premier code breakers at the National Security Agency.

At the moment, Teller was more interested in the paper records, which included a large nautical chart of the Florida coast, from the Keys all the way up to Nassau Sound north of Jacksonville. Along that 450-mile stretch of coastline, seven beaches had been marked by red circles—all of them relatively secluded, well clear of the major tourist centers and resorts.

He showed the chart to Procario. "Looks like they've

been doing this for a while. They wouldn't need seven landing points for a single trip."

"You think they took the weapons to one of these spots and dropped them off?"

Teller shook his head. "I don't think so. I think these are drop points for drug consignments."

"I agree. Have a look at this." Procario handed him the contents of a captured briefcase. It was a thick document—over fifty pages—and appeared to be a contract, with parallel texts in Spanish and in Russian. The front page was decorated with heavily embossed gold seals.

"The Russkies *do* love their official crap, don't they?"

"Don't leave home without it." The Russian love of fancy seals and stamps on official documents was well known within the intelligence community, to the point of being an insider's joke.

Teller scanned through the Spanish portion of the document. "Here's the pricing," he said. "Three hundred million rubles . . . or a hundred thirty-two and some million pesos . . . that's what, in dollars?"

"Not sure. Something like ten million dollars, I think. Rubles are around thirty or so to the dollar right now, maybe a bit less."

Teller slapped absently at a mosquito on his neck, continuing to look through the document. "The price has gone up. They offered to rent the Colombians a Kilo class sub and a trained crew for a year for only one million."

"Well, that *was* back in the nineties," Procario observed. "Gotta keep up with inflation, y'know."

"It's still a drop in the bucket, compared with a cartel's income in just one year. I'm interested, though, in why they took the Russians up on their offer. They've been manufacturing their own home-grown narco-subs since the nineties, right? Those only cost a few million apiece."

"Range," Procario said. "The homemade subs have a range of only a couple of thousand miles max, where a Kilo can travel seven thousand miles on one fueling."

"Which means it could reach anywhere on the eastern U.S. seaboard," Teller said. "We need to flag this for the navy."

"Yeah. If those nukes are on board the Kilo now . . ."

"It could mean a *very* bad day for a couple of our cities. C'mon. Let's pack this stuff up and get the hell out of here."

One of the Kevlar-shrouded commandos appeared in the doorway—Captain Marcetti, the young Army Special Forces captain in charge of the ground team. "Mr. Callahan?" he said, using Teller's current "cover for status" alias. "There's something back here you should see."

"Not a couple of nuclear weapons, is it?" Procario asked.

"No, sir. It's . . . you'd better just come and see."

It was another shed built a little farther back in the jungle. Teller could smell it as they approached—a sharp and coppery tang of blood. That, and Captain

Marcetti's subdued demeanor, warned Teller before he reached the door.

Even with the warning, it was a shock.

"God in heaven . . ."

It was hard to tell how many bodies there were—six or seven, at least, of both sexes—but they were in pieces, a savage and bloody tangle of naked torsos, of arms and legs, of severed heads. Several large steel drums half filled with dark liquid stood in the center of the single room. A bloody chain saw rested on a table. There was so *very* much blood . . .

"We found these," Marcetti said, indicating several boxes stacked in a nearby corner containing neatly folded clothing, cameras and personal effects, passports, and wallets. "According to the passports, they were archaeologists. University of the Americas. Ah . . . don't touch those barrels, sir. They're filled with acid."

Teller snatched his hand back. Procario nodded. "The cartels often use acid to get rid of inconvenient bodies," he said. "They only hang them from bridges or dump them in the street when they want to send a message."

"We'll need to check with the University of the Americas and see when their expedition went missing," Teller said. "These people must have shown up, disregarded the keep-out sign, and blundered into the operation."

"Apparently the bastards didn't want to leave any witnesses," Procario agreed.

The casual butchery was appalling, and Teller—who'd seen more than his fair share of blood and death and battlefield horror—had to work to force back a rising gorge. People who could do this, he thought, would feel no compunction about mass murder on the scale of a major city. He needed to get out, into the open air.

Damn it, he needed a *drink*.

"We've got to stop these animals, Frank," Teller said slowly. "We've got to *stop* them."

Teller just wished he knew how they were going to pull that off.

CHAPTER THIRTEEN

Teller was still hurting from his drunk of the night before.

He rarely suffered from hangovers—the secret was to drink lots of water both during and after the binge—but he was still feeling slow and muzzy. De la Cruz had summoned him and Procario to his office at a few minutes past eight that morning, and Teller wasn't sure he was entirely functional yet.

The two of them had flown back to Mexico City the previous afternoon, and, after uploading their after-actions from the raid at Cerros, he'd settled down to do some serious drinking, hitting a bar on Independencia. He'd checked first at Jackie's hotel but been told only that she'd checked out that morning. Calls to both Dominique's and Chavez's cell phones had gone unanswered, and Langley had heard nothing from either officer in the past eight hours; he was becoming worried about them.

He'd struggled out of bed this morning to de la Cruz's phone call. He had news, the CISEN officer had said, and it was not good.

"I regret to say," de la Cruz said when they entered his office forty minutes later, "that Señor Chavez is dead."

"Dead!" Procario exclaimed.

"I am afraid so. And your other colleague, Miss Dominique, has disappeared. We . . . fear the worst."

Teller went cold, adrenaline shredding the remaining fog of the hangover. "What the hell happened?"

De la Cruz gave a small shrug. "They were on their way to the airport yesterday morning. Apparently there was an ambush. Eyewitnesses say a man on a motorcycle placed a small package against the driver's-side door of their vehicle, which exploded seconds later. Probably a remote-controlled device. Señor Chavez appears to have been killed instantly. The woman, we were told, was injured and taken to a local hospital with minor injuries, but she was discharged later in the afternoon. We do not know where she is at this time—but the hospital records tell us that she was released into the custody of two CISEN officers. She did not show up at the airport to catch her flight, she did not return to her hotel, and she did not return here. She has simply . . . disappeared."

"You have names for the people who picked her up at the hospital?" Procario asked.

"Of course. Cobos and Martinez. However, we have no one named Cobos in CISEN, and everyone named Martinez has been otherwise accounted for. We fear that she has been abducted."

"It's possible that she's gone to ground," Teller said. "In hiding."

"That, too, is possible, of course. We have been checking at hotels throughout the city. So far, we have found nothing."

"God," Procario said. "If one of the cartels has her . . ."

"That is what CISEN is assuming at the moment," de la Cruz said. "I am very sorry."

"Yeah," Teller said, his voice dark. He was thinking of that stack of bloody body parts in that shack in Belize, the stink, the horror. "So am I. And if anything happens to her, someone else is going to be damned sorry, too."

MARIA PEREZ HOUSE
LA CALLE SUR 145
DISTRICTO IZTACALCO
0934 HOURS, LOCAL TIME

"Damn it, Barrón, this is stupid. You should not have brought her here." Maria Perez was furious. "We know they have this house under surveillance. You killed one of their operators on the street outside just three nights ago!"

Barrón gave a careless shrug. "It was necessary, Miss Perez. A temporary measure only. And because of your uncle . . . well, the police are not about to bother you."

"Barrón, the woman is an American! *Una espía yanqui.*"

"It means nothing. With the police and the government in our pocket, we can do what we like. Our friends with the police are watching. They will not permit the North Americans to operate here."

"So you hope."

"*Con calma, puta.* The woman herself is our insurance. The CIA will negotiate for her release before they attempt a rescue. They know what will happen to her if they fail."

"Juan would never have agreed to this!"

"Your boyfriend is not running this operation, woman. And you will do what you are told. Understand?"

Perez glared at Barrón. The man was Sinaloan and a Zeta Killer, and not to be trusted whatever Juan Escalante might have to say about it. The Sinaloans were perfectly capable of setting her and Juan up for an assault by the army, using the *yanqui* woman as bait.

"*Whore! I said, do you understand?*"

"Yes. Yes, I understand."

She'd argued with Juan about this insane idea of uniting the Sinaloan and Zeta cartels. The Sinaloans were pigs, brutal and vicious and utterly without honor. If the Zetas were brutal at times, it was because sometimes brutality was necessary—but the Sinaloans reveled in torture and rape and blood. She'd heard so many stories, *horrible* stories . . .

She looked through the open doorway at the prisoner.

The woman lying on the bed seemed to be young and attractive, though the gag and blindfold made it hard to see her face. She was tightly tied at wrists, knees, and ankles, with her feet drawn up close by a short length of rope connected to her hands. The two Sinaloan thugs who'd brought her in last night had been taking turns guarding her, one always sitting there beside the bed. Earlier that morning, both men had been there. She'd listened to them discussing their captive as she served them breakfast, talking about what they planned to do, and some of what they'd been saying had made her blood run cold. She knew the prisoner had heard them; worse, that she'd understood what they were saying.

The poor woman . . .

There was nothing Maria could do for the prisoner, however. To help the woman would mean her own death, probably a slow and agonizing death. Not even the niece of Jaime Perez Durán could interfere with *el negocio del cártel,* with cartel business, not without suffering the consequences . . . and with the emphasis decidedly on *suffer.*

At least they hadn't started the rough stuff. *Yet.*

CENTRO DE CISEN
MEXICO CITY
0940 HOURS, LOCAL TIME

Teller looked up at the huge face on the flat-screen wall display, disbelieving. "Excuse me, but I think there's a glitch in the signal," he said. "I didn't catch that last."

In fact, the signal was fine. De la Cruz had set up the

video conference call in one of CISEN HQ's briefing rooms, using a secure satellite feed.

"I said," the face of Jack Wentworth said, looming above him, "that we're pulling you out. You've completed your mission. It's time to extract."

"Not without Jackie, it isn't."

"Captain Teller, there is nothing we can do about Dominique. She's an operative. She knew the risks. Her loss is . . . regrettable, but we have what we went into Mexico to get. Now we need to cut our losses and focus on priorities."

"Priorities!"

"Our priority right now is that Kilo sub—and what it may be carrying."

"Hey, check my MOS," Teller said, referring to the military occupational specialty, the nine-character code describing the job of every person in the U.S. military. "Not a word in there about me finding subs at sea. Maybe you got confused, JJ. The navy is tasked with tracking hostile submarines. Not me."

"Until the situation is resolved, it *is* your job. I want you both back here in Washington this afternoon for a full debriefing."

"You already have everything we found in Belize," Procario said. "You don't need us."

"Too many people have died on this op," Teller said. "I'm not compounding it by running out on a fellow intelligence officer."

"Leave no man behind," Procario added. "*Or* woman."

Teller glanced at Procario with a silent "thank you."

On the big wall display, Wentworth shook his head

slowly. "Look, I know what you men must be feeling right now. Grant . . . Dominique . . . Chavez . . . Good people, all of them. It's just too bad that—"

"Jackie isn't dead yet, damn it!" Teller shouted. It was all he could do not to lunge across the conference table at the big display screen. "Not until her body turns up down here—or her head shows up in a box on your fucking desk! We need to find her!"

"I *beg* your pardon, Captain," Wentworth said in frosty tones. "What we need is to find those nuclear weapons before they are deployed. *If* Ms. Dominique is still alive, she could be anywhere—Mexico City, Hermosillo, Veracruz, Guadalajara, Monterrey . . . We do not have the assets in place to conduct a search of every possibility."

"You've got me," Teller said, taking his seat once more. Reaching into his jacket, he extracted a pen, held it up, and clicked it twice. "And we have options."

"I'm with Captain Teller on this," Procario added.

"If you are referring to ghost technologies—" Wentworth began, but Teller cut him off.

"There is a *lot* we can do here," he said, interrupting, "but we don't have the time to discuss it with you now. We're not coming home. Not without Jackie."

"I must intercede," de la Cruz said. He'd been sitting at the far end of the conference table, listening to the discussion but not participating. "I agree with Mr. Wentworth. There is nothing more that you gentlemen can do here, and in view of the, shall we say, public perception of your actions last night, I do not believe it wise for you to remain. CISEN will extend every effort to locate Ms. Dominique and free her. I promise this."

"He's right," Wentworth said. "I was trying to keep this civil, but you two stirred up one hell of a hornet's nest, calling in an ops team."

So *that* was how they were going to play it. Teller leaned back in his chair, arms folded. He was pissed. "*We* stirred it up? Are you freakin' nuts?"

"Your former deputy chief of station got greedy," Procario added. "If you want to lay blame."

"And the ops request *was* approved," Teller reminded them.

"The operation will be brought up for formal review," Wentworth said, ignoring them. "We had hoped you two would be able to handle things . . . more discreetly."

"Well, maybe you should have a talk with the drug lords about that," Procario said. "They're the ones with an army down here. They're the ones killing anyone who gets in their way."

"They butchered seven civilian archaeologists," Teller said, "apparently for no reason other than that they were in the wrong place at the wrong time."

"The civilians are not our concern," Wentworth told them. "What *is* our concern is that someone has leaked details of your operations down there to the Mexican media. I understand that the ambassadors of Mexico and Belize are delivering joint messages to the president this afternoon protesting illegal military operations on their sovereign territory. I can tell you right now that the president, State, INSCOM, and quite a few other people up here are not happy with you at the moment."

"We had a good chance to secure the nukes," Procario said. "What were we supposed to do—use local assets?"

Teller glanced at de la Cruz, sitting at the end of the table, looking for a reaction to this. The CISEN officer appeared absorbed in his laptop at the moment, however.

"Both ops were quiet and slick," Teller pointed out. "In and out. No collateral damage."

"Have you seen the headlines down there this morning?"

"No."

" 'U.S. Troops Attack Chetumal Warehouse.' 'U.S. Troops Invade Belize Soil.' They're playing it up big."

Both raids—the one at Cerros and the simultaneous raid on the airport warehouse next to the Chetumal Airport—had gone down, so far as Teller could see, with absolute perfection, a rarity in any military operation. There'd been no U.S. casualties at all, and no civilians caught in the line of fire. A total of twelve narcoterrorists had been killed and ten captured; the only thing that had gone wrong was that neither the Russian submarine or the missing nuclear weapons—the whole point of the double raid—had been found. Hell, they hadn't even turned up any drugs.

"Is that the *real* reason you're yanking us out?"

Teller demanded. "Bad media coverage? Political expediency?"

Wentworth's face darkened. "Our reasoning is not for you to question, Captain. Getting on a plane and returning to Washington is now your *sole* concern. Do you understand me?"

Teller laughed. "Oh, yes. I understand very well."

On the street a few minutes later, Procario looked askance at his companion. "You're not going back, are you?"

"No, Frank, I'm not."

"You're a cowboy, you know that?"

"I've heard that." "Cowboy" was slang within the intelligence services for someone who did it his own way, someone who shot from the hip and didn't necessarily check in for guidance from headquarters. *Not,* in other words, a team player.

"What do you have in mind?"

"Using a ghost tracker to find Jackie."

"You don't trust de la Cruz, do you? That's why you cut Wentworth off before he could say more."

"That's right. We can't trust *anyone* down here, especially anyone with the government. The *narcotraffi- cantes* have been three steps ahead of us all along, and we know they get their information from corrupt government and police officials."

"They're not all corrupt."

"No—not *all*. But we can't afford to risk any breach of security. If Wentworth had spilled the fact that we, and presumably Jackie, had been carrying ghost trackers, then de la Cruz—if he's a black hat—would have told Jackie's abductors. They would then either kill her or find her transmitter. And we would be back to square one."

Ghost-series transmitters were wireless microphones/transmitters printed on a sliver of plastic small enough to fit inside the barrel of a working ballpoint pen. They had a range of a mile or a little less under ideal conditions. When Teller had pulled out his pen and clicked it during the video conference, he'd been suggesting to Wentworth that they would be able to track Jackie by means of her transmitter. He'd not expected the idiot to begin discussing ghost technology with de la Cruz in the room, however. As it was, ghost-series trackers were in widespread use all over the world to thwart kidnappers and cargo thieves. U.S. citizens couldn't own them—that was illegal unless you were a law enforcement professional—but it was quite possible that CISEN officers like de la Cruz knew all about the things.

That worried Teller.

"Okay, so how do we cover the city? Or did you buy Wentworth's assessment that she could be in some other city by now?"

"Chances are she's still here in Mexico City," Teller said. "They would be running a risk moving her somewhere else, and they probably think they don't need to move her."

"Sounds reasonable."

"We can tap into the Cellmap feed and locate clusters of bad guys throughout the city. Then we check out each cluster with a FIDR." The acronym rhymed with "spider."

"We'll need a helicopter."

"Gray Fox?"

"That's what I was thinking," Procario said. "We'll need armed backup and special gear anyway to pull this off."

"I'll put in a call to Ladyville," Teller said.

Marcetti and his team should still be at the Belize lily pad. The CH-47 crew and some of the commandos had taken the prisoners back stateside yesterday, but the rest had gone back to the lily pad in case an assault was also needed on the *Zapoteca* or some other target objective turned up. Teller had Marcetti's number. He remembered that the man had been as shaken by the butchery at Cerros as Teller was, and thought he would help them if he could. One thing long experience had taught Teller: The members of elite teams—marines, SEALs, Special Forces, ISA commandos—all shared an absolute devotion to the concept that no one *ever* was left behind.

The thought of doing so for political expediency was guaranteed to send such people ballistic, and Teller was guessing that Marcetti was no exception.

"What do you want me to do?" Procario asked.

"Sir, I want you to check out the hospital where they took Jackie. I'd kind of like to validate de la Cruz's story." Teller tended to return to military protocol when he really needed Procario's help—and this had become a deeply emotional issue.

"And after that?"

"After that, we'll see. But I'm expecting that we'll be going in hot."

MARIA PEREZ HOUSE
LA CALLE SUR 145
DISTRICTO IZTACALCO
1350 HOURS, LOCAL TIME

"Abra la boca," the voice said.

Obediently, Dominique opened her mouth, and the woman slipped in a spoonful of hot soup—broth and chicken, tomatoes, and corn, mostly, she thought. She was still tied, still blindfolded, but at least that damnable gag had been removed. The woman continued to feed her. Earlier, she'd untied Dominique long enough to take her into the bathroom.

Dominique didn't try to carry on a conversation, though. She could sense at least one other in the room, and once she caught a murmured exchange of conversation between the woman and a man—one of the men who'd been joking with a friend about cutting her into pieces a few hours ago. When the woman spoke to her, it was with curt, brief orders, but Dominique thought she sensed a kindness there behind the mask.

She hoped so, hoped she wasn't letting desperation make her delusional. She heard the spoon scrape across the bottom of the bowl, then opened for a final spoonful.

"Allá," the woman said. *"Eso es todo."*

"Mil gracias," Dominique replied. A thousand thanks.

"¿Le gusta agua?"

"Si. Por favor." A glass was held to her lips, and she gratefully took a long drink of water. *"Muchas gracias."*

"De nada."

The gag was stuffed back between her lips, the knot at the back of her head tightened. She lay back down on the unseen bed. The guard retied her wrists to her ankles, leaving her helplessly trussed, a piece of meat.

She could still feel the reassuring presence of the pen clipped inside her bra, and she thanked God once again that they hadn't stripped and searched her when they'd tied her up and dumped her on the bed. She'd expected to be raped and tortured as soon as they got her here—assuming they didn't just shoot her outright and dump her body on the street—but she had the feeling that they were waiting for someone else to arrive before anything like a thorough interrogation.

Interrogation, she knew, *would* come. They knew she and Chavez were CIA; de la Cruz had burned them from the start, the filthy, bought-and-paid-for bastard. Presumably they wanted to know what she knew, details on the Cellmap program, for instance; maybe they wanted to know what the Agency had uncovered so far about nuclear weapons on the *Zapoteca,* or the mission of the Kilo submarine.

At the very least they would demand the identities of other Agency operators in Mexico—the ones they did not get from Nichols when he had sold out.

Operators like Teller and Procario.

The pen and the ghost transmitter hidden inside gave her at least a shadow of hope.

Hope that Teller was out there looking for her.

Hope that he was on his way.

HOTEL HILTON
CIUDAD DE MÉXICO
REPÚBLICA DE MÉXICO
2127 HOURS, LOCAL TIME

"So what the hell was it the DEA guy owed you for, March?" Teller asked.

They were sitting at the desk in Teller's room at the Hilton, a laptop open and displaying a graphic street map of central Mexico City. Small blue dots were scattered across the map in haphazard randomness; at the center of the screen was a green aircraft icon. The icon remained motionless as the map shifted and turned around it.

"A few years ago, an op went bad in T-town," Marcetti told them. "A couple of DEA operators were trying to pull off a wired buy, but the opposition made them, and things turned pear shaped. I took a covert team in across the border at San Diego and got them out."

"Sinaloa Cartel?"

"Uh-uh. Tijuana and Oaxaca, working together. That was 2008, right after the big shoot-out between Sinaloa and Tijuana, though."

"I remember reading about that one," Teller said. Fourteen cartel members had died and eight were wounded in the gun battle at the U.S. border.

"Yeah, well, the targets were pretty nervous, on their guard, you know? They grabbed the DEA people and were threatening to execute them. We brought them out."

"So now one of them's willing to loan you an RQ-4?" Procario said. "Sweet."

Teller had feared that it might take a long time—a day or more—to track down Marcetti and get him up to Mexico City, but he'd managed to get him on the phone and explain the situation. Marcetti, four of his men, and several crates of equipment from the lily pad had been on the way to Benito Juárez International less than three hours later in a private Beechcraft rented at Chetumal.

Using the Black Hawk DAPs, it turned out, was not even a remotely viable option. The UH-60s were expensive aircraft with a lot of highly classified hardware on board, and there was no way to sideline them for an operation over Mexico City, especially when the local news media were screaming murder over Mexican nationals killed or captured by American troops at Chetumal. Marcetti had thought a moment, then promised to make some phone calls during his flight to BJI.

"We really do appreciate you dropping everything and coming up here, March," Teller told him. It hadn't taken long after the ISA team's arrival for the three of them to get on a first-name basis. "I just hope you don't land in hot water over this. We're not even supposed to be here now."

"Hey, glad to help out. I've had the REMFs yank the plug on me a time or two. I don't care where the orders come from, I do *not* leave my people in the field." He chuckled. "Besides, we were just sitting on our assets down there in Ladyville. They scrubbed the op on the *Zapoteca,* you know that?"

"I figured that," Teller said. "Everyone's sure the nukes are already on their way to the States. Besides, the bad press down here is making Washington *real* leery of doing anything else to piss off the Mexicans."

"Right. So we were finishing prepping the DAPs with long-range tanks for a ferry flight to McDill when your call came in. The rest of the team went back with the helos, but a few of us just decided we were overdue for some leave time. No reason not to take it in sunny Mexico, right?"

"Well, we're glad to have you on board," Procario said. He nodded at the computer display. "And we *really* appreciate your buddy's toy."

Marcetti's phone call to a friend in the DEA had resulted in an unexpected addition to the team's arsenal in Mexico City.

A Global Hawk.

The United States had been tracking drug smugglers using unmanned aerial vehicles—UAVs—over Mexico for more than twenty years. Most of those overflights had been made with MQ-1 Predators, operating along the U.S.-Mexican border, with the intelligence they picked up shared with the Mexican authorities. Predators had a range of only 675 nautical miles, however, and the nearest was deployed at JBSA—Joint Base San Antonio, 600 miles from Mexico City. A Predator would have been able to arrive over the target, but it would be a one-way flight. Teller could just imagine the news headlines if a Predator crashed outside of Mexico City—or tried to land at Benito Juárez.

The RQ-4A Global Hawk, however, was a whole different breed of bird. Over 44 feet long and with a wingspan of better than 116 feet, it was more than twice the size of the Predator, with greater speed, much greater range, and an astonishing mission endurance of thirty-six hours. By the time Marcetti and his men landed at Benito Juárez, an RQ-4A based at JBSA had been fitted out with a Field Intensity Directive Receiver (or FIDR) keyed to the frequency broadcast by Dominique's ghost-series transmitter, and was being readied for takeoff. With a range of well over 15,000 miles, the Global Hawk had arrived over Mexico City an hour and a half after takeoff. If need be, it could circle above Mexico City for over a day. If it came within a mile of Dominique's transmitter, it would send the signal back to JBSA and to Teller's laptop.

To narrow the search, Teller had provided Marcetti with the Cellmap data showing clusters of cell phones carrying the network-mapping virus. Analysis showed lots of lone signal sources, but twenty-five clusters of two or more targets within the Mexico City metropolitan area; a simple flight plan algorithm was now guiding the Global Hawk above each concentration in turn. Though he was impatient to get started, he and Procario had agreed to wait until after dark to reduce the chances of the Global Hawk being spotted while it was at low altitude. The aircraft was quite stealthy and should be able to avoid local radar, but it had to stay well below 5,000 feet in order to have a chance to pick up the signal. In daylight people would be able to see it, and that could give the game away. For several hours, Procario kept the Global Hawk circling 50,000 feet above the uninhabited slopes of Mount Tlaloc, thirty miles east of the city, waiting for the sky to grow dark.

An hour ago, they'd brought the Global Hawk in, routing it well clear of the airport and bringing it down to just 2,500 feet above the streets. Technically, since this was an unauthorized violation of Mexico's sovereign airspace, the Mexicans would be perfectly within their rights to shoot the UAV down. At thirty-five million dollars apiece, not counting the development costs, the Global Hawk was an expensive toy—far too expensive for the price to come out of Teller's pocket if he broke it.

Fortunately, the authorities were unlikely to bring the eleven–ton aircraft down inside the crowded city. The biggest danger, Teller thought, was running into a small private aircraft, and the Hawk's onboard radar navigation systems should be able to keep it well clear of any such threat.

"*Got* her!" Procario jumped up from the keyboard as a rapidly pulsing chirp came from the speaker. "By God, we *got* her!"

"Jesus!" Teller exclaimed. "That was fast! Where?"

Procario turned the laptop so that Teller could see the screen. "You're gonna shit yourself."

"I take it," Captain Marcetti said quietly, "that we have a target now."

"That's Iztacalco," Teller said, looking at the aircraft icon positioned above the slowly turning mosaic of city streets. Two tight clusters of blue dots were visible on the map. He leaned forward, translating coordinates. "Shit! It's La Calle Sur 145! The Perez house!"

Procario grinned. "Damned straight. They took her right back to the place we were surveilling the other night."

The computer was chirping the announcement of the receipt of signal. Procario now jacked a headset into the computer and started listening. "The signal's weak," he said, "but we're getting it all. Heartbeat . . . so she's alive. And some muffled sounds that might be conversation in the room with her."

"Let me hear."

Procario handed him the headset, and Teller listened. He could hear words in Spanish, a fuzzy backdrop to the steady *the-thump the-thump the-thump* of Jackie's heartbeat, but it was hard to make them out.

"What do you hear, man?" Marcetti asked.

"I'm not sure. Might be an argument." He listened a moment more. "Two men . . . and a woman, too. Not Jackie. Maybe the Perez woman? Something about . . . the woman wants to untie her. One of the men just called her a *puta* . . . a whore, and said she shouldn't stick her nose where it's not wanted."

He strained to hear, strained harder to understand. "Shit. Someone named Calavera is on the way."

" 'Skull?' " Procario asked, one eyebrow raised. "Seems a bit melodramatic."

"These people excel in drama," Marcetti said. "The bloodier, the better."

"We'd better saddle up and get over there," Teller said, "before things get *really* ugly."

CHAPTER FOURTEEN

VICENTE HOUSE
LA CALLE SUR 145
DISTRICTO IZTACALCO
2231 HOURS, LOCAL TIME
20 APRIL

It had taken less than an hour for the eight of them, traveling in two vehicles, to thread through the city's streets from the Hilton to Iztacalco. Teller and Procario had gone up to the OP house and awakened an angry Vicente.

"*¡Diablo! ¿Tienes una idea qué hora es?*" the informant had demanded of the men at his door.

Teller glimpsed a pretty, younger woman in the hallway behind the man, clutching a robe tightly at her throat. "I am sorry, Señor Vicente," he'd replied, speaking Spanish. "But you can blame it on your neighbors."

Vicente's eyes had widened, he'd glanced out the door, looking up and down the street, and then he'd motioned the men inside with a hurry-up motion of his hand. "If they discover that I am helping you—" he began.

"With a little luck," Teller told him, "your neighbors will not be a problem for much longer."

"God willing," Vicente said. "But you will forgive me, *señor,* if I believe that when it happens. You Americans, you come and then you are gone. The Mexican police . . . half of them work for the cartels, and the rest are never around when you want them. But the cartels, and the evil they bring, they are *always* here."

In the third-story room upstairs, they began setting up their equipment—the triple-M scope and the satcom link back to Langley first. Langley, Teller thought, might not be particularly thrilled to hear from them. He and Procario weren't even supposed to be here now, and Marcetti and his team technically were working for INSCOM. Still, they knew some people at the Agency who would be willing to work with them backchannel, and the satellite feed allowed them to keep tracking the Cellmap data.

Once the connection was complete, Teller brought up the street map showing central Iztacalco. As he zoomed in for a close look, two clusters of blue dots defined themselves, one on the west side of La Calle Sur 145, one on the east. Closer still, and he could see the specific houses.

"So," Procario said, looking over his shoulder. "Now we know how Grant and Dominique got spotted when they were surveilling the Perez house."

"An overwatch," Teller agreed. "Looks like six in

the Perez house, and . . . Christ. Twelve in the other. I think what we have here, March, is an ambush."

"You're right. So, how do we take them down?"

"We need some tactical intel," Teller said. He moved the cursor over one of the blue dots in the Perez house and clicked on it. A phone number came up. A long moment passed. Then data scrolled down the side of the screen, personal information on Federico Ortega Noreno—his address in Mexico City, driver's license statics, arrest warrants, prison records . . .

"Looks like a street-level thug," Procario said. "Since he turned twenty-one he's been in jail more than he's been free. Theft, breaking and entering, aggravated assault, auto theft, narcotics possession with intent to sell . . ."

One by one, they identified the owners of each of the cell phones in both target houses. One, Maria Perez, had no police record—though she was listed as a "person of interest" both because she was the niece of a Los Zetas big shot and because she was the *novia,* the girlfriend, of Juan Escalante.

Only one target appeared to be more than a street-level cartel soldier. Enrico Barrón was listed as a deserter from the Mexican Army, was suspected of being a member of the Sinaloan Cartel, and was thought to be a member of Los Matazetas, the Zeta Killers. Except for the desertion, there was nothing on his rap sheet; his army records, though, were reasonably impressive: *sargento primero*—first sergeant—with twelve years in service, eight of them in GAFE, the Mexican Army

Special Forces. Like Escalante, he'd been trained in the United States, including both the Western Hemisphere Institute for Security Cooperation at Fort Benning, Georgia, and Airborne training at Fort Bragg. He'd applied for Ranger School at Fort Benning, too, but the request had been denied.

He'd also gone through the CIA's clandestine ops course at the Farm, supposedly to prepare him for paramilitary operations with CISEN. Graduates of the orientation course did not leave with case officer skills, but they did gain an awareness of "how the magic was made."

That one, Teller thought, would be dangerous.

The twelve targets at the overwatch house, just three numbers up from the Vicente place, all appeared to be relatively low-level cartel operators. Three had at least some military experience, though, and one, Carlos Mora, was listed as a former sergeant with the Guatemalan Kaibiles.

Another one to watch out for.

Within a few minutes, Procario had the MMMR set up and returning a through-the-walls image of the inside of the Perez house, the black-and-white image displayed on the screen of a second laptop. Procario adjusted the aim of the triple-R transmitters and soon had the unit focused in what appeared to be an upstairs bedroom. "Got her," he said.

Anxious, Teller leaned over the marine's shoulder, studying the laptop screen. One guard, a male, sat in a chair at the back of the room, an assault rifle beside him as he held an invisible magazine in front of him.

That was Ortega. A female lay curled up on the fuzzy crisscross pattern of mattress springs beneath her, arms behind her back, which was turned toward the guard. At the extreme limit of image magnification, Teller could see the metal parts of what appeared to be a ballpoint pen resting vertically between her breasts.

They scanned the rest of the house, top floor to bottom, though the southwestern corner—perhaps a quarter of the building's floor space was, from this angle, masked by the walls of the next-door house to the south. Millimeter waves could penetrate a couple of feet of concrete, but they lost a lot of resolution as they did so, and internal walls and staircases further obscured the view.

Still, the watchers had a pretty good map of what was going on inside. The woman—Maria Perez—was alone in another bedroom upstairs, sitting upright on a bed. Five other people, all male, were downstairs, one moving about in the kitchen—Barrón, according to the Cellmap—and the other four in what was probably a nearby living room, sprawled on chairs and a sofa watching television.

As the team collected information, they began hammering out a plan. Clearly, the overwatch group was part of an OP keeping an eye on the Perez house. An attack on the Perez place would bring those twelve running, or at least alert them so that when the strike force came out the front door they would be gunned down in the street. Somehow, both cartel groups had to be neutralized—and at close to the same moment, to avoid having the Perez group kill their prisoner and to avoid having the strike force trapped by the opposition's overwatch gunmen.

Six men to take on eighteen in two locations, three to one. The odds might be even worse than that, since there could be people in those houses who weren't packing cell phones, and there was that portion of the Perez house interior that was blocked.

The odds weren't looking real good.

They had an equalizer, however, a force multiplier, in the MMMR gear. Traditionally in hostage rescue takedowns, the hardest part about the assault was figuring out just where the hostages were being held, where the defenders were, and how many defenders were close enough to harm the hostages once the shooting started. The MMMR showed them all of that, and more, by rendering the walls of the Perez house all but invisible.

One of Marcetti's men, Staff Sergeant Rogers, was in the process of unpacking and assembling a second force multiplier—a Barrett M-107CQ, broken down into pieces and carried in a foam-padded aluminum case. A second man was unpacking the ammunition.

"Okay," Teller said. He indicated the Cellmap screen data. "Taking down the Tangos in the Perez house should be pretty straightforward. But we can't hit the second house from here."

That house, now identified as Hotel Two, "Hotel" for "hostage," was on the same side of the street as the Vicente house, and separated from it by two intervening houses. Microwave radiation could pass through brick walls—even a single thickness of concrete blocks—but two or more such barriers tended to block them off.

Marcetti used his ballpoint to indicate a path on the Cellmap screen. "It looks like we could take the team up to the roof of Hotel One back here," he said, "and that would keep it out of Hotel Two's line of sight, at least until we're on the roof. The rooftop is flat. We have what looks like a ventilator there . . . and this over here might be a trapdoor leading down."

"The through-wall shows a stairway underneath," Procario said. "It'll be a bottleneck, though."

"Hey, better going down than going up," Marcetti replied. "And with a sniper able to interdict the hallway next to the stairs, we're in, no worries."

Hostage rescue and building close-assault teams always preferred to come in through the roof if at all possible if there was more than one floor in the target structure. In a firefight in a stairwell, it was *always* better to be the guy up on top, able to drop grenades down the stairs at the guys below.

"The rooftop trapdoor will be locked."

"Breaching charge, shotgun, or a bolt cutter, whichever seems right for the job."

"So how about Hotel Two? We don't have the numbers for two separate assaults."

"No," Marcetti said, "but we have claymores. *That* ought to even the odds a bit."

"That'll do," Procario agreed. "So . . . one sniper. If

he works without a spotter, one man to plant the claymore. He could either come back here and be the spotter or join the assault."

"Better yet," Teller said, "our extra man plants the claymore, then works his way south along here—sticking to the shadows in front of the houses. Crosses the street somewhere around here, out of sight of Hotel Two . . . then works his way back north up the west side of the street to here. That looks like a fence, doesn't it? He would then have a line of sight to the front of Hotel Two, could set off the claymore when necessary, and provide covering fire for our E&E. And that leaves five for the actual assault team."

"Are you volunteering for claymore duty?"

"Actually," Teller said, "no. I'm going to be on the assault team."

"Ex*cuse* me?" Marcetti shook his head. "You know better than that, Chris."

"I brought you in on this op. I'm going in with you."

Marcetti indicated the other four men in the room, all of them clad in black combat utilities, with combat vests, weapons, and night-vision devices already laid out and ready on the bed. They were listening with a range of expressions running from openly amused to carefully neutral. "The five of us have been training as a team for months. We know *exactly* how we're all going to move, react, and fire. All it takes is one guy to turn left instead of right, and you have a friendly fire casualty—or, worse, the mission is compromised."

"I know all that. But *you* should know that the hostage over there is . . . someone I know. Someone I care about, a *lot*. I'm going in with you guys."

"That makes it worse. If you have an emotional attachment, it can cloud your judgment. I don't need that fucking grief in a CQB."

CQB—close-quarters battle. It was the most difficult, most challenging form of combat, a firefight where your opponent might well be hidden just around that next corner or emerging from a closed door at your back. Hostage rescue units trained as teams endlessly until each team member knew where every other team member was at every moment, could *feel* his presence even when he was out of sight.

"How about this?" Teller asked. "That hostage over there isn't going to be trusting *anybody* right now. She was handed over to the Tangos by CISEN. If you go in there without me, you might have to fight her to get her out."

Teller felt Marcetti's cold stare at that one and knew just how thin an excuse it was. Jackie was well trained and highly experienced; she would know what was happening the instant a team of black-clad commandos burst into her room shouting, "Stay down! Americans!" She wasn't about to confuse Marcetti's team with more Mexican drug lords, and she absolutely was *not* the sort of person to go into hysterics at the wrong moment.

Hell, even if she had been, there was always the field-ready expedient of knocking her unconscious and hauling her out over someone's shoulder.

That stare dragged on for an uncomfortable number of seconds. Then Marcetti threw up his hands. "Okay. You're in. But you will stay out of our way, and you will do exactly what you're told, right?"

"Absolutely."

"And I'm OIC, understand me?"

"You're the officer in charge. *Sir.*"

Marcetti sighed. "I'm probably going to regret this . . ."

"I can handle the claymore, boss," one of the ISA men said.

"Okay, Patterson." Marcetti looked at Procario. "You qualified to play sniper?"

"Former marine," Procario told him. "Expert rifleman. Scored two-forty-five out of two-fifty on my last qual. Distinguished Marksman Medal, McDougal Trophy, *and* President's Hundred."

"Okay! Okay! You've got the job."

"Uh-oh," Teller said. He was looking again at the MMMR screen, where one of the men from the living room was trudging up the stairs to the second floor. "Looks like we might have some trouble here."

MARIA PEREZ HOUSE
LA CALLE SUR 145
DISTRICTO IZTACALCO
2250 HOURS, LOCAL TIME

Dominique heard the second man enter the room. It was Loudmouth, as she'd named him, the bigmouthed, vulgar one that liked to taunt her about what he was going to do to her. Of them all, he was the one who always managed to make her blood run cold. The others were bad, although the Perez woman was decent enough. At least she saw to it that Dominique got to eat once in a while—and use the rest room. Loudmouth, though, was terrifying.

"So, how's our girlfriend?" he boomed. The floorboards creaked beneath his shoes as he walked closer. A sudden, sharp crack sounded as he slapped her butt. Even through her jeans, the blow stung. "Ready for a little action?"

His voice was slurred, his Spanish sloppy and imprecise. *God, he's drunk,* she thought. *Not good . . .*

"C'mon, Renaldo," the other voice said. "You heard the orders. Hands off the merchandise until the Skull says differently."

"Well, I don't know about you, but I'm tired of waiting for Mr. Skull." The hand on her hip was caressing now, rough and insistent. "He won't be here until tomorrow morning. I think we have a perfect right to sample the goods, don't you?"

"You stick it in, he's going to cut it off, you know that?"

"And who's going to tell him? You?"

"Her, maybe."

"Ah. Just my word against hers, right?" Another stinging crack brought tears to her eyes beneath the blindfold. "And you never know, right? She might like a little rough loving! And if not, she might have a real good idea of what I'd do to her if she does tell."

Dominique heard a chilling click, and then she felt a cold blade pressing against her cheek. "How about it, girl? Are you going to . . . cooperate? Be a good girl?"

Dominique managed a nod. They already knew she understood Spanish, and at this point resistance would just result in her being hurt more. If she played along, she might buy some time.

"Good," Loudmouth said. "Let's see what we have here."

She felt him fumble with the rope tying her ankles to her wrists, felt the sharp snick of a blade, and the rope parted. She was still tied hand and foot, but at least she could stretch out her legs. Incongruously, it felt wonderful.

Rough hands rolled her over onto her back. She tensed, expecting the worst.

A phone chirped.

Dominique felt the man's hands leave her and heard his curt *"Aló? Sí."* A moment passed, and he said, *"Pero . . . no. Intiendo. Sí, señor. ¡Sí, gracias! ¡Con mucho gusto! ¡Sí, mil gracias!"*

The man's demeanor felt changed. She sensed him turn away. *"Nada va a pasar a esta mujer,"* he told the other man. *"Absolutamente nada."*

Nothing is to happen to this woman.

"What was that about?" the guard asked, still in Spanish.

"Orders," Loudmouth said. "Very *special* orders."

Dominique heard him stalk from the room.

Reprieve.

She drew a long, relieved breath and worked at stretching her stiff knees.

VICENTE HOUSE
LA CALLE SUR 145
DISTRICTO IZTACALCO
2254 HOURS, LOCAL TIME

"That," Procario said, "was fucking brilliant!"

On the laptop display, the male target fondling the woman on the bed had just turned away abruptly and was now going back down the stairs.

"It was also damned risky," Marcetti said. "What if the bastard knew the voice?"

Teller flipped his cell phone shut. "I figured that having 'Juan Escalante' call him would be quite a surprise. He also sounded pretty drunk."

Moments before, they'd engaged yet a third force multiplier, keying in through the satellite network to turn one of the cell phones in that upstairs bedroom into an open microphone. They'd heard the phone's owner, Renaldo Pascua Sosa, speaking with the guard in slurred, drunken tones and then asking if Jackie was going to cooperate with him. With Pascua's phone number on the screen, Teller had pulled out his own phone and keyed in the number, identifying himself as Juan Escalante.

In curt, rough Spanish, Teller had told him that he wanted nothing to happen to the "package," and that Maria would tell him if it did. He'd then told the man that he, Escalante, was trusting Pascua with an important task: delivering the package to another safe house, which would be identified later. If he did, and the woman was not harmed in any way, Escalante would pay Pascua one million pesos—about $75,000.

Even for a narcoterrorist, that was a fairly substantial chunk of change. Pascua's rap sheet identified him as a street-level soldier with the Sinaloa Cartel, a deserter from the Mexican Army. Bank records showed just under half a million pesos in Banamex, a bank in Mexico City, which suggested that a million pesos would grab his attention.

"If they're all drinking," Procario pointed out, "someone else may get ideas."

"Right now, we have Pascua protecting Jackie for us. We need to get in there and take those bastards down before things unravel."

"You also need a new phone," Procario said.

"Why?"

"You just connected to an infected cell phone." He indicated the Cellmap image, where a new blue dot had just winked on across the street from the Perez house and three houses south from Hotel Two.

"Hell with it," Teller said. "Let's get in harness and get on over there."

MARIA PEREZ HOUSE
LA CALLE SUR 145
DISTRICTO IZTACALCO
2258 HOURS, LOCAL TIME

Maria Perez sat on the edge of her bed, her cell phone pressed to her ear. "Juan, I wish you would come here."

"I can't, beloved. Not tonight. I'll be there with Mr. Morales in the morning."

"The men here . . . I'm afraid for the young woman's safety!"

"It's not important. Just so long as she is still alive when we get there."

"Juan . . . I hate this. I don't want to be a part of it!"

"There's nothing that can be done about it. It's out of my hands. That woman is going to be our insurance that the Americans don't interfere with our operations here, or in the north. If she gets hurt along the way, well, that's just the way it is, understand?"

"Juan . . . one of the men here, Pascua. He's been talking about cutting off her fingers and her ears! You can't let him do that!"

"What is that woman to you, Maria?"

"She is a *person*. A human being! Not a . . . a package!"

"You do not understand."

"Look . . . I *know* what . . . what you do! Who you work for! But I never wanted to be part of anything like this! Kidnapping and torture and—"

"*¡Cálmate, chica!*" She heard Escalante sigh. "Very well. I will call Renaldo and have a talk with him. No rough stuff. Okay?"

"I want out of this, Juan. I don't want to be a part of this any longer!"

"I'm sorry, little girl. In this business, there *is* no way out."

"But—"

"Ah! My wife is coming. I must go."

He broke the connection.

STRIKE TEAM FOX ONE
DISTRICTO IZTACALCO
2315 HOURS, LOCAL TIME

Teller moved with the line of ISA commandos from shadow to shadow as they worked their way between the houses on the west side of the street. The alleys here were quite narrow; in some instances, the walls of one house nearly touched those of the next. After crossing the street far enough to the south to avoid being seen by observers at Hotel Two, they'd made their way north until they were in a tiny lane, clogged with garbage, immediately behind Hotel One.

So far, so good. A dog was barking somewhere, but the team appeared to have made it to the back side of Hotel One without alerting anyone. He looked up the sheer wall of the building, at peeling paint and ancient water stains, and felt his back twinge.

He'd been resolutely ignoring the wound in his back since he and Jackie had survived the firefight in the hotel. The wound wasn't bad, a scratch, really, and he had gauze taped over it, but it *hurt*, damn it, when he moved certain ways—and he was about to have to move in certain ways.

"Ready?" Marcetti asked, looking up the back wall of the house.

"Yeah," Staff Sergeant Gerald Rogers said; turning, the man pressed his back against the wall and lifted his boots to press against the wall opposite. "Let's get it on. Climbing."

Teller watched Rogers using an alpinist's chimney climb to begin the ascent. In black utilities and gloves, with a black ski mask over his face, the man was almost invisible in the deep shadow between the houses.

The ISA team had brought plenty of gear for the assault. Teller was carrying an MP-5SD3 strapped across the front of his combat vest—an H&K submachine gun with an integral sound suppressor and retractable buttstock. He had a laser sight clamped to the receiver housing.

His own .45 was holstered at his hip; in the combat vest, he was carrying two M-84 stun grenades, plus two of the more lethal M-67s. He was wearing a LASH II headset connected to his tactical radio, which kept him in constant communications with the other team members, including Procario—designated "X-ray"— back at the OP. Like the others, he wore AN/PVS-21 NVD, which let him see both by amplified and by natural light.

"How we doing?" Marcetti asked over the tactical channel. "Fox Two?"

"Claymore is placed," Patterson's voice said through the molded plug in Teller's left ear. "Moving to position. Ten minutes."

"X-Ray, Fox One. What do you see?"

"Looks quiet," Procario's voice said. "Perez is in the second bedroom. She was on the phone a moment ago, but I wasn't listening in. Right now, I'm tapped into Pascua's phone, and he's in the living room. One guard with the hostage. The other five are downstairs. Hold it. Pascua looks like he's taking a phone call. Let me listen in . . ."

A rope came down from overhead. Marcetti grabbed it and began climbing. The other commandos waited their turn.

"Shit!" Procario's voice said, explosive. "Trouble!"

"Talk to me, X-ray."

"Escalante—the *real* Escalante just called Pascua! They're arguing right now about the money Chris promised him!"

It was Teller's turn to begin his ascent. He tugged on the nylon line and began climbing, knowing that the shit had just hit the fan.

With the assault team not yet in position.

MARIA PEREZ HOUSE
LA CALLE SUR 145
DISTRICTO IZTACALCO,
2316 HOURS, LOCAL TIME

Dominique heard the bedroom door bang open. *"¡Puta!"* Loudmouth shouted. "Whore! What is going on?"

Angry hands grabbed her, and the blindfold was yanked from her face. She blinked, the light in the room painful after hours in darkness. Loudmouth glowered down at her, backlit by the glare of the room's ceiling light fixture.

"Hey, calm down, Renaldo," the guard said. "What's the problem?"

"I don't know—but this bitch knows, and I'm going to find out right now!"

"Are you crazy?"

"Twenty minutes ago I get a call from Mr. Escalante, promising me a million pesos to make sure this whore stays healthy, okay? *Five* minutes ago, I get a call from Mr. Escalante, and he doesn't know anything about it! And his voice . . . his voice was different, too. Someone is fucking playing games with me!"

"How would she know about that? She's been right here the whole time."

"Yeah—but how carefully was she searched when the CISEN guys brought her in, huh? Maybe she has a bug on her, a wire. Maybe they're listening in to us right now! Well, I'm going to find it, and when I do I'm going to take it out of her skin!" The big man took a step back, spread his arms, and looked up at the ceiling. "You hear me up there, gringos?" he shouted in thickly accented English. "I gonna to kill the little bitch! You hear me?"

VICENTE HOUSE
LA CALLE SUR 145
DISTRICTO IZTACALCO
2316 HOURS, LOCAL TIME

Frank Procario leaned his cheek into the Barrett .50's stock, peering through the digital feed sight. A triple-M receiver mounted over the barrel let him see in millimeter waves through the rifle's scope, giving him a low-resolution through-walls view of exactly what he was aiming at. He could hear Pascua's voice over the open mike feed from Pascua's own cell phone, and he could see the man's blurry image as he stood above Dominique's bed, arms spread, head back, as he screamed at the ceiling.

"You hear me up there, gringos?" the man yelled in English, the words slurred by alcohol. *"I gonna to kill the little bitch! You hear me?"*

"I hear you," Procario said quietly. "Gray Fox, X-ray. We have a situation here. Request permission to engage."

CHAPTER FIFTEEN

VICENTE HOUSE
LA CALLE SUR 145
DISTRICTO IZTACALCO
2316 HOURS, LOCAL TIME
20 APRIL

Procario peered through the .50 caliber rifle's scope, finger tightening ever so slightly on the trigger. The scope mount, with a much smaller aperture than the other MMMR receivers, did not yield nearly as much resolution through the eyepiece. Pascua was a man-shaped blur, just barely identifiable as a human being. Even so, Procario could make out details enough to draw down on the target's center of mass—just a bit to the right of where Pascua's heart was positioned in his chest.

The former marine had given a lot of thought to this shot. All along, the plan had been to take out the armed guard seated on an invisible chair in the background. Pascua, though, clearly was the more urgent of the two targets in the room. He was closest to Dominique, and he was raging, acting out of control enough that Procario didn't want to try guessing what the man might do next.

A more serious matter was the wall between Procario and Pascua. Fifty-caliber rounds were designed to penetrate barriers; the round loaded into the Barrett's chamber now was a Raufoss Mk 211, which could penetrate two inches of rolled homogenous armor.

The front wall of the target house was constructed of concrete block, with an outer layer of painted wood and inner layers of drywall and plaster, offering far less of a barrier than two inches of steel. Even concrete, however, could deflect an armor-piercing round like the Mk 211, and if Procario's shot was off by even a few inches, he might hit Dominique, or at the least spray her with high-velocity fragments of concrete and round casing in a 30-degree cone bursting out from the wall. The Mk 211 possessed a heavy tungsten carbide penetrator inside a soft steel cup, packed in behind a charge of RX51-PETN high explosive and an incendiary compound in the projectile's tip. The explosives would punch through the concrete, and the penetrator would keep going to hit the target.

In fact, the Raufoss Mk 211 round was intended as a multipurpose antimatériel projectile, meaning that it could disable a vehicle's engine block or ignite the aviation fuel inside an aircraft but was not intended for use against personnel. The Red Cross had repeatedly tried to have the round banned, and there were various legal challenges to its use. For Procario, however, the question was not whether the round was a humane weapon but whether or not it would do the job that *had* to be done.

Taking a very educated guess, he adjusted his aim point slightly, moving it farther from Dominique . . . and away from a vertical pipe buried in the wall that would definitely deflect the round if he nicked it.

He listened a moment longer to Pascua's drunken rant. *"You hear me?"*

"I hear you," he said. "Gray Fox, X-ray. We have a situation here. Request permission to engage."

"X-ray, Gray Fox," came back. "You are clear to engage."

"Copy clear to engage. I'm taking the shot."

He took a breath . . . released partway . . . held . . . squeezed . . .

MARIA PEREZ HOUSE
LA CALLE SUR 145
DISTRICTO IZTACALCO
2317 HOURS, LOCAL TIME

Dominique lay on her back in the bed, watching Loud-mouth rage . . . and then his chest opened up like a hideously blossoming flower, accompanied by a searing crack from somewhere behind her and toward the foot of the bed. Blood splashed from the man's back in a spray that painted the far wall so close to the seated guard that he fell out of his chair with a clatter. Loud-mouth jerked back a step and collapsed to the floor, his head and right arm very nearly severed from his body.

"¡Madre de Dios!" the guard screamed, his voice cracking. He picked himself up off the floor, mouth gaping through a mask of Loudmouth's blood.

He'd dropped his rifle. He reached for it . . .

VICENTE HOUSE
LA CALLE SUR 145
DISTRICTO IZTACALCO
2317 HOURS, LOCAL TIME

Still leaning into the weapon, Procario shifted aim slightly.

That first shot would have made a god-awful racket inside the house, and the bad guys were now alerted that something was going down. The Barrett .50 had a five-round magazine, however, enough for him to engage each of the targets one by one before he reloaded, choosing the order of execution by determining which target posed the greatest threat to the op, first, and to Jackie Dominique second.

"One Tango down," he murmured into his throat mike. "Acquiring on second target."

MARIA PEREZ HOUSE
LA CALLE SUR 145
DISTRICTO IZTACALCO
2317 HOURS, LOCAL TIME

Dominique knew immediately what was happening. Someone—Chris? Please, God, Chris?—was outside with an MMMR and a Barrett .50, taking down Tangos by literally shooting them right through the concrete-block walls of the house. That meant that a hostage rescue op was under way, that people—*her* people—were going to be coming through that door any moment now.

Stooping, her guard picked up the rifle he'd dropped when Loudmouth had exploded in such spectacular fashion.

Wrong move, kid, she thought.

With a thunderous crack, the left side of the man's head vanished in a spray of blood and brain and chips of bone and his body twisted around sharply with the impact and collapsed, sprawled in a bloody tangle across the legs of his dead partner. A small, round hole appeared in the gore-splattered wall behind him, and then she noticed that there were *two* holes, punched through by the devastating power of the sniper's penetrator rounds.

She decided that it would be a good idea if she got under a bit of cover, just in case other cartel gunmen came through that door before the rescue team did. There was a bit of space between her bed and the wall. She rolled over the edge of the bed, falling with a thud onto the floor, then rolled so that she was completely under the bed.

She could hear shouting on the floor below, and the pounding of boots on the stairs.

FOX ONE
MARIA PEREZ HOUSE
LA CALLE SUR 145
DISTRICTO IZTACALCO
2318 HOURS, LOCAL TIME

Teller was halfway up the back of the house when he heard Procario's quiet voice over the tactical channel.

"One Tango down. Acquiring on number two." Teller heard the second shot, a crash of thunder transmitted over the radio. "Second Tango is down. Hostage has rolled off the bed and is now underneath the mattress."

Good girl. Hostage rescues turned into real nightmares when civilians began jumping up and cheering in the middle of a CQB assault. Then again, if Jackie wasn't in the military, neither was she a civilian. She was highly trained and disciplined. She would know what was happening and do what she could to stay alive during the next crucial few minutes.

No battle plan ever survives contact with the enemy. Von Moltke's maxim was blending now inevitably with the chaos of Murphy's Law. Their meticulous planning and careful preparations all had been thrown off by the "situation" declared by Procario, whatever it was. The Tangos inside Hotel One would be alerted now—as would the overwatch force in Hotel Two. Fox One was not yet on the roof, much less through the rooftop trapdoor, and Fox Two was not yet in position to watch the front door of Hotel Two.

For the next few seconds, *everything* would depend on X-ray, on Procario, back at the OP.

They needed to get inside, fast, and Teller began climbing faster. His back was already shrieking at him, but now he felt something tear. He could only hope it was the adhesive tape holding the gauze in place and not something more organic.

Using his boots to gain what purchase he could against the peeling paint of the building's wall, he kept hauling himself up . . . and up . . .

. . . and then anonymous hands reached down and grabbed the straps of his combat harness, hauling him up and over the wall at the top of the house.

"Thanks," he managed.

"Don't mention it, old man," Marcetti replied.

Old man? He grinned. He wasn't *quite* at the age where he would have to retire from field work just yet. He'd held his own against the Klingons at the Farm . . . when was it? Had that just been a week ago?

He followed Marcetti across the rooftop at an easy lope, uncomfortably aware that they were now in plain sight of anyone on the upper floor of Hotel Two across the street, less than thirty yards away. Originally, they'd planned to roll over the back wall of Hotel One and belly-crawl across to the rooftop door, but it was too late now for such niceties of technique.

One of the ISA commandos stood above the trap-door, holding an M-1014. "Kick it in!" Marcetti snapped.

The M-1014 was the Joint Service Combat Shotgun, in use by various U.S. military services for over ten years. With a removable pistol grip and folding butt-stock, it was ideal for door-kicking, as hostage rescue teams referred to it, especially when firing an Avon round. The M-1030 breaching round was a 1.4-ounce frangible shotgun slug made of powdered steel bound in wax, designed to shatter dead bolts, hinges, or locks and then immediately and harmlessly disperse without injuring possible hostages on the other side.

Bending over the door, Staff Sergeant Schmidt aimed the shotgun at the rusted padlock and pulled the trigger. There was a flash and a boom that echoed off of surrounding houses as the lock and part of the wooden trapdoor disintegrated in flying fragments.

A ladder led down into a darkness only slightly relieved by the AN/PVS-21 unit over his eyes.

"X-ray, Fox One!" Marcetti called. "We're through. Sitrep!"

"Four Tangos on the top landing now, second floor. One of them moving toward objective bedroom. Engaging . . ."

They heard the sharp crack of the rifle from across the street toward the south . . .

MARIA PEREZ HOUSE
LA CALLE SUR 145
DISTRICTO IZTACALCO
2318 HOURS, LOCAL TIME

Enrico Barrón had just reached the bedroom door when an explosive detonation cracked from the hallway's east wall, a couple of yards to his right. Chunks of concrete and bits of metal slashed across the side of his face and arm, and a pencil-thick hole appeared in the wooden door a few inches in front of his eyes.

"*¡Diablo!*" he cried, hurling himself backward, stumbling, then falling to the floor. He didn't know how a sniper could have targeted him through a solid wall, but he did know what was happening. The Mexican military used Barrett .50 sniper rifles, and the powerful BMG rounds they fired—the acronym stood for "Browning Machine Gun," the weapon for which they'd originally been manufactured—could easily punch through concrete.

Was the sniper firing blind? Barrón didn't think so, though it was possible a police assault team was putting BMGs through the walls of the house randomly in order to cause confusion at the beginning of an attack. More likely, the expected American force, CIA or DEA, was launching an attack, and *they* wouldn't risk hitting the prisoner by accident.

There were rumors—hints of technologies on American TV and in novels—that the CIA had devices that *could* see through walls.

That shot that had just missed him had come *entirely* too close to have happened by random chance.

"Carlos!" he cried at the man who'd been behind him in the hall. "Grab the girl! Grab the girl now!" He remained motionless on the floor as he yelled. If the bastards outside *could* somehow see through walls, they would think that they'd hit him.

VICENTE HOUSE
LA CALLE SUR 145
DISTRICTO IZTACALCO
2318 HOURS, LOCAL TIME

"Tango three down," Procario said, still watching through the triple-M scope. One of the four men in the hallway outside Dominique's door had dropped to the floor, but the next in line was reaching for the knob.

Over the open microphone line, he could hear someone yelling, *"¡Agarra la chica! ¡Agarra la chica ahora!"*

The Tango was through the door.

FOX ONE
MARIA PEREZ HOUSE
LA CALLE SUR 145
DISTRICTO IZTACALCO
2318 HOURS, LOCAL TIME

Master Sergeant Randolph Cameche was first down the ladder, closely followed by Marcetti, Schmidt, Rogers, and finally Teller. Each man hit the floor and moved immediately, making way for the next man down.

The hallway was dark, though their NVD amplified what light there was. A lot of light spilled from around the 90-degree bend to the left in the hallway up ahead. Closed doors to left and right should be empty rooms; Maria Perez's door was directly ahead, a bright strip of yellow light showing at the bottom. The landing at the top of the stairs leading down to the first floor was ahead and on the right.

In close single file, each man touching the man ahead, the assault team started forward.

VICENTE HOUSE
LA CALLE SUR 145
DISTRICTO IZTACALCO
2319 HOURS, LOCAL TIME

Maria Perez had heard the racket—at least three loud shots, they had to be gunshots—plus a fourth, deep-throat boom that sounded like it was right outside her door. Her first impulse was to stay put, perhaps even to hide—but all she could imagine was that Barrón or Pascua had decided to execute the prisoner.

Rising from her bed, she hurried to the door and yanked it open.

Directly in front of her, nightmare shapes, black clad, hunched over, their faces looking like those of huge alien insects in a bad sci-fi movie were moving directly toward her. To her right, down the hallway toward the front of the house, two gunmen stood outside of the prisoner's door, a third was lying on the floor.

Maria screamed.

FOX ONE
MARIA PEREZ HOUSE
LA CALLE SUR 145
DISTRICTO IZTACALCO
2319 HOURS, LOCAL TIME

"Fox One, X-ray," Procario's voice called. "Perez is—"

At that moment, the door at the end of the short hallway opened, and an attractive young woman in a translucent negligee took one step into the hall, saw the advancing assault force, put her hands to her face, and shrieked.

"—coming out the door in front of you," Procario finished. "Tangos are now in Jackie's room."

First in line, Cameche lunged forward, grabbing the woman around her waist and knocking her down and back into her room.

Marcetti was next; with his H&K planted against his shoulder, he rolled around the corner and immediately began taking fire from the doorway opening into Dominique's room. Nine-millimeter slugs slapped against his tactical vest, knocking him back a step, but he leaned into his weapon and squeezed the trigger, sending two three-round bursts down the hall, striking the drug-gang member and splintering the doorjamb. The integral silencer softened the shots to triplets of dull clicks; the sound of bullets shredding wood was louder.

Teller followed Marcetti, Schmidt, and Rogers down the hallway, reaching the door before the gangster's body toppled out and onto the body already on the

floor. There was a ragged hole in the door caused by
the tungsten carbide penetrator from one of Procario's
rounds. No blood.

He heard someone shouting on the other side of the
door. *"¡Venga! ¡Ven aqui, chica!"*

Hang on, Jackie, he thought with fierce determination. *Help's on the way!*

VICENTE HOUSE
LA CALLE SUR 145
DISTRICTO IZTACALCO
2319 HOURS, LOCAL TIME

Procario was trying to watch the whole firefight unfold
at once, and it was proving too much for one man. Normally, a sniper had an observer, an assistant at his side
to help keep track of enemy targets as well as to sound
off on hits, but this time there just weren't enough men
to cover everything, and an observer was a luxury he
would do without.

He'd seen one Tango go through, closely followed
by two more—but then he'd glimpsed movement in the
bedroom opposite the short hallway down which the
assault team was moving. He'd shifted his aim to cover
Perez, since she was the most immediate threat to the
strike team. Until she proved otherwise Maria Perez
was a noncombatant, though they all knew better than
to trust her.

Procario checked to see that she didn't have a
weapon—through his MMMR scope she was stark
naked—and gave the warning. As Cameche tackled

her to take her out of the line of fire, he shifted his aim back to Dominique's room, then bit off a curse.

One Tango in the door, aiming up the hall . . . no, *shooting* up the hall as Marcetti rounded the corner. The other two—they'd spotted Dominique under the bed and were on the floor now, trying to grab her and drag her out.

He took aim at the gunman in the door, his cross-hairs centering on the back of his head . . . but Marcetti had already returned fire, and the Tango crumpled across the body already on the floor. Inside the room, one Tango was hiding behind the door, a pistol raised in his hands, while the other hauled Dominique to her feet, clutching her close against his body.

Stalemate. He couldn't tag the Tango behind the door because the strike force was now lined up out in the hallway to either side of the same door—and someone, he thought it was Teller, was in the way. He couldn't shoot that Tango without risking hitting one of his own men, and he couldn't hit the one holding Dominique without possibly killing her.

"Fox One, X-ray," he said. "Okay . . . you've got two Tangos in there, one right behind the door—to your left of the door, about two feet—and one Tango holding Jackie about five feet straight back from the door. Shit."

"What is it, X-ray?"

"Tango two has a gun against her head. I can't get a clear shot, damn it, *I can't get a clear shot!*"

FOX TWO
LA CALLE SUR 145
DISTRICTO IZTACALCO
2320 HOURS, LOCAL TIME

Randy Patterson was moving at a dead run. He'd estimated ten minutes to work his way carefully back
down the street, crossing at a point where the occu-
pants of Hotel Two couldn't see him, and working his
way back up the west side of the street. He'd been
crossing the road when he'd heard Procario call a situation and receive permission to fire.

Yeah, old Murphy, God of Battles, was out in full
force tonight. As he ran, he heard the first, loud crack
of Procario's .50 up the street, followed a couple of seconds later by a second. The hollow boom of Schmidt's
combat shotgun had sounded next, and then the Barrett
had fired a third time. A moment later, he heard the
high-pitched crack of a 9 mm pistol inside the house.

Leaping a pile of garbage, he landed in the tiny front
yard of the house south of Hotel Two. The building was
a ruin, partly burned out, the yard littered with empty
cans and bottles, rags and paper, and hypodermic nee-
dles. A really great neighborhood.

Across the street and to the north, he could see the
front door of Hotel Two opening, light from inside
spilling into the night.

He was holding the firing trigger in his hand.

Normally, the M-18A1 claymore was detonated by
an M-57 firing device known as the "clacker," connected to the mine by a long cable, or by using tripwires

or other mechanical firing devices. This time, though, the firing trigger was a radio transmitter; a three-number code was punched into the handset, and then the ENTER key was pressed, a two-stage trigger designed to prevent accidental detonation from garage door openers or cell phones.

Patterson still wasn't in position, but he could see gunmen spilling out of Hotel Two's front door. The claymore was resting upright on its two pairs of scissored legs in the street, in plain view of anyone emerging from the house.

He had to detonate the device *now*.

Pulling his glove off so he could better manipulate the keys, Patterson punched in the code.

FOX ONE
MARIA PEREZ HOUSE
LA CALLE SUR 145
DISTRICTO IZTACALCO
2320 HOURS, LOCAL TIME

"Damn it, I can't get a clear shot!"

Teller turned and placed one hand against the wall to his left. According to Procario, there was a Tango immediately behind that wall, just a few inches away. Teller couldn't see him, but Procario could through his MMMR scope.

"X-ray," Teller called. "Where's my hand in relation to Tango one?"

"Move it a little to your left . . . good. Now down . . . yeah! Right there. Your hand is right next to his head."

That told Teller that the Tango was crouching, right *there,* waiting for the assault team to come through the door.

Jackie might be in the line of fire, though. "If I shoot straight through, will I hit Jackie?"

"Angle your fire to the left. Jackie's to your right."

"Got it."

Teller exchanged a look with Marcetti, who nodded. The ISA captain raised a gloved hand and snapped off a string of commands using sign language alone. *Schmidt . . . ready with the shotgun! Stand here . . . angle the weapon down! Rogers, ready with a flashbang!* Out loud, he added, "X-ray, if you see your shot, take it."

"Copy."

Marcetti held up three fingers and performed a silent countdown. *In three . . . two . . . one . . . go!*

Teller pulled the trigger on his H&K. The weapon's selector only allowed single shots or three-round bursts, not full-auto, but he tapped off five triplets in a good simulation of full rock-and-roll, the 9 mm rounds splintering soft drywall, cracked plaster, studs, and joists.

At the same instant, Schmidt's M-1014 boomed, the noise deafening in the narrow hallway, the weapon angled sharply to fire downward toward the floor in order to avoid hitting Dominique. The doorknob and a square foot of the door smashed in and the door flew open. Leaning around the door frame, Rogers underhanded an M-84 stun grenade—colloquially known as a flashbang—into the room.

The flashbang gave them a decided edge. The dazzling strobe effect of a white-hot burning mixture of aluminum and magnesium generated a glare measuring over a million candela, and the bang hit 180 decibels within five feet of detonation. The flash was enough to blind people in the room for about five seconds, while the noise overwhelmed the senses, causing shock and disorientation.

Teller just hoped that it would be *enough* of an edge.

FOX TWO
LA CALLE SUR 145
DISTRICTO IZTACALCO
2320 HOURS, LOCAL TIME

Patterson pressed the three-number code. The last digit was a 1, and he chuckled as he said, "Press one for English, dudes." Then he pressed ENTER.

The flash bounced off the walls of houses on both sides of the street, as did the crack of the explosion. The gentle curve of the claymore unit, with its embossed FRONT TOWARD ENEMY across the convex face, contained a flat layer of C-4 explosives behind seven hundred steel balls embedded in resin, each about an eighth of an inch in diameter. When the C-4 went off, the steel balls hurtled out in a fan-shaped cloud spanning 60 degrees and traveling at almost four thousand feet per second.

The ideal range for the weapon was fifty yards, which allowed for a good dispersion pattern, but Patterson had been forced to set the mine on the street in front of the target house, in this neighborhood a range of less than four yards. That meant the claymore's projectile cloud was still tightly focused when it struck Hotel Two's front door, sweeping through the first few emerging gunmen like a vast, bloody scythe.

Patterson reached his planned hide a moment later, dropping the detonator and unclipping his H&K. The fact that he'd been rushed had resulted in a less than perfect shot. The front door and part of the wall to either side had disintegrated, and three or four gunmen, at least, had been cut down.

Someone at the house had seen him moving into position, and automatic gunfire began snapping and hissing around him an instant later.

Kneeling behind a rotted and crumbling fence, Patterson returned fire. The H&K SD5, excellent for close-in CQB, was less than optimum out on the street. At a range of over forty yards, he couldn't see the red dot from his laser sight and had to aim at moving shadows spreading out into the street.

He heard the boom of Schmidt's combat shotgun to his left.

At the same instant, he saw someone emerge from the open front door of Hotel Two, someone carrying what looked like a length of pipe balanced on his shoulder.

Oh . . . *Jesus!*

CHAPTER SIXTEEN

MARIA PEREZ HOUSE
LA CALLE SUR 145
DISTRICTO IZTACALCO
2320 HOURS, LOCAL TIME
20 APRIL

The gunman was holding Dominique tightly from behind, a pistol pressed up against the side of her head. *"¡Oye!"* the man screamed. *"¡Oye, ustedes allá! ¡No fuego! ¡Tengo la chica aqui!"*

Then everything began happening at once.

The gunman crouching beside the door with a drawn pistol crumpled as bullet holes loosed blossoming puffs of plaster dust beside him. At the same instant, the bedroom door seemed to explode, with chips of wood whirling past her face. A black tube with rows of holes down the side skittered through the opening and across the floor, passing to her right.

Dominique knew immediately what it was—a flash-bang stun grenade. She squeezed her eyes tight and twisted away to her left, bending forward as far as she could.

The flashbang detonated somewhere behind her, the strobe of dazzling magnesium-aluminum light so brilliant it glared through her eyelids, the concussive blast quite literally deafening. The man holding her tightened his grip convulsively; Dominique's wrists and legs were still tied, but as the grenade's multiple detonations slammed at her senses, she snapped her head up and back, connecting *hard* with her captor's nose.

Black-garbed men wearing ski masks and night-vision devices were storming in through the open door.

FOX ONE
MARIA PEREZ HOUSE
LA CALLE SUR 145
DISTRICTO IZTACALCO
2320 HOURS, LOCAL TIME

They were taking a hell of a chance, Teller knew, but it was a justified one, more justified than it might have seemed at first glance. The man holding Dominique needed her alive, needed her as a bargaining chip, as a get-out-of-jail-free card, as a guarantee that the American strike team wasn't going to shoot him out of hand. He knew that the moment he pulled the trigger, he was a dead man, so he was far more likely to open fire at the strike team than at his prisoner.

Hostage rescue teams rely on three key assets in a takedown: surprise, overwhelming firepower, and sudden violence of action. The team had lost the element of surprise, but violence they still possessed in abundance. Storm into that bedroom hard enough, loud enough, and violently enough and the gunman would almost certainly freeze, just for a moment—and in that second or two while his brain was juggling the problem of killing the hostage or killing his attackers, of surrendering or fighting or running, the strike team would have its chance.

Of course, that reasoning wasn't foolproof. In combat there are never certainties, only probabilities, possibilities, and the nightmare of plain random chance. The gunman's finger might tighten on the trigger because of shock or muscle spasm, and then Dominique would be dead.

If the team did nothing, if they let the gunman negotiate an escape, Dominique would almost certainly be killed anyway as soon as he no longer needed her.

All they had to ride on was the flashbang and sheer violence of action.

Marcetti, Schmidt, Rogers, and Teller rolled around the doorjamb and through the shattered door, moving left and right to gain separate angles on the target. Three bright dots of laser light danced across the gunman's head inches to the left of Dominique's face.

Then they had some unexpected help from Dominique herself. As he came through the door, Teller saw her bend far forward, then snap her head back, smashing the gunman's nose with the back of her skull. His grip loosened, and she pitched herself forward, *almost* breaking free—

Her head was clear. Teller tapped the trigger of his H&K at the same moment as Marcetti and Rogers, and the cartel gunman spun to the side.

At the same instant, a fist-sized hole opened in the bedroom's east wall between two others already there, emitting a spray of concrete and plaster dust. The gunman's throat and upper chest simply came apart in a dark scarlet spray, his head literally torn from his body.

"Clear!" Marcetti called.

"Clear!" Teller, Rogers, and Schmidt echoed, pivoting with their weapons to check every corner of that blood-drenched room. The flashbang, Teller noted, had rolled under the bed and set fire to the sheets, and flames were beginning to lick against the wall.

No matter; they had plenty of time yet. Teller stepped forward, stooping to help Dominique.

But something was horribly wrong.

FOX TWO
LA CALLE SUR 145
DISTRICTO IZTACALCO
2320 HOURS, LOCAL TIME

Patterson saw the shadow with the pipe on its shoulder turning to face him, saw another shadow stoop and point. He began tapping off three-round bursts, trying to hit those shadows . . . but then there was a flash and a streak of motion, something hurtling straight toward him faster than the eye could really register.

The rocket-propelled grenade hissed a few feet above his head, then struck the brick wall of the ruined shell of a house behind him. The blast picked him up and smashed him sideways through the rotting fence.

He lost consciousness when he hit the street.

VICENTE HOUSE
LA CALLE SUR 145
DISTRICTO IZTACALCO
2320 HOURS, LOCAL TIME

An instant after dropping the hammer on the remaining Tango in the bedroom, Procario saw the flash from the RPG out of the corner of his eye, saw the streak and the detonation of the five-pound rocket across the street, saw Patterson hurled through the fence and sprawling onto the pavement.

"Man down!" he called. "Fox Two is down!"

Swinging the long, heavy barrel of his Barrett .50 to the right, Procario looked for a target. *There* . . . two men just emerging from behind the front wall of the Vicente house and entering the street. One carried the empty tube of an RPG-7 launcher; the second was pulling a fresh round from his backpack and helping the first man reload.

"No you don't," Procario said, and he squeezed the trigger.

The man carrying the grenade launcher came apart.

FOX ONE
MARIA PEREZ HOUSE
LA CALLE SUR 145
DISTRICTO IZTACALCO
2321 HOURS, LOCAL TIME

Teller heard Procario's call of "man down" over the tactical channel, but his mind was grappling with another problem, even more immediate, if subtle. Three of the four bodies in the bedroom had been struck by BMG rounds, and the result was a charnel-house horror of blood and body parts, so much so that the west wall of the bedroom was almost completely covered by gory splashes of the stuff.

What was wrong?

He pulled his combat knife and cut through the ropes tying Dominique's hands and legs. Her eyes opened, but she was having trouble focusing. He pulled off the gag. "Are you okay? Jackie! Are you okay?"

"What?" she said. "Chris? I can't hear you."

The assault team had been wearing earpieces that automatically blocked out gunshots and louder noises, but Dominique had caught the full force of the detonating stun grenade. She would be okay . . . she *had* to be okay . . .

As he turned to help her sit up, he glanced out through the smashed-in door at the two bodies laying outside in the hall.

Then it clicked, and he shouted the warning, *"Threat to the rear!"*

MARIA PEREZ HOUSE
LA CALLE SUR 145
DISTRICTO IZTACALCO
2321 HOURS, LOCAL TIME

Enrico Barrón had been playing dead for almost three minutes now, lying on the floor, his legs beneath Jose Flores's dead body. Through slitted eyes, he'd seen the assault team—Americans, with those black utilities, vests, and NVDs they *had* to be Americans—move down the hall in single file, blast open the door, and storm through into the bedroom. His pistol lay on the floor next to his hip; his hand was inching toward the weapon. His hand closed on the grip as he heard the Americans shouting, "Clear!"

With both Carlos and Juan dead, they would be checking the bodies, and they would find that he was unhurt. Clearly, they were wearing some sort of ballistic armor under those tactical vests, or the vests themselves were armored, because Jose had pumped three rounds into one of them without visible effect.

He would have to shoot at their heads, which were protected only by wool balaclavas and the plastic and metal complexities of those night-vision goggles they wore.

"Threat to the rear!"

Damn! What had given him away? He lunged to his left, jerking his legs out from under Juan's body, raising his weapon as he did so, squeezing the trigger again and again and again. Gunshots banged loud in the narrow hallway; one of the American commandos staggered, hit . . .

Barrón was on his feet and running down the hall toward the stairs.

VICENTE HOUSE
LA CALLE SUR 145
DISTRICTO IZTACALCO
2321 HOURS, LOCAL TIME

The RPG gunner was dead, torn in half by Procario's shot, but other cartel gunmen were racing across the street now, headed toward the front of the Perez house. One of them ran toward Patterson's still form, motionless on the pavement.

Procario swung the muzzle back to the left, tracking just ahead of the running man, his finger tightening on the weapon's trigger.

Nothing happened.

Damn it to hell! A rookie's stunt; the Barrett .50 fired from a five-round magazine, and in the past four minutes or so he'd engaged five targets. His chamber was locked open, the magazine empty.

Swearing viciously, Procario thumbed the mag release, then groped for a fresh load sitting on the table beside him. He snapped it home and chambered the first round just as the running cartel gunman reached Patterson, standing directly over him, and began firing his M-16, emptying a twenty-round magazine into the motionless body.

A terrible, icy calm descended over Procario as he watched the gunman reload, then turn and begin jogging toward the front of Hotel One. Other men were crossing the street from Hotel Two, all of them heavily armed. The temptation to shoot the man who'd just killed Patterson was almost overwhelming, but Procario suppressed the impulse. The cartel force was storming into Hotel One now, cutting off Fox One's route of retreat. This wasn't about simple-minded revenge.

It was about which tactics would best help the team inside that house.

FOX ONE
MARIA PEREZ HOUSE
LA CALLE SUR 145
DISTRICTO IZTACALCO
2321 HOURS, LOCAL TIME

Teller scooped up his H&K as the gunman in the hallway fired wildly into the room. Marcetti was hit, a round striking him in the right shoulder and spinning him around. Schmidt triggered his shotgun; the frangible round splintered a section of wall as the cartel gunman got to his feet and started running. Teller and Rogers both fired three-round bursts, tracking the man as he vanished behind the bedroom wall . . . and then the target was gone.

Lunging forward, he brought the weapon up to his shoulder as he rolled around the doorjamb and into the hall.

A few feet ahead, Cameche stepped into the hall just ahead of the running gunman, between the fugitive and the stairs, his own H&K raised. *"¡Alto!* Drop it!"

The gunman dropped his pistol—its slide was locked open over an empty chamber—and raised his hands. *"¡No fuego!* Don't shoot!"

Teller came up behind him, spun him around to face

the wall, kicked his feet apart, and roughly searched him for weapons. He had none. As Cameche grabbed the man's collar and rammed his face against the plaster, Teller used a plastic zip-strip to bind his wrists behind his back.

"Patterson is dead," Procario's voice said over the tactical channel. "You have five . . . no, six, repeat *six* Tangos, M-16s and one AK, all coming in through the front door."

The shock of having lost a team member was like a heavy slam to the gut. The op had gone seriously sour. Jackie was okay—he *prayed* she was okay—but one of their team members was dead, and the rest of them, minus Procario, were trapped on the upper floor of Hotel One. *Not* good . . .

Teller grabbed the prisoner's collar and shoved him into the second bedroom, tripped him, forced him down onto the floor. The woman, Maria Perez, lay on the bed, her wrists zip-stripped behind her, her eyes very wide. Standard operating procedure for a hostage rescue: Anyone you didn't know, even an unarmed civilian, was handcuffed or zip-stripped, both to keep them from wandering around in a firefight and to keep them from grabbing a weapon and becoming combatants.

"X-ray, Fox One," Marcetti said. His voice sounded taut with pain. "See what you can do about our friends on the stairs."

"Copy. Target acquired."

MARIA PEREZ HOUSE
LA CALLE SUR 145
DISTRICTO IZTACALCO
2322 HOURS, LOCAL TIME

Carlos Mora Barquin reached the first-floor stairs at the back of the house and looked up. He couldn't see anyone up there, but he heard the thud of booted feet, heard someone speaking in English. He slapped Julio Mazariegos on the shoulder and pointed. Go!

The *yanqui* commando outside had been a nasty surprise, as had the claymore outside of the safehouse. That mine had shredded three of his boys before they'd made it out the door, and the commando had killed two more. Jorge had been killed by a sniper after firing his RPG.

Mora's training with the Guatemalan Kaibiles had given him a keen understanding of close-quarters tactics, of fire and movement. He'd been to this house several times, learning the location of each room, wall, and corridor. It was a small house, with the upstairs smaller than the first floor—just two bedrooms on the second floor plus several closets and a bathroom at the front of the house, and with a ladder going up to the roof. The attackers would be toward the front of the house, in the first bedroom . . . about *there* . . .

Circling his arm rapidly, he sent the rest of his men up toward the second floor.

VICENTE HOUSE
LA CALLE SUR 145
DISTRICTO IZTACALCO
2322 HOURS, LOCAL TIME

The stairway leading from the first floor to the second was toward the back of the house, and that presented Procario with a nasty problem. The angle, shooting down from the third floor of the Vicente house, was such that his shots had to pierce Hotel One's front wall, at least one interior wall, and the floor in order to reach the line of men now ascending the stairs. The BMG round had tremendous penetrating power, but he wasn't sure that after going through the concrete at the front, it would have the power to punch through the floor as well, especially since there were twelve-inch vertical joists supporting the floorboards at two-foot intervals.

He picked the first man in line, now halfway up the steps, tracked him . . . drew breath . . . held . . . *squeezed* . . .

MARIA PEREZ HOUSE
LA CALLE SUR 145
DISTRICTO IZTACALCO
2322 HOURS, LOCAL TIME

A loud crack snapped through the house, splinters flew from the banister beside the steps, and Julio yelped. "I'm hit!"

"Keep moving, *'mano*!" Mora yelled. "You move, they can't hit you!"

That wasn't entirely true, but he needed to keep his people from breaking. Even the ex-soldiers among them didn't have that much training, and charging up the stairs inside a darkened house was a tough thing to ask even of elite Fuerzos Especiales. That last round had punched down through the floor, and that made the rush even more unnerving.

If they could just reach the landing at the top of the steps . . .

FOX ONE
MARIA PEREZ HOUSE
LA CALLE SUR 145
DISTRICTO IZTACALCO
2322 HOURS, LOCAL TIME

Teller was waiting as the head of the first Tango in line appeared above the steps. The hallway was dark, but through his NVDs the man was brightly lit. The red aim-dot from Teller's laser sights rippled across the man's upper chest, and then Teller tapped a three-round burst into the target, knocking him backward.

Schmidt and Cameche each tossed grenades at the same moment—one M-67 and one M-84. The flashbang went off first, filling the stairway with a sun-bright flare of raw light, the fragmentation grenade detonating an instant later with a shrill bang.

Screams sounded from the darkness downstairs. Marcetti yelled, *"Go! Go!"* and Teller advanced to the top of the stairs, H&K at the ready.

Three bodies lay at the bottom of the steps, entangled in splatters of blood, two of them still moving. Teller loosed two more bursts into the tangle, silencing the screams; a fourth body lay motionless halfway down the steps.

"You have two Tangos downstairs," Procario's voice said over the tactical channel. "They're moving back down the main hall . . . they're moving into the living room, the big room at the front of the house."

Confident that no one was waiting down there in the darkness to pop them as they came down the stairs, Teller led the way down the blast-broken steps, picking his way over the first body, and across a gap where two steps had been partially torn away by the frag grenade.

"Tangos are preparing to engage," Procario said. "Hold your position."

As he came off the stairs, Teller could see the entrance to the living room twenty feet ahead. He dropped into a crouch, weapon aimed at the opening.

A loud crack sounded from the living room, and someone screamed. "One Tango down," Procario reported, and then a second BMG shot rattled windows. "Two Tangos down," and then an explosion hurled bits of furniture into the hallway. "Second one had a grenade," Procario added. "Tangos neutralized."

"Let's go," Marcetti asked. "Watch out for snipers. *Their* snipers."

"According to Cellmap, Hotel Two is empty," Procario said. "You're good to egress."

That was comforting, but the team didn't relax. There was always the chance that someone *without* a cell phone had remained behind with a rifle.

Holding the prisoner's bound arms, Cameche steered their captive out the front door, with Teller and Dominique close behind. No shots were fired, but sirens shrilled and growled in the distance, coming closer. As Teller stepped out onto the street, he glanced up and saw a yellow glow flickering inside the upstairs front bedroom—the fire started by the flashbang. In this neighborhood, a house fire could be a serious danger to the entire block.

Teller didn't know if those were fire sirens approaching or police, called in by reports of a running gun battle on Calle Sur 145, but either way the assault team needed to get clear, and quickly. The local authorities would not take kindly to Americans shooting Mexican citizens, no matter what the provocation.

Schmidt and Rogers found Patterson's body sprawled in the street and picked it up between them.

No man left behind.

"The Perez woman," Dominique told Teller. "She . . . she tried to help me."

"Hey, March?" Teller said. "I think we can let the woman go."

Marcetti nodded. "Do it."

Cameche cut the zip-strip binding Perez's wrists.

"Sorry about your house, Miss Perez," Teller said. "But you're free to go."

"¡Por favor, no!" she cried. Tears were streaming down her cheeks as the words tumbled out. She shifted to English. "Please, please, let me come with you! If . . . if *they* know that I survived, they will think I helped

you! You . . . have no idea what these people can do, what they *will* do!"

"We have a pretty good idea, Señorita Perez," Marcetti said. "We *do* know that you're the niece of Jaime Perez, and the girlfriend of Juan Escalante, however. We're going to want you to answer some questions for us."

"Anything!" she replied. "Absolutely anything! I . . . I am *sick* of this life."

Together, they hurried down the street to the Vicente house.

Fifteen minutes later, they were crowded into the upstairs bedroom. The street outside was crowded with fire trucks and emergency vehicles; rotating light bars sent waves of red and blue and white light across the faces of the nearby buildings. Police were cordoning off the bodies in the street as firefighters played streams of water into the bedroom of the Perez house.

Antonio Vicente stood in the hallway, hands on hips, managing to look furious and terrified at the same time. "You no should do this!" he cried in broken English. "If the drug lords, they suspect you have been here, in my house, my life is not worth a single peso!"

"We got them all, Señor Vicente," Marcetti said. He was sitting on the bed with his shirt off, allowing Rogers to apply gauze pads and medical tape to his bloody shoulder. The bullet had gone clean through, breaking his clavicle, scapula, and one rib, but first aid measures had stopped the bleeding, and the wound was not otherwise serious. "No one knows you helped us."

"The police outside, they are talking to my neighbors. If they come here and search—"

"They will need a federal search warrant," Procario said, interrupting. As in the United States, the police needed a warrant to enter a citizen's home. "By the time they obtain one, we will be long gone."

"If you want to come with us, Señor Vicente," Teller said, "I'm sure we can find room for one more."

"No. No . . . I will stay here. Mexico is my country."

"How about it, March?" Teller asked. "We're not going to be needing our walking-around cash, are we?"

"That's a thought. Jackie? The case is over there, by the table. Give it to Señor Vicente, please."

Inside the briefcase were almost one million pesos—over $75,000—in bills of various denominations. The money had been issued to Teller and Procario by the Agency, money to survive in the streets, if necessary, to bribe officials, or to tracelessly hire vehicles. They'd spent some of it to rent cars and hotel rooms while they were in Mexico, but most of it was still there.

Vicente stared at the money, uncomprehending, at first. "*Ese . . . ese es por mí?*"

"You've been a good friend, Señor Vicente," Marcetti said. "And you've been of incredible help, both to us and to your country."

"Just one thing," Teller said. "I urge you to move, and quickly. If you won't come with us, then sell the house and move someplace else. The man who first told us about you—"

"Señor de la Cruz?"

"Yes. He . . . is not to be trusted."

"But . . . he is National Security. Like your CIA, no?"

"Like our CIA, yes," Procario told him. "But he arranged to have our friend Jackie here kidnapped. And he probably arranged to have that army here tonight, to ambush us. The whole thing tonight was a trap."

"*Dios mio . . .*"

"Chances are, he won't bother you," Marcetti said. "But it's better to be safe."

"*Gracias,*" Vicente said, closing the briefcase. "*Mil gracias, por los todos.*"

After Vicente had left, Dominique looked at Teller. "Just how dirty do you think de la Cruz is, anyway?" she asked. "I couldn't tell if he was behind killing Ed and having me picked up, or if maybe cartel thugs forced him."

"I think he's *dirty* dirty," Teller said. "He was trying to plant misinformation from the beginning—al Qaeda smuggling nukes to attack Mexico, remember? Then it was *his* suggestion to put Escalante under surveillance, and him who introduced us to Vicente."

"He ordered me and Ed out of the country," Dominique said.

"Yeah—and you were picked up by a motorcycle almost at once, weren't you? The bomb was meant to kill you, but when he found out you were alive, he showed up with a couple of cartel bully-boys to make you disappear."

"I checked at the hospital," Procario said. "There was no visitor's log, but the charge nurse told me there were three CISEN officers in to see you, including de la Cruz. She identified his file photo and said he'd been the one to order you held after you were treated, and *then* he ordered you released so you could go with him. And later he told us he didn't know where you were."

"Shit," Marcetti said. "De la Cruz told you about Vicente? That means the cartels know about him, too. He's dead. I'm surprised they didn't attack the house tonight."

"They probably didn't attack because we were the prime targets," Teller said. "And if he gets out of town fast, he should be okay. That's why I lit a fire under him."

"We might talk to someone at the U.S. Embassy," Procario said. "They might be able to help him. Maybe grant him asylum."

"Good thought," Marcetti said. "Neither the Zetas nor the Sinaloans are particularly forgiving in nature."

"So how about us?" Dominique asked. "How are we getting out of here?"

"Already taken care of," Procario said with a grin. "Our plane is waiting for us at BJ International. All we need to do is get there."

CHAPTER SEVENTEEN

OVER THE GULF OF MEXICO
0815 HOURS, LOCAL TIME
21 APRIL

As promised, the Beechcraft Model 400 Beechjet was waiting for them at Benito Juárez International, a small twin-turbofan passenger jet that could seat up to nine passengers. Procario had pulled some strings with IN-SCOM to have the jet chartered and readied for them, knowing that they'd likely have to make a fast exit.

The toughest part had been waiting out the police and fire officials in the street. Long after the fire was out, they'd been probing about within both Hotel One and Hotel Two, collecting shell casings and other evidence, bagging bodies, and talking to civilians. It wasn't until after six that the Americans had finally gone down to the street, gotten into their rented cars, and driven to the airport. If the police had noticed the rentals from their license plates and made inquiries, there was no sign. Most likely, the authorities were assuming that the gunfight was another shoot-out between rival drug factions—something that had been increasingly common over the past decade—and hadn't gotten around to thinking about the possible involvement of U.S. intelligence. De la Cruz would know the truth, but he seemed to have vanished. Teller had tried phoning him, intending to transmit the Cellmap virus, but got no answer.

No matter. Once the number was entered into Teller's infected phone, the virus would jump to the new number whether the connection was active or not.

De la Cruz would know that he was burned. He'd probably gone into hiding, though the team took extra precautions getting to the airport. A last-ditch attempt to kill them was not impossible, and Teller was concerned that the rental cars were now hot.

Their weapons and special gear—all save their personal sidearms—had gone into airport storage for collection by the Agency later. Teller had waved a diplomatic immunity pass at security, and they'd been airborne shortly after 0730.

They were flying northeast, en route for Eglin Air Force Base on the Florida panhandle some 930 nautical miles from Mexico City, with a total expected flight time of a bit over two hours. Eighteen minutes after takeoff, they crossed over the beach south of the refinery at Tampamachoco and were out over the Gulf of Mexico, free and clear.

Teller at last began to relax somewhat.

"You okay?" he asked Dominique. "How're your ears?"

"Fine, Chris, better. They were ringing last night—I couldn't hear much of anything coming out of that house. But I'm okay."

"We . . . took an awful chance."

She laid a slim hand on his wrist. "Chris, it's *okay*. You did what you had to do. If you hadn't, I wouldn't be here now."

Teller nodded, but he wasn't happy. If that cartel gunman had tensed when the flashbang had gone off, if he'd shot her . . .

He was angry, too, that he'd missed an obvious warning flag: Enrico Barrón, lying on the floor of the Perez house with no blood on him—an impossibility if he'd been hit by Procario's through-the-wall cannon. Close-quarters assaults stressed putting a round through a downed Tango's head if there was any doubt, but he'd been so anxious about reaching Jackie that he'd looked at Barrón on the floor and not really *seen*, not until it was too late.

Still, they wouldn't have a prisoner now if Barrón had been dead—and Jackie had come through the ordeal temporarily deaf, but in one piece. All in all, not a bad evening's work.

Teller's normal good spirits were reasserting themselves now that they were out of the combat zone. He rose from his seat and walked forward, joining Procario, who was sitting opposite the prisoner.

Enrico Barrón looked at Teller incuriously, then shrugged, looking away. "You have no right to do this, gringo," he said. His English was excellent. "I have not been properly extradited to the United States. When I engage a lawyer, he will have me free so quickly that your fucking heads will spin."

"*Really,* Señor Barrón?" Teller asked. "And what makes you think we're going to allow you to talk to a lawyer?"

He looked startled. He shifted uncomfortably in the seat; his hands were still zip-stripped behind him. "You *have* to! It's my constitutional right, both in Mexico and in the United States!"

Procario picked up on Teller's game and laughed. "Let me tell you something, Enrico," he said. "So far as we're concerned, you are a shithead narcoterrorist, and right now you have no rights whatsoever. If we give the word, the pilot of this aircraft will take us down to twelve thousand feet, we pop open that cabin door up there, and you get to swan-dive headfirst into the Gulf without a parachute. And you know what? No one, *no one* would ever know what happened to you."

"I vote for ADX Florence," Teller said. "You know about that, Enrico? That's the federal supermax prison in Colorado. Lots of Muslim terrorists there . . . but I think there are a few drug dealers, too. Juan García Ábrego? He used to head up the Gulf Cartel. I think someone from the old Medillín Cartel is still rotting in there, too. You could sit down and have a chat with your buddies, maybe . . . except, no, that wouldn't be an option, would it? Supermax facilities are kind of strict. Solitary confinement for twenty-three hours a day. No contact with other inmates. Kind of like sensory deprivation, and it goes on and on and—"

"You can't do that without a trial!" Barrón cried. "And you can't try me without a lawyer!"

"Don't tell us what we can or can't do, Enrico," Procario said, his voice low and dangerous. "You tried to kill us back there, an ambush for the *yanqui* intelligence officers. The woman was bait, wasn't she?"

"I'm saying nothing!"

"You don't really need to say a thing," Teller said, giving his best innocent-boy grin. He leaned closer, looking closely into Barrón's face. "We know you worked with de la Cruz to set up the kidnapping and the ambush. And . . . we know all about 'Skull.'"

In truth, they knew only that someone called Calavera had been on his way out to the Perez house, but Teller was guessing that Skull was a nickname for a cartel big shot.

Barrón confirmed that guess, as his pupils enlarged and his nostrils flared. He was afraid. "I am telling you nothing."

He didn't sound quite so sure of himself now, though.

"Well, it sounds like the Supermax for you, then, amigo," Procario said easily. "Actually, it'll be easier all the way around if you just disappear. We turn you over to the CIA, they interrogate you for a year or two, and then . . . poof! No one ever finds out what happened to you."

"You're bluffing. Your own laws make it illegal to torture me . . . even to threaten me with . . . what is it called? Waterboarding. Making me think I am drowning."

"You think we're bluffing?" Teller asked, grinning.

"If we don't tell anyone that we have you in the first place, Enrico . . . if we turn you over to people who won't even mention to their bosses that we have you in custody . . ." Teller shrugged. "Who's to know?"

"*Anything* could happen to you, Enrico."

"But you can't do that!"

"Try us," Procario said.

Teller chuckled. "Ever hear of NDAA 2012?" he asked. The National Defense Authorization Act of 2012, quietly signed into law by President Obama on New Year's Eve of 2011, had created a raging firestorm of controversy by effectively repealing the Fourth, Fifth, Sixth, and Seventh Amendments of the Constitution—not, in Teller's opinion, one of Congress's better moves. "Among other things," he said, "it gives the U.S. military and certain other agencies the power to arrest anyone, anywhere, *including American citizens,* and to hold them indefinitely without access to an attorney or to trial by jury. Now if Congress is willing to treat American citizens that way . . . how interested do you think they'll be in protecting *your* rights?"

"Look," Barrón said, licking his lips. "I am rich. I could make both of you rich! Rich beyond your wildest dreams!"

That caught Teller's full attention. Until this moment, he'd assumed that Barrón was a relatively low-level soldier in the ranks of the Zeta Killers. There'd been nothing on his rap sheet suggesting more, though his military training might have given him special status. Now, his attempt at bribery suggested either that he had access to a lot more money than did the typical street-level cartel soldier, or that he had some very high-ranking connections indeed—Joaquín Guzmán, perhaps.

And if he was in tight with Guzmán, he might know about the Iranian agent photographed with Guzmán's lieutenant, Hector Gallardo. Or about nuclear weapons smuggled into Mexico from Pakistan.

In fact, he might know a *lot*.

"Not interested," Teller said. "We know how much blood there is on that money."

"Yeah, too many strings," Procario added. "Besides, right now, I hate to tell you, friend, but you don't have shit. You can't go to the bank. You don't have your flunkies with you. You don't have wireless service. We went through your wallet a while ago and found a few thousand pesos—but we already have that. You have *nothing,* except our good will."

Teller shrugged. "You know, Enrico, I don't think you can afford us."

"*Every* man has a price," Barrón said. He sounded desperate now.

"Maybe."

Teller leaned back in his seat, thinking. He remembered reading about one Mexican government official—López Parra, a commander in the Mexican federal attorney general's office in charge of northern Mexico—who'd been found to be receiving 1.5 million U.S. dollars *per month* from the Gulf Cartel. One estimate had suggested that 95 percent of the Mexican AGO was in the cartel's pocket.

One of the most serious aspects of the war against

narcoterrorism was the scope of corruption extending across both sides of the line between Mexico and the United States. When profits of billions of dollars were involved, large-scale corruption was inevitable. Teller knew of one late-1980s scandal involving tons of cocaine going north on board Immigration and Naturalization Service buses, which didn't have to stop for checks at the border, and of another involving the Texas National Guard.

No one, it seemed, was beyond the reach of the cartel billions.

For as long as he'd been an intelligence officer . . . no, longer . . . ever since he'd been a kid growing up in the rugged country outside of Juneau, Alaska, when he'd found himself in a tight spot, he'd tried to honestly answer just one question: *What's the next* right *thing to do?*

"You know what, Enrico?" Teller asked after a moment's thought. "You're right. I *do* have a price."

"Anything! You have but to name it! A million dollars? Ten million? That's fucking *pocket* change!"

"No. My price is what you know about Iranians and Hezbollah operatives in Mexico, nuclear weapons, and a Russian submarine."

Barrón seemed to consider this for a moment. "If . . . if I tell you about what I know . . . you will let me go?"

"No," Teller said. "Absolutely not. But we can see to it that you're handed over to civilian law enforcement authorities in the States, and that you get to hire a lawyer."

Teller could see the calculating light come on behind Barrón's eyes. "What guarantee do I have that you would keep your word?"

"That's a great question coming from a narcotrafficker, isn't it?" Teller asked Procario. "The bastard wants to know if we're going to keep our word."

"Yeah." Procario chuckled. "Tell you what, Enrico. I promise, on my honor as a U.S. Marine Corps officer, that if you answer our questions and tell us everything we want to know, I will *not* personally shove you out of the cabin door of this aircraft."

"No guarantees," Teller added. "You're the one answering the questions, not asking them."

"I should warn you that we do have ways of checking up on your story," Procario said. "You lie to us, and the deal is off. You go to Supermax . . . or you disappear."

"You want the truth? I can tell you all about the submarines!"

"We're not talking about the little toy submarines you guys are building in your basements," Teller said. "We want to know about the Kilo class Russian sub rented from a group of Russian mafia for three hundred million rubles. It was docked beside some Mayan ruins in the jungle at Cerros, in northern Belize, and it sailed north on or shortly after April 17."

That was the date the satellite surveillance photos that seemed to show the sub at Cerros had been taken. When the ISA strike force had launched its assault on the nineteenth, the sub had been gone.

"The eighteenth," Barrón said. "The submarine left on Friday the eighteenth."

"What time?" Teller asked.

"I don't know. Early, well before sunrise. I heard they had to get out of the shallows of Chetumal Bay, out past Ambergris Cay and into deep water, before they could be spotted from the air."

"How do you know all this?" Procario asked. "Were you there?"

Barrón shook his head. "I was at the Iztacalco safe house, providing security. I heard about it from my boss."

"Who is that?"

"Agustín Morales."

"Yes?" Teller prompted. "And who is he?"

The shutters seemed to come down behind Barrón's eyes. "You said you knew him."

A misstep . . . but not a serious one. Barrón had not mentioned the name Morales. He *had* reacted at Teller's mention of "the Skull," however. Were the two names the same man?

"We know about Calavera, of course," Teller told him. "What I meant was, who exactly is he in the organization?"

A shrug. "One of El Chapo's lieutenants."

"Is he as high ranking as, say, Hector Gallardo?"

"No. I don't think so. It's . . . hard to tell, sometimes. People move up in favor . . . people move down. Calavera's star, it is in the ascendency right now."

"Oh? And why is that?"

"Because he was the one who was approached by Pasha. And it was his idea to rent the Russian submarine."

"Pasha?"

"The Iranian. That was his code name. I forget his real name."

"So what are the Iranians doing in Mexico, Enrico?"

"I don't know."

"Ah! Wrong answer," Procario said. "Sounds like you're going for a swim."

"No! I swear I don't know! There was some sort of top secret plan, something brought in by the Iranians, but that was all Escalante and Guzmán! Pasha, he came to Guzmán with this idea he called 'Operation Shah Mat,' okay?"

"Shah Mat?" Teller asked.

"Yeah. Don't know what that means. But to make it work, the Iranians wanted us to set up a truce between the damned Zetas and Sinaloa. Escalante—he had connections with both groups, so he set it up. That way, the Zetas wouldn't screw up the operation with us, and vice versa, you know? And Agustín Morales, he had the idea for using the submarine."

"And where is the submarine going?" Procario asked.

"I . . . I don't know."

"Damn! Wrong answer *again*," Teller said. He looked at Procario. "I'll go talk to the pilot."

"We *know* what's on board that submarine," Procario said. "Do you?"

"No."

"You sure?"

"Look, there was a . . . a shipment of some kind coming in on a cargo ship! I don't know what it was. No one told me!"

"Uh-huh," Teller said. "And I suppose you don't know where the sub was going?"

Again Teller caught a look behind Barrón's eyes, calculating, evasive. "No. We . . . we often use submarines to move merchandise to *el norte*. Florida . . . the Gulf Coast . . ."

"I see." Teller decided to try a different tactic. Clearly, while Barrón was trying to bargain with the two INSCOM officers, he was still far more terrified of his own people than he was of them.

That gave Teller something with which he could work.

Torture was not an efficient way to get information out of a prisoner, not when he would say anything, anything at all, to make the pain stop. Even if Teller had been inclined to use rough treatment on Barrón—and he was not—there were so many ways that the use of torture could backfire. The issue was still extremely sensitive; waterboarding—bringing suspected Muslim terrorists close to drowning in order to get them to reveal details of terror plots against the United States— had been banned by President Obama. When a prisoner knew something of vital importance to his captors . . . if that information might save thousands or lives . . . or millions . . . *was torture ever justified?*

Teller didn't think it was. Sometimes, though, during a tough interrogation, it was useful to create the impression that torture *was* an option. The trouble was that most of America's enemies knew by now that American law forbade the use of any form of physical torture, and that most American interrogators wouldn't dare use it.

There might still be one threat Teller and Procario could use.

He clapped Barrón on the shoulder. "Okay, amigo, I'll tell you what. We're going to let you go."

Procario looked up at him, startled. "What the hell?"

"No, I mean it. There are some things you're just not going to tell us. We understand that. As soon as we get to Eglin, we'll put you on a private plane to take you straight back to Mexico."

Barrón's eyes narrowed. "What's the catch?"

"No catch at all. We'll just let CISEN know how very helpful you've been in our investigation—Miguel de la Cruz in particular. You know . . . so they can protect you."

Procario saw immediately what Teller was doing. "That's good. We could also pass the word to the *federales*. Oh, and Juan Escalante, too."

"Sure," Teller said. "He'll pass the word both to Guzmán and to the Zetas. I imagine they'll be *real* interested in knowing that you're back in the country."

"Sounds good," Procario added. "We'll arrange to transfer you directly to CISEN officers. So they can arrange for you to be in protective custody."

"*¡Hijo de puta!*" The words were a shrill, panic-stricken scream. Barrón's eyes bulged in his face as he broke into a cold sweat.

"Now, now," Procario said gently. "Language. There are ladies present."

"*You bastards!* I won't survive for one hour!"

"Oh, I don't know about that, amigo," Teller said. "I've seen the handiwork of some of your former friends. That young couple strung up from a bridge in Nuevo Laredo? And then there was a CIA agent named Henrico Garcia. Looked to me like they kept him alive for a *long* time after they started working on him."

"Hey, how about Garcia?" Procario asked. "That was your boss's work, wasn't it? Morales? Or did you help?"

Teller nodded. "You *do* know that sending Garcia's head back to Langley was tantamount to declaring war on the CIA, don't you?"

"That wasn't me! It was Morales!"

"Yeah, we know all about Agustín Morales," Teller said. "He came to work for us, but it turned out he was doubling. Betrayed Garcia, who was also working for us. Who was it who tortured that poor guy to death, huh? Your boss Morales? Were you in on that? Or did they bring in a special interrogator?"

"You know, I think you *were* there when they cut Garcia up," Procario said. "You wouldn't be this scared if you hadn't seen it yourself. Maybe you even helped."

"No! No! I had nothing to do with . . . *please!* You can't do this thing!"

Teller tsk-tsked loudly. "There you go again, Enrico, telling us what we can and can't do. Bad habit."

"Just how long do you think they'll keep you alive, Enrico?" Procario added. "While they're working on you, I mean, taking you apart one small piece at a time. I imagine it will be at least a few days. A week, maybe?"

"Longer," Teller said.

"I think so. Will you still be alive when they slice off your genitals and sew them into your mouth?"

"Oh, I think we can count on that, Frank," Teller said, his tone casually conversational.

"Yeah, if they're careful, he won't even bleed to death. Especially if they use a hot iron to cauterize the wound."

"Hell, he'll probably still have his eyes at that point, so he can watch what they're doing. Betcha they save the eyes for the very last—"

"Stop it! Stop it! *¡Por el amor de Dios!*" He was sobbing now, pulling and wrenching desperately against the plastic strip around his wrists. "I don't know where the submarine is going, I *swear* I don't, but I heard Morales talking to Escalante about a couple of *norteamericano* cities burning soon, and that it was going to be Aztlán's Fourth of July!"

Teller studied Barrón's contorted features, then exchanged a nod with Procario. Barrón had broken, and it looked genuine. "What cities?" Teller demanded.

"No! You gotta promise me you're not going to let those people get hold of me!"

"Tell you what," Procario said. "Tell us everything you know—and I mean *everything*—and we'll turn you over to the U.S. Marshals Service in Florida. You'll stay with them for a while, someplace cozy and safe. If we find out you've been dealing straight with us, we'll put in a good word for you, let them know you cooperated with us."

"If they decide to prosecute," Teller said, "you'll end up in prison, but you know what? Even Supermax is better than what'll be waiting for you back home if we spread the word that you helped us. If we find out you've lied about *anything,* we send you straight back to Mexico, and we make sure that Sinaloa and Los Zetas both know *exactly* how much you told us. Me and Frank here will be running a pool, taking bets on how long you stay alive and in one piece."

"Yeah, your friends back there," Procario said, "they don't really seem to be the kind to forgive and forget, y'know?"

"So," Teller added, "let's start with two stolen nuclear weapons on board a Russian submarine. We want to know exactly what time they left Belize, and we want to know where they're headed."

"And after that," Procario said, "you can tell us everything you know about Aztlán."

"I don't know where they're going," Barrón said. Tears streamed down his face. "I *swear* I don't know."

"Lo sé," a woman's voice said from a seat behind them. Maria Perez spoke only broken English, but she'd been listening in—and evidently she'd understood. "I know. Juan, he tell me."

Teller turned in his seat to look at her. She was wearing a robe and fuzzy slippers given to her by the woman living with Antonio Vicente, covering her flimsy nightgown. Her face was drawn and haggard. Dominique was sitting next to her.

"What did he tell you, Señorita Perez?"

"Que Irán tiene dos bombas—bombas atómicas— por dos ciudades en los Estados Unidos."

That Iran has two atomic bombs for two U.S. cities.

Teller felt a cold chill at this, the first independent verification that there really were two nukes out there. Even Castro, the merchant sailor off the *Zapoteca*, had thought the cases containing the weapons had held precursor chemicals for drugs.

"*¿Que ciudades, Maria?*" What cities?

"New York *y . . . y* Washington."

"Why are you telling us this, Maria?" Procario asked.

"We've been talking together back here," Dominique said. "She's telling the truth."

"Yes, but—"

"*Trust* me. She's telling the truth."

Procario arched an eyebrow at Teller. "Girl talk?"

"If Jackie thinks she's telling it straight, I trust her," Teller said. He looked at Perez and switched to Spanish. He wanted to be certain she understood. "Maria, did Escalante ever tell you why?"

"Only that it would be . . . *como fuegos artificiales*. How you say? Like fireworks. Like fireworks to mark the birth of a new nation," Perez said. "Aztlán."

Teller reached for his phone.

This stuff couldn't wait until they landed at Eglin.

PRESS ROOM
THE WHITE HOUSE
WASHINGTON, D.C.
1105 HOURS, EDT

"Mr. President!"

"Yes. In the front."

"Tom Kellogg, *Arizona Republic*. Is it true that yesterday you told the secretary general of the United Nations that you have not ruled out compliance with UN demands that a popular referendum be held on independence for several southwestern states, including Arizona?"

"I don't know how you got that story, Tom. My conversation with Mr. Hernandez *was* private. What I told him, however, is that it is this administration's solemn goal to resolve the situation in the Southwest peacefully, fairly, and democratically. You, yes."

"Marlene Connelly, CNN. Mr. President, there has been talk of actual civil war in the Southwest, and there are rumors that you have authorized additional active-duty military forces to join National Guard troops already in the region. How do you respond to that?"

"Marlene, let me be perfectly clear about this. There is no chance of these disturbances spreading to become civil war. What we are faced with here is criminal gangs engaged in rioting and looting, aided and abetted by drug-trafficking cartels from across the border with Mexico. National Guard and active-duty troops have been dispatched to the region in order to keep the peace. And we *will* keep the peace, ladies and gentlemen, I promise you."

Randolph Preston watched the president from the wings, along with several assistants and secretaries, together with the ubiquitous Secret Service. He had to admit that the president was doing a good job of keeping the lid on things. Just one week had passed since the first demonstrations and riots in Los Angeles, and things out there had exploded far more quickly than anyone could have imagined. By this time tomorrow, *everything* would be different.

He glanced at his watch. A busy day today. Another few minutes of this, and in another four hours he was meeting with that Iranian agent at a particular bench out on the Mall.

Tonight, he flew to San Francisco.

Because things were going to begin happening very quickly now.

Very quickly indeed.

CHAPTER EIGHTEEN

CENTRAL INTELLIGENCE AGENCY
MCLEAN, VIRGINIA
1425 HOURS, EDT
21 APRIL

Teller still felt a bit travel dazed. From Mexico City to
Eglin Air Force base in two hours, a quick stopover for
refueling, then north to Ronald Reagan National Airport, with a helicopter flight for the final eight miles
from there to the CIA headquarters facility at Langley.
He was tired, dirty, and hungry—he hadn't eaten since
late afternoon yesterday, and he was not in the best of
moods. Wentworth and the Agency suits didn't sound
particularly pleased by the intelligence they'd developed after taking off from BJI, and he had the terrible
feeling that they were going to choose not to believe
their story.

"And you really believe these people?" JJ Wentworth said, making a face. "This drug trafficker, Bar-

rón, especially. You claim he just told you all of this . . . what, out of the goodness of his heart?"

Teller exchanged a glance with Procario. The two of them were in one of Langley's palatial electronic briefing rooms, together with Wentworth, Larson, and an assistant Ops director named Charles Vanderkamp. Dominique had mentioned that he was her department head—and the guy who'd sided with de la Cruz about pulling her out of Mexico.

Dominique was elsewhere in the building—Teller wasn't sure where—and he wondered why Vanderkamp was *here* rather than talking to her. Enrico Barrón, Maria Perez, and Captain Marcetti and his people all had gotten off the plane at Eglin. Barrón, as promised, had been turned over to the federal marshals, along with Perez, who'd been put in protective custody. Both of them would be wanted for more questioning before this thing played out.

Also put off the plane at Eglin had been the body bag containing Randolph Patterson.

"It wasn't out of the goodness of his heart," Teller replied evenly. "The guy was scared shitless."

"You used emotional torture on him," Vanderkamp said. "In doing so, you two broke a number of regulations, though, since you're not with the Agency, we're not certain yet of where you stand legally in all of this."

"Barrón was willing to tell you anything to keep from being sent back to Mexico City," Wentworth said. "His testimony cannot be independently verified."

"Since you two deployed to Mexico," Larson told them, "we've developed new information. A reliable informant in Pakistan has told us that those stolen nukes are, in fact, in the hands of al Qaeda—just as we suspected all along."

"You guys are fixated on al Qaeda," Procario said. "There *are* other threats in the world, you know."

"As I told you once before," Larson said with an almost sorrowful shake of the head, "al Qaeda has been our chief suspect all along. They have been too weak and divided since the Abbottabad assault to manage normal operations—but we believe that if they do have nuclear weapons they will attempt to deploy them against us, for reasons of revenge if nothing else."

"Have you given any thought at all," Teller asked, "to the possibility that someone is employing disinformation here? Trying to make you look for al Qaeda when in fact it's the Iranians."

Wentworth laughed. "Why would Iran be trying to smuggle nukes into the country? They hate al Qaeda, and they know what would happen to them if they attacked us."

"Maybe that's why they're trying to put the blame on al Qaeda, a little thing called 'false flag'—we've done it a time or two ourselves," Teller said, exasperated. "Look, did you guys get anything out of the Cellmap data? Some of those contacts must be talking about smuggled nukes, or Iranian agents . . . or something called Operation Shah Mat."

"Mm, yes," Wentworth said. "The new system has

been sending back a great deal of data . . . a very great deal. Look at this."

He tapped out an entry on the glass tabletop in front of him, and both the table and the wall-sized display screen behind him brought up a map of the United States. Blue dots were everywhere, clustered in major cities and especially thick in the American Southwest. There were also dense concentrations in D.C. and New York and in most of the other Eastern seaboard cities, stretching from Tampa, Florida, to Portland, Maine.

Larson placed his thumb and forefinger on the tabletop and moved them together, zooming out from the map until it included Mexico as well—also awash in blue splotches.

"Every one of those is a cell phone on your Cellmap network," Larson said. "Over fifty thousand in the United States, at last count. At least that many more in Mexico, and more and more coming onto the network all the time. We simply do not have the manpower or the computer power to trace every one of those targets, identify them all, and we certainly can't eavesdrop on their conversations."

"That shouldn't be that hard," Teller said. "They can run keyword intercepts easily enough."

"We would need to enlist the Puzzle Palace computer center to process the data on that scale," Wentworth said, "and that, I fear, is going to take time. More time than we have."

"The Puzzle Palace" was an insider's nickname for the National Security Agency. The NSA, America's electronic and signals-intercept intelligence agency, possessed over a dozen acres of supercomputer hardware beneath its headquarters building and at its Tordella Supercomputer Facility, both at Fort Meade, Maryland.

"Time? They have enough computer hardware to crack just about anything," Procario said. "And a keyword intercept would be easy to set up for this. 'Nuclear weapon,' 'Shah Mat,' 'bomb,' 'destroy Washington,' that sort of thing."

Keyword intercepts had been in use since the 1980s, when intelligence agencies had discovered that you could turn an ordinary telephone into a covert listening device without even having to plant a bug or have the telephone connection open. A sufficiently powerful computer with word-recognition software could quietly sit at Fort Meade, mindlessly listening to tens of thousands of telephone conversations at a time, and only yell for human help if it caught certain words.

"The NSA gets something like six hundred and fifty million electronic intercepts per *day,*" Larson said. "And the NSA does not play well with others. *Their* priorities will be taken care of first."

"I should also remind you that it's illegal for the NSA to eavesdrop on American citizens," Wentworth said. "Technically, it's illegal for any of us—but there *are* ways around the roadblocks, of course. Even so, the NSA is simply not going to get involved in something that will take so much computer time and not have some sort of a payoff for them in return."

"That's crazy," Teller said. "We're talking about

someone detonating a couple of nukes, one in Washington and one in New York!"

"That has not been independently confirmed," Vanderkamp said. "Our information now is that those suitcase nukes are still in Pakistan. They were never put on board the *Zapoteca*."

"What about the seaman I talked to in Chetumal?" Teller asked. "He told me there were two crates, each seventy-five or eighty pounds . . . about right for Lebed's missing nukes."

"I saw your report," Wentworth said. "As before, we have no confirmation. Those could easily have been precursor chemicals for the manufacture of methamphetamines or heroin."

"If you hadn't fucking pulled the plug on the ISA team down there," Procario said, furious, "you could have gotten rad counters on board the *Zapoteca*! Maybe *that* would have given you your damned confirmation!"

"We pulled the ISA team because we had reason to believe the nukes were not on board, in fact had never been on board . . . and because the assaults at Chetumal and at Cerros together caused a major international incident. If they'd stormed a Mexican ship in a Mexican port it would have been *much* worse."

"Which brings us to the main reason we asked you to come in to see us today," Wentworth said. "You've managed to piss off quite a few people here—not to mention your boss at INSCOM."

"MacDonald?"

"Colonel MacDonald, yes. It seems you didn't request formal permission to leave the country."

"I thought you people took care of that! We were working for you."

"And we thought *you* had taken care of it." Wentworth smiled. "Our various agencies try to work together, but we must observe the rules, you know. Otherwise it all collapses into chaos."

"But we're getting a hell of a lot of flack now," Vanderkamp said, "from the president's office on down. Gunfights in the streets. Explosions. Fires. Pitched battles. You two managed to turn Mexico City and a couple of other places down there into war zones."

"I should point out, gentlemen," Procario said, "that right now Mexico *is* a war zone. Gunfights in the streets? Nothing new there. Last I heard something like forty thousand people had been killed in Mexico's drug war just since 2006, including a lot of innocent bystanders. We carried out our mission, killed a few narcoterrorists, captured a prisoner, and brought home some important intel. We *survived* the war zone. We didn't create it."

"Speaking of that prisoner," Wentworth said, "you did not properly extradite him. That was kidnapping. And the Perez woman did not have a passport and must be considered to be an illegal immigrant. There are going to be serious charges in this—"

"Serious charges!" Teller flew up out of his seat. "What *should* we have done, turned Barrón over to CISEN? Killed him ourselves?"

"Sit *down*, Captain Teller," Wentworth said, cold.

"I will *not*! We did what you people wanted us to do—bailed your asses out by giving you new eyes on the ground and a tool to patch things along until you could reestablish your Mexican network. Now you tell us you can't use the tool, and you're going to charge us with human trafficking! *What the fuck is going on here?*"

"Let's just sit down and take it easy," Larson said, moving his hands in gentle "calm down" motions. "We're not charging you with human trafficking . . . or anything else, *if* you cooperate with us."

Reluctantly, Teller took his seat once more. He was angry. "We are not going to quietly let you hang us out to dry," he said. He muttered something else under his breath.

"What was that?" Larson asked.

"Fucking Klingons," Teller replied. He made a brushing motion with his hand. "Never mind. Inside joke."

Procario put his hand on Teller's arm, restraining him.

"What is it you want from us?" Procario asked.

"Your final after-actions," Wentworth said, "will not mention the interview with that seaman off the *Zapoteca* or the interrogation of Enrico Barrón. You two went beyond your authority there. Well, mistakes were made, as they say. You may have misinterpreted our instructions."

"There is no evidence that stolen nuclear weapons are being smuggled into the United States," Larson added, "or that the drug cartels are somehow aiding and abetting such a plot."

"You also mentioned several other names," Wentworth said. "Reyshahri, an Iranian VEVAK agent. A Hezbollah operative named Hamadi. Iranian and Hezbollah involvement in Mexico is . . . debatable. Your report will not mention them."

"What about Yussef Nadir Suwayd?" Teller asked.

"I beg your pardon . . . who?"

"Jackie Dominique learned about him from de la Cruz. He was going by the name Pablo Tomás, but the CISEN files identified him as a Hezbollah agent. He was one of the guys who attacked us in the Estrella Hotel. You could ID him from the cell phone pics I sent you."

Wentworth smiled. "I thought you said de la Cruz's information could not be trusted?"

"It can't, but I believe him on that one."

"Why?"

"Because it contradicted his party line—that al Qaeda is trying to smuggle nukes into Mexico, maybe as some sort of extortion attempt against the Mexican government. That story is totally nuts, but he clearly didn't know that al Qaeda and Hezbollah hate each other *almost* as much as they hate Israel—or us."

"If he'd made it up," Procario said, "you would expect him to have done his research, to get it right. We think he was misinterpreting data they really did have in their files, not making it up."

"I don't buy it," Vanderkamp said with a shrug. "The information could have been mistaken either way."

"No, but it sets a strong probability," Teller said.

"Intelligence work always deals with probabilities, not certainties."

"That may be," Wentworth said. "But I have *this* certainty for you. You two will submit your after-action reports to us for editing, and show them to no one else. *No* one. We're classifying all of this material, and you will not reveal it to anyone else, and that specifically includes INSCOM. There are political ramifications here that you are not aware of."

Teller looked at Procario. "Thought so. It's a hatchet job."

"I beg your pardon?" Vanderkamp asked.

"Somehow, the intelligence we developed in Mexico has become . . . inconvenient. You're trying to bury it."

"We are trying," Wentworth said, "to prevent a . . . call it a public relations disaster of unprecedented proportions. The president is trying to calm public fears, public backlash against Latinos in the United States. These . . . these wild tales of Mexican drug lords working with Iranians to smuggle nuclear weapons—they're tossing gasoline on the fire."

"Five men of Latino descent," Vanderkamp said, "were lynched in Chicago last night. A private militia in Idaho has threatened to shoot any Latino they see on sight. Mobs have started fighting each other in Los Angeles—black, white, Latino, Asian. They're at each other's throats right now over this Aztlán thing."

"We're not trying to bury your intel," Larson said. "We've analyzed it and concluded that the scenario it suggests is so extremely unlikely, it must be mistaken.

And if any part of it were to become public . . . well, that could have extraordinarily serious ramifications."

"You know," Teller said, "there's an easy solution here. Those weapons are on board a Kilo class submarine currently somewhere off the eastern seaboard."

Reaching out, he moved his finger and thumb on the tabletop map, zooming in with sharp clarity to a stretch of beach along Virginia's east coast. Created from aerial reconnaissance photos, the map showed exquisite detail—houses, swimming pools, cars on the roads, and the white turbulence of waves breaking along the shore.

"If their targets are Washington and New York City," Teller continued, "there really are only a few places they could put them ashore." He slowly moved the map image, their viewpoint drifting north along the coast. On the big screen on the wall above the table, the terrain had the look of ground slipping away beneath a low-flying aircraft. "Those weapons are small, but they're heavy and awkward. They'll need to put them ashore in a small boat or raft, and they need to do it where the submarine won't be seen. They can't approach D.C., not very closely. A Kilo wouldn't make it very far up the Chesapeake Bay. Too shallow for it to stay submerged, and the Potomac River isn't navigable for anything larger than a speedboat. So it's too risky to try that route.

"No, if they want to put a weapon ashore, it would be from the Atlantic Ocean itself—maybe along here, Chincoteague Island . . . or farther north . . . Assateague, south of Ocean City. Or up here south of Bethany Beach, in Delaware. Those beaches all are a little over a hundred miles from D.C., right? Two major ways they could go—Route 1 up the coast, or Route 50 from Ocean City across the bay at Annapolis. More choices if they stick to back roads. A car meets the boat at night on the beach with a prearranged signal. A few hours later, the weapon is parked on the street near the White House."

"What's your point?" Larson asked.

"If we know the Kilo is going to be off this stretch of coast—that's maybe, what? A hundred thirty, a hundred fifty miles, maybe, from the mouth of Chesapeake Bay to the mouth of Delaware Bay? It should be easier to find it there than somewhere out in the middle of the ocean."

"Find that sub," Procario said, "and *that* will be the confirmation you want."

"I'll remind you gentlemen that we don't even know there *is* a submarine," Vanderkamp said.

"We found the contract with the Russians at Cerros!"

"Yes, but not the submarine."

"Jackie spotted the IR footprint of the thing!"

"Mm, yes. But that data is subject to . . . interpretation. Ms. Dominique is not a trained photo analyst."

"I'm beginning to think you people wouldn't accept the facts if we deposited that Kilo on Langley's north parking lot!"

"Are you aware, Captain," Larson said, "that there have been rumors of a Kilo submarine being sold to the drug cartels for decades, literally? Are you aware of the name we have for it?"

"No. What?"

"Sasquatch. Because there is never any proof it exists."

"We zapped you photos of the contract," Procario said. "That should be enough proof for anyone."

"Not if the opposition is deliberately attempting to obscure what's really happening," Vanderkamp pointed out.

"And what do *you* think is really happening?" Teller demanded.

Wentworth shook his head. "Captain Teller, this interview is at an end. We—"

"Look, has the navy already been brought in on this?" Teller asked. When there was no immediate answer, he looked at Wentworth. "Damn it, you've got to look! Even if we're wrong, you can't afford to take that chance! We're talking about a couple of small nuclear weapons here!"

"Both the navy and the U.S. Coast Guard have been alerted," Wentworth said.

"I know," Teller said. "We had INSCOM flash COMSUBLANT this morning. There are some L.A. class subs operating out of Norfolk that—"

"That's all well and good," Wentworth said. "But, honestly, we don't expect anything to come of it. Kilo submarines are extraordinarily quiet, incredibly hard to find and track. The chances of anyone finding it are . . . astronomical."

"Then I suggest," Teller said quietly, "that you get your ass in gear and start looking *hard*. Or else you start evacuating the city."

"*That* certainly is not an option," Wentworth said. "Gentlemen, we appreciate your concern. We truly do. But sometimes officers in the field get . . . a little too close to their missions. A little too emotionally involved. You both know as well as I do that raw data must be properly assimilated, properly analyzed, and properly fit together with the other pieces of a *very* large and complex puzzle. Your efforts in Mexico are deeply appreciated, and we *are* grateful. Don't think we're not. And we will do what we can to . . . control the fallout from your more, ah, aggressive actions down there. But your reports will not mention contradictory material that will only confuse the issue more. Am I clear?"

Teller stood abruptly. "Clear. C'mon, Frank. We're outta here."

"Your security oaths are on file. Play the cowboy on us, Captain, and you *will* be in prison for a very long time."

"I don't think so," Teller said as he reached for the door.

"What do you mean?" Larson demanded.

Teller gave him a cold smile. " 'And ye shall know the truth, and the truth shall make you free.' "

WASHINGTON MALL
WASHINGTON, D.C.
1445 HOURS, EDT

A shadow fell across Preston, and he looked up. "You have the advantage of me, sir," he said.

"I would say that I have you in *checkmate,* sir," the other man said.

"Eagle?"

He nodded. "Duke."

The man sat next to him on the bench. Preston glanced around in all directions, but no one was close.

Of course, if the CIA had Preston under observation, they could be training a long-range microphone on him at this moment. Or the bench could have been bugged, though he'd selected it randomly. The large yellow plastic shopping bag resting by his feet was how Reyshahri had recognized him.

There was also a radio, a small boom box, beside him on the bench. He switched it on, loud. If they were under audio surveillance, the music—harsh and urgent—should provide enough white noise to drown their conversation.

"It's good to meet you at long last, Mr. Duke," Reyshahri said. "My superiors told me to tell you . . . the information you've provided us has been extremely useful."

"Simply establishing my bona fides," Preston replied. "You have no other reason to trust me."

"Why this meeting, then? It's dangerous to meet."

Preston shrugged. "I *did* want to know who I was working with. To take your measure. I'm a good judge of character."

"You know absolutely nothing about me."

"I know you are Saeed Reyshahri, that you are a *sarvan* in the Vezarat-e Ettela'at va Amniyat-e Keshvar." He stumbled a bit at the Farsi pronunciation but managed to recover. "I know you are dedicated, competent, and thorough. Ten years with the Sepah, three with VEVAK. You've trained Hezbollah and are well thought of by your superiors. Colonel Salehi wrote an absolutely glowing report in your record. You live in an apartment in the Hassan abad-Shomali district of Tehran and have a wife, Hasti, and a daughter—"

"How do you know all of this?"

"It is my job to know things, Captain." He hesitated. "You are ready for tomorrow?"

"I am. My associate and I meet the submarine tonight."

"Two weapons, five-kiloton yield. Your choice of targets, one here, one in New York City."

"Our choice, yes. So that no one else knows where they are."

"Good. And detonation is by telephone?"

Reyshahri nodded. "We arm the weapon, leave it, and dial a number later, from a safe distance. Our confederates in New York City do the same with theirs."

"And the number?"

"What?"

"The phone number that detonates the weapons."

"Why should I tell—"

"In case something happens to you, of course! I can still detonate the weapons if you do not."

"I . . . see." Reyshahri appeared to think it over, then shrugged and recited a ten-digit number.

Preston commited it to memory. "One number, two warheads?"

"Yes."

"Then I think that's everything, Captain Reyshahri. I will walk away from here first. You stay here a few moments, in case someone is watching. I will leave the yellow bag under the bench."

"What's in it?"

"Something to help you with your mission here in D.C." He stood, looked around again, then picked up the blaring radio and switched it off. "I wish you the very best of luck, Captain. *Khodawbeh ham-rah*."

He walked away, leaving the VEVAK agent on the bench.

KILO CLASS SUBMARINE
SUBMERGED OFF BETHANY BEACH
DELAWARE
1505 HOURS, EDT

Captain Second Rank Sergei Alekseyevich Basargin pressed his face up to the eyepiece of the periscope, slowly panning the instrument to take in the sweep of white-sand beach. The view was repeated on a television monitor on one bulkhead of the control room. North, a pair of large cranes framed the entrance to Indian River Inlet; automobiles, quite a few of them, could be seen moving north and south on Highway 1, which ran directly above the beach along this stretch of coast.

April was early in the beach season—the waters of the Atlantic were still bitingly cold—but quite a few beach umbrellas and sunbathers were visible on the sand. Automobiles had been driven down to the high tide line. Fat, wealthy, pasty skinned Americans enjoying the sun.

Well, not all were fat. One of the crewmen laughed and pointed. "Ha! Look at *that* bikini! Why does she even bother?" Others laughed.

The submarine was just over five kilometers from the shore in water just twenty-five meters deep at midtide. That was excruciatingly shallow; the Kilo, seventy-five meters long from prow to screw, measured just fourteen meters from her keel to the top of her sail. That left precious little room for maneuvering, and a mistake could end with the vessel embarrassingly grounded off the coast of Delaware.

His orders called for him to get closer inshore yet, but he was not about to try that in daylight. Already, there was a serious danger that an aircraft overflying the beach would see the dark shadow of the submarine lurking beneath the surface.

He increased the magnification on the digital periscope camera, zooming in a bit closer on the young woman who was spreading a blanket out on the beach. The image was blurred and wavering, but the watching crew was certainly enjoying the show.

Basargin, in fact, was not an officer in the Russian Federation Navy—not any longer. Money for that organization was extremely tight, had been tight since the collapse of the Soviet Union. In 2009, Basargin had been forced to retire—"beached," as his British colleagues so quaintly put it. Three years later, some former comrades of his had approached him with an offer. They were working with the *mafiya*—one of the dozens of criminal networks that were about all in the *rodina,* the motherland, that worked any longer. They'd managed to secure a diesel submarine, one of the older Project 877 Paltus boats, and they were going to rent it to certain clients in Mexico for one year. A crew of former submariners with 877 experience had already been gathered in St. Petersburg. All they needed was a captain.

The operation was fairly straightforward: to take the boat to a designated point in northern Belize, and there take on board two men and a small cargo. He was then shown two locations on a chart where those men and their sealed crates would be deposited—at night and on deserted beaches.

The journey would be made slowly and submerged, using the snorkel all the way. Secrecy was absolutely vital. Basargin knew that drugs were involved. What else could it be? It didn't matter. The Americans, hungry for an inexhaustible supply of drugs, were what kept the drug lords in business—and there would always be people willing to move those drugs, for a percentage of the fabulous profits involved.

The two clients stood silently a few meters away, watching the monitor. The Arab, Hamadi, watched the display of skin with unbridled disgust, the Mexican with dull disinterest.

"We will go in tonight, as planned," Basargin told them. "You will be able to watch for your signal on that monitor."

"I no mind tell you," Hamadi said in heavily accented

Russian, "I happy to go in shore. You submarine ship . . . is crowded, and is stink."

Basargin smiled at the Palestinian. "Crowding and the stink one can get used to," he said. "For most of us, the problem is boredom."

A sudden burst of cheering sounded through the control room, and Basargin looked up, then smiled. The young woman had just removed the top of her swimsuit.

He let them watch a moment more, then gave an order. "Conn! Bring us around and take us away from the beach. Dead slow! If you kiss the bottom I will fine you your wages for the voyage!"

Despite the view, he sought the safety of deep water.

They would return after dark, when Bethany Beach was deserted.

CAFETERIA
CENTRAL INTELLIGENCE AGENCY
MCLEAN, VIRGINIA
1532 HOURS, EDT

Teller collapsed into a seat at a table in one of the Langley headquarters cafeterias. Jackie Dominique was there waiting for them, a tray in front of her.

"God," she said, looking at his face. "That bad?"

"Worse. Why do you ask?"

"They've completely reversed course," Procario said, joining them. "One-eighty. There are no nukes in Mexico."

Teller gestured hypnotically with his hand. "These are not the nukes you're looking for. Move along."

"Shit."

"How about you?"

"They questioned me about James's murder," she said, "and about my conversations with de la Cruz. Oh, and they asked me a lot of questions about you two."

"Yeah," Procario said. "They're scared we're going to tell someone that the nukes are already on the way to Washington."

"But why?" Dominique asked. "Did someone get to them?"

"I don't think so," Teller said. "This smells more like a major preemptive ass-covering."

"What do you mean?"

"I think they're having trouble finding that Russian sub," Procario said. "A *lot* of trouble. There's a very, very good chance that those bombs are going to make it into a couple of our cities."

"Okay . . ." She sounded uncertain.

"What happens," Teller said, "if they tell everyone, the president, the Pentagon, Congress, that a couple of suitcase nukes are on the way—and then the nukes go off?"

"I guess," she said slowly, "I guess people would wonder why they didn't get the information sooner . . . or why they didn't do something to stop them."

"Bingo," Teller said. "Whoever is now in charge of what's left of the government begins looking for scapegoats. You *knew* those nukes were coming, and you did *nothing*?"

"And," Procario added, "if they warn everyone and nothing happens, because it *is* a false alarm, the entire U.S. intelligence community looks like fucked-up shit."

"Ah," she said. "Weapons of mass destruction in Iraq."

"Right," Procario said. "It's budget-cutting time in northern Virginia—and guess who's been crying wolf?"

"And," Teller went on, "if they tell no one and the nukes go off . . . well, *damn*! I'm sorry! Our very best intelligence said there was no threat! But, you know, if you increase our budget a couple of hundred percent, we'll make sure this doesn't happen again next time."

Dominique looked shocked. "Chris, that has got to be the most goddamn cynical thing I've ever heard!"

"This is D.C. It's a cynical town." He shrugged. "It's happened before."

"*What's* happened before?"

"Major, credible warnings getting ignored by the people in charge. Pearl Harbor. Tet. The World Trade Center—*twice*. In 1993 and on 9/11."

"Those didn't involve nukes!"

"Doesn't matter." He looked at Procario. "Hey, Frank. Whatcha want to bet they've already done statistical studies on the results of a five-kiloton detonation on the Washington Mall and decided it's survivable?"

"Could be. It wouldn't touch Langley, that's certain. Not five kilotons." Procario frowned. "I do wonder, though, if the Mall is going to be ground zero."

"Halfway between the White House and the Capitol Building." Teller shrugged. "Seems logical to me."

"There *are* other targets in this town, Chris. And five kilotons? It would wreck the Smithsonian buildings, yeah, and the Capitol Dome is so exposed it would be pretty badly damaged. But the D.C. Trade Center and the Washington Aquarium, the IRS Building, those would probably shield the White House pretty well."

"So where do *you* think the nuke is headed?" Dominique asked.

"I'm wondering about the Pentagon," Procario said.

"Jesus Christ."

"Doesn't really matter, I suppose," Teller said. "Either way, a lot of people are going to die."

Dominique reached over and put a hand over his. "You're not giving up, are you, Chris?"

"No. No, I'm not. But I *do* think we need to shift tactics . . ."

CHAPTER NINETEEN

Captain James Franklin Garret stood behind Sonarman First Class Ted Laughlin, studying the multicolored display popularly called "the waterfall," a cascade of colored lines indicating intensity and bearing presented on a 42-inch plasma LED screen above the sonar workstation. There were a *lot* of targets out there. This stretch of the U.S. eastern seaboard was among the busiest sea lanes in the world, and the *Pittsburgh*'s underwater ears were picking up the screws and wake wash of some hundreds of vessels, from speedboats and pleasure craft to a monster oil tanker slowly emerging from Delaware Bay. The sounds picked up by *Pittsburgh*'s passive sonar system were also being played from an overhead speaker, a muted and unintelligible cacophony of growls, thumps, whirs, and chugging noises.

"If he's out there, sir," Laughlin said, his right hand raised to his headphones, "he's masked by all of that background crap."

"That's what I was afraid of," Garret said. "The bastards *do* know how to hide."

The Flight II Los Angeles class attack submarine, SSN-720, carried a number of sophisticated sonar systems: an AN/BQG-5D wide-aperture flank array, an Ametek BQS-15 close-range high-frequency active sonar, a BQQ-5D low-frequency passive and active attack sonar, SADS-TG active detection sonar, and, now trailing far astern of the slowly moving vessel, a TB-29 thin-line passive towed array. The system was tied into the vessel's BSY-1 integrated sonar/weapons control suite, known affectionately by those aboard as "Busy-one."

A half billion dollars or so of Buck Rogers high-tech packed into the *Burgh*'s 362-foot hull, and they couldn't locate a single diesel-electric boat that wasn't that far removed from its ancestors, the U-boats and Gato class subs of sixty years ago.

"Can I assist with maneuver?" Garret asked. The *Pittsburgh* currently was cruising southeast, her towed array positioned to pick up noise radiating from the southwest—down the coast of the Delmarva Peninsula. By turning to a different heading, Garret could fine-tune the sensitivity of the directional sensor suites.

"I don't think so, sir," Laughlin replied. "If you want to nail this guy, you're going to have to go active."

Garret had been considering just that for hours now. It went against the grain; sub drivers were thoroughly conditioned to maintain silence—to *listen* rather than to actually reach out and tag an unseen opponent. Passive sonar simply listened, picking up the ambient sounds around the submarine. The *Burgh*'s onboard sonic library of collected sounds could actually identify an individual vessel by the distinguishing characteristics of its screw and engine noises, and the joke was that a good sonar operator—and Laughlin was one of the best—could eavesdrop on the conversations in an enemy sub's wardroom. The disadvantage was that it was not discriminatory; you heard *everything* out there that might be making noise, including whales, shrimp, a bewildering zoo of talkative fish, and the thunder of waves breaking on the shore.

Active sonar, on the other hand, sent out a powerful burst of sound, precisely like the echolocation chirp of a bat or a dolphin, and listened for the reflection back from the target. Active sonar gave a precise bearing and range to a target but had two disadvantages. Their direct range was limited to about 20,000 yards— roughly eleven to twelve miles—and sending out an intense pulse of sound was like sending up fireworks, a declaration to everyone in the water who might be listening, saying "here I am."

Garret had received his current orders from COM-SUBLANT that morning, and he still wasn't certain whether this was an unscheduled preparedness exercise or the real deal. A Russian Kilo was reported somewhere along the East Coast between Cape Lookout and Cape May and inside the 200-nautical-mile line. Three L.A. boats had been in position to intercept; *Pittsburgh* was the most northerly of the three, returning to Norfolk from a long deployment in the Med.

If this *was* for real, it was a potential nightmare scenario: Kilos were damned quiet—holes in the water, as the sonar team called them—and the U.S. Navy was concerned that someone might one day use one to slip a nuclear weapon into a U.S. port. For this reason, the scenario was practiced frequently, usually with other American submarines broadcasting Kilo noises from their library databases.

His orders, though, had specified a Kilo possibly operating in the service of either Mexico or Colombia, which meant a Bigfoot—a sub hired by one of the drug cartels to smuggle their damned merchandise into the United States.

The implication was almost insulting—using navy assets for drug intercepts. That was the Coast Guard's job, after all. Garret was a thorough-going professional, though, and that meant he followed orders. Drug boat or not, he was going to nail this bastard.

He picked up an intercom handset. "Conn, this is the captain."

"Conn, aye."

"Come to new heading, two-zero-zero, maintain speed ten knots."

"Come to new heading, two-zero-zero, maintain speed ten knots, aye, aye, Captain."

"Okay, Laugh," he said. "We're going to go active. How are we fixed for CZs?"

KILO CLASS SUBMARINE
35 NAUTICAL MILES OFF BETHANY BEACH
DELAWARE
1828 HOURS, EDT

"All stop," Captain Second Rank Basargin said. "Maintain silence throughout the boat."

The submarine drifted gently to a halt thirty-five meters beneath the surface in water sixty meters deep. They should be safe enough here, at least for the time being. Sunset was at 1943 local time—about another hour and a quarter. Two hours after that should see darkness enough to again approach the shore, and to surface when they saw the signal; it would take three hours, traveling at twelve knots, to return to Bethany Beach. They might have to wait a few hours more, however, if a periscope scan of the shoreline showed people enjoying the beach at night.

So 2200 hours at the earliest, and midnight would be better. Putting a raft into the water and waiting for its return might be an operation of two hours or so. Dawn at this latitude was at 0616 hours; they would need to be well clear of the shore by 0430.

Plenty of time.

He picked up a hand mike. "Sonar, Captain. Report."

"Normal traffic, Captain," the sonar officer's voice came back. "Nothing closer than fifteen thousand meters."

"Very well." He looked at the two passengers, who were hovering nearby, clearly anxious. "And now," he told them, "we wait."

CHESAPEAKE BAY BRIDGE
KENT ISLAND, MARYLAND
1815 HOURS, EDT

Officially it was the William Preston Lane Jr. Memorial Bridge, but everyone knew it simply as the Bay Bridge, a double, four-mile span crossing the Chesapeake Bay between Annapolis and Kent Island, tucked away behind the west side of the Delmarva Peninsula. Teller was at the wheel as they paid the four-dollar toll, then accelerated smoothly onto the southern lane, steadily climbing until they were soaring out over the waters of the bay 186 feet below. The sun had just set behind them in a blaze of yellows and scarlets, and Teller switched on his headlights.

It had taken them over two hours to get clear of the Washington Beltway, then thirty miles more on Route 50 to Annapolis. They still had a long stretch of highway in front of them, another sixty miles or so to Ocean City.

"I never got to ask you, Jackie," Teller said, "just what Maria told you on the flight this morning that convinced you she was telling the truth."

"Our 'girl talk'?"

"Frank didn't mean anything bad by that."

"Yeah, and it really pissed me off," she told him. "It was condescending and sexist."

"I think," Teller replied slowly, "that often women will tell women things that they would never tell a man. Doesn't that constitute 'girl talk'?"

"Only when it's saturated in testosterone, Chris." She sighed. "But . . . yeah. Women do talk. And she told me that our friend Escalante liked to beat her up. She'd been looking for a chance to get out—but Escalante had money and she didn't. She was trapped."

"You trusted her because of that?"

"I've been there."

"Oh? How was that?"

"I was married ten years ago—"

"*I* didn't know that!"

She shrugged. "Never came up. Hey, I didn't tell you *everything*."

"Obviously not." Teller smiled at her.

"I was a kid, okay? Stupid and in love, which is another way of saying stupid. I was married for one year, five days, and ten hours—but, hey, who's counting? When the VCR bounced off the wall next to my head, I decided it was time to cut my losses and get out."

"Sounds like a good choice."

"It was. And that's how I know Maria was telling the truth. She was scared and she was stuck."

"Until we came along."

"Until we came along. She saw an opportunity to get out of Iztacalpa and off to *el norte*."

"Except that if the Agency decides they don't need information from her, they'll send her packing straight back to Mexico."

"I know. They'll kill her. It stinks."

"It'll stink more if those nukes get to where they're going." He concentrated on the driving for a moment, as the support girders flashed past with a monotonous rhythm. "You're really convinced she was telling the truth?"

"I'd stake my career on it."

"Well, we're both staking our careers on it, then."

"You think we'll find them in Ocean City?"

"One of them, anyway. I figure if we do prove someone's trying to off-load a nuke in Delaware, they'll be a bit hotter to find that sub before it reaches New York." He smiled at her. "Maybe they'll even let Maria stay in America."

"Maybe they'll let *me* stay with the Agency."

"Is that important to you?"

She was silent for a moment. "I don't know," she said finally. "Not anymore. I thought I was doing good, once. Helping to save the world. Saving the American way of life. But lately it's all been politics and game after game of cover-your-ass. There are times . . ."

"What?"

"There are times I want out as badly as Maria wanted out of that relationship with Escalante."

"I know what you mean. They tell you to go save the world. Then they say you have to do it with your hands tied behind your back."

"So how are you going to find the Delaware nuke?"

"Cellmap's going to help us."

"Your virus has spread to the Delmarva Peninsula?"

"There are some targets, yeah. The big concentrations are around the big cities, of course, especially

D.C., Philly, and Baltimore—but there are a few in Dover, a few in Salisbury and Ocean City. I figure we're seeing the end branches of the supply network."

"Low-end dealers?"

"Right. Most of them, anyway, dealers and some street gangs that deal. But somewhere out here, there are some people waiting to take delivery on a suitcase nuke and transport it into Washington."

"The Iranian. Reyshahri."

"I think so."

"Have you looked for his name in the Cellmap data?"

"Yeah. Haven't found it. He probably has his phone account under an alias."

"You're aware that 'Shah Mat' is Farsi," Dominique said.

He nodded. "It means 'the king is dead' or 'the king is thwarted.' It's where chess gets the word 'checkmate,' which means the king can't move, can't escape, and the game is over."

"So are the Iranians behind the plot? A nuclear strike against the United States?"

"Good question. It's hard to see what they would get out of it, though. If we prove they launched an atomic attack against us—hell, we'd bomb them back to the Stone Age, as Curtis LeMay used to say. Maybe even retaliate with nuclear strikes of our own.

"And what do they get out of it? Three to five kilotons isn't enough to wipe out a city. It would do terrible damage, yeah, and could kill tens of thousands of people. But we're talking about something a third the size of the Hiroshima device."

"Radioactive contamination," Dominique suggested. "The center of the target cities might be unusable, uninhabitable, for decades."

"Maybe. It would hurt the economy, certainly, and our economy is hurting quite enough right now, thank you."

"I keep wondering about what Maria said about the nukes being like fireworks for the birth of a new nation."

"Aztlán," Teller said, nodding. "I know. Me, too. I can see Mexico being behind that program. Hell, they've been agitating for an independent Hispanic Southwest for years now, and nuking Washington might give them the opportunity to try for a quick revolution. But Iran? Uh-uh. It just doesn't make sense."

"Do you really think Mexico would attack us?"

Teller shook his head. "Nah. They're having enough trouble just staying intact as a country. They don't want a war with us."

"The drug cartels?

"They're crazy . . . unpredictable,. Crazy enough to try to nuke the U.S.? I don't see what they'd get out of it."

"So we're faced with some imponderables," Dominique observed. "The Mexican drug cartels want, what? A new country that they run, where drug smuggling is legal?"

"Could be."

"While the Iranians are covertly involved . . . but the risk of being linked to a nuclear attack on the United

States is just too damned big. And there's no payoff for them, no reason to do it."

"Well, they *don't* like us," Teller suggested. "And they might think that if a couple of nukes can push us into social or economic chaos, it would keep us out of their hair. They're heavily invested in Iraq and in Syria, and they want us well clear of what they see as their turf." Teller frowned, thinking about that for a moment.

"What?"

"I'm not sure. But it *almost* makes sense. With us out of Iraq, the Iranians have been moving in big-time. Everyone knows it, though people in our government don't like to admit it. Certainly, Iran is strong enough as the power behind the Iraqi presidency to block any policies or decisions the Iranians don't like.

"And Syria is enough of a mess now that the Iranians might decide to move in and prop up their puppets there—Hezbollah. That's making Israel *very* nervous right now. It's making Washington nervous, too, maybe nervous enough to intervene militarily."

"Would we really invade Syria?"

"To stop Iran from gaining an empire that stretches from the Med to Afghanistan? An empire that borders Israel, our one solid ally in the region? Yeah. We might. But if the U.S. is tied down by what looks like a nuclear terror strike on a couple of our cities . . . infrastructure wrecked, government in a shambles, economy shot to hell . . . yeah . . ."

"So now we know why the Iranians are involved,"

Dominique said. "It's a diversion to keep us from interfering with their plans for the Middle East."

"Maybe so. The thing is, it's still such a long shot for Tehran. *Incredibly* dangerous for them, if we figure out that they're behind it. I don't think we know the whole story yet."

"Well, if we can find this Reyshahri character . . ."

"Exactly. Him or Hamadi. That's what I'm hoping for, anyway. I have a few questions for those guys."

"Unfortunately, you can't threaten to send Reyshahri back to Mexico to make him talk."

"No. I'm still working on that part."

They were descending now, driving once again over solid ground as they passed between the flat green expanse of Terrapin Beach State Park to the left and the neatly ordered rows of sailboats and pleasure craft docked at the Chesapeake Bay Beach Club Marina on the right. Behind them, the sunset light was beginning to fade.

"I still don't understand how you plan to find the bad guys," Dominique said after a while. "All we know is that the destination for one of those nukes is D.C."

"We know it pretty much has to come ashore on the Delmarva Peninsula," Teller said. "Somewhere on the beach between the mouths of Delaware Bay and Chesapeake Bay, right? That narrows the search a lot."

"That's still a hell of a long beach."

"But if we can spot a few blue dots gathered on the beach, like they're waiting . . ."

"Ah. A light dawns. But why do you think it will be tonight?"

"Well, tonight or tomorrow. We don't know exactly. But . . . well, top submerged speed for a Kilo is twenty knots, maybe a bit more. It's about sixteen hundred nautical miles from Belize to the Delmarva Peninsula. We know they left early on the morning of the eighteenth. At twenty knots, the trip would have taken something like three and a third days. That puts them off the coast of Delaware around noon today."

"You don't sound certain."

"I'm not sure they made the trip flat out, at twenty knots. Going that fast, they're going to make noise, and our submarines and sonar nets might hear them coming. Not only that, but at more than about twelve knots, the water passing outside your hull makes so much noise you can't use your own passive sonar. Makes you deaf to anything else in the water."

"So they might not be here yet."

"Today is the earliest they could possibly be here, if they decided to risk getting picked up by our sonar, yeah. If they chugged along at a nice, sedate twelve knots all the way from Belize, the trip will take five and a half days, which means they'll arrive Wednesday. Two more days."

"Okay. How daring do you think they're going to be? Twenty knots? Or twelve?"

"I honestly don't know. If the Iranians are running things, I expect they'll take it slow and cautious. If the Mexican cartels are calling the shots, they might opt for quicker—which means a smaller window during which we could find them. They might have known we were hunting for them; they sure as hell knew once we raided Cerros. But even on the seventeenth, they knew we were interested in Escalante. Hell, de la Cruz put us onto Escalante in the first place, had us watching him. He knew we were here looking for the *Zapoteca,* and the nukes. I suspected he sidetracked us with Escalante, and passed the word to the *Zapoteca* and the Kilo crew that they needed to make a fast exit and a faster passage north."

"Makes sense. There was already a risk that we were going to intercept the nukes en route to the States. So even the Iranians would agree that a quick passage was better."

"Even if it meant we might hear them with our sonar nets?"

"The more I think about that, the more I think it probably wouldn't make that big a difference. Passive sonar picks up everything, and the eastern seaboard is pretty noisy. *Lots* of traffic. We'd need to know right where they are, pretty close, and use active sonar to find them—and *that* doesn't depend on how noisy or how fast the target is. They might have decided it was worth the risk."

"So all we have to do is watch for blue icons on a hundred-and-thirty-mile stretch of beach."

"Unless the navy finds them," Teller said. "I'm counting on an intercept at sea."

"You know of something to up the odds of spotting the Kilo?"

"Let's just say I've managed to introduce a competitive element to the hunt."

KILO CLASS SUBMARINE
15 NAUTICAL MILES OFF BETHANY BEACH
DELAWARE
2125 HOURS, EDT

The ping seemed to come in from all sides of the submarine at once, a sharp, ringing chirp that every submariner knew and feared: *They've found us!*

"Sonar!" Basargin snapped. "Where did that come from?"

"Bearing zero-six-five, Captain," the sonar officer replied. "Range uncertain. It sounded like a convergence zone bounce, however."

So they still had time. Not much . . . but enough, possibly, to complete the mission.

Turning, he looked at the two passengers. "Time to move," he said. "And *quickly*. There is going to be a slight change in plans."

USS *PITTSBURGH*
72 NAUTICAL MILES NORTHEAST OF BETHANY BEACH
2125 HOURS, EDT

"Bridge, sonar! Submerged contact, bearing two-four-five! First convergence zone, range seventy to seventy-five nautical miles!"

Gotcha, Garret thought, grinning.

Finding a target using sonar was not as straightforward as sending out a ping and listening for the return echo. Sound traveling underwater can behave in strange ways, depending on depth, salinity, and water temperature.

In particular, sound waves can be focused in much the same way that a lens focuses light, allowing active sonar to probe much farther than might otherwise be the case. Convergence zones, or CZs, are concentric rings of focus surrounding the transmitting submarine from which echoes can be received across much longer distances than might otherwise be possible. Each ring tends to be narrow—only about 5 nautical miles wide—and the CZs are spaced out as nested circles about 30 to 35 nautical miles apart. If the first zone was at a range 35 nautical miles from the transmitter, the second would be at 70 miles, the third at 105.

Garret had been fishing for the Kilo. As the *Pittsburgh* moved slowly toward the coast of the Delmarva Peninsula, she periodically sent out a single sonar pulse and listened for a return. The convergence zone was so narrow that the sonar crew had to send one pulse with every four or five nautical miles traveled, attempting to catch the target just as it entered the CZ's focus.

After several hours, the tactic had paid off; an underwater target had just been picked up two rings out. It might be an American submarine—but that was extremely unlikely. The next nearest boat searching for the Kilo was the *Columbus,* SSN-762, and she should now be some ninety miles to the south. Fifty miles southwest of the *Columbus* was an older L.A. boat, the *Norfolk.* No other submarines were supposed to be in this area.

"Designating target as Sierra One," the sonar operator announced.

"Paint him again. See if he's moving."

"Aye, sir." A pause. "Target Sierra One is moving, but slowly. Course two-seven-one, speed three to four knots. Sir, he's only about fifteen miles off the beach."

"That's our playmate," Garret said. "Helm, come to course two-four-five, ahead full."

While the official top speed for Los Angeles class attack subs was twenty knots underwater, they typically could hit thirty to thirty-three knots or a bit more.

It would take them two hours to get into range of the target.

TELLER
OCEAN CITY, MARYLAND
2131 HOURS, EDT

They'd pulled into a parking place on Caroline Street, just off the boardwalk. That space was a lucky find. The city was jam-packed with tourists.

Ocean City had started off as a small and secluded resort and fishing town on Maryland's Eastern Shore, but the opening of the Bay Bridge decades before had provided an easy route from the population centers of D.C. and Baltimore, and the place had quickly grown to become one of the largest vacation spots on the East Coast. The city's native population stood at something just under 8,000, but during the peak summer months the influx of tourists could push that number to well over 340,000.

Late April was early for the summer crowd, but Ocean City was still bustling well after dark. The boardwalk was ablaze with light, as were the streets and storefronts, shops, arcades, and motels inland, and milling crowds surged along every sidewalk. For the past several years, many seasonal businesses—bars, hotels, amusement parks, and the like—had begun opening on St. Patrick's Day instead of the more traditional Memorial Day in order to push the season just a little earlier.

"I wasn't expecting crowds like this," Dominique said, peering over the steering wheel through the car's front windshield. A bar called the Purple Moose was busy enough to do justice to Times Square.

"Neither was I," Teller said. "It's a little late for spring break."

"Are there any contacts here?"

Teller had his laptop open in front of him, displaying a map of the beach area from Virginia Beach to Cape May.

"Lots," he replied with glum frustration. "With this many people, I guess the dealers are out in force."

"If it's this crowded now," Dominique said, "what's it like in July?"

"Worse," Teller replied. "Much, *much* worse. I was here once a few years ago, and the traffic was backed up halfway to Salisbury." That was the largest city on Maryland's Eastern Shore, about thirty miles inland.

"So what do we do?"

Teller studied the map for a moment more, zooming in to focus just on the stretch of beach from Ocean City to the Delaware border.

"We need," he decided, "to get away from the crowds. Our Iranian friend is going to want privacy, and he sure as hell isn't going to find it here."

Dominique turned the key, gunning the car to life. "Okay. Which way?"

Teller considered this. South, the way was blocked by the Ocean City inlet through the barrier island on which the city was built. Beyond that, the beaches were largely deserted; that was Assateague Island, most of which was taken up by a state park in the north and the Assateague Island National Seashore to the south.

"Assateague Island?" Dominique asked, leaning over to look at the screen. "Long white beaches and herds of wild ponies."

"Maybe," Teller said. Then he shook his head. "No. This early in the season the beaches might well be deserted, but Assateague has only one point of access—here, the Verrazano Bridge."

"That's in New York City."

"Different Verrazano Bridge. If I were trying to smuggle a nuke ashore, I think I'd prefer to have several routes, so I didn't get trapped on the beach."

"So . . . north?"

He nodded as he closed the laptop. "North."

CHAPTER TWENTY

REYSHAHRI
INDIAN RIVER INLET, DELAWARE
2215 HOURS, EDT
21 APRIL

Captain Saeed Reyshahri sat behind the wheel of the Dodge Avenger they'd rented at Reagan International, looking out into the ocean's blackness. Fereidun Moslehi sat in the passenger seat, a set of French UGO low-light optics strapped to his face. Available commercially from Thales Optronique, the day/night unit included a second-generation image-intensifier tube that allowed 4X magnification under extreme low-light conditions. For the past couple of hours, they'd been taking turns with the unit, swapping it back and forth as they studied the night-shrouded ocean.

"I am growing tired of this," Moslehi said. "How much longer?"

Reyshahri looked at the luminous face of his watch.

"Three more hours," he said. "Assuming they get here tonight."

There was, in fact, no telling whether the submarine would reach this beach today, tomorrow, or even the next several days after that. There were so many variables—the Russian captain had promised to make the passage from Belize as swiftly as possible, but if he'd encountered American naval elements along the way and been forced to reduce his speed, or even lie in wait to avoid being heard, he could be several days late.

The plan did allow for that possibility. According to their orders, Reyshahri and Moslehi were to drive down onto this stretch of beach each night for five nights and watch between the hours of 2100 and 0200, waiting for the expected signal.

"I hate the waiting," Moslehi said.

"As the Americans say," Reyshahri replied, "it goes with the territory. The operations plan is a complex one. The planners could not anticipate every possibility."

"There are other ways this could have been done. Faster, more certain ways."

"More risky ways."

Operation Shah Mat had been designed to allow for failure or mischance at every step along the way, every step except this one—arguably the most important. He and other operatives had allowed themselves to be smuggled across the line between Mexico and the United States, knowing that if some of those operators were intercepted, others would succeed. The freighter

Zapoteca had been hired from the Mexican drug cartel that owned it through multiple false fronts, to avoid any connection with Iran, and false leads had been planted so that if the nuclear weapons were intercepted, blame would naturally fall on the Sunni heretics—especially al Qaeda. There were even different possible targets, a long list of them, any of which would work as a place where a small nuclear weapon could be detonated with great effect. The agents who actually deployed the weapons had been given a great deal of latitude in the placement; if one target proved to be blocked or otherwise unusable, the agents themselves could decide on an alternative.

The one deadly weak link in the plan was *here*, where the Iranian agents on land had to meet with the submarine and receive the weapons. This was where the Russian submarine was most vulnerable, most likely to be detected. If American intelligence had learned of the plan, this was where they might track the Iranian agents, to this beach, to catch them and the weapons together.

Reyshahri looked away from the ocean, studying the night. South, perhaps a kilometer away, a point of light flickered against darkness—American civilians enjoying a bonfire on the beach. Beyond that, on the horizon, light glowed from beach houses and private homes, and from the streetlights and businesses of a town called Bethany Beach.

There was no sign at all of American surveillance or a military presence.

Of course, American intelligence was very good at

using technologies that at times seemed downright magical. Their satellites, for instance, could easily pick out this car sitting on the sand just above the high-water mark from hundreds of kilometers up, might even be able to photograph his license plate.

The question was whether the American intelligence analysts knew that this one vehicle out of millions offered a potential threat.

In truth, Reyshahri was more concerned about those he was forced to work with on this operation. The Mexican drug lords, especially, could not be trusted. They were greedy, and they were mindlessly vicious in a way that appalled Reyshahri, with a lust both for blood and for drama that could easily jeopardize a mission that depended on invisibility to remain off the enemy's radar. As for the Aztlanistas, the gangs and the political extremist groups seeking independence for U.S. states in the southwest—their passions made them careless, and their outspokenness made them targets for government surveillance.

Even the man sitting here next to him, in Reyshahri's opinion, was a weak link. Moslehi, code name Kawrd, was a member of Quds Force rather than VEVAK, the regular Iranian secret service. Quds Force was . . . less than dependable. They certainly were very good at what they did; they were members of an elite group within Iran's elite Revolutionary Guard, subject to iron discipline and superb training—but that also meant they were motivated by the passions of their ideology. Quds Force was designed to export the Iranian revolution to other nations, to Iraq, Lebanon, Afghanistan, and Yemen in particular. Their ideological intensity could make them blind sometimes, blind especially to their own weaknesses.

That made a professional intelligence operative like Reyshahri as nervous as did the smugglers of drugs and people across the U.S.-Mexican border.

A case in point was the recent purported attempt by Quds to assassinate the Saudi ambassador to the United States. More than anything else, that had been a rather clumsy effort by the American government to accuse Iran and damage Tehran's relationship with various of her allies. However, an overeager operative with a connection to Quds Force *had* allowed himself to be sucked into an American sting operation and given the Americans the ammunition they'd needed. Tehran had been quite busy after that trying to repair the damage to the government's global image.

VEVAK would not have allowed itself to be so easily deceived.

"It's about time for me to take the night goggles for a while," he told Moslehi.

"Good. My eyes are . . . wait."

"What?"

"The signal! I see it! Two shorts . . . a long . . . and repeating!"

"Let me see."

He accepted the goggles from Moslehi and pressed them against his face. Looking in the indicated direction. He scanned the horizon slowly . . . there! A single tiny light winked against the horizon. Short-short-long. Short-short-long . . .

Once he knew where to look, he lowered the goggles and saw the light winking without magnification.

"That's it," he said. Handing the NVDs back to Moslehi, he turned the key and started the car. Reaching down, he turned the car's headlights on, repeating the signal: Short-short-long. Short-short-long. "Very well, my friend," Reyshahri said. "It won't be long now."

KILO CLASS SUBMARINE
3 NAUTICAL MILES OFF INDIAN RIVER INLET
DELAWARE
2218 HOURS, DST

The Kilo submarine surfaced gently, water cascading off the rounded surface of its hull. Captain Second Rank Besargin emerged from the hatch in the vessel's long, low sail moments later, using binoculars to scan the coast to the west. That fire on the beach just to the south—that could be trouble. Swinging slightly to the right, he studied the stretch of beach where he'd seen the signal moments ago through the periscope.

It was too dark. He picked up the intercom handset. "Sail, Bridge," he said. "Flash 'surfaced' recognition signal."

High above him, on one of the periscope masts, a light flashed, using a different code this time: Short-long-long-short. Not the Morse Code *U* for *utets'ya,* which meant being enclosed or cooped up, but *P* for *pover'ii,* which meant surface. A moment later, the reply came—a set of automobile headlights repeating the code: Short-long-long-short. Short-long-long-short.

"Break out the raft," Besargin ordered. "*And* the cargo. *Quickly!* The American submarine will be on us soon!"

Men began spilling out of the forward deck hatch below him.

TELLER
FENWICK ISLAND, DELAWARE
2242 HOURS, EDT

They'd driven ten miles north along the Coast Highway, Route 1, entering the state of Delaware from the south and passing through a resort town called Fenwick Island. Just to the north, the beachfront homes and resorts tapered off, and Dominique had pulled off onto a dirt track that gave access down through the dunes to a deserted stretch of beach.

This, Teller had thought, was more like it—an empty expanse with no nearby houses or signs of habitation, though there were some condominiums on the west side of the highway, well back from the beach and more or less screened from the waterline by dunes and lines of brush and small trees. The barrier island here was quite narrow; they were sandwiched in between the Atlantic and Little Assawoman Bay, which meant that if the smugglers were spotted here they'd be more or less trapped. The only way across to the mainland here was Route 54, two miles to the south. Three miles north, past Fenwick Island State Park, was the town of South Bethany—more motels, more resorts, more beach houses . . . but more choices for someone trying to find alternate routes away from the coast.

He'd booted up the laptop again and was studying the constellation of blue Cellmap dots showing from South Bethany up to Bethany Beach. He picked one more or less at random, an isolated icon on the Bethany Beach boardwalk, and opened a program that let him listen in, using the target cell phone as a bug. Illegal as hell, but he was running out of ideas.

It took a moment to make the connection. His laptop was using a mobile hotspot to provide him with Wi-fi service, linking him by satellite to the larger computers back at Langley. Then his laptop's speaker hissed, and he and Dominique were listening in on a conversation perhaps five miles north of their parking spot.

"Yeah . . . what the dillio, dude?"

"Jes' coolin', m'man. What can I do ya for?"

"The usual, man. Eight-ball o' white."

"Y'got four yards?"

"Four! Shoo, you shittin' me? That stuff is taxed!"

"Hey, watch the six o'clock, man. Times is tough, nah-mean?"

"All I got is a coupla Cs, man."

"Shit. That there'll buy ya a teener, no more."

Teller switched the link off. A drug deal, going down on the boardwalk. He'd been able to hear something like carnival music in the background, mingled with crowd sounds and ocean surf. Were such deals really that public? Apparently so. He'd always imagined such goings-on taking place in dark alleys or deserted buildings, not in the middle of a crowd. Damn it, where were the cops?

He knew the answer to that one, though. Local police forces were stretched to the breaking point. That street dealer probably had some friends spotting for him, to let him know when a cop was approaching.

The flood of drugs coming north into the States and the lure of quick and easy money would only put more stress on the system.

Where, Teller wondered, was the breaking point?

Briefly, he considered giving the Bethany Beach police department a call—but they wouldn't be able to act on what he said, not on an illegal wiretap.

His cell phone buzzed. It was Procario.

"Yo," he said.

"You have Cellmap running?"

"Yup."

"Take a look off the beach just south of Indian River."

"*Off* the beach?"

"Just do it."

Teller thumbed the map view on his laptop, moving to the north. At first, he didn't see anything, but when he zoomed back out a bit, two blue dots appeared out in the ocean, tucked in close alongside each other perhaps half a nautical mile offshore. The Indian River Inlet was just under ten miles north of where they were parked now.

Curious. There were no blue dots anywhere along that stretch of beach. What the hell were two people with Cellmapped phones doing half a mile out in the water? It was possible, he thought, that there was a party boat out there—but his first thought had been that someone might be coming ashore.

They needed to get up there *now*.

"I see them," he said, gesturing to Dominique to start the car, to get going, and *fast*. "Did you get in touch with the McDee earlier?"

"I did."

"Better let her know about this contact. And . . . it might be a good idea to have the Activity in on this."

"Way ahead of you, buddy."

"We're headed for the beach south of Indian River Inlet now."

"Right. I'll let you know if I hear anything new."

"The McDee?" Dominique asked, one eyebrow arched.

"Colonel Audrey MacDonald," Teller replied. "A woman whose career is devoted to making my life a living hell. Fortunately, like me, she doesn't care for Klingons."

"Whoa there, cowboy. You're going way over my head."

He sighed. "Colonel MacDonald is my boss at IN-SCOM. I report to her—at least I do when I'm not playing with your friends at the Company."

"Klingons?"

"The CIA isn't real popular with most of the other intelligence agencies, okay? We call it the 'evil empire.' Or the 'Klingon Empire.' "

"Ah."

"No offense."

"I *may* forgive you. And why is it a good thing that Colonel MacDonald doesn't like us?"

"Larson, Wentworth, Vanderkamp—they seem to have convinced themselves that there's no danger of those nukes coming ashore from the sub."

"Yes . . ."

"So I told Frank to give MacDonald a call. She likes him, I think. If *I'd* called her, she wouldn't have listened. But Frank told her that the CIA was screwing the pooch on this one, and that it gave INSCOM a clear field."

"For what?"

"To try to find that sub."

"I see. Did it occur to you that the Agency might still be on top of it? They just wanted *us* to stand down, so we were out of the way?"

"That's stupid."

"No more stupid than having different agencies competing with each other, like it's some kind of game. What will you do next—drag in the FBI? Homeland Security? How about the NSA?"

"If I have to, yeah. It *is* a game. It just happens to have some extremely serious consequences if we lose."

"It doesn't work that way, Chris. INSCOM is supposed to provide military intelligence to the army and DoD. The CIA provides foreign civilian and political intelligence to the president. The FBI handles domestic security. You're going to have different agencies tripping over one another, and why? Because you want INSCOM to get the credit?"

"Fuck the credit. You know as well as I do that things aren't all clean and nice and neat in the real world. We have a direct threat to the United States here, and I really don't give a damn how we stop it, okay? U.S. intelligence—and by that I mean *all* of the intelligence services, all sixteen of them—they . . . *we* are this country's last line of defense before someone, the military or the president or Congress, has to take direct action."

"Ouch," Dominique said, reacting to Teller's anger. "I think I hit a hot button, didn't I?"

"I dunno. Maybe." Teller hesitated, wondering how much to share. "I had a good friend, a mentor. DIA, army intelligence. Back in 2000, he was part of a secret data-mining project called Able Danger, looking at intelligence intercepts right here in the United States. He actually uncovered two of the three terrorist cells operating in Virginia—the very same cells that went on to launch the 9/11 attacks, and he did so a whole *year* before the government will admit that those tangos were in the country, even now. But the DIA refused to share that intel with the FBI because of . . . legal issues. What was the army doing eavesdropping on people inside America's borders? He also briefed the DCI personally three times. Nothing was done, *nothing*— and three thousand Americans died."

"My God."

"When the finger pointing started afterward, U.S. intelligence was blamed. It wasn't intelligence. It was the sheer glacial *stupidity* of bureaucratic turf-holding and empire-building and ass-covering. That last line of defense I mentioned just doesn't work when the people who put it there don't pay attention."

"And your friend?"

"Forced to take early retirement. He was . . . inconvenient." Teller laughed, a bitter sound. "They called him a cowboy."

"So . . . you really don't care who catches the bad guys."

"Of course not. If the Klingons want the glory, they're welcome. If they want to pretend everything is fine so they can blame someone else, that's fine, too. *Just so someone stops the Tangos from setting off those nukes.*"

"Which explains why you're freelancing." The term meant that Teller was working for himself now, not for one of the agencies.

"Hah. I wouldn't have put it that way, but hey, if no one else will, *someone* has to do it."

"And you could go to prison for it."

Teller had given that a lot of thought. When he'd walked out on Wentworth and the others back at CIA headquarters, he was no longer on loan to the CIA, nor was he working again under the aegis of INSCOM. He was on his own, a captain in the U.S. Army, with no particular authority of his own.

Even as just an army captain, though, he was still under oath. *To support and defend the Constitution of the United States against all enemies, foreign and domestic . . .*

There was his personal credo as well. *What's the next right thing to do?*

"Then I go to prison," he said. "But I figure that won't happen."

"Why not?"

"Because we're going to *catch* those bastards. I just hope MacDonald was able to redeploy some subs off-shore."

"Subs?"

"The absolute best way to catch a sub is with an-other sub," Teller told her. "I figured MacDonald would talk directly to either COMSUBLANT or the Joint Chiefs and scramble some L.A. boats to the area." He gave Dominique a sidelong look. "So how about you?"

"What about me?"

"I asked you to drive out here with me. You were taken off the op, too. Why'd you say yes?"

"Oh, Jesus, Chris, *someone* has to look out for you."

REYSHAHRI
INDIAN RIVER INLET, DELAWARE
2246 HOURS, EDT

Reyshahri stepped out of the car and walked down to the high-tide line. A strong offshore breeze whipped at the jacket he was wearing and tasted of salt.

He turned his binoculars toward the bonfire down the beach. From here, he could make out eight or ten people—probably teenagers—huddled around the fire. The breeze brought snatches of shouts and laughter across the sand.

All of them were turned inward, facing the fire—and that meant their night vision was ruined. They would not be able to see a raft approaching the beach through the surf.

Swinging the binoculars back out to sea, he studied the night, the pounding surf. There were no more signals from the submarine now. The plan had called for them to submerge right out from under the raft once it was loaded. Mohamed Hamadi would bring the first package ashore. The second, with the Mexican, Hector Gallardo, would head for a second rendezvous on a beach along the southern coast of Long Island.

At least . . . that was the plan. Reyshahri knew better, though, than to expect any given plan to go right. There was always *something* . . .

He heard the drone of a small motor above the hiss and crash of the half-meter surf. Reaching into a jacket pocket, he pulled out a flashlight, aimed it out to sea, and flicked the switch on . . . off . . . on . . . off . . .

Moslehi joined him. "I see them." He pointed. "There."

He handed Reyshahri the NVDs. He put them on, and the black ocean shifted to lighter shades of gray beneath a silver-gray sky. Yes . . . there. He could see the raft a hundred meters out, moving toward the shore with the gentle but irresistible movement of the swell.

With *two* figures aboard.

Minutes passed, and the raft drew closer, guided in by Reyshahri's flashlight. The craft was a commercial Zodiac, a rigid-hull rubber boat with a 90-horsepower outboard motor for propulsion. As the boat lifted and surged toward the beach with the tumble of a final wave, Reyshahri and Moslehi splashed out into the water a few meters, grabbed hold of the safety line around the boat's gunwales, and helped haul it up onto the beach.

"Welcome to the United States," Reyshahri said in Farsi as the two men aboard clambered out and helped drag the boat across the sand.

"The Great Satan, you mean," one replied in the same language. "Sunrise."

"Eagle," Reyshahri said. Sign and countersign.

"I am Hamadi."

"Sarvan Reyshahri. This is Moslehi." He looked into the Zodiac. "I take it our plans have changed."

Hamadi nodded. "They have. An American submarine picked us up an hour or so ago. The submarine's captain did not want to be trapped against the coast."

"We follow the backup plan, then," Reyshahri said, nodding. "Let's get these into the vehicle."

An American submarine just off the coast. What did that mean? A chance encounter? That was possible. The American navy had major port and base facilities at Norfolk and Portsmouth, less than 250 kilometers to the southwest of this beach.

It was also possible that the Americans knew something of the plan. If they did, they might be closing in now.

Almost, Reyshahri wished that he had a cell phone.

He did not carry one while on a mission—*ever*. American intelligence had ways of tapping into cell phone conversations, and they were rumored to be able to use them for electronic eavesdropping as well.

"The two of you," he said as they climbed into the car. "Do you have phones?"

"Of course," Hamadi said.

"Get rid of them. *Now*."

"Don't be ridiculous," Hamadi said. "How are we supposed to coordinate—"

"*Now!* Throw them away!"

Both men pulled cell phones from their pockets and hurled them away into the darkness.

"Good," Reyshahri said. "Now we can proceed."

"I think, Saeed," Moslehi told him in Farsi, "that sometimes you are too paranoid."

"Quite possible," Reyshahri replied. "But the Americans have not found us yet, and I intend to keep it that way."

"I wondered why you didn't want *me* to carry a phone, when we joined up in Arizona."

"We *know* they can listen in on conversations," Reyshahri replied. "Any signal sent through the air cannot be considered secure."

"Yes, but a phone that's not even on?"

"I would put *nothing* past the Americans," Reyshahri said, "and it is imperative now that we remain invisible."

With the car loaded, the packages in the trunk, Reyshahri gunned the engine, moved up the beach to the dirt road that led to the highway.

Turning right onto the main road then, they sped north into the night.

CHAPTER TWENTY-ONE

TELLER
INDIAN RIVER INLET, DELAWARE
2315 HOURS, EDT
21 APRIL

Traffic was light on Route 1 this late at night, but the highway was not entirely deserted. As they drove north from Fenwick Isle, they'd encountered several other vehicles—particularly as they passed through the resort towns of South Bethany and Bethany Beach.

Now they were driving through a wilder, more desolate stretch. Teller continued to stare at the laptop screen with intense concentration, watching as they drew closer and still closer to the two blue dots that had just come up out of the sea.

"Whoa," Teller said suddenly. "Slow-slow-slow-slow . . . here! Right! Turn right here!"

Dominique swung the car off of the highway and into the mouth of a hard-packed sand road leading up over a dune and then down toward the beach. The headlights showed empty sand and the roll and splash of the waves.

"Shit," Teller said. He'd been expecting to see two men coming ashore in a boat. Pulling a flashlight from the glove box and his pistol from its holster, he slid out of the car.

"The two contacts?" Dominique asked.

"Yeah, the ones that came ashore from the ocean. They're *here*."

She was out of the car now as well. She'd left the engine running, and the headlights glared across sand, surf, and black water. "There's a fire on the beach over there."

"No. According to the Cellmap, we're within a few yards of them. Maybe over here . . ." He probed ahead, probing through the dune grass with his light.

"What's that down there?" Dominique asked, pointing up the beach toward the left.

"Let's see." They jogged down the beach together. Teller's flashlight fell on a wet gray shape.

"A Zodiac!" Dominique exclaimed.

"Yeah." Teller laid his hand on the outboard engine, then snatched it away. "Still hot. This is definitely how they came ashore."

"But where are they?"

"Look." He shone the light on the wet sand. Footprints, a number of them, led from the Zodiac up the beach.

"The tide's coming in," Dominique said, "but it hasn't had time to reach those prints."

"No." Teller swept the flashlight up across the empty

beach. "I think they're gone. But we can't have missed them by more than a few minutes." Holstering his pistol, he reached for his cell phone instead.

He punched in Procario's number. "Frank? We're here. The beach is deserted."

"I'm still reading two contacts. Looks like they're in the dunes at the top of the beach."

"I think they ditched their phones."

"Shit."

"We have a Zodiac—empty. Footprints going up the shelf, and then they're lost above the high-water line. Just loose sand. It does look like vehicles have been here. I see ruts from tires, lots of 'em. I'm thinking the boat came ashore and was met by somebody in a car."

"We'll have a forensics team there in half an hour."

"Good. Maybe they can check the Zodiac for radiation, and confirm that a weapon was on the thing."

"Right."

"You have anything on the two phones from the database?"

"No names. Both are registered with a corporate account."

"What account?"

"Manzanillo Internacional."

"Manzanillo . . . wait. Isn't that the import-export company that owns the *Zapoteca*?"

"The very same."

"Okay. Maybe if they find the phones, they can get evidence pointing to individuals. There's got to be a log somewhere linking specific phones to specific people."

He signaled Dominique, and the two of them headed

back to the car. There was nothing more they could do here.

"So, which way do you think they went?" Procario asked him as he slid into the driver's seat. Dominique took the laptop and began looking for nearby blue icons.

"I'm not sure," Teller said as he started the vehicle. "The main highway back to the Bay Bridge is south of here. North, Route 1 goes up to Dover, then on to Wilmington."

"I'm looking at a map now," Procario told him. "At Wilmington, they could pick up Interstate 95. That becomes the Jersey Turnpike and takes them straight to New York."

"Yeah, but if they want to hit D.C., their best bet is south to Ocean City, then west to the Bay Bridge. Straight line and no tolls." Teller thought for a moment as he backed the car around and headed back up the dirt track toward Route One. "Look, we need to cover every possibility. We need some really major high-tech help here."

"We're on it. NEST has already been alerted."

"Excellent," Teller said. They reached the highway, he glanced left, then right . . . and then turned left, toward the south. "We're hot on their trail now."

INSCOM HQ
FORT BELVOIR, VIRGINIA
2320 HOURS, EDT

Procario switched off his phone. "They missed them," he told Colonel MacDonald. "But it can't be by very much."

They were standing in the INSCOM Ops Center two levels beneath the street, along with several senior army officers—Colonel Steven Devendorf and Colonel Andrew Howard, as well as the director of the DIA, Lieutenant General Patrick Granger. A civilian was present as well, the deputy director of human intelligence, George Haupt. Together with several aides, they were standing around a large light table, studying the computer-generated map spread out there and on the wall behind them.

Devendorf brought up a window showing the target beach and the two blue icons. He pointed at a time stamp running in the lower left corner. "Right. This is at 2258 hours 30 seconds . . . the targets are moving. Here . . . 2258:40, both of them move *quickly* about ten yards north, then come to rest."

"So . . . they're on the road then at 2300 hours," Procario said. "Chris's call came through at 2316:12, so they must have pulled in there, say, 2315."

"And left again at 2320," Howard said.

"So they're twenty minutes behind the bad guys," MacDonald said. "Maybe twenty-two. What's the speed limit on that part of the highway?"

"Fifty-five," Howard replied. "We already checked that."

"So if the Tango is cautious," Procario said, "he's twenty-one miles ahead of them. If he's pushing a bit, doing sixty in a fifty-five, it's more like twenty-two."

"God," Haupt said, studying the map. "The terrorists could already be in Ocean City! That's just eighteen miles south of that beach!"

"They're off the barrier islands, certainly," Granger observed.

"Can't we get the local police in on this?" Haupt asked. "Maybe set up roadblocks?"

"We're working on it," Granger said, "but it takes time to get authorization and clearances. Just like getting a warrant."

Haupt slammed a fist on the display table. *"We're the federal fucking government, fer chrissakes!* If we have to shut down the whole state of Delaware to catch these people, then we do it!"

"Yes," Granger said. "We'll do it, if we have to. But NEST has been alerted and is on the way in. They should be able to pick them up easily enough."

"NEST" stood for Nuclear Emergency Support Team. When it was created by President Gerald Ford in 1974, it had been designated as the Nuclear Emergency *Search* Team, presumably because the word "support" sounded less uncertain, a bit less desperate than did "search." Tasked with investigating any radiological incident, including accidental spills or reactor leaks, it was also equipped to help locate nuclear weapons or radioactive material in terror incidents. Since 1975, NEST had responded to thirty nuclear terror threats.

All had been false alarms. It looked like they'd hit the real deal this time.

MacDonald looked at Procario. "Just how certain are you that this is for real?" she asked him. "Captain Teller is not known for his . . . steadiness."

"Chris Teller is one of the steadiest men I know,

ma'am," Procario replied. "And look at the sequence. We have solid intel that two nuclear weapons are being put on a Russian Kilo. Three days later, two Cellmap icons come ashore in Delaware, out of empty ocean. What the hell else would be going on out there?"

"Drugs," Howard suggested. The others looked at him, and he shrugged. "Hey, it's a narco-sub, right?"

"If there's even a chance that it's smuggling nukes," Devendorf said, "we need to find them."

MacDonald's Bluetooth flashed, and she held her hand to her ear for a moment. "MacDonald. Yes . . . okay. Thank you." She looked at the others. "That was Admiral Dolan," she said. "One of our attack submarines has made contact with an unidentified submarine object off that part of the coast."

"When?" Granger demanded.

"About two hours ago. Our sub is attempting to close with the target now."

"What else do we have in the area?" Granger wanted to know.

"Two other Los Angeles subs, and a large number of surface ships and helicopters are moving now from Norfolk and Philadelphia. Sounds to me like half of the U.S. Navy."

"But we still have a nuclear weapon ashore," Devendorf said. "We need to put together the best plan for nailing these bastards."

"What NEST assets do we have?" Granger asked.

"Right now . . . two muon imagers, a dozen ZBVs, and three ZBAs," Devendorf said.

"Not much to cover this much territory," MacDonald

said. "D.C. and Baltimore and Philly and New York City. All high-value targets."

"Our intel said D.C. and NYC," Procario said. "If the bad guys haven't been alerted yet, they'll still be targeting those cities, not the others."

"Agreed." Granger nodded. "Where are the muon scanners?"

"One's outside D.C., sir," Devendorf said, "the other's in Newark. Where do you think we should put them?"

"The one targeting New York City," Procario said, "that depends on whether the bomb is being sent in from Long Island or from New Jersey, doesn't it?"

"We don't need to worry about the New York bomb now," Granger said. "Our best information now is that that weapon is still aboard the sub. The navy will catch it."

"Okay," Procario said, but he was worried. What if the navy didn't get that sub? "Look, just in case . . . we need a detector as far down the Jersey Turnpike as they can manage. South of all of the bridges and tunnels leading from 95 across to Manhattan."

"Edison," Howard said, enlarging one section of the map, zooming down on a tangle of highway overpasses.

"Where's that?" Granger demanded.

"Near Perth Amboy, sir. South of 95's interchange with Interstate 287—that's Staten Island, and would give them access either to the Holland Tunnel or Brooklyn."

"Okay," Granger said. "Sounds like you already have this worked out."

"The NEST people have been running scenarios," Howard told him. "If we don't catch that sub in the next ten hours or so, though, we're going to need to fall back on another plan."

"Good enough." Granger pointed at an area farther south. "I think the D.C. scanner needs to go up at the Bay Bridge. Major choke point there."

"Sounds good, sir."

"And the ZBVs should probably concentrate on all the main highways between D.C. and Baltimore. Route 1, 95, 295 . . . all of them. Just in case."

"How about the ZBAs?" Procario asked.

"Where are they?"

"Two at Edwards," Howard said, "the other one at JB MDL."

"Joint Base McGuire-Dix-Lakehurst," Granger said, nodding. "Central New Jersey. That one can patrol the New Jersey Turnpike. Have the others patrol around D.C."

Procario pointed. "One can patrol over the Delmarva Peninsula, from the Bay Bridge to Ocean City," he suggested. "The other can concentrate on the Baltimore–Washington Corridor."

"Very good," Granger said.

"But what if they get through?" Haupt said. "Should we call for an evacuation?"

"Jesus," Granger said. "What a nightmare *that* would be! Over half a million people trying to get out of D.C. at once?"

"And we thought the Beltway rush hour was a

problem," Procario said. "But you know . . . *there's* an idea . . ."

"We're *not* going to order an evacuation," Granger said. "Not yet. Not until we're *sure* we know what we're dealing with here."

"An evacuation wouldn't kill as many people as a five-kiloton nuke," Devendorf observed.

"I'm not so sure about that," Granger told him. "It would also have half a million people stuck in their automobiles out in the open, going nowhere. Emergency vehicles blocked. If the warhead went off, we could actually lose *more* people than we would if everyone was at home. If the blast happened in central D.C. at night, casualties might be fairly low."

"We should still alert the city government," MacDonald suggested. "So fire and police are ready."

"Good idea." Granger looked at Procario. "What was your idea, Colonel?"

"If we can get authorization, General, then what Mr. Haupt suggested is dead-on." He pointed at several spots on the map. "Get the police to put up roadblocks here . . . here . . . over here . . . any of these towns in Delaware and Maryland where several roads meet. Use army personnel if we have to, to get enough men—"

"That's still a needle in a haystack, Colonel," Granger said. "And . . . do you have any idea of the size of the traffic jams that would cause?"

"Exactly, sir. And if people are stuck in their cars, not going anywhere—well, neither are the Tangos, are they?"

Granger blinked, then smiled. "You know, I have a

feeling that the commuter rush hour tomorrow morning is going to be a real bitch."

TELLER
OCEAN CITY, MARYLAND
2345 HOURS, EDT

"Which way now?" Teller asked.

"I'd take 50," Dominique said. "That way."

Heading west, they sped through the night.

"It would be nice if we had at least a make and model on their car," Dominique said. Traffic was still light, but there *were* other vehicles on the highway. The double red pinpoints of taillights showed on the horizon up ahead.

"I know. We don't even know if we're on the right road."

The problem, he'd decided, was impossible. Going north on the Coast Highway, then turning west on Route 9 or 16 actually offered a more direct route toward the Bay Bridge, but the roads were smaller, two lanes, with more small towns and lower speed limits along the way. Turning south had put them on an expressway, which was faster, but longer in miles. Teller was also realizing how many choices of route there were—at least a dozen different back roads winding across the flat expanse of Delaware and Maryland's Eastern Shore.

"So what's our plan?" Dominique asked him.

"Okay . . . there's a major bottleneck at the Bay Bridge. We can join the NEST unit there and use the laptop to tap into INSCOM or Agency files and help ID Reyshahri."

"The NEST people will have file photos and Agency downloads, too, I'm sure."

"Yeah. I guess I just want to be in on the capture."

"What if Reyshahri went north?"

"Then he's heading for Route 95 and the Baltimore–Washington Corridor. Or he'll take back roads and small towns straight across to the Bay Bridge. I'm betting on the bridge."

"You don't think he might decide the Bay Bridge looks too much like a trap?"

Teller chewed on this for a moment. "I see your point. Damn, I was just looking at time."

"We don't know that they have a time deadline," Dominique pointed out.

"No, but the longer they're moving on the highway, the more chance there is for us to find them."

"Balanced against the possibility that we would shut down the Bay Bridge and check all traffic funneling across." She tapped out some commands on the laptop. "Going north to 95, then southwest to Washington . . . that's only about 165 miles or so . . . compared with 155 taking the high-speed southern route . . . or about 110 miles if they stick to small towns and head straight for the bridge."

"Damn. That's not much difference at all. I guess the question to look at is how much of a hurry they're in."

"Do they know we're on their trail?" Dominique asked. "That might make a difference."

"Hard to know for sure, but . . . oh, Christ."

"What?"

"I just thought of something. Why would the two Tangos off the sub ditch their phones *after* they came ashore?"

"Someone waiting for them on the shore told them to? Otherwise they would have tossed them into the water."

"That's the only explanation that makes sense. And that means that either the Tango on the beach is *super* cautious . . . but not cautious enough to get rid of the phones earlier on—"

"Or that he knew the cell phones have been compromised," Dominique said. "Okay. We'll assume they know about the phones."

"Not only that. There's another giveaway."

"What?"

"Just a second." He pulled out his cell phone and thumbed the speed dial for Procario's number. "Frank?"

"Right here," Procario's voice said.

"When you alerted people—did that include the navy?"

"MacDonald called her contacts at Norfolk, yeah. And we just had word an hour and a half ago that one of our subs spotted a submerged contact off Indian River."

"Okay. Before they put that Zodiac ashore? Or after?"

"Can't say for sure, but it's a good bet that it was before."

"And we can't rule out the possibility of ship-to-shore communications," Teller said. "Okay, that tells me what I need to know."

"You have an idea, Chris?"

"I think so. If this Reyshahri character knows we spotted that sub offshore, he knows we must be looking for him."

"Okay . . ."

"Which means he's not going to walk into a box-trap like the Bay Bridge. I suggest you concentrate your search to the Baltimore–D.C. Corridor."

"I'll pass that along. We have NEST assets deploying there already."

"Good. One more thing?"

"Shoot."

"Think one of the ZBAs out of Edwards could swing by and pick us up?"

"I'll see what they can do. Where are you?"

"Westbound on Route 50—ten miles outside of Ocean City. Maybe twenty miles east of Salisbury."

"Okay. I'll get back to you."

"What," Dominique asked as he switched off the phone, "is a ZBA?"

"Z Backscatter Aircraft. Goes along with Z Backscatter Van, a ZBV. A mobile screening system. Uses backscatter X-ray imaging to see inside cars and trucks, and all it needs to do is drive past—or fly past in the case of a helicopter."

"Backscatter X-rays. Like the X-ray units at airports now? Instant voyeur?"

"Yup. It's a way to unobtrusively find all sorts of contraband—illegal immigrants inside a van, say, or plastic explosives, or drugs. And the NEST units are outfitted with something called RTD—Radioactive

Threat Detection. Picks up low-level gamma radiation or neutrons at a distance, so it can detect nuclear weapons."

"I had no idea they could do that. I thought you couldn't separate radiation from a man-made source from natural background noise."

"Actually, we've been able to distinguish the two since, oh, the late seventies or so. We haven't advertised it, because we don't want the bad guys to know what's possible. On the other hand, letting them know means they're not as likely to try smuggling WMDs into the country. So lots of it's not classified—but we don't talk much about it, either."

"If that technology means driving down a city street and performing strip searches on people who don't even know it's happening—maybe you don't *want* to talk about it."

Teller grinned. "There is that. Like the show you put on for me and Frank down in Mexico. Really nice, by the way."

"Thank you. Bastard."

"Hey, most espionage is surveillance, right? Some surveils are just a little more personal than others."

"What kind of range are we talking about?"

"Something like fifteen hundred feet. Used to be you had to be pretty close—say a hundred yards—to detect low-level radiation. The real problem is time. It takes fifteen seconds, more or less, to scan one vehicle. Four a minute—two hundred and forty an hour. But we're going to have thousands of cars to examine."

"So . . . where has it gone?" Dominique asked after a moment. She sounded sad.

"Where's what gone?"

"The Fourth Amendment, of course. The one that says you need a warrant to conduct a search, and that people have a right to be secure against unreasonable searches of their homes, papers, their personal stuff—and their own persons."

"I've been wondering about that for a long time," Teller admitted. He was thinking again about the damnable NDAA of 2012. That American lawmakers would even *think* about trampling on the rights of citizens so completely showed how seriously broken the system was.

Teller had always considered himself to be a firm constitutionalist. His oath was to the Constitution, and the ideals behind it. *Against all enemies, foreign and domestic . . .*

Then again, if protecting the citizens' right to privacy meant accepting wholesale death and devastation . . .

"Damn it, Jackie, what's worse?" he continued. "Using high-tech to peek inside of people's cars and trucks, or into their homes or through their clothing? Or watching a mininuke vaporize downtown Washington?"

"I know, I know. But do you remember what Ben Franklin had to say about that?"

" 'Those who sacrifice liberty for safety deserve neither liberty nor safety.' That one?"

"Yes."

"It's not what Franklin actually said—but it sounds like him. I don't know, though."

"What?"

"Franklin was a notorious dirty old man. Maybe he

would have enjoyed cruising down the streets of down-town Philadelphia in a ZBV, looking through all those layers of clothing women wore back then."

"I think you've been hanging out with too many exotic dancers," Dominique said, angry. "Some of us prefer to keep a little mystery in our lives. Or maybe a bit of dignity."

"And some of us," Teller added, "don't want to see our cities destroyed, even if it means conducting illegal strip searches."

"I know. I'd just be happier if I knew the Peeping Tom bit is *strictly* line of duty, for emergencies only, and not just one more facet of bureaucratic thuggery, bullying, or nanny-state tyranny."

"If you figure out how to guarantee all of that," Teller said, "you let the rest of us mortals know how to do it, okay?"

CHAPTER TWENTY-TWO

REYSHAHRI
EAST OF NEWARK, NEW JERSEY
0055 HOURS, EDT
22 APRIL

"No," Reyshahri said, studying a roadmap with the help of a penlight. "We do not want the turnpike."

"But that's Route 95 South," Moslehi protested. He was at the wheel. "It will take us straight into Washington!"

"It will also take us through toll booths," Reyshahri replied. "Places where they might be checking every vehicle, looking for us."

"We don't know that," Hector Gallardo, the Mexican, said from the backseat. He spoke English, since he didn't speak either Arabic or Farsi, and Reyshahri didn't speak Spanish. "You are too cautious, Captain."

"We will not take unnecessary risks," Reyshahri replied. "We are also going to avoid the toll bridges across the Susquehanna River—and for the same reason."

"How do we get across, then?" Hamadi asked.

"The Conowingo Dam," Reyshahri said, still studying the map. "We'll take the exit for Route 7, then Route 2. Once we're through Newark, we'll take 273 West . . . something called Telegraph Road. That will put us on Route 1 and take us across the river at Conowingo."

"And that will be . . . what? Another forty, fifty kilometers to Baltimore?" Hamadi asked.

"I agree that we are being too cautious," Moslehi said. "Small, winding country roads through the middle of nowhere! This will take us all night!"

"Patience." Reyshahri said, looking out the window. They were passing one of the enormous shopping malls so beloved by the Americans, and deserted at this late hour. "The Americans must suspect we are here—and they likely know why. We will not make it so easy for them to find us."

"The Americans are not going to stop every vehicle to look for us," Moslehi said.

"I agree," Gallardo said. "You act as though the American intelligence agencies possess magic."

"We don't know what American intelligence can do," Reyshahri said. "It's best not to be surprised, yes?"

"You are in command," Moslehi replied. He did not sound happy about it, however.

"Yes," Reyshahri said. "I am in command."

Although he wished otherwise.

USS *PITTSBURGH*
OFF CAPE MAY
0115 HOURS, EDT

"Bridge! Sonar! Contact, Sierra One, bearing three-zero-four, range ten thousand yards!"

"Sonar, this is the captain. Keep banging him! I don't want him to twitch without us knowing about it!"

"Aye, Captain. He appears to be on a heading of zero-eight-zero, eight knots. Looks like he's trying to reach deep water."

"Where is he relative to the line?"

"Contact is still inside the twelve-mile limit, Captain. I would guess three miles."

Garret exchanged a glance with Commander Malone, his exec. "I think the son of a bitch has run out of running room." He raised the intercom handset again. "Radio shack, bridge. Get off a message to COMSUBLANT. 'Submerged contact, probable Kilo, confirmed and in range. Please advise.' And give them our position."

"Aye, aye, sir."

It had taken several hours to run the bastard down. The *Pittsburgh* had made several quick dashes toward the coast, punctuated by sudden stops while the sub's active sonar had blasted through the water ahead, "banging" in submariner's slang. Finally, they'd closed the range until they were no longer hearing echoes coming back from convergence zones thirty-five or seventy miles ahead. The contact was just under five nautical miles away now—and Cape May was at his back. He wasn't going to be able to reach deep water without running past *Pittsburgh*.

Normally in this sort of situation, *Pittsburgh* would have moved over to the attack, but this was not exactly a normal situation. Either the Kilo was Russian or it belonged to a Latin American country—Mexico or Venezuela—but no one seemed certain of the details. In either case, the contact was not overtly hostile, the United States was not at war with the submarine's owner, and it seemed unlikely that Norfolk would tell him to blow the contact out of the water, even if he was well inside the twelve-mile limit.

On the other hand, intelligence believed that the submarine's operators were a major Latino drug cartel, and the last word he'd received from Norfolk had recommended that he use caution in his approach—that the contact might well be carrying nuclear weapons.

That tidbit alone had given Garret reason to hesitate. Kilos were attack boats; they didn't carry ballistic missiles. A Kilo class submarine running under the Russian flag *might* carry torpedoes with nuclear warheads, but if this boat was working for Venezuela or for a drug cartel, any onboard weapons would be strictly conventional.

That suggested that if this Kilo was carrying a nuke, the weapon was something else—a suitcase nuke, perhaps, or a wired-in-the-basement do-it-yourself job.

Which meant there were *no* guarantees if one of *Pittsburgh*'s torpedoes detonated on the target. Atlantic

City was just thirty miles to the northeast. An underwater detonation here could drop radioactive rain across parts of the New Jersey coast and kill thousands.

"Bridge, radio shack," a voice said from the overhead speaker. "Message from COMSUBLANT."

"Let's hear it."

"Message reads 'Use best judgment to force contact to surface.' Signed Kellerman, vice admiral, COMSUBLANT."

"Very well." Garret considered the order. *Use best judgment* was tossing the ball squarely back into his court, meaning that if he screwed up, it was his career on the line.

Assuming, of course, that *Pittsburgh* and those aboard her survived the encounter.

"Weps, this is the captain," he said. "Status on tubes two and four."

"Captain, weapons officer. Tubes two and four have warshots loaded—Mark 48 ADCAP."

"Sonar, bridge. Range to target."

"Bridge, sonar. Target Sierra One now at ninety-five hundred yards."

"Fire control. Power on, tubes two and four."

"Power on, tubes two and four, aye, aye, Captain."

"Weps, I want a wire-guided detonation one hundred yards in front of the target. Do not, repeat, do *not* hit him. This is a warning shot only."

"Warning shot only, aye, aye, Captain." A pause. "Weapons warm and ready to fire, Captain."

"Tube two. Make tube ready in all respects." From this moment on, things would get noisy. The target certainly knew *Pittsburgh* was out here, thanks to the now constant sonar pinging.

"Tube two is flooded, Captain. Outer door open."

"Firing point procedures." Garret waited a beat. If he was wrong . . . "Match bearings and *shoot!*"

Garret felt the lurch through the deck plating as the torpedo, weighing more than a ton and a half, slid from Tube Two.

"Two fired electrically, Captain." A pause. "Torpedo running hot and normal."

The Mark 48 ADCAP torpedo—the standard anti-ship weapon for all U.S. submarines—was wire guided, a crewman at the weapons station guiding the warshot by sending command signals down a slender wire unspooling behind the torpedo as it traveled through the water. Though the publicly stated speed of a Mark 48 was "in excess" of twenty-eight knots, the weapon's actual top speed was closer to fifty-five knots.

At a range of 9,500 yards, the warhead would reach the target in just under six minutes.

KILO CLASS SUBMARINE
OFF CAPE MAY
0121 HOURS, EDT

"Captain! *Torpedo in the water!*"

"Where?"

"Bearing two-six-four!"

"Conn! Hard right rudder!"

"Hard right rudder, Captain!"

"Thirty degrees down planes! Put us on the bottom!"

"Thirty degrees down plane, Captain!"

Basargin felt the deck tilt sharply beneath his feet. They were still in relatively shallow water here—less than forty meters. The Americans set their torpedoes to detonate beneath the keel of a target vessel. It was just possible that the Russian submarine could slip deeply enough quickly enough that the incoming torpedo would strike the bottom.

"Torpedo now passing in front of us, Captain! Range . . . about—"

The detonation thundered through the submarine, slamming Basargin against the periscope housing and rocking the vessel savagely to starboard. A second shock followed as they kissed the bottom.

"Are we still in one piece?"

"That appears to have been a warning shot, Captain. A shot across our bows."

Basargin's first loyalty was not to the men who'd hired the services of the boat, himself, and his crew. So far as he was concerned, this accursed mission had ended when he'd sent the Mexican and the Persian ashore.

"Captain, radio room. We are receiving a message by transponder."

"What is it?"

"Two words, sir, in Russian. 'Surface now.'"

"Mr. Shuvalov! Are we in international waters yet?"

"It's close, Captain. But probably another four . . . perhaps five kilometers."

He nodded. "They have us. Blow ballast, Mr. Khristenko. Take us up, if you please."

"Aye, Captain," the diving officer replied. "Surface the boat!"

For an anxious moment, he feared the submarine was damaged, that it might not rise. Then the deck tilted, bow going up, and he heard the roar of ballast tanks being blown.

TELLER
EASTON, MARYLAND
0135 HOURS, EDT

The traffic had been backing up for an hour, becoming a sea of red brake lights stretching forward into the night. Outside of Easton, Maryland, Teller and Dominique finally had pulled off the road next to an open field. Minutes later, a CH-53E Super Stallion, the largest and heaviest helicopter in the U.S. military, had dropped out of the sky, spotlights glaring out of the darkness in a display that must have had other motorists thinking of UFOs and alien abductions.

The huge aircraft touched down in the field, its seven-blade rotors still turning. Together, Teller and Dominique had left the car, running bent forward to avoid the still-turning blades. If not a UFO, Teller thought, it was at least a black helicopter—*all* black save for a serial number stenciled on the tail boom in gray. Pounding up the lowered rear ramp, the two entered the aircraft's cavernous cargo deck, and in another moment they were airborne, flying north across that river of slowly moving vehicles.

"Welcome aboard!" a marine crew chief greeted them, bellowing to be heard above the Super Stallion's thunder. "You Dominique and Teller?"

"Yeah!"

"Good! If you weren't I'd have to kill you and kick you out! Here, put these on!"

He handed them helmets with built-in communications gear and noise-suppression headsets. Once hooked up to the intercom, it was easier to hear and talk.

A second man greeted them forward. "I'm Major Walthers," he said. "Welcome aboard NEST Two/Two. They said you had an idea for finding our target."

"I think so," Teller told him. "We need to get up to the Baltimore–D.C. Corridor. And I need to access this." He patted his laptop case.

"We can do that. Or you can use our network."

Much of the huge cargo bay on the helicopter transport was walled off, providing space for computer workstations for two technicians and for the massive backscatter X-ray equipment. Walthers led them forward and into the control center, giving them what he called the fifty-cent tour.

"It's called Z-Backscatter," he explained, pointing to a large flat-panel display screen on the starboard-side bulkhead. "That's because it uses wavelengths reflected by what are called low-Z materials—that's low-mass elements like carbon and hydrogen, molecules like water. Here . . . Kaminsky." He pointed at the line of cars visible in ordinary light on a smaller monitor to the side. "Give 'em a show."

"Sure thing, Major."

The technician did something to the touch-screen controls on his console, and a car appeared in shades of gray on the large screen, frozen motionless, viewed from overhead and to the right. The vehicle itself appeared ghosted, with even the engine block almost invisible. The tires were more easily seen than the hubs or axles. A man, a woman, and two kids seemed to float in space, their clothing vanished, their faces oddly plastic. Teller glanced at Dominique. She met his eyes, then looked away with a small shrug. He could almost hear her thought. *I'd just be happier if I knew the Peeping Tom bit is* strictly *line of duty . . .*

The technician grinned. "Hey, that's a nice set on the—"

"*That* will do," Teller snapped, his voice cold. "Save it for the bad guys."

"Hey, I didn't mean any—"

"Just keep it professional," Teller told him. Briefly, he considered pinning the man's ears back, but he was wearing civilian clothing at the moment, and he didn't want to turn the conversation into an officer-enlisted pissing match.

He clearly heard Kaminsky mutter the word "asshole" in response. Probably the guy had no idea the high-tech helmets they were wearing transmitted even words that were all but whispered. He let it go.

"Ah, yes," Walthers said, embarrassed. "Really dense materials—lead or uranium, say—will reflect well, but the low-Z radiation passes right through steel as easily as it does glass . . ."

Teller found himself wondering, though, not about the physics of the surveillance equipment but about that family. What were they doing out on a normally empty stretch of Maryland highway at one thirty in the morning? The kids in the backseat looked like they were asleep. Maybe they'd left Ocean City that evening, hoping to drive all night and reach their home, wherever that might be, by morning. From the look of that middle-of-the-night traffic jam down there, they weren't going to make it.

"We've used this technology before," he said, feeling weary. "We don't need the physics lecture. Let's just get it to where it can do some good."

REYSHAHRI
CONOWINGO DAM, MARYLAND
0150 HOURS, EDT

It was only about fifty kilometers from the point where they'd turned off the main road north in Delaware to the bridge and dam they were looking for across the Susquehanna, but the trip had taken them almost an hour. Telegraph Road had turned out to be a long, single-lane highway with a speed limit of fifty-five, but slowed by stretches where the speed limit had been reduced to thirty. The others in the car were becoming increasingly agitated and impatient.

Now, however, they were back on Route 1, heading south across a narrow road that was actually the top of a dam across the river. "Once we're across," Reyshahri told them, "we'll be safe. No more toll roads or bridges. We'll take the long way around Baltimore to avoid the Key Bridge or the Harbor Tunnel. We will have our choice of roads south."

"I, for one, dislike the change," Hamadi said. "We should have stayed with the original plan. What about New York?"

"The New York part of the operation," Reyshahri told him, "is unnecessary. We have the freedom to make our own decisions. And we are doing so."

"*You* are doing so, Captain Reyshahri. If the mission fails because of your delays, it will be entirely your responsibility."

Reyshahri did not reply, focusing instead on the driving. The road across the dam was narrow, with no shoulders, and he felt hemmed in, almost claustrophobic.

He wondered if his decision to spare New York City was due to caution or because he actually pitied the Americans.

Reyshahri had questioned the necessity for using the nuclear weapons at all, during his briefing back at VE-VAK headquarters, in Tehran. Colonel Ebrahim Salehi, his commanding officer, had merely shrugged. "Those are our orders, Saeed," he'd said.

"But to launch a nuclear attack on America, sir—" Reyshahri had been horrified. "Such a strike will kill thousands and leave two cities in ruins. If they learn that it was us, they will not rest until our nation lies in ruins."

"Then see to it that they do *not* learn, Captain. We

will place clues, through our network in Mexico, that the attack was either by al Qaeda or by the Mexican cartels themselves."

"There must be other ways to destabilize the United States."

"Are you questioning your orders, Captain?"

Reyshahri had sighed. "No, sir. But to take such an extreme step . . ."

"Operation Shah Mat is intended to deeply shake the American economy, its government, and its military's internal command and control. The creation of a free Aztlán will be possible only if the Americans are so . . . distracted by the attack that they cannot respond."

"I understand that, Colonel."

"If you are feeling soft about American casualties, Captain, remember that the United States has been carrying out a covert war against us for years. It was they, we are certain, who produced the so-called Stuxnet virus that destroyed the centrifuges at Natanz, delaying our nuclear program. And the Americans were working with the Jews when Mossad sabotaged our ballistic missile facilities near Tehran. They were probably behind the attack on Estafan as well."

"I am aware of all of that, Colonel. But there is an enormous difference between covert sabotage and the detonation of two nuclear weapons."

"A weapon is a weapon, a means to effect an end, Colonel. We have acquired two nuclear weapons—two very small nuclear weapons—and their use will cause the United States to draw back to within its own borders to deal with its own more pressing problems. And that leaves us free to pursue our ambitions in Iraq and in Syria, without American interference."

"Yes, sir."

"If you do not have the stomach for this, we can find another officer who does."

Reyshahri had stiffened to attention. "I can do it, sir."

"Good. I would hate to lose so promising an officer."

What would have happened, he wondered, if he'd refused the mission? Reassignment, certainly. Demotion, possibly. Questioning by Internal Security, probably—with just a chance that they would investigate his loyalty to the regime.

He was thinking of Hasti, his wife, and his daughter, Mehry, as he drove off the bridge and left the Susquehanna behind them. It was not unknown for the families of men accused of treason to . . . disappear.

He would have to see this through, no matter how distasteful the assignment might be.

NEST 2/2
ABOVE HAVRE DE GRACE, MARYLAND
0155 HOURS, EDT

With a cruise speed of 150 knots, it had taken the CH-53E Super Stallion just twenty minutes to fly from Easton to the port of Havre de Grace, at the mouth of the Susquehanna River. They could see the city lights of Havre de Grace out the big helicopter's windows to port, the smaller town of Perryville to starboard, as they swung northwest and flew up the midchannel of the river.

"Not much traffic up here," Major Walthers observed.

"Exactly," Teller replied. "The traffic jams haven't hit this far north yet." They would.

"So what are we looking for, anyway?"

"A vehicle. We don't know the make or model. At least two passengers. And a small nuclear weapon."

"Chris thinks they'll want to avoid toll roads and bridges," Dominique added. "Only if they want to reach Washington, they *have* to cross either Chesapeake Bay or the Susquehanna River."

Teller nodded. "Right. Their first choice would be the Bay Bridge, of course. No toll going west, but it's such an obvious direct route to D.C. *and* such a major bottleneck that I don't think they're going to try that way."

"I'd have to agree," Walthers said. "But NEST is setting up a muon detector at the Bay Bridge anyway, just in case."

"Right. The only other way from the Eastern Shore into central Maryland is to swing way north, past the top of Chesapeake Bay at Elkton, then head southwest, which brings them to the Susquehanna. There are just three vehicular bridges across the river in Maryland—Route 40 and Route 95, both of which are toll bridges, and the Conowingo Dam. The next nearest crossing is way up in Pennsylvania somewhere."

"So you think they're trying to cross at Conowingo?"

"Good chance. I just hope we're ahead of them."

"What, they might've already crossed?"

Teller turned his laptop to show Walthers. "I've been using Tracker."

Highway Tracker was software designed for use by law enforcement agencies and government organizations. You entered starting time and completion times and a point on a map, and the program downloaded data from Highway Department Web sites and law enforcement networks on factors such as heavy traffic, local speed limits, and construction. A moment later, it showed you on a computer-generated map just how far a target vehicle could have traveled in the requested period of time.

One of the sets of routes Teller had plugged into his laptop had generated a red field that covered everything from the Indian River Inlet north through Newark, then southwest toward the Susquehanna. One tentacle of blue extended just past the bridge at Conowingo and down Route 1 toward Baltimore.

"If they've been driving steadily for two and a half hours, no stops, no delays, they could have covered about a hundred twenty miles by now. That puts them here, about five miles southwest of the dam and maybe eight or ten miles northeast of Bel Air."

"Unless they've been breaking speed limits," Walthers pointed out.

"True . . . but if you were carrying a small nuke in your trunk and there was even a remote chance that the opposition knew about it, would you risk a traffic stop?"

"No. I suppose I wouldn't. But what if they're headed for New York City?"

"A possibility, but not a likely one. The NEST units up there will be covering the approaches to Manhattan. They're setting up a muon detector on I-95, too."

"What the hell is a muon detector?" Dominique asked.

"*Big* unit," Walthers explained. "A transmitter and a detector. It sends a stream of muons—a kind of subatomic particle—between the two. Muons pass through everything without slowing down—everything except for those elements that are *really* dense. Plutonium and uranium, specifically. Set it up at a bridge or a toll booth, transmitter on one side and detector on the other, and it sounds an alert if something passing between them reflects the muons instead of letting them through. It's the best tool we have for sniffing out nuclear weapons."

"So we don't have a portable system for that yet."

"Not for muons, no. If you want portable, you need the mobile Z-backscatter units, vans and helicopters. We've had backscatter vans patrolling the streets for a while now. Helicopter units are a bit more recent." Walthers studied Teller's display for a moment longer. "So you're suggesting we go to the dam and then work our way southwest on 1?"

"Right. I understand other NEST units are covering

D.C. farther south. But if we can tag this character before he gets close to a major city, I'll be a lot happier."

"You're thinking a dead man's switch?"

"It's a possibility."

"So, when we find him . . . what then?"

"I don't know," Teller replied. "I'm still working on
that part."

CHAPTER TWENTY-THREE

INSCOM HQ
FORT BELVOIR, VIRGINIA
0201 HOURS, EDT
22 APRIL

"There they go," Procario said.

The INSCOM Ops Center was crowded now with personnel, including CIA, DIA, and NEST officers. General Granger, Haupt, and Devendorf all were present, along with Wentworth from the CIA and the WIN-PAC officer, Larson, both looking haggard after being woken by late-night phone calls. One woman—Diane Cosgrove—had arrived from the White House, dispatched to INSCOM HQ by the national security adviser himself, Randolph Edgar Preston. The ANSA, she'd informed the group, was unavoidably in California that night, but she was there to observe the op and to advise the president in his place.

The president, she'd just informed the group, was on board *Marine One;* on his way out of the city.

Just in case.

It was a surreal scene. Formerly the Information Dominance Center, a cyber warfare facility, the INSCOM Ops Center was an exact replica of the bridge of the USS *Enterprise* out of *Star Trek: The Next Generation*. The place had actually been designed by the guy who'd created the *Enterprise* set. Any outside observer walking in would have thought he'd walked into *Star Trek*.

The big display on the wall was showing a dizzying drop into a chaotic blur of night, glaring light, and spray. The image was being transmitted real-time from a camera mounted on the helmet of a U.S. Navy SEAL as he dangled fifty feet above the deck of a Kilo class submarine nine miles off the coast of New Jersey. The deck of the submarine swung and rolled alarmingly; two more SEALs hung suspended below the one with the camera, bulky with tactical vests, weapons, and equipment. The surface of the black water was lashed to white froth by the helicopter's rotor blast. Two faces, tiny and pale, looked up toward the camera from the submarine's sail.

"Now we find out if they're going to let us come aboard," Colonel Devendorf said.

"Garret said they'd agreed to surrender," George Haupt pointed out. "If they don't go through with it, he'll put a torpedo up their ass."

"That may not be a good idea," Granger said. "We don't want to detonate a nuke that close to our shoreline—or sink that Kilo and have it leaking radiation onto our continental shelf."

"Then we'd better hope the bastards decide to play nice," Procario observed.

"Do our people know there's a nuke on board that sub?" MacDonald asked.

"Of course they do," Procario said. "They have to know what they're looking for, right?"

The USS *Pittsburgh* was still submerged out there somewhere, but with her radio mast and periscope above water. Garret had radioed a situation report shortly after the Russian submarine had surfaced, and INSCOM had immediately dispatched a platoon from SEAL Team Two out of Little Creek, Virginia, on board an HH-60H Seahawk Naval Special Warfare helicopter.

The VBSS team was fast-roping onto the Kilo's forward deck now, an extremely dangerous evolution to carry out in the middle of the night in a rough swell. The winds had been picking up, and there'd been some rain squalls passing through the area.

The SEALs, trained for operations in all weather, day or night, had gone in anyway. They were armed with H&K submachine guns and clad in black combat armored vests, night-vision devices, and tactical harnesses, which gave them a nightmarish look as they descended on the wallowing surfaced submarine.

The first two men on the line hit the deck and moved toward the open forward hatch; the camera view slid precipitously down, hit with a jar, and then began moving toward the hatch as well. The camera view swerved, jiggled, and swooped, and for a moment the watchers at INSCOM were treated to an up-close look at the rungs of a metal ladder as the SEAL descended through the forward hatch. The voices of the team members called back and forth to one another over the tactical net.

"Arc Five! Moving to the control room!"

"Arc Three! Going down one deck . . . entering torpedo room . . ."

"*Nazahd! Nazahd!* Move back!" A number of the SEALs spoke fluent Russian. *"Rukee v'vayrh!"*

The scenes on the display showed cramped spaces, harsh lighting, men in blue jumpsuits backing out of the way of the VBSS boarders, putting up their hands in response to the harsh, shouted orders. It looked, Procario thought, eerily like one of those first-person shooter computer games, where you could see a gloved hand holding a weapon as the virtual soldier wound through a maze of passageways and rooms.

There was a small difference with this version, however. "Game over" did not mean a chance to start a new round of play.

"G'deh Kapetahn?" one of the SEALs demanded.

"I am Captain Second Rank Basargin," one of the blue-clad men replied in good English, stepping forward. "I *do* apologize. We appear to have suffered a failure of our navigational equipment, and have accidentally strayed into your waters."

"So *that's* how they're going to play it," Granger said.

NEST 2/2
ABOVE BEL AIR BYPASS
BEL AIR, MARYLAND
0210 HOURS, EDT

"I've got something!" Kaminsky yelled. "I've got a package!"

Teller looked up from his laptop and studied the gray-scale image on the big display.

The vehicle was a Jumbo SUV of some sort, too heavily transparent for him to guess the make and model. Two males were riding up front; the faint outlines of an AK-47 floated on the backseat. Brick-sized packages glowed with silvery-gray opacity everywhere—under the seats, tucked up inside the wheel wells, and massed in a sizable pile in the cargo space at the vehicle's back.

"I don't know," Walthers said. "Does that look like a bomb?"

"It's low-Z material," Kaminsky replied. "RTD is negative. No radiation."

"It could also be shielded in lead. What do you think, Mr. Teller?"

Teller studied the image a moment. "I think what you have there is a drug shipment—cocaine, maybe heroin. Stashing it inside the wheel wells is an old, old trick."

"So, do we nail 'em?"

Teller thought about it. They were probably looking at several tens of millions of dollars of cocaine packed into that car . . . and at addiction and misery for thousands of people.

What, he wondered, was the right thing to do? If they stopped to deal with that car and it turned out to be just drugs, they might miss the vehicle with the D.C.-bound nuclear weapon. If they just let the drug van go . . .

"Can we call the police?"

"Not a good idea, sir," Walthers said. "They wouldn't have probable cause for a search, and we don't really want to admit that we're flying around up here peeking inside people's trunks, do we?"

"Very funny."

"I'm not getting through to the county police," Dominique said, her cell phone pressed to her ear. "They may have been called out to throw up roadblocks farther south."

Teller called up another program. Sure enough, when he opened Cellmap, a cluster of blue icons turned up on the Bel Air Bypass: two on the highway, one— his own cell phone—showing just to one side. Might the handoff of the weapons have been made to some known East Coast dealers? He sighed. "Okay. We'll have to deal with it ourselves. They *might* have the weapon hidden under all of that low-Z stuff in the trunk, and we simply can't take the chance that it's not them."

"Right." Walthers picked up an intercom handset. "Okay . . . Skipper? We need to stop that SUV."

REYSHAHRI
BUSINESS ROUTE 1
BEL AIR, MARYLAND
0214 HOURS, EDT

"What is going on over there?" Moslehi asked.

"Sounds like a helicopter," Hamadi added.

Reyshahri had left the Bel Air Bypass moments before, in search of a twenty-four-hour gas station. He wanted to fill the rental's tank before beginning the run past Baltimore and down into Washington, and they all needed to stretch their legs and use the facilities. A convenience store with the unlikely name of Wawa offered gas, rest rooms, and food.

They'd just stepped out of the store when their attention had been grabbed by the low-voiced growl and *whup-whup-whup* sound of a helicopter, a big one. It sounded like it was coming from the bypass, only a kilometer or so to the west. A bright light came on, a glare in the sky behind the Saturn car dealership across the street from the Wawa.

"I don't know," Reyshahri said. "But I think it wise if we go another way."

They might be searching the major highways.

The four of them climbed into the car, Moslehi, this time, at the wheel. "Which way, then?"

Reyshahri pulled out a road map, studying it around his sandwich. He ate with some diffidence, taking small bites; he wasn't entirely sure he trusted this thing they called a "sub." He'd specified something called "buffalo chicken," avoiding ham, pork, bacon, anything prohibited by Islamic law, but the sauce was so spicy he wasn't sure what was in the thing.

"We need to get around Baltimore," he said after a moment. "And that means to the west, so we don't have to go across the Key Bridge or take the Harbor Tunnel. Here." His finger came down on a road. "We go a few more blocks down this street, then right onto Hartford Road. Single lane. We'll take that southwest until we find something that will get us around Baltimore."

"Wonderful," Moslehi said. "*More* small, backcountry roads."

The strange sandwich, actually, was quite good. He took another bite, a larger one this time.

"Just drive," he said around a mouthful.

NEST 2/2
BEL AIR BYPASS
BEL AIR, MARYLAND
0220 HOURS, EDT

The helicopter had come down in front of the SUV, forcing the vehicle to swerve onto the grassy center median. As the Super Stallion hovered, Teller, Dominique, and Walthers had descended the aft ramp, the two intelligence officers with pistols drawn, Walthers packing an M-4 carbine. The two men in the SUV had tumbled out, one of them waving the AK, but Teller had fired two quick shots into the man and knocked him down. The other had stepped back from the car, hands raised. "Don't shoot, man! *Don't shoot!*"

"Let's see what you've got in the car," Dominique said. She went to the driver's side and popped the rear hatch.

"Hey . . . you guys DEA?" their prisoner demanded as Teller moved him well back from the car. "You *feds*? You need a warrant, man! We know our rights!"

"Why don't you talk to your friend here about your *rights,*" Walthers told him, stooping to pick up the AK. The wounded man, clutching his chest, was bleeding heavily.

Teller pulled an automatic pistol from the prisoner's waistband, handed it to Walthers, then spun him around, tripped him, and put him facedown on the grass. "Anything?" he asked Dominique, who was looking through the back of the car.

She emerged from under the open rear hatch with a plastic-wrapped brick in each hand. "No bombs. Just these."

"*Bombs?* Shit, man, we ain't got no bombs!"

"Shut up."

Dominique tossed the bricks back inside. "Looks like . . . I don't know. Three, four hundred kilos of cocaine."

"Four hundred kilos?" Teller did a fast calculation. "What is that," he asked the prisoner, "maybe fifty, fifty-five million dollars on the street?"

"Look, you don't want to mess with this, man! You don't want to mess with *us*!"

"Walthers, you have something to take care of that cargo?"

"Right here, sir."

"Do it." Teller leaned over and roughly secured the prisoner's hands with a zip-strip. "Okay. I suggest you stay right there. This won't take a minute."

Walthers tossed the AK and the handgun into the back of the vehicle, then pulled a gray cylindrical object from his tactical vest. He pulled a circular cotter pin from the top and tossed it in after the weapons.

"Don't look at it," Teller warned his prisoner.

The AN-M14 incendiary grenade went off with a dazzling flash of TH3—thermite—burning at some 4,000 degrees. Flames licked up inside the back of the van. A few moments later, droplets of molten iron began dripping through the back floor and melting into the SUV's gas tank.

Orange fire blossomed into the night, the fireball roiling above the blazing vehicle.

The prisoner screamed, "No! You've *killed* us, man! You've *killed* us!"

"So what's the deal? You owe that money to someone else? Ah, I see. You owe your supplier something like eight million, but you need to distribute the stuff to pay him back, right? And all of your operating capital just went up in flames. Too bad."

The man on the ground was sobbing now. "Man, you don't know what they'll *do* to me!"

"Oh, I have a pretty good idea," Teller said, though he wondered if the sheer bloody viciousness common within the Mexican cartels had worked its way north into the United States yet. "Tell you what. The police will be along in a few minutes. I suggest you tell them everything and have them put you into protective custody." He looked up. "How's the other one?"

"Dead," Walthers said.

"Too bad. Well . . . take it easy, fella."

"Please don't leave me!"

"Oh, I hardly think your distributors will come looking for you out here. You just wait for the police, okay? They'll help you out."

"Who are you guys?" The question was a shriek.

"Actually," Teller told him with an exaggerated sense of drama, "we're no one at all . . . and we were never here."

Moments later, they were airborne once more, leaving the towering pillar of orange flame behind them in the night. Traffic was light, but there were a few vehicles on Route 1, and several were stopping. Just to be sure, though, Dominique put in another call to the county police, and another to the state highway patrol.

"It's not every day you get to burn fifty million bucks," Walthers said.

"No," Teller said. He was studying his laptop's screen again. "But we couldn't do much else. Couldn't admit how we found it. And I sure as hell didn't want to let that carload of shit go!"

"Think the police will figure out what happened?" Dominique asked, switching off her phone.

"They'll find cocaine residue in the wreckage," Teller said. "Probably even intact bricks, the ones in the front wheel wells. They'll probably release an official story saying a rival drug gang did it. In any case, I don't think they'll ask too many questions. When that guy tells them he got pulled over by a black unmarked helicopter . . . well, that might warn them off."

"But we didn't find the bomb," Walthers said. "Where next?"

Teller pecked out some more characters on the keyboard. He shook his head, then turned the display for the others to see. "I think we're too late to catch them," he said. "Too many choices."

Something like three and a half hours had elapsed since the weapon had come ashore. The data, fed into Highway Tracker, showed a vast bright red octopus spreading tentacles across northern Maryland, some of them already pushing through the city of Baltimore, others stretching around to the west.

"We can't assume that the bad guys stayed on the main highways, like 1 or 95. Back on the Eastern Shore, there weren't that many different routes. On this side of Chesapeake Bay, and south of the Susquehanna . . . well, take a look. *Lots* of choices."

"And not enough of us," Walthers said, looking at the screen.

"We can't just give up!" Dominique said.

"No. No, we can't. But I think we need to move in closer to the target and give some thought to just exactly what it is they're after."

Banking sharply, the Super Stallion turned south, heading for the vast yellow glow of Baltimore's lights spreading across the horizon.

REYSHAHRI
BUSINESS ROUTE 1
BEL AIR, MARYLAND
0525 HOURS, EDT

"Where the hell are we?" Gallardo demanded in English.

"Just outside the National Security Agency," Reyshahri replied. "The NSA. It's back there on the other side of those trees."

"Maybe we should detonate here," Moslehi said, driving. "It would end our traffic problems, at least." He suddenly tromped on the brake as a red car cut sharply in front of them. "Abortion!" he shouted in Farsi, shaking his fist.

"Gently, my friend," Reyshahri said. "We do not want an . . . altercation. Or a traffic accident."

Traffic had been very bad for the past half hour, as more and more cars crowded onto the early-morning expressways. After they worked their way slowly across the Maryland countryside north of Baltimore, Reyshahri had agreed at last to merge with the Baltimore Beltway; all roads, it seemed, led to Baltimore—at least in northern Maryland.

Reyshahri's concerns about traveling on major freeways appeared to have been unfounded. The smaller, one-lane country roads were treacherous in and of themselves, not because American military or law enforcement personnel were patrolling them, but because it was so easy to take a wrong turn and end up lost. Fortunately, the major highways north and west of Baltimore weren't as bad as he'd feared they would be.

Swinging around to the south of the city, then, they'd taken the exit for 295, the Baltimore–Washington Parkway. Now they were passing the cloverleaf with Route 32, Fort Meade, and the site of the supersecret NSA—though they'd just passed a brown and white exit sign saying NSA, EMPLOYEES ONLY.

"The NSA," Hamadi said, grinning from the backseat. "*That* would be a worthy target!"

"And how would that help our cause?" Gallardo asked. "Destroying a spy's nest will not destroy the United States."

"Always *your* cause," Hamadi said, sneering. "It would be enough to strike at the Great Satan and singe his beard!"

"Señor Gallardo is right," Reyshahri said. "Our target is the American capital."

"I still question whether attacking Washington will help our . . . allies in Mexico," Moslehi said. "Destroying a few hundred buildings, killing a few million people—how will it help your Aztlán?"

"We're an hour away from the downtown," Reyshahri told them. "Wait, be patient, and we will see."

"An hour *if* we get through this damnable traffic!" Gallardo said. "Where is it all coming from?"

"It is something," Reyshahri told him, "called 'the morning rush hour.' We'll get through it. You'll see."

Moslehi had to step on the brakes more and more often, though, and soon their pace had been slowed to a crawl, as red taillights flared and flashed in front of them.

INSCOM HQ
FORT BELVOIR, VIRGINIA
0540 HOURS, EDT

"A fresh report from Arclight," MacDonald said. Arclight was the name of the naval operation to secure the Kilo submarine off the Delaware coast and to find the nuclear weapon on board intended for New York City. "After a careful search, they have not found the nuclear weapon."

"What, you're sure?" Larson demanded.

For answer, MacDonald held up her phone, on which a text message showed. "You want to argue with them?"

"No . . . no. But it makes no sense."

"I think it does," Procario said. "Think of it like this. The Kilo—which is under contract to a drug cartel, but crewed and skippered by Russians—is approaching the beach to drop off the first weapon, okay? But then they find out the *Pittsburgh* is hot on their trail. What do they do?"

"Drop off *both* weapons," Granger said. "That way they're not caught red-handed."

"Right. Besides, those Russian sailors aren't being paid enough to go up in a nuclear fireball—and probably don't want anything except for the job to be over so they can all go home." He grinned. "It's *so* hard to get good help these days."

"So the question becomes whether the two weapons are together, or if one got put on a separate car and is heading for New York."

"The defense of New York City," Granger said, "is

the responsibility of the local NEST headquarters. Because Manhattan is an island, it'll be a little easier to protect. NEST and police are already screening all traffic at all of the bridges and tunnels." He gave a wry smile. "I gather rush hour is turning out to be a bitch up there."

MacDonald typed at a keyboard, and the wall display behind her lit up with a satellite photo-map of Washington, D.C., the hub of a vast wheel with dozens of spokes converging on it. Green icons clustered around the city about where the D.C. Beltway was, an attempt at putting up a barrier against incoming traffic.

The barrier was woefully inadequate, showing far too many gaps and spaces.

"Our problem in D.C. is a bit tougher," she said. "They may be approaching the Beltway on one of the main highways—95, 270, 197—but we don't know. There are lots of smaller streets and roads, unlike the approaches to New York City. And once they reach the Beltway they have literally hundreds of streets to choose from. We can't possibly cover them all."

"Then we pray we get real lucky," Granger said. "Because we don't have many fucking options here."

NEST 2/2
OVER GREENBELT, MARYLAND
0610 HOURS, EDT

"My God," Teller said, looking out one of the Super Stallion's windows. "What a nightmare."

Dawn would break over the D.C. area in another

twelve minutes, but from fifteen hundred feet up the sun was already beginning to nudge above the horizon, filling the eastern sky with light while the land below was still in gray shadow. Teller was watching the endless river of red taillights below as cars nosed ahead bumper to bumper on the Baltimore–Washington Parkway, filling every lane, barely making any progress at all.

"The good news," Dominique observed, "is that the bad guys might not be able to reach their target."

"Targets," Walthers reminded them. Teller had received a call from Procario moments before, alerting them to the fact that a search of the Russian Kilo had turned up nothing, and that the presumption now was that both nuclear weapons were somewhere in that gridlocked mass of traffic below.

Teller grunted. "Targets. What I'm afraid of is that the bastards will decide to trigger the warheads because they know they're stuck. *Worst* case of road rage ever."

"You think they might do that, Chris?" Dominique asked.

Teller frowned. "No, actually. A hell of a lot of thought went into this operation, y'know? They will have particular targets in mind—probably a menu—and they won't change the plan unless they're absolutely forced to do so."

"Okay, people," Walthers said. "We're making another pass."

For hours, the Super Stallion had been swooping over the lines of traffic below, using Z-backscatter to scan vehicle after vehicle. They'd checked hundreds of vehicles already and turned up nothing. Eventually, they'd gone back up to 12,000 feet and refueled from an airborne tanker out of Edwards, then returned to the search, checking hundreds more.

There still were thousands, *tens* of thousands, left to go.

"So how do we figure out what's on their menu?" Dominique asked. "I'm not very good at reading minds."

"Let's look at everything we know about the enemy's plan," Teller said. "It's called Operation Shah Mat, which means 'the king is thwarted' in Farsi. Checkmate. It may have originated with Iran—brought to Mexico by their agent Pasha—but the Mexican cartels are providing a lot of the muscle. The whole thing is linked to the Aztlán independence movement—people who want to create a new country carved out of the U.S. Southwest. We can assume the drug cartels want to bring that about to provide themselves with a safe haven—no laws against drugs. The Iranian motives are less clear, especially since they stand to lose so much by attacking us with nukes."

"That actually seems pretty clear to me," Dominique told him. "You figured it out on our drive out to Ocean City yesterday, remember?"

Teller thought for a moment. "No." He was, he realized, exhausted. How long had it been since he'd last slept?

"If the United States is badly destabilized first by the attack itself, then by what amounts to a civil war in the West, they have a free hand in places like Syria and Iraq."

"Oh . . . right. I wasn't convinced. That was just me grasping at straws."

"But it makes sense. The Iranians want us out of the Mideast, and a second American civil war would give them the diversion they need."

"For some very ambitious empire building," Teller added, nodding. "A damned dangerous game—but they did set things up to blame al Qaeda, whom they hate anyway. Larson's 'reliable informant' in Pakistan. De la Paz, who tried to convince us it was all an al Qaeda plot against Mexico. Yeah . . ."

"It's probably not an *official* Iranian plan," Dominique pointed out. "The ones behind it might just be a few loose cannons in their intelligence service."

"Or at least that's what they would claim if we caught them," Teller said. "Sure. They'll make certain that even if we can trace the nukes back to them, we won't have a solid enough case to justify full-scale retaliation. Now . . . who are the players?"

"Pasha," Dominique said. "The Iranian organizing and running the op in Mexico and the U.S. That's probably Reyshahri."

"And Hamadi. Hezbollah, and therefore working for the Iranians. For the Mexicans, we have Juan Escalante. Brokering a deal between Los Zetas and Sinaloa." He paused, frowning.

"What is it?"

"I just realized something. Agustín Morales. Calavera. A high-ranking member of the Sinaloa Cartel. He lets Galen Fletcher recruit him as a CIA agent, along with Henrico Garcia. And there's someone else—the

CIA deputy chief of station in Mexico City, Richard Nicholas."

Teller began typing rapidly on his laptop's keyboard, entering a password and bringing up a classified personnel file on an encrypted satellite channel. A photograph showing Nicholas's face—young, blond, ambitious— gazed back out of the screen at him.

" 'Current whereabouts unknown,' " Teller said, reading. " 'Wanted for questioning . . .' Yeah, I'll just bet he is."

"Nicholas was the traitor at the Mexican station."

"Right. Poor Galen found out that Nicholas had sold out the Agency's network down there. He must have found out that Morales had been recruited as well— and that he was still working for Sinaloa." He kept typing as he spoke.

"What are you looking for?"

"This," Teller said, pointing at a block of text on the screen. "Okay, thanks to Fletcher, we know Nicholas was a traitor. He sold our entire Mexican network to the cartels. That's why Frank and I were sent down there in the first place."

"Okay . . ."

"Nicholas would have recruited Garcia and Morales. It's certainly hard to imagine that Morales could be brought in—*under his real name*—without some pretty high-level intervention."

"Right, that doesn't make any sense at all," Dominique said. "Why would he use his real name? If he was even suspected of cartel involvement . . ."

"So that our people could access his Mexican military

records when he applied for training in the U.S.," Teller said. He typed in another password, bringing up another face, heavy and swarthy, with a thin mustache. "Here he is. Agustín Morales. Mexican military intelligence. Armored Corps. Special training in the U.S., including the Farm. Nothing at all here about him working with the cartels, but I'd be willing to bet that the information is there somewhere. Or it *was*."

"Someone tampered with the records?"

"Someone high up in the Agency—or higher. Look, Galen Fletcher recruited him—but Galen was old school, and *very* thorough. He would have checked Morales out six ways from Sunday. Ah . . . here." He pointed.

"What is it?"

Three columns of text came up on Teller's screen, side by side. "The connection I was looking for. Look . . . Agustín Morales was recruited by Galen Fletcher, but it was Richard Nicholas who first contacted Morales, and who brought him to Fletcher's attention. If Nicholas was dirty, he probably knew Morales was dirty as well. And Nicholas was appointed by—"

"Randolph Edgar Preston," Dominique said, reading over Teller's shoulder. "The president's national security adviser."

"I'm beginning to get the feeling," Teller said slowly, "that this thing goes a *lot* higher than we thought."

CHAPTER TWENTY-FOUR

NEST 2/2
OVER GREENBELT, MARYLAND
0621 HOURS, EDT
22 APRIL

The NEST Super Stallion was making yet another pass, flying low beside the line of traffic, checking vehicle after vehicle with its Z-backscatter scanner. As the morning light grew stronger, the traffic jam was becoming more monstrous, an impossible gridlock. Up ahead, the police had established a roadblock and were letting cars through one at a time after a close check. Teller had also seen a gamma detector truck moving up the highway's shoulder. A long arm, like that of a cherry picker, was extended out from the trailer, dangling a box on the far side of the traffic lane. The device, he knew, allowed the truck to fire X-rays through a target vehicle and capture them on the other side, and also to pick up gamma radiation. An ancestor of the ZBVs, they'd been in use for well over a decade at major U.S. ports, checking incoming cargo containers for radiological or nuclear devices.

"Fletcher must have killed himself when he saw how far the rot had spread," Dominique said.

"He reported the fact that Nicholas had turned," Teller said, "but I suspect he was told to be quiet about it."

"Preston?"

"Preston. The national security adviser is, among other things, the funnel for intel from INSCOM and the CIA and the NSA to the president's desk. I can't imagine what else would have made Galen snap. When he realized that Preston was dirty . . ."

Teller let the thought hang. Poor Galen. Old school, yeah, and as straight and as honorable as they came. Honor, however, didn't seem to have much of a place any longer in intelligence work—or in D.C.

"So why didn't Preston warn us off of Escalante? Why weren't we pulled out of Mexico? I mean . . . Preston would have known."

"Not necessarily," Teller told her. "Our friends Wentworth and Larson had their own ideas about what was going on in Mexico, remember?"

" 'There are no nukes in Mexico,' " she said, eyes widening. "Jesus! They never told him!"

Teller grinned. "This may be the first time in history that bureaucratic CYA actually worked to someone's advantage!"

"So . . . did Fletcher know about the nukes?" Dominique asked.

"No. He would have told someone. All he knew was that the Mexican station was compromised by someone he'd recruited, and that ANSA was telling him to back off."

"So where *do* the nukes come into it?"

"I think Preston learned that the Iranians had purchased two Russian suitcase nukes," Teller said. "As ANSA, he would have been privy to Trapdoor. And he would have had access to the Iranian secret service, through Nicholas and the Iranian Embassy in Mexico City. He may have . . . encouraged them. Maybe even worked out the plan to use the nukes to destabilize the United States and give Aztlan a chance to take over."

"Why? What would Preston gain from having the American Southwest break off and start an independent country?"

"I don't know," Teller admitted. "The Iranians would see it as a chance to get us out of the Mideast. By blaming al Qaeda or the drug cartels, they keep their hands clean. Plausible deniability. But someone else is pulling the strings—Preston. And I don't know why."

"So how does any of that help you figure out the bad guys' menu?" Walthers asked.

"It doesn't. But if it's the Iranians, that tells us that Shah Mat was meticulously planned as a surgical attack," Teller told him. "*Surgical.* That's the key."

"If they only have warheads measuring a few kilotons," Dominique pointed out, "it would *have* to be, wouldn't it?"

"Right. With a blast yield of less than five kilotons, they can be sure of *complete* destruction across only a few hundred yards, with severe damage going out to a couple of miles or so from ground zero. We know that originally they had one target in D.C., another in New York City. They *might* still have a warhead going to Manhattan in a second vehicle, but right now I'm thinking both weapons are on the way to D.C. If so, they've probably selected two targets in Washington."

"Maybe they plan to detonate both together," Walthers pointed out. "Double the boom."

"No," Teller said, shaking his head. "Doesn't work that way. If they could guarantee both warheads would go off at *precisely* the same instant, maybe—but the two blasts would interfere with one another to some extent. And if one went off even a fraction of a second before the other, it would destroy the second warhead— vaporize it, not detonate it. So their best bet would be to select two widely separated targets, at least a mile or two apart. The targets must be determined by military logic. They would probably have a list—number one, two, three, and so on, with the idea that if target one is blocked, they go to the next one down on the list. With two warheads, they'll just select the top two."

"But how do we figure out what that list is?" Walthers said. "Or the target order?"

"We take a very hard look at what they're trying to do. Maria Perez told us the attack would kick off Aztlán independence. That means their targets must have been chosen to create the maximum amount of chaos throughout the U.S., and probably hamper our ability to respond militarily."

"The White House," Walthers suggested.

"Possible. Not, I think, likely, but it's certainly on the list, for morale purposes if nothing else."

"Why not likely?" Walthers wanted to know. "The president is the commander in chief of the armed forces. Kill him and you cut off the military's head."

"Because when it's all said and done, the president is a figurehead more than anything else. He issues big-picture strategic military orders, sure, but he has military officers to advise him, the Joint Chiefs. *They're* the ones who decide where to send the troops, who to attack, what to defend. They're at the center of the military's C^3—command, control, and communications. And they're at—"

"The Pentagon!" Dominique exclaimed.

"The Pentagon," Teller agreed. He had a satellite map up now on his laptop, centered on the Washington, D.C. metro area, and he put a red marker over the huge gray pentagonal building located on the west bank of the Potomac River. "I've been thinking about that for a while. Destroy the Pentagon, and local military commands will have to make their own decisions. At the very least, command and control for our military would be completely disrupted for hours—more likely days." He drew some lines on the map, checking distances. "Two miles from the White House, and with a clear line of sight. So that warhead might very well get the White House, too. For the second warhead . . . how about the Capitol Building?" He zoomed in for a closer look, then placed a second marker. "Maybe here. A whole row of buildings with the offices of congressional representatives—the Rayburn Building, the Longworth Building, the Cannon Office Building . . . Put a warhead somewhere along Independence Avenue, smack between these offices and the Capitol Building, and it takes out most of the members of the House of Representatives, all of the ones that are in town at the moment, at any rate."

"Most of them are," Dominique pointed out. "In town, I mean. There's a House debate going on this week about the use of troops in the Southwest."

"You're right. They might also try for the Senate office buildings northeast of the Capitol."

"Even a small nuke anywhere on Capitol Hill is going to take them all out," Dominique said. "That whole complex is only about half a mile across."

Walthers had pulled out a small plastic disk, a circular slide rule, and was peering at it closely as he manipulated it. "Say three-tenths of a mile . . . one-kiloton yield . . . yeah. One hundred percent deaths from radiation within two to fourteen days." He looked up. "And that's just from the initial radiation exposure. Fallout will kill a lot more in a footprint stretching downwind."

"It'll be bad," Teller said. "And not just for congresscritters." He measured again on the map. "The dome is a little less than three miles from the Pentagon, so the two blasts can be sequential, not simultaneous. About a mile and a half from the Capitol Building to the White House. Not a clear line of sight—but with two weapons going off, and most of official Washington caught between two blasts, even very small ones . . ."

"They decapitate the whole government," Walthers observed. "Militarily and politically. Man, that would be one world-class diversion."

"Wait a minute," Dominique said. "Their first choice was to hit New York City with one of the bombs. How did *that* figure into their plan?"

"My vote would be for Wall Street, and an attempt to cripple us economically as well. If our banking system collapses, we won't be interested in what's happening overseas—or even in California. But this would be almost as good. Look . . . almost directly on a line between the White House and the Pentagon . . ."

"The Federal Reserve," Dominique said.

"Wall Street would have been more effective, probably," Teller said, placing a third marker. "But nuking D.C. would do a job on the U.S. economy as well."

"So we're starting to get a menu," Dominique said. "Pentagon and Wall Street, and when New York was closed to them the list became the Pentagon and the Capitol Building. The White House has to be on the list as well, but after those two. What else?"

"CIA headquarters?" Walthers suggested. "Fort Meade? Fort Belvoir?"

"I don't think so," Teller said. "Those would be pretty unlikely as Shah Mat targets. The Iranians are also going for global impact, I would imagine. They get to point and say, 'See? The Americans had it coming! *Allah akbar!*' But that sort of thing works best with high-profile targets like the Pentagon or the Capitol Dome. Besides . . . destroying the CIA or the NSA just doesn't advance the Mexican agenda. Langley's not worth a damn—no offense, Jackie."

"None taken. I'm beginning to agree with you."

"Oh?"

She sighed. "Last night you told me that U.S. intelligence is our last line of defense for this country, before we have to take overt action or get into a war. But from where I sit the Agency is a lot more worried about its bureaucratic turf than it is about an enemy attack. It's . . . discouraging."

"Yeah, it is that," Teller agreed. "All we can do is keep soldiering, and try to figure out the next best thing we should do. At this point *we* are the line."

"So what *is* the next thing we do?" Walthers asked.

"We get in touch with INSCOM and NEST HQ," Teller decided. "Let them know what we've come up with. Suggest NEST concentrate most of its search effort around the Pentagon, the Capitol Building and the nearby offices, the White House . . . maybe the Federal Reserve, too. That'll cut the search area down by a hell of a lot."

"And us?"

Teller looked at the big screen, which showed yet another gray-tone image of a ghostly car and its naked passengers. No suitcase nukes. No weapons. *Nothing* . . .

"Let's head downtown," Teller said. "Who knows? Maybe we'll get lucky."

REYSHAHRI
MARYLAND AVENUE NE
WASHINGTON, D.C.
0815 HOURS, EDT

"Okay, I admit it," Moslehi said from behind the wheel. He was grinning. "You were right. Look!"

The stately white dome of the Capitol Building had just emerged from behind the trees and varicolored row houses lining the sidewalk. Reyshahri estimated that it was now less than a kilometer away. He glanced at his watch. It had been a long and exhausting drive—almost three hours to work through the traffic from outside the Beltway. On the car's radio, a morning news broadcast was talking about the ongoing riots in California, about declarations of martial law and the use of federal troops.

After passing the NSA, he'd ordered Moslehi to take an exit onto something called Powder Mill Road, winding tree lined across the Maryland countryside. Traffic here was still heavy—many other drivers, apparently, had had the same idea—but at least it was moving. Eventually, they'd reached Beltsville, Maryland, where they'd picked up an old friend—U.S. Route 1—and turned south.

They'd made a right onto Rhode Island Avenue shortly after that, to avoid the gridlock building up around the Washington Beltway. When they passed under the Beltway a short time later, they'd been able to see the mass of vehicles frozen motionless on the overpass. For the next hour and a half they'd zigzagged through the narrow streets of suburban communities like College Park, Mount Rainier, and Arboretum, still in bumper-to-bumper traffic, edging along from stop sign to stop sign, but at least *moving*.

After working their way through a suburb called Trinidad, they'd turned right onto Maryland Avenue NE, just two and a half kilometers from their destination.

With Moslehi at the wheel, Reyshahri could study the people they passed on the sidewalks. It had occurred to him some distance back that all of the faces he was seeing were *black* . . . and that bothered him.

Although he'd been in the United States before, this mission was his first time in the country's capital. His training back in Iran had presented the United States as sharply divided between the rich whites, who controlled all business, all government, all banks and all religious institutions, and the vast ocean of black and Latino people at the bottom of the social and economic ladder. He'd seen the poverty, the stark desperation, of the Chicano population in California. In Tehran they'd taught him that the plight of American blacks was even worse, that not only were they were desperately poor but that the Muslims among them were prevented from following their faith.

Somehow, what he was seeing on the streets of northeastern Washington didn't match the image he'd carried in his head. The streets were clean and lined with trees, the houses neat, the people well dressed. Automobiles were parked end to end on the streets— few of them brand-new, but few rusted and worn, either. Compared to the poorest classes in his own country, these people were fabulously wealthy.

The thought that by tomorrow most of these people, these *innocents,* would be dead or dying was disturbing.

Past Stanton Park, more and more of the faces on the sidewalks were white. Now the Capitol Dome rose directly ahead—the seat of American political power both in America and throughout the world.

Constitution Avenue NE came in from the left. A man in shorts and a T-shirt and carrying a bottle of water jogged past on the right. On the other side of the street, a group of twenty or thirty kids straggled along the sidewalk, moving toward the Capitol Dome— part of a school field trip, no doubt. Reyshahri had heard the term "tourist Washington," but never really understood it.

Reyshahri told himself that it was . . . *necessary,* sometimes, that the innocent die for the greater good.

"Start looking for a parking place," Hamadi said. "We're close enough now."

"No parking . . . no parking . . ." Moslehi said, reading signs. "No parking . . ."

The Senate office buildings went by on the right. Then they passed an entrance to the Capitol Building on their left—with stop signs, barriers, and a guard shack manned by several men in blue uniforms, bulletproof vests, and automatic weapons. More heavily armed guards were at the entrance to the offices on the right, watching the traffic. Security was tighter than Reyshahri had thought it would be. Was that because the city had been alerted? Or was it always this way?

Parking was allowed in front of Upper Senate Park, but every space was full. They kept driving, past heavily tree-lined parks. At First Street NW they turned left, driving slowly between the Capitol Building and the Capitol Reflecting Pool. No parking . . . and police up ahead were erecting some sort of barricade.

"We should just detonate now!" Hamadi said. "They are searching traffic!"

"This is not a suicide mission, Mohamed," Reyshahri told him. "We plant the weapons, we walk away, we detonate them by remote control. *That* is the plan."

The line of cars going south on First Street had stopped. A large white van was coming toward them on the left, moving north.

"Besides, the weapons must be armed," Gallardo said.

"Turn right here," Reyshahri said. It was the beginning of Pennsylvania Avenue. The street had only one lane going each way, but there were four lanes given over to diagonal parking, one to each side and two in the middle.

Better yet, there was a construction site on the right, at the corner of Constitution Avenue and Third Street NW.

With parking spaces. "There," Reyshahri said. "Pull in there."

As Moslehi parked, Reyshahri turned to face the two men in the back. "Underneath the front seats," he said. "Pull out the plastic vests."

"What are these?" Gallardo asked.

"Your disguises. Put them on, then get out of the car."

Reyshahri could hear the fluttering roar of a helicopter nearby.

"Drop the weapon in that Dumpster over there, then get back in the car. We don't have much time."

NEST 2/2
OVER HOUSE WEST FOUNTAIN
0852 HOURS, EDT

"Jackpot!" Walthers cried. "One of our units tagged them!"

"Where?" Teller demanded.

"Close! In front of the Capitol Building."

The scan image was coming through on the screen, relayed from one of the ZBVs patrolling the area immediately around Capitol Hill. The target was a ghosted four-door sedan, with four male passengers. Two bright white masses, like thick, heavy suitcases or travel trunks, were riding side by side in the trunk.

"*Both* of them!" Dominique exclaimed.

"Get us over there!" Teller ordered.

Walthers talked to the pilot, and the helicopter started to rise.

"Damn it!" Walthers cried. "They *lost* them! The target turned onto Pennsylvania Avenue and they *lost* them!"

The Super Stallion was rising now, passing low above the Rayburn Building. They'd been flying south of the Capitol Dome, searching vehicles along D Street SE from the air.

"Did they get a license?"

"Negative! You can't *see* a license plate on the

backscatter, or the color—and by the time they reached the police on the ground, the vehicle had disappeared!"

Teller looked out of a port-side window. The distinctive glass roofs of the United States Botanic Garden passed below, then the green waters of the Capitol Reflecting Pool.

"Get us over Pennsylvania Avenue," Teller said, "and start scanning cars!"

REYSHAHRI
PENNSYLVANIA AVENUE NW
WASHINGTON, D.C.
0853 HOURS, EDT

They'd backed into one of the diagonal spaces, and Moslehi and Hamadi had gotten out of the car. Each was wearing a bright, yellow green plastic vest of the sort worn by D.C. construction workers, and a white helmet. Operation Shah Mat had never been intended to be a suicide mission. The idea was to plant a weapon, arm it, then drive off, using a cell phone trigger to detonate it later from a safe distance. Where the weapon was to be planted had been left up to the operatives. Favored hiding places included on the street underneath a parked car, tucked away in the corner of a public parking garage, or inside a Dumpster at one of the construction sites that so heavily populated official Washington. Because each weapon was so heavy and bulky—sixty-five pounds—Reyshahri had acquired the construction helmets and vests when he and Moslehi had passed through Washington a couple of days ago. His contact here, the man who'd called himself "Duke," had gotten them somehow and passed them on to him in the yellow plastic bag at the park bench on the Mall.

It was a good disguise. Americans, Reyshahri had noted, never paid attention to people whom they assumed belonged there. Two men hauling a heavy case across a sidewalk or tossing it into a Dumpster would be suspicious—but if they looked like city workers, then passersby, even police or security guards nearby, wouldn't give them a second glance.

The helicopter's roar was getting louder. Looking back over his shoulder, Reyshahri saw the black aircraft coming low across the Reflecting Pool, its rotor wash lashing the water into a white frenzy. "Arm the bombs!" Reyshahri screamed. *"Arm the bombs!"*

NEST 2/2
OVER THE CAPITOL REFLECTING POOL
0853 HOURS, EDT

"Damn it, I can't *see*!"

Teller wished he could be up in the cockpit, where they would have a decent view of Pennsylvania Avenue. The backscatter scanner was too slow to show what was happening in real time; Kaminsky touched a control, and three parked ghost-cars slowly drew themselves on the screen side by side . . . all empty.

"We need someone on the ground!" Teller said.

"Tell the pilot to find a clear spot to hover, and drop the rear ramp!"

Dominique saw him draw his pistol and chamber a round. "I'm coming, too!" she said.

"No!" he told her. "I want you to coordinate with the police and other NEST units! Tell them we have the bad guys spotted, and where. Have them cordon the area off." He looked at Walthers. "After he drops me off, have the pilot pull back. Two miles at least."

"Damn it, Chris, that's sexist bullshit!"

"No. It's command-control bullshit! If this goes bad here, we need someone in the air to coordinate the search at the Pentagon."

And yeah, he thought, *I don't want you caught in the blast, Jackie.* He didn't say that out loud.

"I got them!" Kaminsky yelled. "On the big display screen, a ghosted car slowly appeared. Two men sat in front, while two bent over the opaque white suitcases in the trunk, comically nude.

"Get me down there, close as you can!" Teller yelled. He grabbed a startled Dominique with one arm, pulled her close, and kissed her hard. "See ya!" he said.

The rear ramp was grinding open, flooding the rear of the Super Stallion's cargo deck with morning light. Holding the pistol, Teller trotted down to the end, dropped to his knees, and peered out. He was over the broad, curving esplanade along the western edge of the Reflecting Pool. He took a moment to judge the helicopter's forward drift, then rolled off the ramp, dropping five feet to the pavement.

He hit with a sharp jolt but took the shock with flex-ing knees, collapsed into a roll, and nearly went into the pool. The helicopter thunder grew louder as the aircraft began moving forward and up once more, the rotor wash a living thing tearing at Teller's clothes and exposed skin.

Just ahead, the esplanade opened onto Pennsylvania Avenue NW. Teller turned left and jogged onto a patch of green parkland with scattered trees, a part of the landscaping surrounding the eastern end of the Wash-ington Mall.

He could see all the way down the Mall from here, a distance of over a mile to the slender white needle of the Washington Monument thrusting into the morning light. Dodging in among the trees, he crested a low rise, jogging toward the intersection of Pennsylvania Avenue with 3rd Street NW.

And then he saw them—sixty yards ahead, two men in bright yellow vests and white helmets standing by the open trunk of a white four-door sedan. One was holding something like a large fat suitcase, balancing it over his shoulder. Both men were distracted, staring up into the sky as the Super Stallion peeled away toward the northeast.

He had to get closer. Sixty yards is a *long* reach for a handgun, with little guarantee of accuracy. Holding the .45 Glock in both hands, he bent into a crouch and started zigzagging between the parked cars.

One of the Tangos, the one without a suitcase nuke on his back, saw him and pulled a handgun of his own from beneath his shirttail. The other was lugging the heavy suitcase across the sidewalk, angling toward a construction Dumpster on the grass.

The one with the gun opened fire.

The windshield of a Ford next to him crazed as a round punched through. At a range of thirty yards now, Teller came to a halt, brought the pistol up in a two-handed grip, and squeezed off five rounds, shifting from one target to the other. The gunman kept firing as well, putting a second round into the side of the car with a harsh, metallic thud and sending another snapping through the air somewhere above Teller's head. Teller moved forward, trying for a better angle past the parked cars. The one with the suitcase was partially obscured now by a parked pickup truck; he shifted his aim back to the one with the pistol, squeezed off four more rounds, and saw the man stagger and twist, one hand clutching at his side. He fired again at the other man as he emerged from behind the truck, saw the man crumple to the pavement beneath his heavy load.

The white car jerked forward, tires squealing, open trunk flapping with the movement. Teller took aim, squeezed the trigger . . . and realized his .45 was out of ammo. *Shit*.

Thumbing the Glock's magazine release, he dropped the empty magazine and slapped in a fresh one just as the car jumped through the intersection against the light. Horns blared, brakes shrieked, and then two cars slammed into each other, but the white sedan made it through the intersection, accelerating quickly.

"Two Tangos down!" Teller yelled—and then he realized that in his excitement he hadn't brought along a tactical radio. Reaching the suitcase nuke, he pulled his cell phone out of a pocket and speed-dialed Dominique.

"Chris!" he heard her say.

"Yeah! Two Tangos down, and we have one of the weapons. Get the NEST guys here fast as you can! Two more Tangos now in white four-door sedan, Virginia plates, partial license Charlie Mike 3, heading northwest on Pennsylvania Avenue. We need to stop those bastards now!"

"Walthers says we're on the way," Dominique told him. "And we've contacted the Capitol Police."

"You!" someone shouted behind him. "Drop the gun!"

"They just got here," Teller said, turning. A policeman was coming across the street toward him, a pistol aimed at Teller's chest. Other law enforcement officers were converging on the scene, including one member of the Park Police riding a Segway. "Hello, Officer."

"Drop the weapon!"

"Federal officer," Teller said, carefully pulling out his wallet and flipping it open to his ID. "And that suitcase on the sidewalk is a small nuclear weapon. You'll want to cordon off the area until NEST gets here."

The cop squinted as he looked at the badge and read the credentials, then lowered his pistol slightly. "A fed? Jesus! Is that really a nuke?"

"Yes. This is not a joke," Teller said with deadly seriousness. "This is not a drill." The Segway rolled up, and Teller pointed at it as the cop stepped off. "And I'm requisitioning that vehicle."

"Hey, wait just a—"

"A horse would be better," Teller added, climbing onto the contraption, "but since Congress took away your horses, I'll have to make do with what's available."

The Capitol Police had had a mounted unit until a few years ago, which they'd used to patrol the Hill, but a cost-cutting move had ended the program. He leaned into the handlebars and the machine whirred into motion.

He thought the things were comical, but Teller had used a Segway before, renting one for a tour of downtown D.C. Like riding a bicycle, you never forgot how. You moved forward by leaning forward, and the transporter sensed the shift in weight and accelerated; you turned by leaning left or right. Top speed was only about twelve and a half miles per hour, but the avenue along the Washington Mall was thick with cars. Slaloming through the traffic, Teller rapidly closed with the white sedan, which had moved a hundred yards down Pennsylvania and come to an abrupt halt behind a D.C. tour bus. He raised his Glock, muzzle pointed at the sky, wondering if he could disable the car . . . but there were far too many people and cars in his line of fire. He leaned forward more, trying to coax another bit of speed from the transporter, and hoped to hell that the batteries were well charged.

The car up ahead was turning . . .

REYSHAHRI
PENNSYLVANIA AVENUE NW
WASHINGTON, D.C.
0856 HOURS, EDT

Moslehi swung the wheel and turned south onto Fourth Street, between the National Gallery of Art and its East Annex. Reyshahri glanced into the right-side rear mirror and caught a glimpse of someone careening through the traffic on a device that looked like a pogo stick with wheels.

The figure had a gun . . . and was catching up.

TELLER
FOURTH STREET NW
WASHINGTON, D.C.
0856 HOURS, EDT

He made the turn onto Fourth Street, still following the white car up ahead. Traffic here was a lot lighter, and the sedan was accelerating. Tucking his pistol back into his waistband, Teller pulled out his phone and thumbed Dominique's number.

"We're back over Capitol Hill!" her voice said. "Where are you?"

He told her. "This has got to be a first!" he added. "The U.S. Army in hot pursuit on one of these ridiculous Segway things!"

He heard the helicopter off to the east, the roar muffled to a dull clatter by the Art Gallery's east building.

Twenty yards in front of him, the sedan swerved suddenly right at a stoplight.

"Target is turning west onto Madison!"

"Chris . . . the pilot says the target is in sight. He wants to know . . . how are they going to detonate those bombs?"

Teller had been wondering exactly that.

He only wished he knew the answer.

CHAPTER TWENTY-FIVE

REYSHAHRI
WASHINGTON MALL
WASHINGTON, D.C.
0857 HOURS, EDT
22 APRIL

They swerved right onto Madison and smashed into the rear bumper of another car, an expensive luxury model. Madison Drive NW was a one-way street running past the northern tier of Smithsonian museums—the Art Gallery, Natural History, and American History. "Back up! Back up!" Reyshahri yelled. *Damn* this traffic! "Get around him!" Horns blared. The driver of the car ahead opened his door and stepped onto the street, glaring as he started walking toward them.

"I can't get through!" Moslehi screamed back.

The man looked furious, stalking toward them, fists clenched.

Reyshahri pointed to the left, through the trees lining the Mall. "*That* way!"

The car nosed left, threaded its way between two parked vehicles, then bumped up onto the sidewalk, crashed past a park bench, and plunged through a light mesh fence into a park area with widely scattered trees. Pedestrians scattered as Moslehi floored the accelerator. They bounced across the wooded area, crashed through another mesh fence, and emerged on the broad, open expanse of the Mall.

Reyshahri suddenly felt very small, trapped in this vast openness between the Capitol Dome and the Washington Monument.

They had to act *now*.

TELLER
WASHINGTON MALL
WASHINGTON, D.C.
0857 HOURS, EST

He followed the sedan onto Madison, narrowly missing a bicycle-propelled rickshaw and eliciting an angry flurry of horn blasts. A silver El Dorado had been rear-ended by the quarry, and the driver was in the street, shaking his fist. Teller could see where the white rental had gone, though, knocking down a mesh fence and careening out onto the mall. He followed—and nearly fell as the Segway hit the curb—but then he was on hard-packed gravel, and then on the sidewalk.

He wasn't convinced the little electric personal transporter would navigate the grass beyond, though, so he swung right again and raced down the sidewalk.

He could see the sedan now, through the trees, heading southwest across the Mall in the general direction of the Air and Space Museum.

How *did* the Tangos plan to detonate their nukes? Some sort of timer would be simplest—but did they also have some sort of remote control device, something that would let them set the bombs off with the touch of a finger?

Would they detonate the weapons if they found themselves trapped, unable to flee?

Sirens wailed and howled as emergency vehicles converged on the Mall. Everywhere, civilians were running, scattering, some screaming, some standing open-mouthed and oblivious.

Behind him, the Super Stallion cleared the trees and thundered toward the Mall.

REYSHAHRI
WASHINGTON MALL
WASHINGTON, D.C.
0858 HOURS, EDT

"You made us get rid of our phones!" Moslehi screamed. "How are we supposed to detonate the weapons now?"

"The idea was never to detonate them while we were still in the city," Reyshahri replied. He'd been planning to buy new phones outside of Washington, or even to use a public phone, but that no longer was an option. The opposition was too close now.

"Yes, but now we *have* to!"

Reyshahri pointed. A young woman in pink shorts and a tight black halter was standing on the Mall, talking into a cell phone. "There! That girl! Run her down!"

Moslehi grinned. "Allah be praised!"

TELLER
WASHINGTON MALL
WASHINGTON, D.C.
0858 HOURS, EDT

Teller reached the crosswalk that headed south directly opposite the National Gallery's main entrance and made a sharp, fast turn. "Out of the way! Out of the way!" he shouted as tourists gaped and screamed and scattered to left and right. "Federal officer! Gangway!" Damn it, with the gridlock outside the city, where had all these civilians come from?

The question of the terrorists' psychology was very much on Teller's mind. These people weren't Islamist fanatics, suicide bombers determined to blow their target and themselves to bits. Reyshahri was a VEVAK officer, which meant he was a professional, and the chances were good that the others in his ops team were professionals as well—or at least that they weren't bent on self-immolation. They'd intended, almost certainly, to place the warheads, withdraw to a safe distance, and either set them off with timers or detonate them by remote control.

That didn't mean they didn't have some sort of backup plan, a way of setting off the bombs immediately if it looked like they were about to be captured and their plan was going to fail. If they were backed into a corner, they might set the warheads off here and now. They might even have some sort of dead man's switch, a device that would trigger the nukes if the man holding the switch closed was killed.

What he needed now was negotiation rather than firepower.

Ahead, halfway across the Mall, he saw the sedan abruptly swerve, apparently trying to hit a woman.

Maybe negotiations wouldn't help either . . .

REYSHAHRI
WASHINGTON MALL
WASHINGTON, D.C.
0858 HOURS, EDT

The car sideswiped the woman with the cell phone. She shrieked and tumbled backward. Reyshahri opened the door and leaped out of the car while it was still moving.

One part of him was horrified at the fact that he'd actually ordered Moslehi to run the woman down. Another part of him was coldly analytical. If he could get the woman's cell phone and punch in the triggering number, the woman would be dead anyway in a pair of searing white flashes of light—along with some tens of thousands of other people in central Washington.

The woman was on her back, still clutching the phone. Reaching down, Reyshahri grabbed it from her.

TELLER
WASHINGTON MALL
WASHINGTON, D.C.
0858 HOURS, EDT

Teller couldn't get any more speed out of the Segway. It was faster than a man over long distances, but Teller knew he could sprint faster than the transporter's top speed. Leaping off of the platform, he raced across the mall as fast as he could run. The sedan had stopped, and one of the passengers was struggling with the woman on the ground, trying to take something from her.

He aimed and fired . . . an impossible shot while running all-out, but the noise might startle the Tango, or—just maybe—he might get lucky. The driver was on the far side of the vehicle, getting out. He heard the shot, raised a pistol, and snapped off a round at Teller.

Teller ignored him as the bullet cracked through the air a foot from his head. He'd just seen what the first Tango was trying to wrest from the woman—a cell phone—and in that instant he knew how the bad guys planned to detonate the two suitcase nukes.

The Israelis had done it first, back in the seventies, assassinating several PLO leaders by calling them and, when they'd identified themselves, sending a triggering signal through a phone line to detonate the bomb planted under the phone hours earlier. The nukes, Teller thought, must have phone receivers wired into their detonators. Call the number, and the closing of the circuit would set off the blast. The two weapons might even have the same number so that both would explode with a single call—and that call could be made from anywhere in the world.

Or by someone standing just a few feet away. Teller was close enough now to recognize the VEVAK officer, Reyshahri, from his file photos. The Iranian finally yanked the phone away from the woman at his feet and began punching furiously at the keyboard. The driver was bracing himself on the sedan now, holding the pistol two-handed and bracing it across the roof of the car. Behind him, the Sea Stallion was settling toward the surface of the Mall, its rotor wash lashing the grass and the gunman's hair.

Teller emerged from the trees bordering the Mall's central open area. To his right, the Washington Monument speared the sky above clouds of soft pink cherry blossoms; to his left, much nearer, less than a thousand yards away, loomed the stately white curves of the Capitol Dome.

Teller ignored everything but Reyshahri, continuing to fire as he ran.

REYSHAHRI
WASHINGTON MALL
WASHINGTON, D.C.
0858 HOURS, EDT

Reyshahri entered the memorized phone number—area code . . . seven digits . . .

He was searching for the CALL SEND button on the unfamiliar phone when something hit him in the side. It didn't hurt, exactly, but the impact was like a hammer blow against his ribs.

Twisting, he saw a man running toward him from the trees, firing a pistol, just thirty meters away. Another round struck him, this time in the hip.

Still clutching the phone, he dropped to his knees, then fell.

TELLER
WASHINGTON MALL
WASHINGTON, D.C.
0858 HOURS, EDT

Teller saw his target drop, but the Iranian agent was still holding the cell phone. How many numbers had the man entered? The other man, the gunman behind the car, fired again, and Teller felt the impact against his left shoulder, a dull thud that staggered him and nearly knocked him down. He turned, shifting his aim—and realized that his Glock's slide was locked open, the magazine again empty.

He watched as the gunman reacquired the target, taking careful aim—

—and blinked, startled, as the man's head exploded in a spray of blood and bone.

The gunman sagged and dropped out of sight behind the sedan. Behind him, Dominique was running from the lowered rear ramp of the Sea Stallion, her pistol raised.

Somehow, Teller stayed on his feet, covering the last few yards to Reyshahri. The VEVAK agent was on his back, next to the woman whose phone he'd stolen. The cell phone was in his right hand, his thumb hovering above the keypad.

"Don't," Teller said. He started to raise the empty pistol, then tossed it away. "Just *don't*."

"My mission . . ." The words were faint, weak, little more than a whisper. At least he spoke English.

"Saeed Reyshahri," Teller said.

Reyshahri looked startled. "How . . . do you know my name?"

"We also know you're VEVAK," Teller told him. "And if you push that button, I promise you that the whole world will know that your people are mass murderers."

"They will know that no matter what."

"Not necessarily. You see . . . I don't think that Iran is really behind this. Shah Mat, you call it? Your country has way too much to lose. I think your superiors saw a way to tie us down so that we couldn't interfere with your plans in the Mideast. But someone else came to you with the idea, didn't they?"

"You appear to know a great deal about us . . . mister . . . mister . . ."

"Chris Teller. We know the Mexican cartels are agitating to start a new country in the American southwest, Aztlán. We know Iran and Hezbollah are helping that along, and we know that the nuclear weapons were supposed to so wreck the American economy and command-control infrastructures that it could happen."

"Yes . . ."

"But Shah Mat still wouldn't have a prayer—not without some major help inside the United States itself. That new country would need money, lots of it. Maybe investment from some major banks? Or a faction within our own government committed to steering things their way?"

"How do you know all of this?"

"It was fairly obvious. The cartels are powerful in Mexico, but they haven't managed to buy Washington just yet. But they might have bought a few individuals."

"Duke," Reyshahri said.

"I beg your pardon?"

"I know my American contact as Duke. He is a member of your government, fairly highly placed. I do not know his name." Reyshahri reached out with a trembling hand, giving the cell phone to Teller. "But I do know it's not worth sacrificing my country's honor for a traitor's dream."

"The weapons. Are they on timers? Any other means of setting them off?"

"A phone call." Reyshahri managed a smile. "Duke has the number. He could still set them off. I don't think anyone else knows the number."

Teller looked up. A second helicopter was landing nearby, and men in protective suits were piling out. NEST had arrived to take charge of the second weapon. Dominique was talking on her phone as sirens wailed in the distance.

"Thank you, Captain Reyshahri."

"If you can . . ."

"Yes?"

"A message. To my Hasti."

"Absolutely. But you'll be able to tell her yourself. We're going to get you to a hospital."

"I have not . . . lately . . . been able to pray . . ."

THE OWL'S NEST
BOHEMIAN GROVE
MONTE RIO, CALIFORNIA
0615 HOURS, PDT

Preston had arrived at Oakland International on the red-eye during the wee hours of the morning and caught a commuter flight up to the Sonoma County Airport. From there, it was a twenty-five-mile drive by rented car through the spectacular mountains of Northern California to a small town on the Russian River called Monte Rio. He'd checked in at the Club château and was still in the process of unpacking his things. A large-screen plasma TV was hung from one red-oak wall. Picking up a remote, he clicked it on and turned the channel setting to CNN.

". . . minutes ago from a traffic news helicopter above the Mall in the heart of Washington, D.C.! We go now to traffic reporter Larry Delancey on the scene."

The image on the screen showed a tangle of movement and confusion on the broad, open swath of ground between Washington's Air and Space Museum and the

National Gallery. Two helicopters were on the ground, their rotors still turning, as a swarm of people clustered around a white car on the grass. Police cars were there . . . and an ambulance.

The trunk of the white vehicle was open, and several men in protective silver suits were leaning inside.

"Thanks, Vicki. It's possible that we've now determined the cause of the massive gridlock outside the nation's capital this morning, as police converge on the Washington Mall in an apparent response to gunfire. We're not sure yet what's going on down there, but I can see men in hazmat suits working on something in the trunk of a car, and it's possible that we are witnessing the outcome of some sort of biological or chemical terror attack. According to our sources, witnesses reported gunfire on the Mall approximately fifteen minutes ago. No word yet on whether anyone was hurt—though from our vantage point five hundred feet above the Mall it *does* look as though someone is being loaded on board an ambulance."

Preston knew immediately what was happening . . . and what needed to be done.

Grimly, with a cold determination, he reached for his cell phone and punched in a memorized number.

He waited for the view of central Washington to dissolve into white noise.

Nothing happened.

Nothing at all.

INSCOM HQ
FORT BELVOIR, VIRGINIA
1545 HOURS, EDT

"Preston knows we secured and safed the nukes," Teller said. "One of the NEST guys said the telephone circuit closed about five seconds after he'd disconnected the power from the detonator."

George Haupt looked uncomfortable. "I don't see how you can accuse Mr. Preston of this . . . this treason. Do you have any idea who he *is*?"

"The president's national security adviser," Procario said. "Or are we talking about some *other* traitor?"

"You people are going to need some very serious proof of these allegations."

"No one," Granger said, "is making any allegations. Not *yet*."

They'd met at Fort Belvoir's underground Ops Center, the B2 level—Teller and Procario, Colonel MacDonald, George Haupt, General Granger, and a half-dozen others. Granger had called the meeting, informing the rest of them that he would be briefing the president later that afternoon.

Teller was exhausted, barely standing. He'd caught a couple of hours of sleep earlier that morning at the DeWitt Army Hospital here at Fort Belvoir, where they'd brought him after the takedown at the Mall, but his sleep meter was still running way on the minus side of the dial. His shoulder, bandaged now, was aching, and between that and the lack of sleep he found he had exactly zero patience with Haupt's obstructionist attitude.

"We have all the proof we need," Teller said. "Colonel MacDonald here pulled some strings and got us some time on the Tordella Supercomputer network earlier this afternoon." He handed Haupt a printout. "Here's what they came up with."

The Tordella Supercomputer Facility at Fort Meade was the heart and muscle of the NSA's code-breaking infrastructure, an array of ultrafast latest-model Cray computers used to decrypt and analyze signals intelligence from all over the globe.

Those machines could also chew through mountains of raw data to identify patterns, and that was what they'd done earlier that afternoon with information sent to them from MacDonald's office.

For five days now, the Cellmap program Teller had planted in a cartel assassin's phone had been silently multiplying and spreading, unseen and relentless, from phone to phone to phone across the entire world. Anyone and any organization that had had electronic contact with the Mexican cartels had been infected; current estimates suggested that the number of Cellmap-tagged phones numbered over a billion.

Making any sense at all of that vast mountain of data was beyond any analyst or department, even beyond any organization including the NSA, but the Tordella computers could still extract particular pebbles of information from the mountain, *if* the analysts knew what to ask.

"What the hell is this?" Haupt asked, looking at the list of names, dates, and locations on the sheet.

"That is a list," Procario replied, "of people tagged

by Cellmap who were in Washington, D.C., up until April nineteenth, who then caught flights out of the city. The computers then looked for correlations in destinations. That list there includes twenty-seven people who flew to one of four destinations in Northern California over the past few days: San Francisco International, Metro Oakland International, San Jose, and Sacramento. We then looked for correlations among those twenty-seven. Eleven, you'll notice, caught commuter flights to Sonoma County Airport, in Windsor. That's about fifty miles north of San Francisco. We also tapped into rental car and limo records. Seems like there's been quite a bit of traffic between Windsor and a little town west of there called Monte Rio."

"Mean anything to you?" Teller asked.

"Should it?"

"It's the location of the Bohemian Grove."

Teller hadn't known much about the Bohemians until he'd looked it up on his laptop a little earlier. It was a private men's club started in San Francisco in the 1870s, originally for journalists but now with an exclusive and *very* private membership that included government leaders and cabinet officials, the CEOs of oil companies, banks, and other large corporations, military leaders, and high-ranking members of the media. Once each year, in July, the Bohemian Club hosted a two-week-long camp-out at Bohemian Grove, located within a secluded old-growth redwood forest just outside of Monte Rio. Nearly three thousand had attended in years past—presidents and future presidents, defense contractors, oil magnates, banking CEOs, Joint Chiefs, corporate executives, senators and representatives . . . it was a long and imposing list.

The festivities had in recent years become somewhat controversial. Membership in the Bohemian Club was strictly males only. The club had lost a State Supreme Court ruling over a discrimination suit in 1986, requiring them to hire female workers during the summer, but even those were required to leave the Grove at sundown. Perhaps more alarming was the public's fear that letting that many power brokers and elitists get together for two unsupervised weeks would inevitably lead to backroom deals, secret agreements between government and big business, and national conspiracies. A couple of years before, a popular History Channel program had run a rather shallow and slanted episode about the Grove, and several of the actors had been arrested for trespass.

"Of those eleven people going to Monte Rio," Procario pointed out, "nine are members of the Bohemian Club, including, you'll notice, Randolph Edgar Preston, the assistant to the president for national security affairs. Also on the list, Mr. James Fitzhugh Walker, of the Federal Reserve; Charles Richard Logan, CEO of North American Oil; Congressman Harvey Gonzales, of East Los Angeles; Robert Avery Delaney, of the First New York Bank of Commerce; Joseph Howard Belsanno, of the President's Commission on—"

"Damn you!" Haupt said, dropping the list as though it had just burned his hand. "I shouldn't even see this! I *can't* see this!"

"Why not, George?" Granger asked.

"Because this stuff is illegal as hell! This . . . this is wiretapping, plain and simple! Without a warrant . . . and on *government officials*!"

"These men," Granger said carefully, "have just conspired to set off two nuclear weapons inside one, possibly two, of our cities in what appears to be a conspiracy to break several of our states away to create a new country. There are times when going outside the normal legal niceties is necessary."

"I can't see this," Haupt said again. Turning abruptly, he left the Ops Center.

"Sandy," MacDonald said to one of her assistants, "have Security detain Mr. Haupt. And make certain they relieve him of his cell phone."

"We're adding false arrest to the list, Colonel?" Teller asked.

"Watch your mouth, Captain," MacDonald replied.

Teller felt secure in the knowledge that the colonel still hated him.

"We're only holding him until this California situation is resolved," Granger added. "We want to make sure that Preston and his friends don't get any help from outside."

Personally, Teller doubted that Haupt was a part of the conspiracy. He'd been left behind in the D.C. area, after all—though Fort Belvoir would have been well outside the probable zone of radioactive contamination if the bombs had actually gone off. It was possible, but most likely the man was nothing more than a chronic bureaucratic ass-coverer. He could see the legal ramifications of

INSCOM's activities and didn't care to risk twenty years in Leavenworth for even marginal association with the Cellmap program.

"So what *are* we going to do about Preston and his cronies?" Procario asked.

"These men have a great deal of money and influence," Teller pointed out. "If they learn we're onto them, they'll either be gone, fled out of the country, or else they'll be holed up behind a few battalions of lawyers."

"That much money can buy safety just about anywhere in the world," MacDonald said.

"This person tried to detonate those weapons this morning," Procario pointed out. "He tried to commit mass murder as well as high treason. And the people with him are accomplices at the very least. I don't care how rich or powerful they are, they cannot be above the law!"

"It's also logical to assume that they know we're onto them now," MacDonald added, "since they know we caught the people with the weapons. They won't be within reach for very long."

"I'm open to suggestions," Granger said.

"Well, given some of the people we're dealing with," Teller said, picking up the list Haupt had dropped, "I'd say we need to occupy Bohemian Grove."

"What, as in that Occupy Wall Street movement a few years ago?"

"Exactly."

"Bad joke," Procario said. "I think you're still running way short on sleep."

"I'll get caught up on the plane."

"Plane?"

"We're going to Monte Rio. McDee? How about booking us a couple of seats, and maybe talking to the ISA?"

It was symptomatic of just how tired he was. He'd never before called the Colonel "McDee" to her face.

She glared at him but reached for her phone.

CHAPTER TWENTY-SIX

"Look, people, it's going to be okay!" Preston was exasperated. He'd not expected the group to begin crumbling so swiftly. "This is a minor setback, that's all! We can still win this if we hold it together and don't panic!"

The eleven of them had gathered in the Owl's Nest common room, a fair imitation of an authentic Swiss chalet. The Owl's Nest was one of a number of rustic cabins tucked away among the redwoods of Bohemian Grove—though "cabin" did the building a serious disservice. Presidents had stayed here, and the decor and furnishings were tastefully luxurious. For the past five hours, they'd been here in this room, discussing the situation and trying to hammer out a consensus.

A number of them wanted to leave. Too many.

"And just how the fuck is the Program supposed to work now?" Logan demanded. "The Iranians let us down! The Mexicans aren't going to be any help at all! This damned Aztlán scheme doesn't stand a chance in hell if the government can still put together a coherent response!"

"We have other options," Preston insisted. "They're still rioting in L.A. and a dozen other cities. Our Mexican . . . friends are still ready to pour money, weapons, and muscle into every border state from California to Texas. And the president's ready to cave on this, I promise you!"

"Cave *how*?" Walker demanded. "By granting Aztlán independence? Or is he just promising more talk with the UN? Mr. Preston, I . . . *we* never bargained for this!" Walker looked around the table, as though trying to assess how much support he had from these men. "It's time to cut our losses and get out! We don't know how much they learned about us from the Iranians. They might know everything!"

"They know nothing!" Preston snapped. "I'm the only one who met with any of them, and they never even knew my name!"

"Mr. Preston is right," Joseph Belsanno said. "Hell, we don't even know if any of those jokers were taken alive."

"We can't take the risk," Robert Delaney said. "All of us, we have too much to lose."

"How many of you agree with Walker and Delaney?" Preston glared at the others around the room, each in turn. Five hands went up—Walker and Delaney, plus

Logan, Carter, and Gonzales. That last was a surprise; Gonzales was online to become *el presidente* of the new republic, once it had been recognized by Mexico and other nations, and its security was reasonably guaranteed.

Then again, Preston reasoned, Gonzales was a politician, always sensitive to the winds of change.

Almost half of the group wanted to run, and some of that number would go straight to the authorities. Preston couldn't risk that.

"I gather you others want to stick it out?" Preston asked.

"I don't see that we have a whole lot of choice," Carl Fuentes said. He was another banking executive, a VP of First Federal of Arizona. He was also the only other Latino in the Program, after Gonzales, and the only one with dirty ties to the Mexican cartels. It wasn't common knowledge, but his uncle was a big shot with the Sinaloa Cartel, and his cousin was Juan Escalante Romero. "If we fold now, there's no hole on earth deep enough to hide us."

"Five yea, five nay," Preston said, "and I cast the deciding vote. We stay and stick this out."

"But what if they come for us?" Walker asked. "Damn it, Preston, I want out!"

Preston looked at the Federal Reserve man with surprise. The small, gray bureaucrat was showing some unexpected backbone.

He would have to do something about that.

"Listen," Preston said, making a show of checking his watch. "It's late—past midnight. I suggest we get some sleep. In the morning, we'll see if anything further has developed. If any of you want to leave, well, we can make the arrangements then. Okay?"

There was a mutter of agreement, and the others began standing and wandering off toward their rooms. Some were in other cabins nearby, Walker and Delaney among them.

A knock sounded at the door. "What?" Preston called, sharper than he'd intended.

Juan Escalante entered and walked over to Preston. "Sir," he said, keeping his voice so low the others couldn't hear, "we may have a problem."

"What is it?"

"Two of my men have not checked in."

Preston considered this. Escalante had flown up to California two days before, bringing with him a dozen *viajeros*—"travelers," cartel gunmen with clean visas, able to travel freely in the United States when necessary to address certain problems when they arose. The Program was paying them to provide some additional security, beside the Grove's usual rent-a-cops.

"They're probably stoned behind a bush someplace," Preston replied.

"I don't think that would be the case, sir."

"Look, put everyone on full alert and keep your eyes open. I don't think it's anything—but we won't take chances." He looked at Delaney and Walker, who were putting on their jackets. "There's something else."

"Sir?"

"Pick a couple of your best boys. I'll have a special job for them in the morning."

"Yes, sir."

"And don't tell any of the others. They're jittery enough."

"No, sir."

Preston watched Escalante leave, stepping back out into the night after Walker and Delaney. The naysayers would all have to be eliminated, of course . . . but carefully, in such a way that the rest of the Program's members thought they'd simply left the Grove. Except for Gonzales. They still needed him as a figurehead for the new country, to give the secession a measure of legitimacy to the rest of the world, if not in Washington.

Was it even possible that the Program had been discovered? Preston didn't see how that could be. They'd been careful. Even the Mexicans, save for a very few like Escalante, had no idea that *norteamericanos* were behind Aztlán—or knew that Aztlán was a scam. The Iranians knew nothing useful, and certainly could not divulge names or identities.

No, the Program was still safe. It *had* to be.

In fact, the worst problem they'd encountered so far—aside from the failure of the nukes in New York City and D.C., of course—was that idiot de la Cruz in Mexico City. Unaware that Escalante was a key member of the Program, he'd actually pointed some CIA operations people at Escalante and his mistress in Iztacalco. He'd not known of Escalante's importance—of how vital it was to the Program that Sinaloa and Los Zetas establish a truce, at least temporarily. When de la Cruz had had the Zeta Killers kidnap a CIA officer and actually hold her there for interrogation, he'd nearly blown the whole operation.

Fortunately, as far as Preston could determine, the CIA hadn't learned anything useful. The only real loose end there was Escalante's mistress—she'd disappeared—but she hadn't turned up in any Agency reports, and in any case it wasn't likely she'd known anything useful. She was probably hiding out somewhere in Mexico City; they'd find her . . . and then that particular loose end could be eliminated.

Even if the CIA or FBI did have some idea of what was happening, it wasn't like there was anything they could do about it. They could have no idea where the members of the Program were hiding, and certainly no evidence that would stand up in court.

No, the Program was still very much alive. The warheads purchased from the Russian *mafiya* had been captured, true, and that meant that Aztlán would probably collapse sooner rather than later. That was okay; the Program's members would still be able to get what they wanted and vanish into the chaos afterward.

If Walker and the others fell by the wayside before the big payoff, that just meant more for the survivors.

WALKER
BOHEMIAN GROVE
MONTE RIO, CALIFORNIA
0104 HOURS, PDT

"I don't trust Preston," Delaney said, a low-voiced mutter in the darkness.

"Neither do I," Walker said. "I'm sorry I ever got mixed up in this."

The two of them were walking across a broad, open area among the towering trees. It was chilly out, and Walker zipped his jacket. The redwoods around them were invisible in the darkness, but their towering bulks blotted out the stars.

"He's not going to let us just walk out of here."

"I don't know. Maybe I can convince him."

Delaney gave a brittle, sarcastic laugh. "Convince? Preston can't be *convinced*. He always has his own agenda."

Walker's cell phone warbled.

Odd. He'd thought he'd switched it off. Pulling it out of a pocket, he examined the screen. There was no caller ID.

Hesitantly, he put it to his ear. "Hello?"

"Good morning, Mr. Walker," a pleasant voice said. "It sounds to us like you're looking for a way out."

Walker's eyes bugged, and he stopped in midstride. Delaney stopped as well, aware that something was wrong. "James? What is it?"

"Who is this?" Walker demanded.

"That doesn't really matter right now, Mr. Walker. Suffice to say that a number of us have been listening in on your conversations yesterday and today. We know that some of you are, shall we say, somewhat disaffected about Mr. Preston. You don't believe the Program can succeed now—and if it fails, the lot of you are going to be in prison so long you'll forget what daylight looks like. The fact that you all are complicit in an attempt to detonate nuclear weapons in downtown Washington, D.C., means you're all facing some serous time in Supermax . . . or worse."

"I didn't know about the nukes!" Walker almost screamed the words.

"Gently, Mr. Walker, gently. Mr. Preston has already decided to eliminate you and Mr. Delaney. That *is* Robert Delaney standing right beside you, isn't it? Yes, I thought so. As I said, Preston is going to get rid of the Program members who want to back out. Keep your voice down, or he may send his cartel thugs after you now."

"Please . . . please . . . where are you? *Who* are you? FBI?"

"Look down at your jackets, please."

Walker did so, and his eyes widened again as he saw three red pinpoints of light dancing across his chest . . . and four more on Delaney's jacket. Delaney saw them as well and jumped as if he'd been burned.

"We are people who could save Preston the trouble and terminate you both immediately," the voice said. "However, we've been listening in on your conversations, and we know you were trying to stand up to Preston a moment ago. We can offer you a chance to get out."

Walker locked eyes with Delaney. The banker couldn't hear the full conversation, but he probably had a good idea of what was going on.

"Yes. Yes! I want out! I'll give you a statement, sworn testimony . . . whatever you want."

"Very well. Do not return to your cabin. Instead, turn to your right and begin walking. We'll talk again in a few moments."

"Wait!" Delaney said as Walker turned. "James! Who was that? Where are you going?"

Delaney's cell phone chirped.

"You'd better answer that, Bob," Walker said. "It's for you . . ."

TELLER
BOHEMIAN GROVE
MONTE RIO, CALIFORNIA
0215 HOURS, PDT

"What I don't understand, Mr. Walker," Teller said, "is what the hell you people thought you'd get out of this."

They were inside a caterer's van parked outside the main lodge. Teller and Procario had entered the Bohemian Grove the day before, getting past the rent-a-cops at the gate with a pass signed by the Grove's owners in San Francisco. The assault team had been able to get through security by posing as caterers for the July VIP event, bringing in their equipment ahead of time.

The Grove owners had been willing enough to cooperate when the FBI flashed their badges. The last thing the prestigious club wanted right now was a scandal, especially one involving club members who'd rented the Grove for an off-season retreat. Once inside, four ISA commandos had taken over the security office, tying and gagging the officers there. Procario, Teller, and Captain Marcetti had turned the caterer's van into their command post. From there, they'd been tracking the members of the Program throughout the camp, watching a flat-screen monitor that showed the

ID'd locations of each of the Program's members and listening in on their conversations through their Cellmap-infested phones.

What they needed more than anything else, though, was the cooperation of the two disaffected Program members, Walker and Delaney. As Haupt had pointed out the day before, the intelligence they'd gathered so far was illegal and would be thrown out of court.

They needed an insider's perspective—and his willingness to testify before a grand jury. With advice from an FBI legal expert, they'd been granted the authority by a federal judge to offer immunity to the program's disaffected members. Teller didn't like it—at some point, these people had agreed to join a cabal dedicated to the secession of all or part of four or five states in the American Southwest, an act that could trigger a civil war and result in the deaths of tens of thousands of American civilians. Walker and Delaney were traitors, nothing less.

Still, the ISA/FBI team needed their cooperation, or every one of the traitors would walk free.

"What would we get?" Walker asked. "We were originally told that the United States is failing. The debt . . . mismanagement by the government . . . the erosion of civil liberties . . . the government deciding it could hold citizens indefinitely like some third-rate African dictatorship . . . The idea was to create a new nation with new laws, where we could kind of start over."

Delaney nodded. "Preston told *me* that it would give people in the Southwest a chance to tell the government, once and for all, what the people down there thought of

Washington's policies lately. Especially about illegal immigration."

"So you're saying it was supposed to be a kind of mass protest movement?" Procario asked.

"That was the line," Walker agreed. He scowled. "But soon it was pretty clear that he had something else in mind."

"What?"

"A new nation that he could *loot,*" Walker said, clenching his fist. "He was setting things up so that there would be a lot of investment in the new country—by the Federal Reserve, by major banks, and by the Mexicans."

"By 'Mexicans' you mean the drug cartels."

"We didn't know about that until later," Delaney said. "But reportedly, the president of Mexico was behind the idea, too."

"Yeah," Walker agreed. "Turns out Preston promised the cartels that they'd have their own country with their own laws—a safe haven for their, ah, activities, money laundering, smuggling, all of that. But the Mexican government is interested in supporting Aztlán, too. They need a place to send their poor and jobless, a relief valve, and they need access to programs like Directo a México for hard cash. But when he told me to set aside the Directo a México reserves for transfer to an Aztlán national bank, I knew he was just after the money."

It made sense, in a twisted sort of way. Each of the groups involved in the plot had its own agenda—the Iranians wanted something to keep the Americans out of the Mideast, the drug cartels wanted a safe haven, the Mexican government wanted a safety valve for their poor. Behind it all was a gang of politicians, lawyers, and corporate executives interested in nothing more than stripping the new nation bare.

"Takes corporate piracy to a whole new level, doesn't it?" Teller growled. He was angry, angrier than he'd been in a long time, almost shaking with barely suppressed fury. Islamic fundamentalists were bad. So were drug cartel thugs. By far the worst, in his estimation, were the enemies who would tear the country apart from the inside, purely out of greed or a lust for power.

"Why would you people do something like this?" Procario asked. "You're all successful businessmen."

"I guess we all had our reasons," Walker said with a shrug. "My career was going nowhere."

"My bank is being investigated by the FDIC," Delaney said. "We're expecting them to bring suit any day now. Mortgage irregularities."

"Same for Carl Fuentes. He's being investigated by the FBI for ties to the Mexican cartels. Logan's oil company is an empty shell right now, on the point of collapse. Carter's personal life is shot; his wife's leaving him. Joe Belsanno has political enemies inside the Beltway who are publishing unsavory things about his connections with certain groups." Walker sighed. "Preston painted us all an attractive picture. A chance to say the hell with it and start over, relaxing on a beach somewhere in the South Pacific with hundreds of millions—maybe *billions*—invested in offshore banks and earning obscene amounts of interest."

"No worries, no cares, no extradition, eh?" Teller

said. "Just warm sunshine, pretty girls, and drinks with umbrellas in them."

"So when did you find out he was going to attack Washington with nukes?" Procario asked. He sounded only mildly curious, but Teller saw the heat behind the eyes.

"A week ago," Walker said. "I wanted out then, but I didn't see how I could pull it off."

"He has those cartel thugs working for him," Delaney added.

"Well, you have your chance now," Teller told them. He didn't like it, but the McDee had told him how to play it. "*One* chance you get, that's all. I can't promise you won't be charged, but the attorney general is willing to cut you a deal if you cooperate with the investigation."

"Anything," Walker said. "*Anything.* I just want this nightmare to end."

PRESTON
BOHEMIAN GROVE
MONTE RIO, CALIFORNIA
0232 HOURS, PDT

Preston's cell phone rang. It was Escalante. "What?"

"I sent two of my people over to the Security Office a little while ago," Escalante told him. "They haven't reported back. I definitely think something's wrong." There was a pause. "And Walker and Delaney aren't in their cabin."

"Shit." Escalante was right. There were too many suspicious things happening. A couple of security guards not at their post might be evidence of nothing more than drunkenness on duty—but this was four men now, plus the two on watch in the Security Office.

It was time to get the hell out—*now*.

"Okay. Meet me at the car."

If someone had infiltrated the Bohemian Grove, they would have the main gate guarded. However, there were several other ways in and out known only to a few—including a dirt road leading down to a spot on the Russian River where Preston had hidden a Zodiac a few days ago. That would get them into town unobserved, where a car was waiting at a local garage.

He didn't like abandoning the others; more than anything, though, he hated abandoning the Program. So many years of careful work, of recruiting, of nurturing to bring the plan this far.

Long ago, Preston had decided that the United States of America was doomed. Even before he'd been tapped as the president's national security adviser, he'd been convinced that the country had, at most, another twenty years before it was engulfed in bloody chaos and economic collapse. He'd begun making preparations then, while he was still a department manager at the Fed. He'd been asked to join the National Security Council seven years earlier, and only last year been tapped as ANSA. Access to security briefings and secret intel from every branch of the intelligence community had only served to strengthen his conviction that America stood at the brink of apocalypse.

The only question was how to take advantage of the approaching collapse. He began—cautiously—to talk to others who shared his belief. Logan was a born-again Christian convinced that Armageddon was at hand; Walker thought that the international fiscal policies he was required to supervise would bleed the nation into economic collapse, and that his superiors didn't care; Gonzales believed passionately that Aztlán was part of the inevitable future march of history. Slowly, Preston had built his little group, playing on their fears and on their convictions. If America was to fall, it wouldn't hurt to nudge things a little—and to do so in a way that would make a few billion along the way. Not in dollars, obviously, or in unstable Euros. Gold, silver, platinum, and certificates of deposit easily converted to renminbi or Australian dollars or pesos or pounds sterling or whatever other currencies remained strong in the coming collapse. Preston had contacts within the PRC, and they'd been quite happy to have the Program invest in Chinese renminbi yuan. China's leaders hoped to internationalize their currency during the next few years, to make it a strong reserve currency.

In fact, the People's Republic, he thought, might be a good place for him to hole up for a while, to reassess and to rebuild. If the intruders here in the Grove tonight knew about the nukes, as seemed likely, they would go to considerable lengths to apprehend him.

He retrieved a pistol from a desk drawer, checked to see that it was loaded, then put on his jacket.

His phone rang. There was no caller ID.

Better not to answer it. During the past few years working with various intelligence agencies, he'd heard rumors, of course, of technologies allowing the government to turn cell phones into listening devices. The only hard information he'd seen on that had been reports of NSA intercepts of terrorist cell phone calls; the wilder stories, to the effect that the government could turn your phone into a listening device even when it was off, he'd discounted.

Now, though, he was beginning to wonder.

At his level, it wasn't necessary for him to know the details of signals intercepts, or the technologies that made them possible. He'd read thousands of reports of phone intercepts in Pakistan, of satellite infiltrations of electronic networks in China, of computer viruses inserted into Iranian nuclear labs . . .

He'd never once questioned how these myriad technological miracles had been worked.

He was met at the door by one of Escalante's thugs, a powerfully built Latino named Herrera holding an M-16 assault rifle. He looked nervous. "Señor Escalante, he says to hurry," Herrera said. "Something here is not right!"

"Let's go, then. *Adelante*."

They stepped out into the cool blackness of the night.

TELLER
BOHEMIAN GROVE
MONTE RIO, CALIFORNIA
0236 HOURS, PDT

The door to the Owl's Nest swung open on Teller's IR imager, and Preston joined the Mexican standing on the front porch.

"All units, November Sierra is in sight," a voice said over the Bluetooth clipped to his ear. The Owl's Nest had been surrounded for over an hour now. Officially, the FBI was running this show, in the form of a Bureau special tactical team, but the real muscle was provided by Marcetti's ISA assault force. Teller, Procario, and Marcetti had left the confines of the van to close on the redwood château where their main target had been residing.

"He's not answering his phone," Teller said over the tactical net. "Get his attention."

Teller's arm, nestled in a black sling to keep it invisible in the darkness, was throbbing. The drugs they'd given him yesterday at Belvoir had long since worn off, but he'd decided not to take more. He wanted to be fully aware, alert, and functional when they took Preston down.

"Randolph Preston," Marcetti's voice boomed out of the night, electronically amplified. "You are surrounded. Raise your hands immediately and—"

It all happened too fast to follow. The cartel gunman raised his M-16 and opened fire, blazing away in a broad semicircle. Preston lunged to the right and started running. The assault unit's snipers opened fire, sending multiple rounds into the gunman, who continued firing until his magazine went dry. Other shots directed at Preston missed as the man dodged behind the massive black bulk of a redwood.

Floodlights winked on, bathing the Grove's central area in a harsh white light. "Damn!" Procario snapped. "Where'd he go?"

"I've got him," Teller said. He'd pulled up a Cellmap

image on his smart phone, showing the blue icon tagged as Preston moving through a graphic map toward the lake. "He's headed for the Owl Shrine. C'mon!" Teller lurched from his hiding spot and raced through the trees, hoping that the surrounding snipers and tactical personnel got a clear ID on their target before opening fire.

The ground was uneven and descending, the path twisting through the enormous trees, some of which were over a thousand years old. Up ahead was the Owl Shrine, a stage next to an artificial lake at the center of the Grove. During the July revels, Teller had learned, the Shrine was the location of the Bohemian Club's Cremation of Care ceremony, as well as the venue for informal daily talks on public policy, government, and economic issues of interest to the attendees.

Teller emerged near the shore of the lake. To his left, a car was pulling up in front of the entrance to the shrine—Escalante. When the driver saw the lights glaring through the trees, however, he floored the accelerator and sent the vehicle squealing around in a half circle, leaving the running Preston behind.

"Preston!" Teller yelled. "Stop! Give it up!"

Fifty yards away, Preston stared at Teller, then turned and ran, apparently trying to make his way around the man-made pond. A startling apparition loomed up above the water—a forty-foot-tall statue, concrete on steel and covered with moss, of a titanic owl. Preston ran across the small wooden stage between statue and water, ducking to slip through beneath a wall of evergreen branches. Teller followed, pounding onto the wooden stage.

Gunfire cracked from the dark mass of evergreens ahead, two shots, and Teller felt the snap of one of the rounds going past. He was backlit, he realized, by the searchlight glare filtering through the forest behind him and immediately took the only option that presented itself, pitching to the side and over a wooden railing, hitting the pond with a noisy splash.

The pond was quite shallow and choked with algae and weeds, but Teller stayed beneath the surface as he moved forward across the muddy bottom. It was an awkward swim, one-handed, with his arm bound and his shoulder screaming at him. Preston, he knew, would do one of two things—run, or stay put and wait for him to emerge from the water. If he ran, other members of the tactical team were already moving to cut him off, and Teller would emerge from the pond, soaking wet and too late to participate in the capture.

If Preston was waiting to see if he had in fact killed the man chasing him, he would be staring into the glare of light in the trees, and his night vision would be gone.

Teller was counting on that as he maneuvered his way through black water and carefully, carefully raised his head above the surface once more.

The bank was lined with stone. Teller pulled his Glock from its holster and edged his way forward, crouched low to avoid silhouetting himself against the light. He could hear lots of noise in the forest around him, men running, men shouting and calling to one another. They'd heard the gunfire and were trying to create a new perimeter, not easy in pitch darkness. If Preston avoided that net—quite possible in the confused tangle

of night and woods—it would mean a drawn-out man-
hunt, with every possibility that the quarry would escape. The Bohemian Grove was something like 2,700
acres, all of it thickly wooded, and plenty of wilderness
beyond its perimeter where a fugitive could disappear.

Teller stopped, holding absolutely still, listening. That
sixth sense that combat operators relied upon was running full-tilt. He could *feel* Preston out there, silent,
waiting, just a few yards away . . .

He couldn't see, though, could see nothing but darkness. Teller sank down lower, closer to the earth, and
took a quiet breath. He needed to flush the fugitive out,
and he could think of only one way to do it. Raising his
Glock .45, he licked his lips, then called, "*Got* you,
Preston! Hands up!"

He heard movement, a rustle off to his right, and a
sharp intake of breath. Teller rolled to the left just as
Preston fired, the muzzle flash piercing the darkness
just five yards away. Teller fired an instant later, aiming
at Preston's muzzle flash. He heard a gasp, a moan, and
the thud of something heavy hitting soft ground.

Cautiously, Teller rose and approached. Lights flashed
and glared through the trees as tactical team members
closed on the sounds of the shots. One light bobbed and
jittered as it came closer. "You got him!" Procario's
voice said.

By the harsh glare of an LED flashlight, Teller could
see Preston on the ground, clutching his chest, still
breathing, his eyes open and aware, a 9 mm automatic
lying on the ground nearby. He was sprawled at the
foot of an unusual statue—not the immense owl on the

other side of the pond, but a life-sized wooden figure of a man in clerical robes, holding his forefinger in front of his lips.

"You . . . don't know . . . who . . . I *am*," Preston managed to say, his voice gurgling a bit, and broken by pain.

Teller knelt beside him, moving his hands to look at the wound. "Randolph Preston," Teller told him. "Adviser to the president, domestic terrorist, and traitor. Anything else we should know?"

He began to work to stop the flow of blood.

EPILOGUE

INSCOM HQ
FORT BELVOIR, VIRGINIA
0915 HOURS, EDT
25 APRIL

"You are *still* in a world of shit, Captain," Colonel MacDonald said. "I wouldn't want you to think any differently."

"Yes, ma'am," Teller replied. He glanced at Procario, who said nothing. The two had been summoned into the McDee's office that morning, interrupting their ongoing round of debriefing sessions. Teller decided it was best to hold his tongue, to stick to "Yes, ma'am" and "No, ma'am" until he knew just how this summons was going to play out.

"Operating independently of this command, without authorization," she said. "Creating an international incident in Mexico and in Belize. Conducting illegal wiretaps of American citizens on U.S. soil. Initiating military action on U.S. soil in violation of the Posse Comitatus Act. I could go on."

"Permission to speak, Colonel," Procario said.

"Well?"

"Just how were we in violation of Posse Comitatus?"

The act was designed to limit the powers of local government to enforce the law on U.S. territory. Contrary to popular belief, it did not prohibit the army from engaging in law enforcement activities—so long as the orders to do so originated with Congress or the Constitution.

"Neither Congress nor the president *officially* gave you any orders to act," MacDonald replied.

Oh, God, here it comes, Teller thought. *They're going to lock us up where the sun never shines, and flush the key.*

He desperately wanted a drink. He'd been holding off for the duration of the debriefings. Now he was wishing he'd submerged himself at Executive Sweets once he'd returned and never come up.

"However," MacDonald said after an agonizing hesitation, "the TJAG is looking into it. The president did grant certain broad powers to government personnel while we were searching for those suitcase nukes. It might be argued that you two were operating under his verbal instructions. The charges of kidnapping and illegal arrest . . . that will probably be covered by the current NDAA."

That again. Teller didn't know whether to be happy that he wasn't facing criminal charges, or furious that his case was actually justifying that piece-of-shit legislation undermining the Constitution.

"Chris *did* save Congress's great collective ass," Procario said, "when he tracked down those nukes. Damn it, you ought to be giving him a fucking medal."

"The language is unnecessary, Colonel," MacDonald told him. "And, believe me, the fact that they didn't incinerate most of Washington, D.C., will mitigate in your favor. Normally, we can't condone cowboy tactics, but in this instance . . ."

Only then did Teller catch the twinkle in MacDonald's usually cold eye, and realize that this was going to work out okay. Damn it, she was *playing* with them!

"Needless to say," she went on, "the public doesn't need to know just how close we came to a major . . . incident in the Capitol. Or about how drug money was connected both to members of Congress and to the White House itself. All of that *will* remain classified."

"Permission to speak, ma'am?" Teller said.

"Yes?"

"What about Preston? When he goes on trial—"

"Randolph Preston is dead," MacDonald said with stiff finality.

"Dead? I thought we got to him in time. The medics were there in—"

"Randolph Preston is dead," she repeated. Obviously she was going to say no more.

Which left Teller wondering. Dead, as in he'd died of his wounds while being medevacked to the hospital? Or dead, as in someone high up in government had decided that they couldn't risk a public trial . . . or that what might come out about cartel connections and federal banking irregularities would be embarrassing for the president? Dead, perhaps, as in "disappeared," locked away at Supermax while the government decided what to do with him?

Teller suppressed a shudder. The NDAA again. "What about all the others we rounded up at the Grove?"

"In custody. Undergoing questioning. Walker and Delaney are cooperating with the AG, as are Logan and the others—all except Escalante, of course. The whole affair is being kept quiet. You can imagine what would happen to oil prices if the North American Oil scandal becomes public knowledge. Mr. Gonzales will be impeached, will probably be indicted on charges of racketeering—his involvement with the cartels. All in all, very, very messy."

"And the Iranian? Reyshahri?"

"At an undisclosed location with the Company. I gather he's cooperating fully. My contacts at Langley tell me they're learning a great deal about the inside workings of Iranian intelligence from him."

"I guess that wraps things up, then," Teller said.

"Almost. You two should know that we're officially shutting down Cellmap."

"What?" Teller was startled. "Why?"

"Wiretapping Mexican citizens engaged in the drug trade is one thing," MacDonald said. "Deliberately wiretapping American citizens is something else."

"It wasn't deliberate. The virus jumps from phone to

phone all by itself. Doesn't distinguish between one side of the border or the other at all."

"Nevertheless, we're hitting the kill switch." The Cellmap virus, Teller had been told, included code that disabled the software if it received a signal from its controllers, a kill switch.

"If this became public knowledge," MacDonald continued, "there'd be a firestorm, maybe worse than the controversy over NDAA 2012. The White House is *very* concerned that this technology be . . . properly controlled. And kept quiet."

Which might well mean they would keep using it, but keep the fact as deeply buried as the knowledge of Z-backscatter vans conducting personal searches without warrants, or a scandal that had reached all the way into the White House.

She *had* said "*officially* shutting down Cellmap."

Fourth Amendment be damned.

"Oh . . . one last thing."

She picked up a single piece of paper from her desk and handed it to Teller, almost tossing it at him.

Teller broke attention to look at it.

"Congratulations, Captain Teller—you were selected by HRC for promotion to major, effective 1 October. I hope you can stay out of trouble at least until you pin it on. Dismissed."

He *really* wanted that drink—it was way overdue.

At the very least, however . . . perhaps Galen Fletcher now had a measure of peace.

MORALES
MEXICO CITY, MEXICO
1345 HOURS, LOCAL TIME

"Mi amigo," Agustín Morales said with a smile, *"estás en uno mundo de la mierda."*

A world of shit. It was a term he'd learned during his training with the U.S. military, one he liked.

Miguel de la Cruz gave another piercing scream, back arching convulsively as the interrogator applied another jolt of electricity. Stripped naked, tied spreadeagle on a large and filthy wooden table with electrodes clipped here and there, de la Cruz was smeared with sweat, blood, and excrement, scarcely recognizable now as human.

"Please!" he gasped, chest heaving. *"Please!* What is it you want me to tell you?"

"Tell me? Why, absolutely nothing. I already know everything. In particular, I know how you risked our entire operation by sending those spies to the Escalante safe house. You jeopardized our operation in the United States. You cost us an important asset, Enrique Barrón, and both he and the Perez bitch are singing to the Americans now."

Morales's pleasant smile darkened. His agents in Florida had reported that both Barrón and Perez were there, in custody. They couldn't be reached . . . now.

There would be other opportunities.

"I didn't know Escalante was a part of it! *Please!"*

"Ah, well, now you know." Morales looked at the

interrogator. "Give him . . . let's say, three days. Let him truly understand the consequences of his ignorance. Then end it."

"*Sí, Calavera. Con mucho gusto.*"

The former CISEN officer turned cartel informant shrieked again as the Skull walked out of the basement room.

He would have to discuss this with El Chapo, the Sinaloan boss of bosses. The Iranian affair had been damned expensive, with little to show for it. The Iranians' promises hadn't counted for much after all.

Much worse was the possibility that Perez, Barrón, or Escalante would give away too much. How much had the enemy learned? How much would they learn?

In the long run, Morales thought, it probably didn't matter that much. A lot of street-level cowboys might get caught. Perhaps a few of the high-ranking ones as well, but not even Escalante knew enough to really cripple the organization.

In the meantime, the *yanqui* government would fuss and fume and debate and pass laws and rescind them, and in the long run not much of anything would be accomplished. There were still lots of people within the American government deeply and solidly in the pockets of Sinaloa, Los Zetas, and the others.

So long as the incredible *norteamericano* appetite for product remained, the organization would continue to thrive.

U.S.–MEXICAN BORDER
2 MILES EAST OF NOGALES, ARIZONA
1725 HOURS, MST

"*Freeze*, dirtball! *¡No mueva!*"

Ernesto Jesús Mendoza scrambled up off the struggling girl, his trousers nearly tripping him as they bunched around his feet. "*No disparar!*" he cried, raising his hands. "Don't shoot!"

"Step away from the gun, *hombre*," one of the men nearby said, gesturing with an M-15—the semiauto version of a military assault rifle. Mendoza had a holstered pistol in the belt at his ankles. "And get away from her."

The posse was a mixed bag of ranchers and county law enforcement. Nathan Spangler, a deputy on the Nogales police force, took another look at the map displayed on his smart phone, then switched it off. "So . . . Ernesto Mendoza?"

"*¿Que*—? How is it you know this?" the man cried, managing to kick free of his pants and belt. "You have no right—"

"I got all kinds of right, amigo," one of the civilian men said. "This here's *my* land, and you boys're trespassing." He looked Mendoza up and down. "Indecent exposure, too, looks like."

"We're not Border Patrol, if that's what you mean," Spangler told him.

"That's right," another rancher said. "We're not *nearly* that nice."

Elsewhere in the small arroyo, other members of the posse were rounding up the other coyotes. There were five of them, plus a dozen filthy men and women. The coyotes had herded four young women together underneath a broad, low-spreading tree brightly festooned with panties and bras and had been in the process of raping them when the Minuteman Patrol had finally caught up with them.

Mendoza managed a terrified smile. "Look . . . we can work this out, yes?" He spread his hands. "I can . . . I can talk to people who will make you, *all* of you, incredibly wealthy!"

The gunshot cracked across the desert. Mendoza's back arched sharply, and then he crumpled to the ground. Behind him, momentarily forgotten, the young Mexican woman, naked and filthy, clutched Mendoza's pistol in two tiny hands.

"Cabrón," she spat, an epithet that meant both "billy goat" and "bastard."

"Son of a bitch," Spangler said, looking down at the body. "Looks to me like the bastard got shot trying to escape."

HAMMER ONE
MEXICO CITY, MEXICO
1820 HOURS, LOCAL TIME

Gunnery Sergeant Antonio Sanchez stared into the electronic eyepiece of his Barrett .50, unmoving, relaxed . . . and bored. Were those two *never* going to stop?

Beside him, James Edward Clarke was restless. "Can't you take the shot?"

"No," Sanchez replied. "I can't. Not without risking hitting the girl."

"Collateral damage is only to be expected—"

"*Negative.* Not on my watch. *Sir.*"

Sanchez was a Recon Marine sniper, and a very good one. He took pride in his work, and he was not going to blow both of those people away with one round just because a stuffed suit out of Langley was getting impatient.

Besides, it was kind of nice that the target was getting to have one last fling before the hammer fell.

The technology was amazing, and Sanchez wished he'd had it in Iraq. More than once, during his three deployments to that unhappy hellhole, he'd nailed insurgents from a mile away *through* a solid concrete wall, but he'd had to take a guess as to their positions. The backscatter device hooked up to his sniper scope and to Clarke's computer monitor was peeking right through the wall of the apartment across Emiliano Zapata Street and into the bedroom.

Those two had been at it for a couple of hours now.

"Who's this guy, anyway?" Sanchez asked.

"You don't need to know."

"Fair enough." Sanchez was a CIA contract employee, hired for certain operations requiring his deadly and precise skills. He rarely knew the names or identities of the people he was brought in to terminate.

Clarke seemed to think about it, then relented slightly. "His name is Nicholas," he said.

"One of ours?"

"He . . . used to work for us."

"I see." Sanchez had been watching the rot spreading through this country. Drug money was everywhere, and anyone, it seemed, could be bought.

Perhaps the rot had spread to Langley as well. *That* was an unsettling thought.

"We're sending a message this evening, Sanchez," Clarke said. "The Company is not for sale."

In his scope, the plastic-looking man finally rolled off of the woman and sat up at the edge of a ghost-hazy bed. The woman sat up behind him, her hand caressing his back and shoulder. "Target is moving," Sanchez said.

"Yeah," Clarke said. "Yeah! *Nail* the bastard!"

"Wait one." He followed the man as he stood up, walked past the bed, and headed toward the apartment's bathroom. Sanchez wanted to be absolutely sure that the woman was out of the line of fire.

He drew a breath . . . let it out partway . . . and gently squeezed the trigger.

TELLER CONDO
ALEXANDRIA, VIRGINIA
1910 HOURS, EDT

Teller's condo was a classic bachelor's pad. Located in the Manchester Lakes of the upscale Kingstowne area, it was just three miles from Fort Belvoir. It had been a long and grueling day talking with the INSCOM investigation team. At least he wasn't going to prison; in fact, they were going to make him a freakin' major.

They'd stopped asking him about his motivations in

going after the cartel thugs at the Perez house and shifted to the details of that contract he and the ISA team had found in the jungle at Cerros.

The Russian submarine, he'd learned, had been thoroughly searched, then finally released. *Another* international incident, that—but one that the State Department appeared to be smoothing over.

Barrón and Maria Perez had been transferred to different secret locations. Barrón was headed for Supermax; Perez would probably end up in a witness protection program, given a new name and a new identity in exchange for her testimony against Escalante.

A brave woman. He sincerely hoped she survived this. It was terrifying to know just how completely the Mexican cartels had penetrated the United States—its government, its police forces, the hearts and souls of over 170 different cities across the country, at last count.

America's last lines of defense were crumbling with horrific speed.

The Aztlán threat, at least, was fading away, at least for now. The riots had all but sputtered out as the National Guard took control of barrios and city centers from San Diego to Chicago. The president of Mexico, under pressure from the U.S. secretary of state, had publicly backed away from endorsing the Aztlán Libre movement.

Congress had promised to look again into the issue of illegal immigration on the border and the influence of Mexican drug cartels in American cities. Teller wondered if that would amount to anything worthwhile at all.

Secrecy. Washington, D.C., was awash in secrets, some well kept, others not so much. It was anyone's guess how the Shah Mat affair was going to shake out. The idea that a cartel-linked conspiracy had reached so high up into the city's halls of power . . .

Teller's thoughts went back to that wooden statue by the pond at the Bohemian Grove. He'd had to look it up later in his laptop: the figure was the patron saint of the Bohemian Club, John of Nepomuk, a priest who, it was said, had died rather than tell a Bohemian ruler, the "good King Wenceslaus" of song and fable, the confessional secrets of the queen.

There were *some* secrets that must be protected at all costs.

Most secrets, he thought, were simply people in power keeping their own screwups hidden from the people, keeping themselves from looking like idiots—CYA on steroids.

Sometimes, however, the people entrusted with power *had* to be exposed, or that secrecy became the means of destroying a nation.

Maybe that was Fletcher's legacy here. A man betrayed, an old-school man of honor who'd discovered that both those under him and above him in the chain of command were corrupt, that the corruption had gone higher and deeper than anyone had suspected. He'd found himself cut off, unable to trust anyone, unable to *tell* anyone what he knew or suspected.

His suicide, though, had highlighted Nicholas's treason, and that, in turn, had led to Preston.

Thanks, Galen, Teller thought.

Teller didn't like the fact of Preston's ambiguous death—if death it had been. Still, he would do what he'd done again. *The next right thing . . .*

His arm hurt, a heavy throbbing pulse. The problem, he thought, was that it was no longer possible to draw clear lines between the good guys and the bad. The Mexican cartels—those were pure evil, no question . . . but Teller was beginning to question issues of right and wrong he'd not questioned before. *The next right thing . . .*

Was it *ever* right to sacrifice the sacred Constitution of the United States when it became . . . inconvenient?

Some questions were just too big—or too painful—to face all at once. Galen Fletcher had run into that.

He needed to think.

It was early yet. He could still drive up to Fourteenth Street . . . have a few drinks, maybe see if Sandra Doherty was on tonight.

Then again . . .

He hadn't had a chance to spend time with Jackie since he'd gotten back from California.

What was the next right thing?

He pulled out his cell phone and speed-dialed her number.

Maybe the Filamena, up in Georgetown, for dinner.

Don't miss Lt. Col. Anthony Shaffer's
New York Times bestselling memoir

OPERATION DARK HEART

"Takes you inside the espionage world, a labyrinth of
secret agencies that do not like to share secrets."
—*Army Times*

Now available, in trade paperback,
from St. Martin's Griffin